MASTER
OF SIN

MASTER
OF SIN

MAGGIE ROBINSON

BRAVA
KENSINGTON PUBLISHING CORP.
www.kensingtonbooks.com

BRAVA BOOKS are published by

Kensington Publishing Corp.
119 West 40th Street
New York, NY 10018

ISBN-13: 978-0-7582-5105-3
ISBN-10: 0-7582-5105-X

First Printing: April 2012

10 9 8 7 6 5 4 3 2 1

Printed in the United States of America

CHAPTER 1

Italy, 1820

Andrew Rossiter was on the cusp of reformation. He could taste it, sweet as the wine Giulietta had passed him at dessert from their picnic basket, bold as the wind that whipped the sails of their little yacht, tempting as the green coast of England would be at this moment. Alas, he was cruising the Mediterranean, the city of Savona in the distance, still steeped in sin, and he was rather bored with it. The only saving grace was the sight of his little son drowsing on a velvet tufted cushion, his small fist curled under a distinctive Rossiter chin—square, dimpled, and determined.

Of course Andrew could not claim the boy. He was Duca Alessandro di Maniero's heir, the product of a carefully orchestrated plot to bring continued glory to the di Maniero name. It would not do for the duca's true inclinations and shortcomings to be revealed to all the world. Andrew had been perfectly willing to assist the duca and the duchessa in their bedroom quest. The hardship was minimal. Giulietta was a lovely young woman, Alessandro bearable, and the price right, even absurdly generous. When they had invited him back to Italy to contribute further to their family, he had happily assented. The weather was perfect, and there had been pressing reasons for him to escape England and his troubled past.

He doubted anyone could rival him for trouble. Or past. Perhaps he was being too maudlin what with all the wine he had drunk this afternoon, but it seemed his luck was bad. Cursed, even. Andrew was blessed with the looks of an angel, which had attracted an earthly devil to snatch him off the streets and use him without conscience from the age of seven onward. Andrew had never been innocent, even as a child, but even his ramshackle upbringing had not prepared him for Donal Stewart. Eventually it was easier to succumb to sin than fight it. If he were honest, Andrew eventually derived some succor from his sexual escapades, but they had long since lost their luster.

That was it—he'd lost his lust. He barked out a laugh and watched his child startle at the sound. The boy's face was quite pink and damp despite the awning over the deck.

"Giulietta, let me bring Marco below. The sun is strong today."

Giulietta looked up from her book, a wide-brimmed straw bonnet shading her face. Even in shadow, she was exquisite, a delicate blonde Venetian beauty who could have married anyone. It was her misfortune to choose a man who was entirely immune to her sex. "*Si,* Andrew. That is perhaps wise."

Andrew laughed again, softer this time. No one called him wise, or at least not often. He'd taken some pains lately to buff the tarnish from his reputation, but he very much feared the black would not ever be completely eradicated. He gathered up the boy, pillow and all, and, ducking his golden head, stepped down into the little cabin. He laid the sleeping child on the bunk and plunked down on the soft chair opposite to watch over him. Marco's favorite nursemaid had remained at the villa. Giulietta had confided that the woman became easily seasick, and wasn't it nice to be just *in famiglia*?

As the duke and his duchess were the closest thing Andrew

had to family now, he had readily agreed. Any opportunity to get to know his little son was welcome. The sail had been blissful so far on a perfect late summer day. The food, the wine, the amenities—Alessandro's yacht had every comfort imaginable. Usually there was a small crew to sail the vessel through the turquoise and lapis waters—Italy's Riviera—but today Alessandro had dismissed them and was alone at the helm, chest puffed, chubby cheeks red with exertion, his few tufts of black hair waving maniacally in the wind. Andrew had done his share earlier with lines and sails and was now pleasantly fatigued, especially after the heavy lunch that had been prepared. If he wasn't careful, he'd wind up as fat as Alessandro, and then requests for his particular skills would dry up.

And would that be such a bad thing? Andrew thought not. There was plenty of money at his bank. Sin paid well, and his investments had been remarkably successful—he was not unlucky there. He might do something useful with his life, though he could hardly think what.

A lassitude crept over him as the boat rocked through the gentle sea swells. He closed his eyes and tried to picture himself back in England. Better yet, Scotland, the place of his birth. It was safe to go back now. His "uncle" Donal was long dead, a victim of his own excessive appetites. Everyone Andrew had loved was dead, save for Caroline, and she was married and quite above his touch despite his every effort.

Bah. He'd come to Italy to run from his past. He closed his eyes and gave himself over to sleep, a sleep not as innocent as his son's but restful nonetheless.

A series of sharp cracking sounds above awakened him, then Giulietta's high-pitched scream. A torrent of Italian followed in voices he didn't recognize. What the devil? His knowledge of the language was limited to directions in the bedroom, and sex was a language without words anyway. He checked on his son. Marco still slept, undisturbed by the noise. He pushed the cabin door open an inch and looked up the polished stairs. Beneath the bright blue sky, two men had surrounded Giulietta. Before Andrew could open his mouth, one untied the ribbon to her pretty hat and tossed it into the wind. Then he held the muzzle of a gun to her ear and shot her.

Holy Mother of God. She slumped to the deck with an ungainly thud, which would have mortified her had she still been alive. She'd been all grace and good breeding, the perfect duchess apart from her rather insatiable behavior in the bedroom. The shooter bent over her and tore the rings from her fingers, the earbobs from her ears. The boat pitched to one side, and the men fought for balance. It was clear no one was at the helm.

Alessandro must be dead, too.

Andrew stood paralyzed. Any second they would clatter down the stairs and come for more booty. Come for Marco. There was no way he and his son could escape. No way out.

If he could hide Marco, persuade the child not to speak—but he was just a baby, not yet three. Anything Andrew might say would be gibberish to him anyway. He was an English-speaking stranger, no matter that he'd been in the di Manieros' household a few weeks.

He looked around the teak-paneled cabin. The gleam of a brass drawer-pull caught his eye. Andrew gingerly slid the drawer open under the bunk where Marco slept. Inside were folded linens, scented with lavender. How odd that he would note the fragrance over the stench of his own fear. He shoved them aside and lifted his son from the bed. Marco was heavy and hot in his arms. Miraculously, he did not wake as Andrew entombed him in the drawer.

Andrew didn't pray. Hadn't since he was a child of seven, when his mother deserted him and Donal Rossiter found him in an alley in Edinburgh. He prayed now with what might be his last clear thoughts.

To go above or stay where he was? The choice seemed simple.

He needed to lead the men away from Marco. He smoothed down his disheveled curls, pulled the knife from his boot, put a smile on his face, and climbed up on deck, shutting the door quietly behind him.

"Good afternoon, gentlemen."

Two pairs of dark eyes turned to him. One face was familiar—Alessandro's cousin, a cherubic-looking young man who bore a strong resemblance to his relative and was obviously keeping very bad company. "I say, Gianni, what have you done?"

Gianni tossed a dueling pistol to his partner. *"Bastardo! Uccidere l'inglese."*

Andrew only understood the first word but imagined he got the gist of the next. It was hard to miss the significance of the gun. He flipped the knife casually at the throat of the man who advanced upon him. The man who had murdered Giulietta and stolen her jewelry as Gianni stood by. Andrew had been good with rocks as a child and was pleased to note that in the intervening years he had not lost his aim. The fellow landed at his feet, but not before the gun discharged.

"Your mamma will be disappointed in you, Gianni."

Gianni's face was crimson in fury. "Shut up," he said in English. "I will be the duca now. I have men at the villa to get the boy. No one has been fooled by that pervert or you. The child is yours. Everyone knows it."

Andrew sent silent thanks up to a puffy white cloud. There was still a chance—Gianni didn't know Marco was on the boat. "What do you mean to do now?"

"I will set the boat on fire." Gianni pointed to the liquid-filled bottles that had been placed along the railing. "This has been a very unhappy accident. All aboard are dead. Even you."

Perhaps his thanks had been premature. Andrew smiled "Go on then. I suppose I deserve to roast now—it will give me a little taste of hell before I get there."

He turned his head toward the rhythmic banging of a small

boat at the yacht's side. Gianni and his late friend must have boarded while Andrew and Marco slept. Would it have made a difference if Andrew had been on deck? Probably not. No doubt he would have been killed as well.

He had to get Gianni back into that boat before Marco awoke. "It will be difficult for you to row back to Savona without your thug here. And it's a pity to destroy such a fine yacht. Part of your inheritance. Are you sure you don't want to take me along to help you sail her?"

His offer was rewarded by a torrent of curses. Stepping back, Andrew watched as Gianni lit the rags. Though his hand trembled a bit, he was too successful.

"Tell the devil hello for me, Rossiter," Gianni said, a feral smile on his face. He hopped overboard and tugged at the towline.

The first of the explosions startled them both. A lick of flame caught the sailcloth on the deck. Gianni pushed off, rowing madly to get free of the *Giulietta*.

"Bloody hell." Andrew looked down at his arm. The sleeve of his white woolen jacket was soaked in bright red blood, although he really couldn't feel a thing. No time to stare and wonder. He had to get Marco off the yacht before all hell really did break loose.

The next hour was a blur of shrieking child, toxic smoke, and wet exhaustion. He couldn't think about Giulietta, her sky-blue eyes forever fixed on their match above. Nor poor Alessandro, slumped over the tiller, staining the deck with his blood, fire encroaching on his expensive leather boots. He'd covered Marco's face with a handkerchief as they slipped into the water, but surely the boy knew that something terrible had happened. His little fists and feet windmilled as Andrew struggled to keep hold of him with one arm, the child crying and blubbering until Andrew wondered if he should just let go. If Gianni discovered he'd been unsuccessful—and he would, since Marco had not been in

the villa to snatch and snuff—they were in mortal danger anyway. A drowning death for both of them would be relatively
painless, or so he'd heard. Who knew what happened at the end
of life? The dead told no tales.

But perhaps Gianni would believe Marco had died aboard the
Giulietta. The seasick nursemaid would reveal the child's where-
abouts. The yacht still burned behind him, flames shooting into
the air. Surely no one, least of all an infant, could survive such a
conflagration. He gripped the child harder, earning a piercing
screech to his eardrum. They floated and flailed for what seemed
like hours until they were saved from almost welcome death by a
fisherman, who hauled them aboard his humble vessel as though
they were the lightly grilled catch of the day. For once Andrew
was glad he spoke little Italian, for he couldn't answer any questions.

The three weeks of recuperation spent in the fisherman's
white-washed cottage had nearly driven Andrew mad, but at
least Marco's babbling was understood. Andrew had a fever and
some festering of his wound, which the fisherman's wife had
tended to with herbs from her little walled garden. Andrew
hoped he'd bought the silence of his saviors through a combination of very fractured Italian and clever little drawings he'd managed left-handed. Donal had seen him educated at a second-rate
school, but at last bits and pieces of his Latin had come in handy.

It was imperative that he and Marco disappear as quickly as
possible, although how he had managed to make a stealthy exit
from the region with a useless arm and a crying child had been
another miracle. Retrieving his belongings at the villa was out of
the question, but fortunately he had more than a few coins and
treasure on him when he plunged into the water.

He always carried insurance. He'd known extreme poverty as
a child and vowed he would never be caught short again. Andrew gave his rescuer his watch fobs, the simple stick pin that

Caroline had given him one Christmas and the rather vulgar diamond ring he bought himself for his twenty-fifth birthday to sell in Savona. His gold watch, alas, was water logged, but went for its pretty etched case.

Andrew had no idea if the fisherman cheated him when he returned with a clinking purse, but would not have minded anyway if he had. The man had saved his son's life and deserved more than Andrew could ever pay him. Andrew himself had been doctored and drugged. Lay for hours as the fisherman's wife picked the ball and splintered bone out of his arm. Fed *zuppa di pesce*. Given the fisherman's own well-washed clothes. His wife had cut off his and his son's yellow curls and rubbed some dark muck on their heads to disguise them as best she could.

The fisherman had posted letters for him. His bank, N.M. Rothschild and Sons, had offices in London, Paris, and Vienna and could be counted on to get him where he needed to go. But where would that be? Andrew expected Gianni and his thugs to descend on him at any moment and drag Marco away.

Andrew's luck, if one could call it that, held until Paris. There the woman he had hired as a temporary nurse abandoned them, simply taking off in the middle of the night. Andrew had awakened to Marco's screams and a sodden bed. He was sure the boy had been toilet-trained before the murder of his parents, but it seemed Andrew now had to find nappies as well as someone to help him manage his son. He spent a day interviewing entirely unsuitable women and was forced to conclude he'd need to do the job himself.

How strange to discover he had paternal standards after the life he'd led. Children were a mystery to him, and this one even more so as they didn't share a language. Andrew thought back to the time when he was "rescued" by a strange man and thought he understood why Marco was so terrified. He'd been a lot older than Marco, but Donal Stewart still played boogeyman in his dreams.

To complicate matters, Andrew still did not look like the Duca di Maniero's familiar urbane guest. He'd cast off his borrowed clothes once they had gotten safely to Paris, but his butchered fair hair still had traces of brown and his arm hung leaden in its sling. It would be difficult restraining the boy with two hands, but with one, he felt significantly outmaneuvered.

But good news had awaited him at his bank, although Marco had made the interview with the manager anything but pleasant. Andrew had written to his old nemesis Baron Edward Christie requesting a return on a favor, and Christie had come through. Odd that a man Andrew had once considered an enemy was responsible for getting him settled in his new life, but everything in Andrew's current world was odd. Of course it was Edward's man of business who had actually secured the deed to a property on a remote island in the Western Isles, but according to his letter, Edward himself had vetted his son's new governess.

Presented with the documents, Andrew was now in possession of Gull House, "a fine, partly furnished historic stone manor house overlooking the Atlantic" and roughly one-third of Batter Island purchased from the MacEwan himself. The "partly furnished" aspect could easily be remedied. He'd see what was needed and order it. Edward hadn't beggared him—the purchase price of the house had been more than reasonable.

There was helpful translation in a separate letter that Batter Island took its name from the Norse word for boat—*batr*—and that the locals claimed the weather was somewhat inclement. Andrew was advised to purchase warm, waterproof clothes.

Andrew didn't care about a few raindrops. The location was essential. Life in the Outer Hebrides would be a welcome change. It was Andrew's own explicit wish to be far away from what passed for civilization. Now that he was entrusted with the welfare of his son, he wished to be as far beyond earthly temptations as possible. It wouldn't do for him to backslide into his old ways. It wouldn't do for Gianni to discover he was still alive, either. With that in mind, Andrew Rossiter was becoming Andrew Ross, and Marco di Maniero now Marc Ross. Andrew was killing off an imaginary estranged Italian wife to explain the inconsistencies in his tiny family unit. He only hoped Miss Peartree, the Italian-speaking governess who had been dispatched to Scotland, would believe it.

The crossing had been brutal, fitting entirely with the harrowing trip across the Continent and through the British Isles. The Sea of Hebrides was firmly in winter's grip. Andrew was fairly sure once he landed; he was done with travel and water transportation of any kind. He was unlucky on boats, although he supposed one could look at it the other way and appreciate he'd merely lost the full use of his arm rather than his life. Andrew was obliged to borrow a crewman's rough coat as poor Marc had vomited all over his greatcoat one too many times to ignore. The child was a poor traveler, much thinner and paler than he'd been under the Mediterranean summer sun, although the gold had returned to his hair. From the looks of the slate-gray sky, a golden sun would not be making an appearance here anytime soon.

Once the boat docked at the settlement's jetty, they were ushered into what was little more than a hut among the crescent of cottages to wait for the unloading of the ferry. Apparently most of its contents were destined for Gull House. Apart from his trunks, there were massive quantities of peat from nearby Mingulay to help heat his new home, as well as mysterious boxes from his London apartments that Andrew would be too tired to unpack. As a sharp drizzle of icy rain pelted the roof, Andrew watched the crew and island men work together to pile everything into a wagon drawn by a rather dispirited horse. More than one trip would be needed, but it was his understanding from the one crewman who spoke some English that the crew would stay overnight in the hut and leave at first light tomorrow, weather permitting.

He supposed the wagon might belong to him, too, but he had no way of knowing. He had overlooked a significant fact about the Western Isles—Gaelic was the main language. He'd not spoken a word of it since he was a child, and then only knew the few words his Highland-born mother had cared to teach him. Donal Stewart had drummed it right out of him in his attempt to make Andrew an Edinburgh gentleman. How he had failed.

According to Edward Christie's letter, there were perhaps fifteen or twenty families on the island—crofters and fisherfolk. All the women and their daughters and babies seemed to be here in the little hut staring and smiling at him, chattering incomprehensibly but making Marc very welcome on a round of warm laps as the wind howled outside. Andrew had heard *"Failte"*—welcome—too many times to count. He was plied with hot tea and oatcakes, but Marc screwed his little face up and refused the unfamiliar food. Even with his purchase of an Italian-English dictionary in a Paris shop, Andrew was making very little headway with his son. It would be nice to discover what the child liked to eat. He would even cook it himself if he had to.

Once the wagon was loaded, Andrew carried Marc out into the sleet. One of the men hopped up to drive them, and the others followed on foot and a few ponies. Andrew wrapped Marc in several thick blankets, pressing him to his chest. If they could simply survive long enough to get to the house, all might be well.

There was nothing especially picturesque about the scenery. Once one climbed the ridge away from the landing, the topography was relatively flat, with gneiss outcroppings dotting the grassland. There were few cottages, but several goats and sheep too stupid to get out of the weather. The wagon rolled south over a narrow cart track until Gull House and the surrounding ocean rose up like a gray storm.

To call the structure a "fine historic stone manor house" was a bit of a stretch. It did not look particularly historic, though it was old enough. According to the deed, at one time there had been an Iron Age fort here at the point, but the pile of rocks in front of Andrew was no fort. The two-story rectangular building *was* stone, but not particularly fine, and not really all that much larger than the crofters' cottages he had passed on the narrow road.

But the view was indeed spectacular. Evidence of gulls and abundant birdlife was everywhere, their droppings on walls and windows that even the driving freezing rain had not washed off. Here and there slates had slipped from the roof to shatter on what passed for the lawn, a mix of nettles and silverweed. If ever any shrubs had ever hugged the foundation, they'd blown away long ago. Andrew frowned. There was no fire from the chimneys, no welcoming peat smell from a hearth. And the warped front door stood wide open to the elements.

With a few hand signals to the driver and the dispensation of coins, Andrew left Marc sleeping in the wagon under the blankets and entered his new home. His first impression was that it was very nearly as cold inside as out. The square reception room on the right was clean but nearly bare of furnishing. The dining room opposite looked slightly better equipped—there was even a moldy painting on the wall.

Andrew was beginning to suspect Edward Christie had the last laugh after all, giving him *just* what he asked for. Andrew had wanted private; he'd wanted simple. He'd suggested the Western Isles himself, having had a romantic notion about them since he was a boy and read of Viking raids. He doubted any factor of Edward's had actually seen the place—the purchase had been accomplished in too short a time. Someone had been sold a bill of goods. And Andrew now had to live with the consequences.

He tiptoed down the hallway as quietly as he ever had eluding a suspicious wife or husband, coming at last to the kitchen. A raggedy serving girl dressed in what appeared to be stray Tartans and tablecloths was bent over an empty fireplace, a pitiful pile of sticks on the hearth. At the sound of his footstep on the bare slate floor she turned and shrieked.

Some of Andrew's childhood Gaelic had come back to him the farther north he'd come. Immersion with the village women earlier had helped a bit. *"Gabh mo leithsceal."* *Excuse me.*

"Does bloody anyone in this bloody place speak any bloody English?" the girl muttered.

She looked like a street urchin. Her brown hair was a nest, her pointed, unfashionably brown face was smudged, and her brown skirts were muddied. She was so very brown. Surely she couldn't be—

"Miss Peartree?" Andrew asked, praying not.

The little wren's mouth hung open like a baby bird waiting to be fed. Then she looked like she tasted the worm. "Oh, good lord. Mr. Rossiter?" She curtsied, nearly tripping on twigs.

"Ross," Andrew replied quickly. "Just Ross. Andrew Ross. There was a mix-up. I didn't mean to startle you. How long have you been here?"

"Fourteen bl-blessed days, sir. I think. One loses track of time when there is nothing to eat and nowhere to sleep and it rains every bl-blessed day when it isn't snowing."

Andrew frowned. "Nothing to eat? Is there no housekeeper employed here?"

The girl looked at her boots. They were crusted with mud, and brown beneath that, too. "There was a woman. But she left."

"She left?"

She raised her sharp little chin and looked straight into his eyes. "She left. Good riddance to her."

Miss Peartree's rather large eyes were, unsurprisingly, brown, but with a few flecks of gold. They were quite her best feature. It was impossible to tell what her figure was like beneath the swaths of fabric she had fastened to herself with what looked like clothespins. Good thing the ferry would depart in the morning. This little baggage and her clothespins and her mud would be on it. Good riddance, indeed. She was in no way what he thought a governess should look like. Or smell like.

"I am afraid there has been another mix-up, Miss Peartree. I find my son and I do not have need of your services after all."

Her wide eyes narrowed. *"È figlio di una cagna."*

Andrew threw back his head and laughed. He may not have much Italian, but this impertinent little creature had just called him a son of a bitch. How right she was.

"Your assessment of my character is no doubt accurate. Be that as it may, Miss Peartree, I'm afraid I find you equally unsuitable to teach my son. I will make arrangements for your passage home tomorrow morning."

She didn't back down. "I have no home to go to. I need this job, Mr. Ross. I'm sorry if I seem—" She looked up to the unhelpful ceiling.

"Insubordinate? Filthy? Certainly disheveled. Whatever you are, I have every reason to believe you drove away my housekeeper." Andrew wondered which one of the kindly hovering women he'd met at the landing she was.

"You try managing here for fourteen days when your trunk is lost and there isn't one single person who speaks a bloody word of bloody English. I speak Italian, Mr. Ross. French. German. Latin and Greek, too, though just for translation. I may not understand Gaelic, but I'm certain Mrs. MacLaren called me a whore."

"You? A whore? For a blind man, perhaps."

She was remarkably quick, but then so was he. The stick merely grazed his left ear.

"You are definitely dismissed." He was not going to be attacked in his own home by this little harpy. Why, if there was a constable on this rock he'd clap her in jail so fast her head would spin. He was about to tell her just that when she folded her arms over whatever it was she was wearing and spoke.

"I signed a contract with Baron Christie."

"But I am not he."

"He assured me he was acting as your representative. His fancy barrister Mr. Maclean drew up the agreement. At least that wasn't stolen. It's in my reticule."

"I don't care where the damn thing is. You are fired."

She shook her head. If Andrew was not mistaken, she created a dust cloud. "I won't go."

"Oh," Andrew said, stepping forward, "you will."

Miss Peartree was spared from deciding to step back or throw something else by an unearthly howl.

"What is that?" she asked, seeming more alarmed by the cry of a two-and-a-half-year-old than the menacing sinner before her.

"My son."

One of the men was bouncing Marc into the kitchen, trying in vain to stop the child's hysterical tears. To wake in another strange place with even more strangers was the last straw for the poor little devil. Before Andrew could go to him, Miss Peartree ran across the floor.

"*Bambino, cosa c'e di spagliato? Povera bambino! E tutu bene,*" she crooned, taking Marc and his blankets from the man. She put a grubby hand on his forehead. "Mr. Ross, your son is very hot." Her hand lingered. "Burning up, actually. Poor mite. You need to light the stove so I can bathe him to get his fever down. Don't boil the water, just heat it a little. Tell this man to get some kindling. What I foraged won't be nearly enough."

Surely Marc was warm from sleep. From woolen blankets. From screaming his head off. "I brought peat," Andrew said stupidly.

"I don't care what his name is! Are you just going to stand there?"

No, he was not. He went back outside and organized the men as best he could, cursing silently in every language known to him. Marc would be fine. He had to be. It was Miss Peartree who needed a bath.

CHAPTER 2

His rehired housekeeper Mrs. MacLaren returned with the wagon's second load. After a bit of creative detective work on his part, Andrew had found her husband among his little work crew. He had persuaded Mr. MacLaren to fetch her from the village, offering them both employment and rooms under his leaky roof by drawing watches and dishes and beds and handing over several more crowns. The MacLarens agreed to work days only, returning to their own seaside cottage, garden, and goats. At least Andrew thought it was a goat. It may have been a sheep. Mr. MacLaren was no artist, and his own right hand did not work as well as it used to. He could barely read his own writing. He should have bought a Gaelic-English dictionary in Paris, if they sold such things. Andrew would send for one at once.

And send for a new governess. He could not possibly tolerate Miss Peartree one day longer than absolutely necessary. Right now she was pointlessly arguing with Mrs. MacLaren about Marc's luncheon. The child, already much improved, was naked, heating a wooden spoon on a bucket, his fever-flushed cheeks rosy and cheerful. The great clatter of pots and pans punctuating the women's conversation had sent Andrew from the kitchen into what he assumed was his library. There were plenty of shelves, but no books.

Andrew started a fire and stared out the sleet-spattered window. He would have to buy books to keep himself occupied, a ferry-load of them. Once, he'd purchased a very naughty set of volumes depicting virtually every sexual position known to man—even some he had not tried personally, and there were very few. Those books would not be unpacked on these shelves where his son might stumble upon them. He expected Edward Christie had crated them up with all his other possessions from the Albany and they were somewhere about. He would burn them, every last depraved page. They'd make a roaring fire and save on peat.

He would give his soul for a brandy. Well, he probably had no soul to give. Donal Stewart had taken it long ago. But surely there must be spirits somewhere in this house. On this island. They were in Scotland, after all. He could walk back through the muck and the wet to the village. He'd not seen a pub through the gloom, but there had been a tiny stone church. He'd make do with communion wine if absolutely necessary.

Andrew sat down at his desk, lay his head down, and closed his eyes. His arm ached like the very devil. He was in a hell entirely of his own making. What had possessed him to trust Christie with these arrangements? He would have been better off going to America and rubbing elbows with wild Indians. Instead he was perched on top of a windy ridge, trapped with a sick child, two unintelligible servants, and a wicked little shrew.

Now that there was a substantial fire in the kitchen, the shrew had removed a few layers of her makeshift covering to reveal a scrawny little body worthy of a twelve-year-old boy. Her dress—brown of course—was the ugliest thing he'd ever seen on a woman. He thought the only thing worse would be to remove it and catch sight of what little there was underneath.

And Edward Christie had met her. Approved of her. Damn the man to hell. He didn't deserve Caroline or all the comforts of life.

There was a tap at the door. Mrs. MacLean poked her head in. *Now what.* Andrew lifted his good hand. "Come."

The woman didn't bother to speak but dropped a tray gently on the bare surface of the desk. She was a mind reader. Or a witch. There on the toleware sat a tumbler of whiskey and a thick ham sandwich. Andrew smiled and swore he still had some of his own magic judging from the blush on the woman's cheeks.

"Thank you, Mrs. MacLaren. You are a godsend in this god-forsaken place. If you weren't already married to your good husband, I'd take you to bed and show you heaven, fuck you sideways and upside down. Lick a path from your toes to your iron-gray head. If I have a bed. I suppose I'll look after lunch. But we wouldn't really need a bed, you know."

He heard the snort from the hallway. *Bloody hell.* Miss Peartree walked in holding his son, now swaddled in a nappy. In the washing of him, she'd lost some of her own grime, though her hair still looked as if Mrs. MacLaren had taken a fork to it.

"I hope when Marc is fluent in English, you will refrain from such disgusting vocabulary," she said primly.

Andrew felt his face darken. It had been very bad of him, he knew. He didn't need this little gremlin to tell him so. "You're one to talk. I've never heard so many bloody *bloodies* in my life."

She had the grace to color. Apparently he had put her in her place and she was done with her lecture. For now. He had a feeling she'd find something else to upbraid him about, and soon. "Marc has swallowed every drop of broth and had a coddled egg besides. I won't let that woman give him milk yet, though. *Goat's* milk, if you please." She shuddered. "Here. Feel his forehead." She offered his son to him, but Marc shied away, clinging to Miss Peartree's bony shoulder. She murmured to him in soothing Italian, but his face remained buried in her nonexistent bosom. "He doesn't seem to like you very much. Why is that?"

Andrew took a long pull of the whiskey. He would have to get much more before night fell, although it really was as dark as sin outside already. "He does not know me well. My late wife and I were separated for most of our marriage."

Andrew was fairly sure she whispered "smart woman" into his son's shorn curls.

"What a pity. He asks for her, you know."

Andrew did. He'd lain awake all through Europe hearing his son cry for Giulietta. "He'll get over it. He must."

"How heartless you are! He's just a baby." She kissed the top of his head and Marc snuggled deeper. "How did your wife die?"

"An accident. Really, Miss Peartree, this is too personal and painful to talk about. You are overstepping your bounds."

Her eyes widened at the rebuke. Her lashes were very long, reaching nearly to her straight brown brows. "I'm sorry. I thought knowing might help me with your son."

"You won't be here long enough." Andrew bit into the sandwich and chewed noisily, hoping to repel her right out of the room.

"Oh, not that nonsense again. Surely you must know all these changes have been very hard on Marc. If I disappear, he'll only get worse."

Andrew looked for his new watch in his pocket, but it had played a part in the negotiations with the MacLarens and it was still on the kitchen dresser. "You have known my son all of two hours, Miss Peartree. Three at the most. I hardly think he'll miss your influence."

"You'd be surprised. *Voi come mi.* You like me, don't you, love?"

"*Ti amo.*" Marc gave her a sloppy kiss and giggled.

Insupportable. That this absolute hoyden had won his child over in a matter of hours when he had worked weeks for a smile. He pointed at his chest and then at Marc. "*Ti amo,*" Andrew repeated. Marc shook his head and stuck a finger in his mouth.

"*Abasso il.* You'll make your teeth all crooked and not grow up to be as handsome as your papa," she said, tickling him under his chin. She turned to Andrew, all business, as though she'd just not shamelessly flattered him. He knew he was not looking his best. There were many reasons. Two of them stood before him. "I've just come to tell you that the old witch and her husband will bring a crib for Marc tomorrow. Do you want him to sleep in your bed tonight or in mine?"

"Since you are temporarily serving as his nursemaid, he may sleep with you." Andrew had woken up urine soaked several nights running. Let her discover Marc's little problem on her own. The child was masterful at removing his diaper well before dawn.

"Very well. I'm going to put him down for an afternoon nap."

"I thought you said you had nowhere to sleep."

"That was because Mrs. MacLaren locked all the bedrooms when she left."

"She what?"

"She locked the doors and took all the keys with her. I had to sleep on the couch in the front parlor, and may I suggest you replace it at the first opportunity? It smells dreadfully of damp."

Just wait until Miss Peartree smelled Marc. "Has she unlocked them now?"

"Oh, yes. She seems resigned to me being here. If I understand her correctly, she believes if children and dogs like one, then one is worthy."

Andrew waited to laugh until Miss Peartree left the library. Once he started, he had trouble stopping. He had gone mad, but he feared he was in good company.

Gemma brushed the hair from little Marc's damp forehead. His temperature was not quite right, but children could quickly spike a fever and return to normal in the blink of an eye. He had eaten well, and now he rested in her Spartan room. She wished she could do the same, but she was a bundle of nerves, startling each time the hail hit the window glass. The ocean roared below, which added to the ominous ambiance of Gull House. During the fourteen days' hideous weather she'd actually seen—and eaten—fish thrown up to the grass by the force of the waves. Waiting for the Rosses to arrive had been beastly, but she was very much afraid their arrival was even worse.

She could not like Mr. Andrew Ross, which was just as well as he seemed to dislike her. She knew she'd made a very bad first impression. She wasn't beautiful or elegant or charming like her Italian mother, or as cultured and correct as her Austrian stepfather. And of course, she was absolutely nothing like her English father—that went without saying. If she didn't know better from her old nursemaid Caterina, she would have believed she'd been switched at birth by gypsies or elves or whichever creatures did such things to innocent babies. She was as good as a changeling, orphaned, homeless, and adrift in the Atlantic.

But she was no longer innocent.

She caught sight of herself in the freckled mirror and rolled her eyes. She was not merely adrift—she had drowned and sunk to the bottom of the sea. If she weren't such a coward she'd climb down the beach path and plunge in the sea to wash, as young men had done in the frozen Danube in wintertime in Vienna. She shivered just thinking about it. Her stepbrother Franz had been a member of an adventurous outdoor club and had been insufferably smug about his bravery. Girls were not invited.

What she needed was a bath. A hot, hot bath, some scented soap. A hairbrush. A complete change of underthings. She sniffed her armpit. Certainly a new dress. This one would have to be burned. Her trunk had gone missing before boarding the boat that took her island-hopping through the archipelago in a storm-tossed ocean. She'd been promised when it was found it would be sent along, but it had not come today in Mr. Ross's belongings. It might never come, which meant she'd have to ask the witch to help her again, but that had worked out very badly before.

Of all the bloody luck. She was stuck here, as good as naked, even if Andrew Ross had other ideas. He'd not get rid of her so easily. She had her contract and would abide by every letter. That baron who hired her had not been entirely forthcoming about the hardships of the job, however. The little boy was adorable, but Gemma had pictured a country house set on a rolling green meadow with sheep, perhaps a bit of salt-scented spray in the air, not this violent, volcanic lump. To prove her point, the windows rattled like gunfire in the endless storm.

And then there was Andrew Ross. Handsome as the devil and knew it, too. Not just handsome—dazzling, golden, kissed by the gods.

Well, perhaps not. His wife was dead, his son hated him, his arm flopped about when it wasn't in its sling, and he'd chosen to bury himself in the outermost reaches of the British Isles. No doubt he had a dark secret, but then didn't everyone?

"Mamma!" Gemma hurried to Marc's side. He was thrashing around, still sleeping, a tiny frown on his perfect face. He was the image of his father.

"Shh, my darling. It's just a bad dream. Gemma's here." She stroked his arm and spoke to him in Italian and English, repeating each idea in the other language. It is what her mamma had done for her, to make sure she knew her father's tongue, even if she didn't know *him*.

She knew him now and wished she didn't. Sighing, Gemma inspected the contents of her dresser. She found a dusty powder puff, two hairpins, and a mostly toothless comb, but as in people, some teeth were better than none. She set about to bring some order to her person, in the very remote chance that Mr. Ross asked her to dine with him. Which she hoped he would not. She'd be better off with the MacLarens in the kitchen, trying to make sense of what they were saying to each other. Who knew? With her facility for languages, she might just add a seventh.

Mrs. MacLaren had set two places in the dining room, so it didn't seem sporting to request that Miss Peartree take her plate and cutlery and go back into the kitchen. The MacLarens were leaving anyway. True to the little pictures they drew, they were going home through what was now a snowstorm to sleep in their own beds. Andrew hoped they wouldn't fall into a ditch and freeze to death, for Mrs. MacLaren's lamb stew smelled delicious and Mr. MacLaren had done a creditable job moving boxes and trunks to where they needed to be unpacked. He wanted them to come back tomorrow and forever. Andrew had many things planned for Mr. MacLaren—planing the front door for example, which continuously blew open unless the heavy hall bench was dragged in front of it. Washing and caulking windows. Climbing up the roof to fix the tiles when he wouldn't get tossed off in a gale to Ireland. Andrew knew he'd lose Mr. MacLaren in the spring when he went back to fishing. He hoped by then Gull House would be snug and comfortable.

He had his doubts, though. If Miss Peartree were still here, his comfort was bound to be a chancy thing.

She had been in a tizzy to discover Marc would be left alone while they ate their dinner, but it was clear even to her that once he'd eaten his own bowl of stew in the kitchen, he was still too sick and tired to keep his little blue eyes open. He'd fallen asleep on Andrew's shoulder as he'd carried him up the stairs to Miss Peartree's room, Miss Peartree trailing a step behind him like a guard dog—some sort of yapping little brown terrier that had been left out in the rain because it rolled in something unpleasant. She had made an effort with her hair, but it was clear to him if he meant to keep her something must be done about her personal hygiene. He'd not have his son cradled in such aromatic arms.

He'd corner Mrs. MacLaren in the kitchen tomorrow morning and beg for some new clothes for the girl. Insist she take a bath, too. Maybe when she smelled sweeter he wouldn't hold her in such aversion. Of course, her tongue would be just as filthy as ever. But Marc liked her. Hell, *loved* her. Andrew supposed he could put up with her for a while until he got his feet under himself again and his arm mended.

He looked around the simply furnished dining room. There was a round table and six turned Jacobean chairs, though he doubted he'd ever fill them with company. A nice seascape in desperate need of a cleaning hung over the Delft-tiled fireplace. A small sideboard, a polished brass chandelier—that was it. There was no carpet, no wallpaper. Andrew found the room suited him, although the echo of Miss Peartree's cutlery was insistent despite her surprisingly ladylike efforts. Her manners were unobjectionable as she dipped her pewter spoon into the white china bowl and fished out carrots and peas and potatoes to chew with her small white teeth.

"Do you not eat meat?"

She swallowed before she answered, another good sign. "Not often."

"You should. You look like a scarecrow."

She put her spoon down on the plate with a clank. "You may be my employer, but it does not give you leave to criticize my appearance."

"It's not just about your appearance. You'll need stamina to keep up with Marc. He's a busy child, into everything when he feels well. In Italy—" He stopped himself. He couldn't tell her of Marc running in the lush villa gardens chasing orange butterflies. Or Giulietta tossing a red ball over his head to Andrew as Marc squealed, jumping up and down, his chubby fists reaching up. Or tumbling with his greyhound puppy, letting the dog lick him all over as he wriggled and laughed. Marc's life had been paradise before Gianni saw fit to end it. Andrew took a sip of wine. There were no palm trees and sultry breezes here, no pretty, light-hearted mother, no ducal father to spoil him. Just Andrew and this ragged little governess.

"I'm sure I can manage," Miss Peartree said tightly.

"Just managing will not be enough. My son should have the best."

"Then why did you bring him here? You are the only *gentleman* on the island." The way she said it let Andrew know how little she thought of him already, and she knew nothing. "He'll have naught but the village children to play with. Do you know there is no school here? The parish priest comes but a few times a year. The islanders' lives are very basic. They steal seabirds' eggs to eat, for heaven's sake."

"How do you know all this when you don't speak Gaelic?"

"I had fourteen days to occupy myself. I walked about, observed. Not everyone was as mean as Mrs. MacLaren." She paused. "Some were worse."

"What did you do to her to put her back up so?"

Miss Peartree's eyes dropped to her bowl. She appeared to be counting peas and spoke directly to them. "She came into the kitchen when I was bathing on the second day I was here. She—she didn't understand."

"Didn't understand what? That you were dirty after traveling and needed to get clean? You do again, by the way," he said baldly.

Miss Peartree's face was very red now. "I know. I'm sorry, but it was too much trouble to go to fill the tub. I ran out of wood—and—and anyway, there was no one to see me. Or smell me. I didn't know when you were coming." She shrugged. "I'd hoped to befriend someone in the village to help me before then."

"Well, you'll have a bath tomorrow, come hell or high water."

Miss Peartree lowered her eyes again. "Yes, sir."

Andrew wondered if he'd heard correctly, but decided not to press her further. He was nearly as worn out as his son. She continued to pick her vegetables out of the stew, but he was pleased to note she allowed one square chunk of lamb to pass her lips.

Her mouth was wide in her elfin face. Now that her hair was combed and pinned, he saw gold threads among the dirty brown in the candlelight. He supposed he shouldn't be too hard on her. She'd lost her luggage and been alone for two weeks in this nearly empty house. "So, tell me what else you've learned about the island," he said, hoping to pass the time until he could fall dead asleep in his own bed instead of at the supper table.

That had been a near thing. Gemma thought for sure Mr. Ross would inquire more closely about her disagreement with Mrs. MacLaren. Thank the Lord he had not. For how could she tell him Mrs. MacLaren had caught her touching herself *down there,* her other hand cupped on her tiny breast flicking a flat brown nipple? She had been incredibly wicked for daytime but had needed release so badly. The past few months had been an absolute horror, and this new job looked to be no better. She had just wanted to unwind the spring that was so tight within her that even her hair hurt.

That day she thought she had the house to herself. Mrs. MacLaren had helped with the bath and then gone back down to the village to borrow fresh clothes for her. Gemma lost all sense of time in the cooling water as she kneaded and stroked with rigorous precision. She had been in the midst of a particularly fine peak and panting accordingly when Mrs. MacLaren discovered her abandon.

It would be hard to say who had been more shocked, but Mrs. MacLaren definitely had the last word, screeching at her, making numerous signs of the cross, and tearing upstairs to lock Gemma out from finding similar bliss on any bed. Needless to say, the housekeeper took the parcel of clean clothes and keys back home. At this point, Gemma's own brown traveling dress could stand up without her.

Gemma didn't think Mrs. MacLaren had told anyone about her sinful ways. While the villagers had been suspicious of her, they hadn't looked at her with the same degree of disgust that the older woman had. Maybe by now the housekeeper had convinced herself that Gemma was washing herself the English way.

She tugged off her dress and unrolled her dingy stockings. She had nothing but her shift to sleep in, and not nearly enough blankets. Gemma stirred at the coals and added another brick of peat. At least for tonight she would be toasty warm. She was looking forward to snuggling with Marc and welcomed his body heat. It had been a long while since she'd shared a bed with anyone, and then it had not been anyone as innocent as Andrew Ross's little son.

Gemma blew out the candle and crawled into bed. She pulled the child to her chest and said her prayers. Tomorrow she would have a bath, and that was nearly as good as being delivered from evil.

Chapter 3

He woke up to a bloody miracle. No, Miss Peartree was right. He'd have to edit himself if he wished Marc not to repeat phrases that were unsuitable for the only *gentleman's* son living on the island. It was a blessed miracle. The sun seemed to be shining, although the gusts were as fierce as ever, billowing the faded curtains even though the windows were closed. Andrew had lain awake most of the night despite his exhaustion, listening to the booming ocean below and the howling wind. He'd better get used to the sounds, for they were all he was apt to hear for the foreseeable future.

He'd discovered some ledgers in the desk yesterday afternoon and had pieced together a sketchy history of his new house. It was more than fifty years old, built on this spit of land for an English gentleman whose interest in ornithology might have been considered excessive, perhaps even unhinged. List upon list of the number of kittiwakes, shags, puffins, guillemots, razor bills, and other seabirds the man observed every spring and summer was rather mind-boggling. There were meticulous pencil sketches in one notebook that were fine enough to frame. But the Englishman had the good sense to leave the island every fall, so who was to say who was unhinged? It was only early December, and already Andrew felt a chill to his bones that seemed permanent.

Andrew reluctantly left the warmth of his covers and went to the window. Scattered diamonds of frost littered the machair on the beach below. The whitecaps were fierce but compelling. He sat in the deep window seat and placed his left hand on the glass. So cold. Too cold for a tramp out of doors, but who knew when the sun would shine again? He was lord of his manor now, should pace his boundaries and look for his ruins.

He was hungry. Judging from the pale yellow sun in the sky, it might be closer to lunch time than breakfast. He'd dress and eat and go for his walk. Exercise his arm as he was supposed to do, squeezing and unsqueezing the hard ball that the doctor he'd consulted in Paris had given him. Andrew had once been fond of exercise—boxing, fencing, and riding—it had kept his instrument in perfect tune. His body had been his fortune. Even if those days were over, there was no reason to let his fitness lapse.

He washed and fumbled with his clothing, cursing the buttons. The house seemed still, thank goodness. No caterwauling child or banging of pot tops. No arguing shrew. Perhaps they'd all taken advantage of the break in the weather and gone off to the village. Andrew hoped something had been left for him in the kitchen to eat. He took the back stairs and pushed the door open.

Steam was rising from an enamel tub, as was Miss Peartree. She had been reaching for a towel draped on a kitchen chair, but at the sight of Andrew had paused for one fatal second. Her wet hair was slicked back from her scrubbed little face and snaked past her waist to rest on her pert backside. Her skin was the color of coffee with far too much cream added, her nipples large and flat and brown, her breasts just the slightest swell over her rib cage. His eyes fixed upon her thatch of curls, mink-brown over slender thighs. She looked like a woodland nymph. A clean woodland nymph.

"Not bloody *again*!"

She clasped her arms around her body. She didn't have quite enough hands to cover herself, not that there was an extra ounce of flesh on her. Andrew stepped forward and handed her the towel. She hastily wrapped it around herself, missing one breast entirely.

Andrew had been mistaken yesterday. What little she had under her clothes was strangely, sinfully appealing. He felt a tug to his groin, which startled him. He hadn't felt real desire in years.

"How dare you?"

She blinked. Her eyelashes were wet. Spiky, tangled. Andrew blinked back but couldn't move any other part of him.

"Don't just stand there! Go away! Go away!" she screamed.

Andrew woke from his trance. What was wrong with him? His feet seemed glued to the floor. He couldn't even find his tongue to say he was sorry

Because he wasn't sorry. Not one bit.

But he did go away, without breakfast. Without a taste of what seemed like the most delicious skin he'd ever seen.

She was so tiny. Everywhere. Almost childlike. He'd never had a sexual interest in children as so many satyrs did. As Donal did. But she was no child. He wondered just how old she was. Twenty? Twenty-five? His hand went to his cock to adjust himself in his breeches. He was rock-hard and nearly in pain. What sort of cosmic joke was being played upon him now? Had he not been punished enough?

Evidently not.

He imagined those perfectly formed legs locked around his hips. He imagined his lips suckling on the cocoa disks of her nipples, teasing them to fullness. He imagined her long lashes fluttering on her cheeks, her wide mouth open in ecstasy as he drove into her.

And he would be alone with her in this house every night, his sleeping son the only chaperone.

God help him. She had to go.

A blast of wind nearly knocked him over. He'd come to the point overlooking where the Sea of Hebrides met the Atlantic. Waves slapped together, sending spray high into the sky. A collision of forces too elemental to ignore. If he were at all fanciful, it resembled what would happen if he and the diminutive yet delectable Miss Peartree ever united in his bed.

It would never happen. It *should* never happen. He'd given all that up to raise his son. No more dallying, no more sneaking around, *no more sin.* He'd done his share for twenty-five years, both involuntary and voluntary. He was two-and-thirty now, the age when many men finally settled down and became leg-shackled. But marriage was forever beyond his touch. No woman could possibly ignore what he had been, what he had done.

He glanced behind him at the forbidding gray box of his new home, its myriad windows focused on the sea. On him. Was Miss Peartree peering out, shaking her little fist at him? Was she packing? No, she had nothing to pack. The ferry had surely left by now, and it returned only every two weeks until the winter weather might make it altogether impossible. He would be trapped with her at Gull House for another fortnight at least.

There were village women. Girls. Not for him, of course. For Marc. They could serve as caregivers until he secured another Italian-speaking governess. Even if he had to wait until spring for someone to come, he could manage. Couldn't he?

He thought of Marc burrowing into the curve of Miss Peartree's neck, happy at last. Bloody, bloody hell.

He'd spent a lifetime feigning interest. Now he'd just have to feign disinterest. It shouldn't be hard. A flat-chested little thing like Miss Peartree had probably never attracted a man. She wouldn't expect or want him to fall at her feet. So he wouldn't.

He was her employer. A father. Celibate.

He didn't even know her first name.

Hortense. Prudence. Brunhilde. More likely Circe, turning him into a pig to root about looking for his lost good sense.

Andrew shook his hatless head. He'd need to find a knitted cap like the islanders wore if he were to go outdoors this winter. He and Marc would need sweaters and scarves and thick boots. The warm clothes he purchased for them in temperate Paris were totally inadequate. He'd go back to the house and make a list—

No, *she* was in there.

There had been no trace of Mr. or Mrs. MacLaren or his son. They were probably in the village. He'd walk down the rutted track and explore. Make new acquaintances. Wave his good hand wildly about gesturing his thoughts. Talk to a goat or two along the way. Andrew turned his back to the sea and set off, hoping when he returned Miss Peartree would be dressed from her pointed little chin to her narrow little feet.

"*Scheiss!* Bloody wonderful!" Gemma slammed around the kitchen, pulling up her towel. She had locked the hall door to the room with a polite little note tied to the door handle. Who would have thought he'd use the back stairs when there were perfectly good front ones to descend? They even had carpet, threadbare though it was. But he'd snuck up on her like a servant when he was supposed to be a gentleman.

Well, he was no gentleman. She'd have to be blind not to notice the look he gave her, like a starving dog staring in the butcher shop window. She was not a chop or a rasher of bacon.

She *would* have to leave. There was no way on earth she could remain here to be hounded and fight off his lust. She'd made all the mistakes she was going to, worked too hard and come too far to find herself in the same predicament as when she left school in Bath and returned to Vienna. She'd allowed herself to be trapped. Never again.

Her father had been no help when she'd fled to London, but at least she'd stolen his seal and stationery and forged a glowing letter of recommendation for herself that had impressed the sniffy Baron Christie. During her interview, she'd rattled off greetings in all her languages and remembered every bit of her boring deportment lessons from Miss Meredith's School for Young Ladies. She had been so very desperate for this job, and now that she had it, she'd be mad to stay.

Two weeks until the next boat came. Two weeks to avoid Marc's father. It could be done. She'd station the crib across the threshold of her room.

Gemma stomped up the back stairs. Perhaps she was mistaken. Maybe Andrew Ross had goggled at her because he'd never seen anybody so unappealing in all his life. He might not see her as a tasty chop but just a scrap of bone. Just because she'd caught the eye of one man—

No, she mustn't think of it. She'd been a fool, but now she was not.

Where in hell were the MacLarens and Marc? They were supposed to come back with fresh clothes for her. She was not ever going to touch any of the clothes she'd been wearing these two weeks.

Mr. MacLaren had delivered the crib on his pony cart, and the little boy had gone back to the village willingly with the couple, already picking up a word or two of their language. To give her privacy in the bath, Mrs. MacLaren had indicated as she'd pointed elaborately between the child, the tub, and the back door, although she'd looked stern and waggled a finger at her as though she expected Gemma would touch herself again given the first opportunity. Not bloody likely with Adonis upstairs sleeping.

Well, he was awake now. And she was freezing and mortified. She wrapped the towel tighter and looked out the window. He was on the point, his unbuttoned jacket blown back by the wind. His fair cropped hair stood on end. He must be colder than she was. He turned suddenly and she ducked back against the wall, heart hammering. She waited, but there was no slam of door or footsteps below. She was safe for the time being.

Taking the toothless comb, she struggled to get her hair untangled, then braided it, wound it up, and pinned it. There was nothing to do but get back under the covers to try to get warm.

Wherever was her trunk? It had been filled with lovely things, ungovernessy things. Her mother would never have permitted her to dress in ugly black mourning clothes, and she hadn't. It had caused a bit of scandal in Vienna, but what she had done out of her pretty frocks was far worse.

She had taken the precaution of buying a few gray and brown dresses for her new job, but buried beneath them in the missing trunk was her favorite bronze silk evening dress and some of her mother's clothes, including a scandalous sheer nightgown that had spent more time upon the carpet than on her mother's body. Gemma had her mother's jewelry, too, if thieves hadn't absconded with it. Of course, she had stolen it herself from Franz's safe. It was only fitting after what he had stolen from her.

Even as a child, Gemma had been fascinated with the gifts that her mother's male friends had given her. The pieces rightfully belonged to her—Herr Birnbaum had not given her mother much in the way of trinkets over the five years that they were married. Francesca Bassano Birnbaum sometimes lamented this fact in the letters she sent to Gemma at school. Gemma wondered exactly how happy her warm-hearted Italian mother had been with her strict Viennese husband, but at least she was financially secure and Gemma's school tuition paid for.

"To grow old alone, *bambina* that is not for me," her mother had said to her time and time again. Worried about losing her looks and her hold on men, Francesca had decided to leave mistressing behind and look for matrimony. She had snared Herr Birnbaum but wasn't able to grow old with him after all.

Even if she never got her belongings back, Gemma heard her mother's musical voice in her head and felt her presence in her heart. Francesca had done her best to raise her, although her methods would be considered unorthodox by most standards.

Which is how Gemma wound up shivering at the ends of the earth, torn between committed loneliness and unwelcome desire for a man who could tempt her from her best intentions. Gemma needed this job, but she didn't need the complication of Andrew Ross. But perhaps given time, she could manage him as she did his son. She wouldn't quit quite yet.

She burrowed under the thin quilts, wondering if she would ever feel warm again. Her mother had often spoken of the warm Italian sun, but they had never, in all their travels together, returned to her home country. Gemma wondered if her mother was ashamed of what she had become—an astronomically priced courtesan sought after by any man with sense and sufficient coin.

Gemma had been born in chilly, gray London, in a rather mean dwelling grudgingly paid for by her mother's longtime benefactor, the Earl of Barrowdown. The earl had lost all interest in his increasing mistress, but he did his duty to his daughter. Just. Gemma's mother had received a small allowance until her figure returned and her fatigue left her. Then, Francesca Bassano clawed her way back on top and left the earl to history.

Gemma had never felt relegated to the shadows, however. Her mother included her often in her amusements, taught her manners, introduced her to art and music. Languages, too, for love was made in many of them. Gemma had been an accomplished young lady until her first mistake cost her her mother's company.

Her second mistake was much worse.

Her third mistake was absolutely necessary.

A young woman alone had few avenues open for employment. A young woman wanted for theft had even fewer choices. Perhaps it was just as well she was freezing to death on this inhospitable rock, far from the gaiety of Vienna and the greed of her stepbrother. She had only taken what she was entitled to, and Franz would never find her here. He would in any case be looking for Gemma Bassano, not Gemma Peartree.

Perhaps she should have changed her first name, too. But she could hear her mother whisper it against her temple, almost feel her silken arms around her. Gemma closed her eyes, imagining the scent of lemon verbena.

She had vials of her mother's signature scent in her missing trunk. Right now she'd trade every vial and silk dress for a set of flannel underwear. She could hear her mother cluck and chide her now. No self-respecting woman would ever disguise her charms beneath such practical garments. As Gemma had few charms to disguise, she was all for practicality at the moment. Warmth was at a premium, and if what she wore extinguished the devilish light in Andrew Ross's eyes, all the better.

She sat up at the sound of the trap rolling on the crushed shell drive. At last! Merciful heavens, to wear clean clothes again was enough to make her weep for joy. Yes, that's why tears were streaking down her face. Gemma brushed them away and waited for Mrs. MacLaren to climb the stairs to her. She wasn't going to shock the woman again wrapped in a bedsheet.

CHAPTER 4

Andrew met the pony cart on the track coming back from the village. His son was seated on Mrs. MacLaren's generous lap, swathed in a thick sweater, cap, and mittens, which must have belonged to one of her grandchildren. His cheeks were rosy and he was laughing until he caught sight of his father. Instinctively he shrank into Mrs. MacLaren's bosom, earning Andrew a look of concern from his housekeeper.

He remembered what Miss Peartree said. If children and animals liked you, it meant something to Mrs. MacLaren. Perhaps he'd have to get a dog to convince the woman he was not a devil, although in his heart he knew he was. His own child was afraid of him. Marc probably felt Andrew was responsible for robbing him of every known thing in his world, including his name. There was no way to explain the truth to him now, or perhaps ever. How could he tell the child he was a bastard, conceived in triangular sin to hold on to ducal consequence? That his parents were dead because of him? Andrew was an expert liar—any lie he told the boy would be preferable to the truth. By the time Marc was old enough, perhaps he'd have a story fashioned that would be palatable.

He gave a falsely good-natured smile to the little group. "Good morning. Lovely day, isn't it?" He gestured to the sun, which showed no sign of hiding behind a snow-filled cloud just yet. The MacLarens nodded enthusiastically and gestured to the pile behind them. Clothes for Miss Peartree, Andrew guessed, too late to do him any good. Her naked image was burned upon his eyelids. "I'm just going for a walk. Carry on."

The island wasn't more than a few miles long and wide, and a third of it was his. He took a breath of bracing sea air and watched the birds career above his head. There must be thousands of them out here. Traces of them were everywhere, from their droppings to the nests tucked into rock and tall grass. He didn't know one gull from another, but the previous owner of Gull House certainly had. Perhaps the next time it was fair enough to venture outside Andrew would take the man's journals with him. He needed to do something to turn his mind from the captivating Miss Peartree, although bird-watching might not be sufficiently engaging.

One night in his new home and he was ready to jump from the rather jagged cliffs on either side of him. Perhaps when his arm was better, he'd teach himself to rappel down them, hunt for eggs himself. He was hungry enough to eat a raw egg right now.

He headed down the sloping track until the village was in sight and peat smoke perfumed the air. The turf-roofed stone houses clustered close together as though they were cold themselves, facing a sheltered cove. He could see quite a few bundled-up people taking advantage of the sunny day in their dooryards, spinning, mending nets, gossiping. Very likely gossiping about *him*, talking about his arrival. A humble sign swung in the wind over what appeared to be a tiny store.

Suddenly, Andrew didn't want to bear their scrutiny. He took an abrupt turn on a footpath that wound along the eastern ridge. The waves thundered and crashed on the beach below, birds wheeled and squawked in the sky. For a place in the middle of nowhere, the noise was deafening, louder to Andrew than London ever was.

But yet, there was nothing whatsoever to do.

Andrew was afraid he'd made a grave mistake asking Edward Christie to secure him property here. It wasn't as if he missed human contact—he'd had quite enough of that, ever dissembling, fawning, flattering to line his pockets. If he never again had to pay a compliment to a portly viscount or an aging dowager, never had to position himself between an unhappy husband and wife, that would be fine. He'd whored long enough.

But how was he to occupy himself here? It wasn't as if he had an estate to run. There was no home farm to oversee, no tenants' roofs to repair, no horses in the stable whickering for a run. The decaying outbuilding to Gull House might garner his attention for a while, although it was more suited to keeping chickens than prime horseflesh. A few chickens wouldn't go amiss, though. Andrew didn't truly fancy eating seabirds' stolen eggs. Perhaps a cow, milk for Marc since Miss Peartree didn't seem to think much of goat's milk.

He'd have to go home and make a list. A long one. And he might solicit Miss Peartree's opinion, if he could focus on a spot over her head and not into her lovely gold-flecked eyes. Sighing, he chose the long way home, hoping the girl would be properly dressed by the time he got back.

After a two-hour tramp exploring the coast of his new domain, Andrew was ready to warm up and eat. His stomach was more than empty, his fingers were frozen, and his gentleman's boots had done nothing to repel the frost on the uneven grassy path. He fumbled at the kitchen door, then held back his laughter as he interrupted his housekeeper and his governess in the middle of a bilingual argument.

Be careful what you wish for. Miss Peartree was now draped in an oversized pea-green sack, the sleeves rolled up in a bunch to expose her dainty wrists. Mrs. MacLaren was running basting stitches up one side of the dress in a futile attempt to fit it to the little governess. There would be enough fabric left over for at least another exceedingly ugly garment should they decide to cut into it, if Mrs. MacLaren didn't cut into Miss Peartree first. It was clear Miss Peartree was not a bit grateful for her new clothes.

"I hope it's safe to come in now," he murmured.

Miss Peartree shot him a scornful look but said nothing. Marc looked up shyly from his pot on the floor and then resumed banging. Andrew couldn't decide what was worse—the domestic intranquility of his servants or his son's attempts at percussion.

"Couldn't we find him something less noisy to occupy him with? A set of blocks or something?" he shouted over the noise.

"You should ask Mr. MacLaren to make him some. He has his tools with him today," Miss Peartree shouted back. Curious, Marc stopped his drumming and stared at the adults. Andrew tamped down his desire to pick his son off the floor. It was enough that the boy wasn't crying when he looked at him.

"What an excellent idea, Miss Peartree. I will directly after I finally have my breakfast. Lunch now, I guess. I was somehow distracted from food earlier. The condition of the kitchen quite— shocked me. I expect I should apologize." Not that he was a bit sorry. Miss Peartree had been a tempting morsel.

Miss Peartree took a step forward, and Mrs. MacLaren yanked her back by her skirts. "I left a sign on the door, sir. I never expected you to take the back stairs."

"No harm done. In fact, there's a great improvement to your person. The bath has done wonders for you. I wish I could say the same about that—that—shall we call it a dress?"

Miss Peartree's lips twitched. "I call it an abomination. You should see what else this evil woman brought me to wear. It seems she still hates me."

"You must admit it's better than what you had."

She sniffed and pinched the material that hid her hips. "I'm not sure about that."

Mrs. MacLaren threw up her hands, stuck her needle back into a pincushion, and snapped the lid of her sewing box shut. She said something in Gaelic with finality.

"Getting you to stand still is a trial, I take it." Andrew went to the sideboard, lifted the linen napkin from a loaf, and began to cut a slice. He was gently shooed away by Mrs. MacLaren, who pointed to a kitchen chair. Andrew obeyed and watched the older woman assemble a simple lunch for him of bread and cheese and pickles, replete with a mug of ale. Marc sidled up to the table, staying a safe distance away.

"Marc, would you like a bite?" He tore off a corner of the bread and held it out. After thinking a long moment, Marc snatched it from Andrew's hand and crammed it into his mouth.

Mrs. MacLaren beamed and patted his son's curls. She set to making Marc a little plate of his own.

"We've eaten already, you know." Miss Peartree frowned. Mrs. MacLaren said something right back that Andrew interpreted as "Marc is a growing boy." The housekeeper filled a cup with milk and placed it and the food quite close to Andrew. If Marc wanted it, he'd have to climb onto the bench and get it. Sit within spitting distance of his father, emphasis on spitting. Andrew inched back a little to make it easier for the child to proceed. He was relieved when Marc hauled his little body onto the scarred wooden bench, straightened himself, and tucked into his second lunch.

Miss Peartree relented and helped herself to a pickle. The three of them sat in companionable silence in the warm kitchen, watching Mrs. MacLaren move capably between the larder and the stove preparing tonight's fish pie dinner. Thanks to the provisions they'd brought over on the boat yesterday, his household was spared from eating roasted gulls or their eggs. One could not precisely go to market with a basket over one's arm out here, although Andrew had seen the store. Perhaps tomorrow if the weather held he'd have the courage to go down and face the islanders and check out the village itself. Maybe he could even bring Miss Peartree and Marc with him.

Marc began drooping over his plate. The governess swept him up in her arms and whispered something in Italian in his ear. He shook his head no but was not defiant. No self-respecting boy would admit he was tired and needed a nap. She carried him upstairs, singing softly. Andrew was left with his housekeeper, who looked as if she'd prefer to be alone in her kitchen kingdom.

He took the hint. Making a great show of patting his belly and bowing, he shut himself in his bookless library. A dozen crates were lined up along the walls. Mr. MacLaren must have taken the liberty of prying them open while Andrew was out on his ramble, but their contents were undisturbed. A very good thing, too, for Andrew did not want to shock the man with his naughty books.

But he had others—histories, novels, scientific treatises. His education had been a hit-or-miss affair, so it had behooved him to teach himself that he might move smoothly in society. One would never guess that Andrew Rossiter was the son of a common Edinburgh prostitute.

Not that his mother was common. She'd been extraordinarily beautiful, a golden angel as he remembered through his little boy's lens. She'd had rich patrons—one of whom had been his unknown father—but when he was seven she had become ill and left him. Disappeared. Whether she was dead or simply in despair, the result was the same. Andrew had managed somehow on his own for a few weeks before Donal Stewart found him.

Andrew was not going to let himself wallow in the unpleasant past. He removed the lid on one of the boxes and unwrapped a small marble statue of Pan. Safe enough. He placed it upon a shelf, then rummaged around for other objets d'art. Many had been gifted to him by grateful patrons, who had far more money than sense. He admired the bric-a-brac for its worth, not for sentimentality. He had little in his past to miss, but much to regret.

Bah. He was doing it again. He shoved the empty box aside and began on the next. Books this time. Leather-bound and gilt-inscribed. He lined them on a shelf methodically bringing them out to the very edge. Andrew was particular when it came to his surroundings—he appreciated beauty and order. How he was going to set Gull House to rights would be a monumental task, although somewhere in the house came the steady tapping of a hammer. Mr. MacLaren had gotten right to work. Andrew's new home's deficiencies needed no explanation, which was fortunate as whatever Andrew said would not be understood. But the Mac-Larens seemed competent and hardworking. He would keep them on, but certainly for his own sanity Miss Peartree had to go.

As if she knew she was in his thoughts, she knocked on the library door, not waiting for an invitation to barge in. She had changed into something else equally huge and hideous, only instead of pea-green it was more vomit yellow. Andrew raised an eyebrow.

"You might have waited for me to say 'enter.' " He could have been doing anything in here—gratifying himself with the image of Miss Peartree's far lovelier appearance this morning, for example.

"Marc is asleep, even through the hammering, poor lamb. I thought I would ask you if you need any help unpacking."

Well, this was something new. Miss Peartree actually looked meek and biddable. Ridiculous as well. "I'm perfectly capable of moving a few books on my own."

"Of course you are. I meant no disparagement. How did you injure your arm, anyway?"

"An accident," he said tersely.

"The same one that killed your wife?"

He had been mistaken. She wasn't here to help but to hound him. "Miss Peartree, you ask far too many questions. Even an upper servant such as yourself should know your place. I cannot think how your previous employer tolerated your inquisitiveness." He plunked a stack of books down on his desk with a deliberately loud thud, hoping to frighten her away. Instead, she took the top off one of the crates and peered into it.

Damn it! Before he could tell her to close the box, she had lifted what was surely one of his more salacious volumes and opened it.

To her credit, she neither blanched nor blushed. There was no sign of a ladylike swoon, no shriek, no revulsion. She looked up at him quite calmly, the book still open in her hands. "Oh! I can see now why you wanted to do this task alone. I know you care nothing for my opinion, but these books should not be around an impressionable child. What if Marc were to come upon them?"

Andrew stalked across the room and snatched the book from her hands. "I have no intention of placing them on the shelves! Nor will I put up with your meddling, Miss Peartree."

She raised her pointed little chin. "You have employed me to help raise your child, sir. I think I should have some influence in what is appropriate for the household."

"You do? I believe I should have even more influence than you, and right now your presence in this household is about to be terminated."

That chin grew more pugnacious. "You cannot sack me every day, Mr. Ross. I won't go. You do remember that I still have that pesky contract in my possession. Any magistrate would uphold my right to this job."

"Your right! You serve at my pleasure, Miss Peartree, and may I say I am getting *none*."

She bristled. "I was not hired to give *you* pleasure, Mr. Ross, but to teach your son. And I will not have you ogling me when I take a bath, either."

"Ogling! You were naked in my kitchen. I challenge you to find a man who would not notice such a thing."

"You *noticed* for an exceptionally long time." She picked up another erotic book and skimmed through it. "Judging from your taste in reading, I begin to understand you. Your poor wife. I feel now more than ever I must clarify the terms of my employment."

This was outside of enough. Andrew was not about to let this impudent creature dictate to him. If she could snoop on him, he could turn the tables. When he had the opportunity, he'd go through her reticule and tear the vaunted contract to shreds. "There are no terms. You are fired, Miss Peartree. I suppose I'll have to put up with you until the next boat comes, but I'll carry you up the gangplank myself when it docks."

She snapped the book shut. "You will not lay a hand on me, sir, if you know what's good for you."

Andrew loomed over her, but she refused to back down. Her face was mutinous, her lips a bloodless thin line of disapproval. He fought back the incomprehensible urge to kiss her. She'd probably bite his tongue in two.

She was driving him mad. He must get hold of himself. Marc needed this woman now, no matter what Andrew thought of her. In just a little over twenty-four hours his son was becoming a happy child again. Andrew truly understood for the first time just how difficult it must have been for Marc all these weeks to be surrounded by strangers who didn't speak his language. Andrew had only been on this island a day, and his frustration was getting the better of him. The only person who understood him was the virtuous, vicious little Miss Peartree, and he was afraid she understood him only too well.

He sighed wearily. "Look here, Miss Peartree, once again we are at sixes and sevens. I assure you my first concern is for my son. Keeping that in mind, I am willing to overlook your argumentative behavior. As we are in absolute agreement about the contents of those books, that is one less impediment between us. Rest assured I will not be laying a hand on you now or in the future. If you can keep a civil tongue in your head, I shall endeavor to do the same, and perhaps we can see what transpires in the next two weeks."

She narrowed her eyes in suspicion. "So I am to be on trial."

"As am I. Should I offend your delicate sensibilities in any way," he said over her snort, "you may leave and I will fulfill the financial obligations of your contract. You'll be paid for the full year, even if you spend a mere two weeks here. Fair enough?"

Her eyebrows knit. "Not really. You might go out of your way to be offensive, ensuring that I will leave. I can think of any number of objectionable tricks you might play."

Andrew sat down heavily at his desk. "Miss Peartree, I'm too tired to play tricks, objectionable or otherwise. I've had a bad few months. I simply want to be left in peace. I want my son to get used to me. That's not too much to ask, is it?"

"N-no, I suppose not."

She looked as if she wanted to say more, but he cut her off. "Well then, that is all. Let me get back to my books. Mrs. Mac-Laren might have need of you in the kitchen if you truly insist on being helpful to someone."

"Unlikely. Are you sure—" She had the sense to stop when he gave his most glacial stare. "Very well. I suppose I'll see you at supper."

"I will dine alone tonight. Here in the library. Please tell Mrs. MacLaren." The last thing he needed was more time spent in Miss Peartree's company. Let her dine in the kitchen with Marc, or even in the dining room. He was not equal to another inquisition or her unsettling effect on him.

"Yes, sir." She wavered a moment and finally turned, tripping on her voluminous skirt. Andrew rose from his chair, shut the door, and turned the key. At least he'd be alone for the rest of the afternoon, unless he was called to referee another fight between his housekeeper and governess. Though they seemed to enjoy hurling insults at each other that neither one could understand.

Miss Peartree was an odd little thing. She didn't have the demeanor of a servant, so it was up to him to school her, if he could stand her company for any length of time. How ironic that a boy from an Edinburgh slum was now more smoothly polished than any lord of his acquaintance.

Over the next half-hour, Andrew consolidated all the erotica and tapped the boxes shut with Pan's hoofed feet. He would store them until he could sell them. No point in throwing good money after bad. He must know someone perverted enough to enjoy this particular collection. He would write to the few he trusted and see if he could recoup his investment.

Which reminded him. He needed to make a list. Needed to replace his parlor sofa if Miss Peartree's nose was accurate. But first he'd line his shelves to help him endure the days ahead. His conversations with Miss Peartree must be limited. Andrew imagined pretty soon he'd turn into a doddering old cripple, talking to himself and counting snowflakes and seabirds.

Something about Andrew Ross smelled to high heaven. A man as handsome as he was shouldn't need dirty books to find his satisfaction. Although, Gemma realized, now that he was out of society perhaps those awful books and his hand would be his only comfort. It wasn't as if she was going to tumble into his bed. Or bend over the parlor sofa like the first picture she saw. That looked most uncomfortable. Her mamma had always advised her a little variety in the bedroom was the key to male happiness, but Gemma had no intention of making any man happy in whatever room she found herself in. Especially Andrew Ross.

It was true she had not entered the library solely to be useful. There was unfinished business between them from this morning. She could not very well have spoken of it over lunch, not that Marc or Mrs. MacLaren would have understood a word. It wanted a private moment, but as soon as she was in the man's presence, he put her back up.

Faced with an hour of idleness, Gemma didn't dare to take advantage of the comparatively fine weather and go outdoors. Marc could wake and would expect her to be nearby. Really, at some point she would *have* to sit down with Mr. Ross, for surely he wouldn't enslave her to his son twenty-four hours a day, seven days a week. They needed to set the conditions for her employment, at least as long as she *was* employed. His daily threats to remove her from his house had already become tiresome. Perhaps a girl from the village could be hired for a few hours a week to give Gemma respite, not that there was anything to do or anywhere to go. Mrs. MacLaren had been prevailed upon to take Marc with her so Gemma could have her disastrous bath this morning, but the woman couldn't be depended on to do her any more favors. They had reached an uneasy truce—or at least Gemma thought they had. Mrs. MacLaren was no longer wild-eyed waving knives around and shrieking like a banshee. Marc's presence had a quelling effect on her, and his father was even more powerful. Mrs. MacLaren seemed besotted by Mr. Ross. Mr. MacLaren had better watch out.

There was no doubt Andrew Ross possessed his unfair share of charm. Gemma had been subjected to a parade of men through her mother's life, but she could not recall any one of them coming close to Andrew's physical perfection. He was so tall, so blond, so very blue-eyed, like a Viking god returning to the Western Isles. Wounded in body and spirit, he was even more appealing. Vulnerable. Although he did not wear mourning for his late wife, it was clear it pained him too much to speak of her.

Unless—

Unless he was responsible for her death. Gemma stumbled as she mounted the stairs to her bedroom. She was becoming fanciful, having read far too many gothic novels. Looks were often deceiving, but surely a man who so resembled an angel could not have killed his wife. Though perhaps he had caused her accident and was so steeped in guilt that he couldn't talk about it. She could not quiz his poor little boy, who refused to even call the man "Papa." It was almost as if Andrew Ross was a complete stranger to him.

Gemma threw herself down on her bed and sighed. There was a mystery here. Oh, dear. Her mother had despaired of her curiosity, calling her a little terrier after a rat when Gemma wouldn't leave well enough alone. "Be careful what you catch," her mamma had warned. "Rats have sharp teeth and they carry disease." Andrew Ross's teeth were blindingly white and even, and he looked clean, but who knew what lurked within? And how could she find out without winding up like the late Mrs. Ross? If he decided to toss her over the cliffs, Mrs. MacLaren certainly wouldn't object.

Didn't she owe it to her own safety to discover what Mr. Ross was hiding? For she certainly wasn't going to get any straight answers from him. A proper governess might not rummage through her master's belongings, but Gemma was not a bit proper, and she hadn't been a governess long enough to teach herself propriety. She was used to living by her wits, and one handsome employer should not drive them from her.

There might be clues in all those books downstairs as to what kind of man Andrew Ross was. Already she knew his taste for sins of the flesh. She'd really like to examine those erotic books a bit more closely to further her education, but couldn't, seeing how Mr. Ross had staked out that room and rarely ventured out of it except to eat and sleep.

Sleep. She had nothing else to do at the moment. And as Mr. Ross had said last night, she needed stamina to deal with Marc. Gemma closed her eyes, listening to the crash of the waves beneath her window. Tomorrow she'd figure out a way to begin her investigation of her employer. For now, she'd steal a nap while she could.

CHAPTER 5

The sun played hide-and-seek with the clouds all morning, but it was still a second day of relatively good weather. In an unprecedented act of civility, Mr. Ross had actually invited Gemma and his son to stroll down to the village with him, but Gemma begged off. Making a great pretense of sneezing and pinching her little nose until it looked realistically red, she convinced him to go by himself and gave him a long list of things to look for in the tiny village shop. As soon as she heard the front door slam, she hurried into the library, plunked Marc down with his favorite spoon and pan, and began her search.

The shelves were lined with books now and interesting bric-a-brac. The boxes were empty, stacked neatly against the wall, but for three that had been nailed back shut. The "bad" books, no doubt. Gemma had nothing with which to pry them open, so she concentrated on other areas. A cursory glance through the desk drawers yielded the same old ledgers and papers relating to Gull House that she had already committed to memory while she was stuck downstairs for two weeks waiting for the Rosses' arrival. She'd almost been desperate enough to bird-watch herself, but the weather had been so inclement she soon disabused herself of that notion.

Wait. She hadn't been waiting for the Rosses. She'd been waiting for the Rossiters. She was almost positive that was the name that Baron Christie had given her in the employment interview. Of course, she had been terribly nervous what with lying left and right, so maybe she had heard the name incorrectly. However, she found a yellowed sheet of foolscap and the nub of a pencil and began her second list of the day.

Name???

There was nothing personal in the desk except for a list that Mr. Ross had begun himself, listing necessary items of furniture for the house. She was pleased to see the addition of a new sofa on it, as well as the word *toys*. There had been very few items in Marc's baggage that could amuse him. As if to emphasize her thought, Marc rapped noisily on the saucepan.

"I hope your father buys you quiet toys. I shall go mad otherwise, sweetheart," she told Marc, taking the sting out of her words with a smile. Not that he knew what she said. She pulled a book down from the shelf.

It was an ordinary history book, no bookplate affixed to the frontispiece with its owner's name. Someone had defaced it during reading. Various words were underlined, and tiny notes were written in the margins throughout. She could be mistaken, but Mr. Ross didn't strike her as a scholar. He seemed too physical to be contained behind a desk for long. She could see him riding to the hounds, swimming across a lake, or boxing, stripped to the waist. When he had come in from his walk yesterday, he'd taken her breath away. His color was high, his fair hair windblown, his eyes sparkling from whatever adventure he'd had.

And then of course he'd ruined it with his smirk when he saw her in that big green bag. Mrs. MacLaren had brought back a frightful compilation of clothes yesterday, too ugly for even the impoverished islanders to wear. Most looked as if they were the remnants of a failed church jumble sale, sent over the water by well-meaning do-gooders. Who in their right mind would ever wear the hideous purple-and-scarlet-striped gown she had on today? It had made her dizzy to see herself in the looking glass this morning.

Gemma put the book back and took down another. More scribbling inside. On the fourteenth book, she finally found some evidence of Mr. Ross's previous life, a newspaper clipping pressed between the pages. It advertised the latest effort by the gothic romance author who wrote the wildly popular *Courtesan Court* series. Those books were a secret sin for the girls at Miss Meredith's—curious that a gentleman would care about such entertainment. To her delight, she swept through the shelves and found a nearly complete set, well-thumbed, if she were any judge. It seemed Mr. Ross had catholic tastes, or at least the taste of a fifteen-year-old girl. No, that was unfair—the series attracted countesses and chambermaids alike. Whoever wrote them must have made a fortune.

For a second, Gemma wondered if Mr. Ross himself was the author. Impossible. No gentleman could have the perspicacity and wit of the anonymous "Lady X" who wrote them. There were several volumes that she had not read, and she put them aside. Surely Mr. Ross would not begrudge her reading in her spare time. If she ever had any. Marc was a handful.

To emphasize that point, he had abandoned his drumming and stood before her, his chubby arms raised. "Up!" he begged.

He was so smart, already picking up English and Gaelic. Her mother had always claimed the best time to teach a child a foreign language was when they were learning their own native tongue. Francesca would have loved this little boy.

Gemma swooped him up for a cuddle, and he settled his nose into the crook of her neck.

"That tickles," she smiled down on him. She wiggled her fingers on his sides, and he screamed in delight, right in her left ear. "Oh, I see you're protecting your papa's privacy. I was bad, wasn't

I, snooping about. I wish you could tell me what I long to know."

"And what is that, Miss Peartree?"

Good lord. Andrew Ross stood like a thundercloud in the doorway. Marc began to whimper. Gemma snatched her list from the desk and stuffed it into her apron pocket. "Oh! You startled me."

"What are you doing in my library?"

"Why, looking at books, of course! I found three I've been longing to know about," she prevaricated, hoping he would confuse what she said now with what she said seconds ago. "The Lady X *Courtesan Court* books. They're among my favorites. You're back from the village rather soon." She set Marc down on the rug, where he picked up the wooden spoon and pretended to eat from the empty pot.

"The shop was closed." Mr. Ross looked as if he wanted to say more, so she went on the attack.

"I'm glad you're back. We need to discuss my time off, so I can actually read these books. You can't possibly expect me to spend twenty-four hours a day seven days a week looking after Marc without any kind of break."

She could see from the surprise on his face he had expected exactly that. "When I was originally hired, I assumed I was coming to a normal sort of household with at least a nursery maid," she continued patiently. "Gull House is *not* normal. Mrs. Mac-Laren cannot be expected to spell me—she has the duties of two or three people as it is."

"I'll look into hiring someone," he said, his voice clipped. "Until I do, I imagine you'll try to shake me down for an increase in your salary."

Gemma felt her face flush, never a good sign to those who knew her. "I never said anything of the kind. The terms Lord Christie and I came to were most generous."

"Then I can't bribe you to go away?"

"You agreed to give me a two-week grace period to see how Marc and I get on. Should I fail that, I won't even want the year's salary you promised me. I'll get on the next boat without a backward glance." *Foolish, foolish.* But he'd set her teeth on edge, accusing her of avariciousness. She needed money like everyone else, especially now that her trunk had gone missing, but was not about to sell her soul to get it.

He gave her a sour smile. "I forgot about our bargain. Before I go employing anyone to please you, let's see if you please *me.* Can you manage being a slave to my son for the next thirteen days?"

"As long as I am not a slave to you! But you're going to have to add staff here eventually. Unless you can't afford to."

His face shuttered. "My finances are none of your concern."

He looked haughty as a duke. Perhaps he really was the runaway son of some grand house, forced to flee to the Continent after killing someone in a duel. Where he met his tempestuous Italian bride who drove him mad with desire. Until she came to her senses and tossed him out on his beautiful bottom.

Gemma *had* noticed. The man's clothes were exquisitely and expensively tailored. He definitely had money. And eclectic taste in literature and the arts and sciences, if she were to judge him by his book covers.

But what healthy young man would choose to bury himself here on this windblown volcanic rock, unless he really was hiding from trouble? Gemma's curiosity had only intensified from her aborted search. The mysterious Mr. Ross was concealing something, she was sure of it.

Just as she harbored one or two regrets of her own.

Marc chose this moment to commence beating on his pot. Gemma jumped a mile

"You really have to find something else for my son to occupy himself with. At this rate, he'll grow up to be a chef and we'll all be deaf."

"There's nothing wrong in good, honest employment. Those that provide nourishment and sustenance to people should be valued, not mocked," she said primly.

"I have greater hopes for Marc."

"Do you want him to follow in your footsteps?"

A look of horror crossed Mr. Ross's face so quickly Gemma was not entirely sure she'd seen it. "I want him to have the freedom to choose what he is to be."

"An admirable goal." Gemma bent to pick up Marc again. "Did you ever do one of your drawings for Mr. MacLaren yesterday? Sketch a set of blocks? They would be far less noisy unless Marc decided to throw them at you. I'm surprised you didn't pack his toys when you left Italy. Surely he had some."

"There was great confusion when Giu—when my wife died. I thought it best to make a clean break."

"Hmm. I cannot agree with you. Children prefer stability. Comfort and familiarity."

"I know that now. Let's agree, Miss Peartree, that I was a very poor father before. I'm learning every day."

Gemma was surprised by his humble admission. Perhaps he wasn't a duke's son after all. Cooing to Marc, she made for the door to leave the man alone with his books.

His words stopped her in her tracks. "I'll have that piece of paper you hid in your pocket."

"I beg your pardon?"

"I shall not give it. You looked as guilty as a child caught stealing from a cookie jar when I looked into the room. The note, please."

What had she written that would damn her? Feeling mulish, she fished the crumpled list from her pocket.

" 'Name?' That's all? What does this mean, Miss Peartree?"

"Uh, nothing, really. I was going to write down a list of books I wished to borrow from you. So that we were clear that I had them, and you couldn't accuse me of stealing them."

"Are you frequently accused of stealing from your employers, Miss Peartree?"

"Of course not. But until I know you better, I did not want to take any chances. Some gentlemen are very particular about their libraries."

"I am not one of them. I would never begrudge anyone their love of reading, one's chance to improve one's mind. I daresay even you could stand some improvement."

"And you as well," she said dryly. It seemed her quick thinking—lying, really—had saved her from an uncomfortable few minutes. She shifted Marc to her other shoulder. "I'm going to take Marc upstairs for his morning rest."

"Before you go, I have another question for you."

Gemma sighed. Escape had been too easy.

"What is your name, Miss Peartree?"

She couldn't help but giggle. "Listen to yourself, sir, and you will have your answer."

"Your *given* name, Miss Peartree. I'd like to know it."

"Why? You are my employer, Mr. Ross, not my friend."

"Nevertheless." He stood, waiting. Well, he could wait forever. For some perverse reason, she did not ever want to hear her Christian name from his lips. It would be too intimate. Too dangerous.

"I'm sorry, sir. My name is *mine*."

The look on his face was most gratifying. Singing to Marc up the staircase, she would save her investigation for another day.

The little brat. He'd caught her red-handed pilfering through his things, and somehow she'd managed to make him feel in the wrong.

And she was perfectly right. Had he expected her to assume all the responsibility for Marc without any respite? Marc had several nursemaids at the villa, and of course there was a raft of other servants seeing to the duca and duchessa. Gull House was a far cry from the luxury the child had known. Its starkness was almost a welcome punishment to Andrew, but Miss Peartree certainly could not have expected such hardship. She'd never stay.

And that was what he wanted, wasn't it? One way or another, he would drive her off. He had to. She was a little brown tick burrowing under his skin, growing in importance every day. She was a danger to his resolve for all she was a blessing to his son. The longer she stayed, the more he and his son would come to depend upon her, and then it would be impossible to get rid of her.

Andrew supposed he should wait to dispatch her at least until her trunk arrived. He couldn't send her out into the world looking like a ragamuffin dwarf. And if her belongings didn't come, he'd have to pay to outfit her from the skin out. That wouldn't be a problem—he had, contrary to her suspicions, plenty of money. More than he could spend in a lifetime here, for sure, even if he bought Marc every toy the child could ever want.

He sat at his desk composing another letter to Lord Edward Christie. His correspondence could not go out until the next boat came, but it helped center Andrew to write of his predicament. He might never even post these daily diatribes, for he counted on Edward's goodwill to stock Gull House with the necessities until he found his own man of business. Whom Christie would hire for him, just as he'd hired Miss Pernicious Peartree. It bedeviled Andrew that he had to rely on Caroline's husband, but he really had no choice.

Andrew hated to depend on anyone but himself. People were bound to disappoint, if not actually cause despair. He'd learned that at a very early age. His son must never know any fraction of the sorrow he'd experienced as a child. Andrew was all Marc had now, and for once, he would do the right and honorable thing.

Even here in this Scottish hellhole.

CHAPTER 6

"**W**hat is your Christian name, Miss Peartree?" He was tired of thinking of her so formally in his nightly fantasies. It was probably something prosaic, like Mary or Margaret, but he really had to know. It had become something of an obsession for him, but from the looks of her, she still wasn't going to tell him.

"I have not given you leave to call me anything but Miss Peartree, nor will I," she sniffed. She crumbled a muffin and handed it to Marc. His son shredded it even further before he popped it in his mouth, fist and all. The boy was blooming and had put on weight under Miss Peartree's vigilant care. Mrs. MacLaren's fine, simple cooking helped, too. Andrew was getting somewhat stout himself. It was impossible to tell the effect on Miss Peartree, however. She was dwarfed in her borrowed clothes. Evidently the largest women on the island had pitched in to donate their shapeless cast-offs. If Miss Peartree stayed, he would have to order her something better than the rough homespun that hung from her tiny frame.

"Elizabeth."

She did not respond except to cut a sausage in thirds for his son.

"Calliope."

She pursed her lips. "My mother was not so fanciful, sir."

"Jane, then."

She shook her head and ate her eggs. "*Bene, e Marc?* So good."

"Goo!" his son shouted.

"*Si.* Yes. Good." Miss Peartree's radiant smile tripped Andrew's hard heart.

She pointed to her plate. "*Uova.* Eggs."

"Eck!"

"Eat yours, love. *Mangia.*"

Marc shoveled his spoon into the eggs and got most of the contents in his mouth. "Goo eck."

"You're making remarkable progress."

"Marc is a remarkable boy," Miss Peartree said modestly. "He is by far the best pupil I've ever had."

"How long have you been at this sort of work, Miss Peartree? If you won't tell me your name, at least tell me your age."

"A *gentleman* never asks a lady her age, even if the lady is in his employ." She blotted her lips on her napkin. Andrew envied the linen.

"Ah, but I have the feeling you don't think me much of a gentleman."

"It does not matter one whit what I think, Mr. Ross. I am interested in Marc, not you. And now that you've brought it up," she said, lowering her voice, "I would appreciate it if you did not always *look* at me so. I thought I made that clear. We are still in our two-week trial period."

Andrew feigned innocence. "What do you mean, Miss Peartree? Evalina? Alberta?"

"As if you'd like to gobble me up like Marc did his muffin."

"Miss Peartree! I assure you I don't want to turn you into a pile of crumbs." Now, to slather her with jam or honey might be a tasty treat indeed.

"And I have no wish to be turned," she said with asperity.

"But I do have an idea which I'd like to present to you if you could divert your attention to something serious."

Andrew took a sip of blistering hot coffee. Mrs. MacLaren must know precisely what he wanted to do with his tongue and was discouraging him in the only way available to her. "I am all ears, Miss Peartree."

"I believe it would benefit Marc if he could share his lessons with a few of the village children. They are as ignorant of the English language as he is. Lessons would be more in the way of play, of course. It would help socialize him, too."

"The boy is not even three years old. Surely he's too young for school."

"Of course. I'm not talking about giving Marc a slate and expecting him to write his numbers. But there is much he could do with two or three little ones like himself."

Andrew looked at his son, who was placing a glob of egg on his spoon to carry to his mouth. The egg slipped between his fingers, and with determination Marc picked up the egg and tried again. Quite a bit of his breakfast seemed to be on him rather than in him.

"Isn't Marc enough for you to handle, Miss Peartree?"

"I'm sure I could manage a few more children for an hour or so a day, sir. For that matter, I would love to start a little school for the older children. Once I pass my trial, of course. When you hire a village girl to assist me. If you employed more people from the settlement and founded a school, you will increase your consequence here. It would behoove you to look after your people."

His people! As though he was a feudal lord. The MacEwan owned the rest of the island, absent landlord that he was. The idea that Andrew had an obligation to anybody was ludicrous.

"I did not employ you to teach the world, Miss Peartree, just one small boy. Cecily. Sarah."

Miss Peartree frowned at him, all traces of good humor gone. "What I am proposing would be of benefit to us all. You'd engender the goodwill of the islanders, Marc would have play-mates, and the local children would have advantages. I'm perfectly capable of tending to Marc and instructing the others for an hour or two."

"I cannot agree. Unless, perhaps—" He broke off, watching the hope return to her piquant face. "If you tell me your name, I might consider your idea."

Miss Peartree crumpled her napkin and pulled Marc from his high chair. "I, too, cannot agree. There is no need for an employer to know anything so personal about his employee."

"Good lord. It's only a name. You know mine. What if I had to write you a bank draft instead of pay you in coin? Is your name so awful you're ashamed of it? Griselda, perhaps? Horatia? Clytemnestra?"

"Good morning to you, Mr. Ross," she said, clutching a sticky Marc to her chest. "If you have need of us, we will be in the nursery."

She stomped off, or stomped off as loudly as someone her slight size could muster. She was just a little slip of a thing, and it was outrageous to Andrew that she could have provoked him so completely. He saw her glistening wet body rising from the bath-tub in his mind's eye at the most inconvenient times, with the resultant effect.

She needed to go. There would be no school or houseful of children here for his son. He'd find some old battle-ax to care for Marc and keep him to the straight-and-narrow path he'd chosen in his newest incarnation. It was a jest of the vastest proportions that his lust had been so piqued by a girl who looked enough like a boy to pass for one, barring her magnificent fall of caramel hair. Andrew dropped his fork on his plate with a clatter and pushed himself away from the table.

How would he spend his day? It was storming again, storming always, it seemed. The ocean beyond the grassy point was gray-green and furious, the rain pelting against the wavy glass.

His arm ached like the devil with the damp, but that was no excuse for him to skip his exercises. If he didn't do what his Parisian doctor ordered, his limb would atrophy—just as his brain was becoming stunted by the lack of stimulation here. He'd been in residence just a few days and already was regretting it.

But where else could he go to keep Marc safe? London was out of the question for so many reasons. People knew him there, knew his past and proclivities. His son would never have a fair chance, and Andrew feared the city's many temptations would wear down his resolve. If one skinny little virgin was driving him to madness, what would he do when faced with actual feminine pulchritude?

He rather thought he could resist the gentlemen now. For so many years he'd not cared where or how he took his pleasure as long as there was some. He'd become endlessly inventive and intrepid in his search for the fleeting moment of passion. But he'd always been happier when involved in a ménage, a soft woman to blunt the rough edges of a male lover.

It had been a revelation to discover that he was not totally Donal Stewart's creature. While nothing had ever been forbidden in his life travels, there were some acts that were preferable. But he was done with all that, done for the sake of his son. He had a hand and a brain, and that would have to do.

Andrew went into the library. All the books were on the shelves now, nothing from his collection of pornography, of course. He and Mr. MacLaren had finally hauled those up to the attics yesterday much to Miss Peartree's satisfaction, where hopefully a platoon of mice wouldn't munch on them. Andrew had spent a good bit of money buying the volumes and someday might sell them for a profit. At the time it had seemed money well spent, as anything to provoke his flagging interest in the sexual arts was welcome. He'd been half afraid then he was losing his touch, and therefore his financial independence.

In his experience, sin had paid very well. There was a roof

over his head and his belly was full. He'd made some lucky investments, which now enabled him to live this life of relative comfort. Oh, Gull House was not comfortable yet, but it was his, and in time he could make it a home.

Andrew picked up the hard leather ball from the desk and set to squeezing. This activity was far more boring than sparring with a partner or riding or fencing, gentlemen's pursuits he'd engaged in to blend into society and keep fit. He'd much rather be squeezing Miss Peartree's sweet bum than the ball, and the pressure of his fingers changed when he imagined he was. It was not quite so onerous when his hands cupped creamy flesh rather than dry brown leather. If she were beneath him, he'd run his hands up her slender narrow back and lose them in her silken hair. Whisper sweet secrets in her ear as he took her from behind. Watch his shaft enter and exit with practiced grace. He knew just how to—

But no. He didn't think Miss Peartree would allow herself to be sweet-talked into anything. She'd probably be fighting him off like a little spitfire hedgehog, all claws and bristles.

That could work, too. His hand picked up the pace with the ball, rolling it in his palm in a feverish pitch until his cock threatened to burst through his breeches. In another minute his smalls would be wet and he'd be the victim of a diurnal emission. The ball skittered across his desk, where it thumped to the floor.

Good lord. What was happening to him?

Weather be damned. He found his greatcoat hanging on a peg by the front door. Mrs. MacLaren or someone had tucked a faded plaid scarf into the collar, which he wrapped around his neck as best he could with one working hand. Razor-sharp rain hit the top of his bare head the moment he stepped out the door. He could, he supposed, tie the scarf around his head like an old village woman. He'd be a laughing stock if anyone saw him, but he wasn't heading toward the settlement. If it caused a few goats' amusement, so be it.

Thus Andrew Rossiter, *gigolo extraordinaire*, toast of the Continent and the British Isles, roamed the cliffs of Batter Island wearing a plaid turban like an old blind dowager. How far he'd fallen. But if the price was keeping his son safe and whole, it was worth it.

He headed to the ring of stones that were all that was left of his Iron Age fort. A thousand years ago, men must have stood here just as he did, watching for Viking longboats. The Norsemen had raided, then settled, these islands for centuries, and the glint of gold and red in some of the villagers' hair was proof that their blood lived on.

Andrew had no idea who his father was. He fantasized it was some rich toff who spent at least fifteen minutes with his pretty mother, but he could as easily be the product of a back-alley coupling with a fishmonger with a few coins. He thought the former was more likely from the few words his mother let slip when she was into the gin. Her beauty was such that she had been very successful for a while, until illness stripped the flesh from her bones and taking care of a seven-year-old boy had proved to be too much.

Ah well. Life was full of crooked turns, and Andrew had taken most of them. Here he was at the edge of his land, buffeted by high winds, a straight shot across the Atlantic to the New World. Should Gull House's amenities pale, he could always start fresh with Marc there. In Boston or Charleston or some such city. He was less familiar with America than he was with the drawing rooms of the ton, but the naïve democracy of the United States might be perfect for him, the bastard-born son of a Scottish whore and his bastard-born son of an Italian duchess. It was something to think about.

If he went, would Miss Persnickety Peartree accompany him? Would he hold her over the railing, catching her gilt and umber hair as she puked? No, likely he'd be doing that with Marc, who was a very poor seaman indeed. The thought of more weeks on the water with the child brought forth a shudder that had nothing to do with the sluice of icy rain dripping down his neck.

For good or worse, this was his home now.

He turned into the wind, unraveling his unusual head gear. Catching it in the nick of time before it blew to Ireland, Andrew tromped along the cliff path, minding the slippery grass. One wrong step and he'd pitch below to the beach. While the sand was brilliantly white, he doubted it would be like landing on a cloud.

He'd have to speak to Miss Peartree about being cautious with Marc out-of-doors. One day the sun might shine again and the child would want to chase his own ball or a butterfly or a swooping bird. It might behoove Andrew to fence off a portion of the property for a play yard for the little boy so he couldn't escape from supervision on his short chubby legs. Add wood to the growing list—the island was virtually treeless.

That would be a project for the spring, however. Soon the ground would be too frozen to pound posts into. By spring, Andrew hoped to have more use of his arm so he could do the pounding himself. It would give him something to do besides lust after Miss Peartree.

No, by spring she'd be gone. Marc would be speaking English and her particular skills would be unnecessary. Andrew would pension her off with a generous stipend.

Or so he hoped. A lot could go wrong in a few months. Hell, there were still days to go before the two-week trial was up. Anything could happen.

But one thing he knew for sure—Miss Peartree would not be joining him in his bed, no matter how much he craved her brown, scrawny little self.

CHAPTER 7

Slick with sweat in his freezing room, Andrew forced himself to wake up. He didn't need to see the images again, didn't need to hear Caro cry.

The dreams usually came in threes, the same three. One inexorably after the other, even though he fought against them in his sleeping mind. What was the adage? Bad luck comes in threes. In his opinion, his share was a bit more than three, but at least his dark nights were limited to those three turning points in his life.

First to appear in the Elizabethan shadow of Reverend Raybourne's School for Boys was Nicky Parker, always young and laughing, always randy. His schoolboy lover who had nearly washed away the staining years of Andrew's guardian Donal. But he and Nicky had never been innocent, even if they were young.

Then came Donal, his eyes vacant. It was not Andrew's fault Donal couldn't find his pills until it was too late, not really. That quack Doctor Copeland would find them scattered on the floor under the bed, just where Donal had spilled them. Andrew had gotten down on his knees to pick them up, but his fingers had been clumsy in his fear, slow and ultimately constrained by the devil whispering in his ear. He might be free for the first time since he was seven.

Andrew knew where that fleeting taste of freedom led. Lovely, lively red-haired Caroline swirled in for a bit, and the third dream took on a watercolor sweetness that was not to last. Couldn't. Andrew had not deserved her then and did not now. To prove that, Nicky reappeared, lying still as death but trapped in his mortal shell. Andrew always woke up before he delivered the coup de grace.

Three memories that reminded him of what he had been, what he was, what he would remain no matter how he tried to change.

Andrew needed reminding. For a day or so he'd caught himself imagining Miss Peartree by his side as something other than an irritating employee. Even in the ridiculously baggy clothes, he remembered her as she rose from the tub, her toasted skin slick and wet. The sharp tongue she gave him could be put to much better use. She could whisper Italian endearments into the crook of his neck instead of Marc's—he even had a few phrases of his own. *Lo desidero che si.* I desire you.

But even she deserved better. He lay back on the pillow, listening to the wind and the waves. He would drag his dreams out for inspection, rub his nose in the stench of them. Torture himself as he was meant to be tortured. He knew what he was—he only needed to be reminded. He was responsible for two deaths and the despoilation of the first and only woman he'd ever loved.

Winter was a time of reflection, of death. How well his three dreams suited the season. They stirred up Andrew's mental sea as the tides and wind eroded the coast beneath his window. There was only his estranged son who held the fragile lifeline to his vessel. He needed to keep Marc safe. He needed to keep Miss Peartree at a distance. The first was easy. The second he would have to work on.

One could only lie abed feeling sorry for oneself for so long. Daylight dawned whether he was rested or not, and Andrew sloughed off his covers and made himself presentable. He breakfasted alone and left word with Mrs. MacLaren to send Miss Peartree in when she was available, then pored over weeks' old newspapers and made some calculations in his account book. He was relieved from his boredom by the tap at his study door.

Andrew bit back his laughter as the governess shuffled into the room. Poor Miss Peartree was head-to-toe in gray garb, a corded tie wrapped around her waist to lift the garment from the floor. He squinted. By God, if he wasn't mistaken, the sash came from one of the ratty parlor curtains. The bulge of fabric around her torso was large enough to store a substantial picnic lunch or possibly a dwarf.

"Don't say one word," she warned, looking like a gorgon. "I'll not be responsible if I'm insulted any more than I am by wearing this attire."

"I would not dream of insulting you, Miss Peartree," Andrew replied, trying to keep an impassive face. "But could they not have found you some children's clothing? Surely they would be a better fit."

She shrugged a shoulder, causing the neckline to gap precipitously and expose a golden curve. Her skin was really the most intriguing color, but Andrew was robbed of further view of it as she snatched the fabric back up to her throat. "I'll not take clothes off the backs of the poor wee things. They have little enough as it is."

"The very reason I've summoned you. Please sit. I know Marc is napping and apt to wake up at any minute so I'll get right to the point. It was two weeks ago today you made your bargain with me."

"A devil's bargain," she muttered.

"Quite. But I cannot argue that Marc is improving daily. He's almost—" He would not compare his son's behavior to how he was in Italy. Likely Marc would never be that sunny child again. "He seems settled with you, and happy. So, I am prepared to extend your employment for another two weeks."

Her brows scrunched. "Infamous! Am I never to have security, Mr. Ross? Or are you waiting for me to show my true colors and throw a book at your head so you can dismiss me?"

"I have excellent reflexes. I think it best if we attune ourselves to the ferry schedule. You yourself may decide this is all too much for you."

"Are you going to hire someone to help me at least?"

"I already have. Mrs. MacLaren's great-niece Mary will come tomorrow. She's just thirteen but has four little brothers, poor girl. Her mother still needs her at home, of course, but we'll work out something to your advantage.

"And I'm beginning to like this idea of a school of yours. I'm writing to Baron Christie to arrange to have some supplies sent our way. Some books for this library, for example. With this weather, they probably will not arrive until months from now, but I wondered if you'd like to include lesson books. For Marc as well. You know better than I what children of varying ages require. That's if you're still here to run the school."

She smiled, transforming her grumpy little face into a thing of true beauty. His heart jumped, and he focused with difficulty on the grotesque gray dress instead.

"Oh! Thank you, Mr. Ross. I'll still be here! You won't be sorry. If we can educate the island children, teach them some English, they'll be more able to navigate the world."

Andrew passed a pen, ink, and paper across the desk. "Their parents may feel differently, you know. Traditions die hard in this part of Scotland."

"I'm not asking them to give up their way of life, just to add to it. It's always advantageous to know another language. Have educational opportunities. To read."

"Um. Yes." Andrew had been completely unlettered when Donal Stewart snatched him from the street. He recalled when he'd been brought to the grand Edinburgh house on St. Andrews Square. It had seemed providential itself that he was to live in a place that bore his own name. The ceilings had seemed miles away, the reception rooms as large as the country kirk his mother took him to once. Donal himself had bathed him in a tub deep enough to dive into. There had been hot tea laced with brandy and endless muffins, and he hadn't said a word when Donal slipped into the vast bed in his new room. Andrew had been lonely, and the comfort of his protector had been welcome. The confusion of the first night became clearer each day, but Andrew was warm. Fed. Eventually sufficiently educated so he could be having a discussion about literacy with a governess.

"And what do you like to read, Miss Peartree? I might include some books for you."

Miss Peartree dropped her eyes. "I enjoy the classics, sir."

"What, not admitting to the gothic novels? You filched the *Courtesan Court* books from my library. I know the woman who writes them."

"Lady X!" The wash of color over her little face told him she probably had stayed up all night a time or two reading Caroline's romances, fantasizing over a ridiculously heroic hero. "Who is she?"

"An old friend." Someone he'd wanted to be much more, even after her marriage. He reached over and tapped the paper. "Make a list of what you might require to set up a school. There can't be above twenty children here."

"Twenty-three," she said, picking up the pen. Trust her to have ferreted out the exact number. "Some are infants, like Marc, too young for sitting still for any length of time. Quite a few are older boys who work alongside their fathers and older girls whose mothers depend on them to watch the little ones. I doubt they could be spared."

"The boats are in for the winter, and if some of the younger children are in your care for part of the day, everyone's load will be lightened. Depending on the details, you might be able to begin lessons before the fishermen leave in the spring."

She looked up at him, her brown eyes sparkling. "This is very generous of you, Mr. Ross."

Andrew shifted uncomfortably in his chair. He was no one's ridiculously heroic hero. But at least the islanders would have a more innocent tutelage than he. "As you said, children deserve opportunities. And it's not as though you'd be tied up all day. A few hours at most, given that children here seem to work as hard as their parents."

Miss Peartree smoothed the pen over the paper in elegant loops. "Where would we hold school, sir? Every cottage that is livable is occupied."

"Well, not here, obviously. I'll not have my peace cut up even if I am suddenly a philanthropist. I thought the church. I believe you said the priest is here only a few times a year. The building stands empty."

"Not really. There may be no priest, but some villagers worship without one."

"You *do* know a great deal about the way things work here, don't you?"

Miss Peartree grinned. "My mother always said I was nosy. *Nasuto.*"

"She was Italian?" That would explain the beautiful biscuit color of Miss Peartree's skin.

"Yes, although she spent most of her life in England." She put the pen down. "Perhaps we should wait on this before you spend your money. You were right to have reservations. The islanders may not think a school is a worthwhile endeavor. And I may displease you yet."

"Nonsense. You've prodded me this far, my Italian *signorina.* Esmeralda. Maria. Concetta. Am I getting close?"

Miss Peartree bit a luscious lip to keep from smiling. "No, sir."

"I believe you like this game we're playing, Miss Peartree.

Domina." She was certainly dominating his waking and sleeping hours in the most profound way.

"I might be."

"It hardly seems fair. You know *my* name." Or his new one at any rate. Andrew Rossiter seemed a shade at the edge of his memory. Only his unpleasant dreams reminded him of who he used to be.

He'd never gone without sexual congress this long in his adult life—he wasn't about to count the nights with just his wicked imagination and his hand for solace. He watched as she screwed up her little brown face and labored over a list that was growing alarmingly long. Even with her brow wrinkled in concentration, he wanted to get his hand on her.

Perhaps before he sent it off he should consult with someone on the island—although how he was to manage that he hadn't a clue. His drawing skills had never been exceptional. His facility with charades, however, had stood him in good stead. Right now he wanted to place a hand over his heart, point to his pointing cock, and invite Miss Peartree to his bed.

"There. That's all I can think of for the moment." She stood, pulling at the elephant-gray folds of her dress. "I'd better get upstairs before Marc wakes and climbs out of his crib. He's a little daredevil, you know."

Andrew felt a stab of paternal pride. His son was coming along splendidly in his language development and seemed sturdy physically. "I'll go up with you."

"That's not necessary. You must have things to do."

Ah, yes. Stare at the books he'd already read and squeeze his exercise ball. Count snowflakes as they swirled by the window. Think of all the inventive ways to fuck Miss Whateverhername-was Peartree. "Nothing is as important as Marc."

He rose with her and walked out into the flagstone passage. The wind whistled through the draft under the doorway, chilling the hall so thoroughly he could see his breath. He missed the warmth of his study already and wouldn't bask long in the body heat of Miss Peartree, who seemed in a rush to get away from him as fast as possible. She hustled up the threadbare stair runner so quickly that her feet got tangled in the hem of her hopeless dress. Before Andrew knew it, she slipped and he was holding her against his chest, struggling not to fall backward onto the flagstones himself. Pain shot through his arm as he steadied them both.

"Oh!"

"Be still or we'll be Jack and Jill, Miss Peartree. I have no wish to break my crown."

She smelled of Mrs. MacLaren's oatmeal soap, clean and comforting. Holding her was like cradling a baby bird, she weighed so little. Like a baby bird, he could feel the thudding of her heart and feel the feathers of her indignation as she sought release. But he couldn't let her go quite yet.

"Mr. Ross!"

So she had felt his manhood rise despite the swaths of fabric. How could he help himself when an angel fell from heaven into his arms? Sweet-smelling, delicate, delicious. He could do nothing less than cushion her against him, pressing her to his needful body. He'd had no contact with anyone warm and willing in months and months.

He glanced down—perhaps she was not willing after all. She had her troll face on, her lips turned down in scorn and her golden-brown eyes mere slits. He put a finger to her blushing cheek. "You needn't look at me like that. I saved your life, you know."

"Let me go this instant!" Miss Peartree spluttered.

"I want to make sure you're perfectly all right. Perhaps you twisted an ankle?" Andrew asked hopefully. He would gladly pat her down to her toes to check for any infirmity, get his hands under that dress to touch the electric velvet of her skin.

"My ankles are no concern of yours." She struggled against him, causing the most delightful friction. "You're doing it *again*."

"Doing what?"

"*Looking* at me!"

He smiled, completely smitten, helpless to resist her even if she looked like she wanted to skewer him with a hatpin. Thank God she was bare headed, her lovely streaky hair whisper-soft beneath his hand. "Well, I can hardly do anything else. You're right here. Quite close. Within kissing distance."

Miss Peartree's lips snapped shut and disappeared inward, leaving an angry line on her rosy face. Andrew felt a rather vicious pinch to his midsection and very grudgingly released her.

"You could say thank you."

"I could, but if you hadn't been at my heels like the hound of hell I might have been more careful."

"Hound of hell? Now you're exaggerating. I simply wanted to watch my son wake from his slumber. My intentions, Miss Peartree, were entirely honorable. Fatherly. I may have come to my responsibilities late in life, but I assure you I take them very seriously. Marc is *my* son, you know, not just your charge."

She had the grace to look a bit shame faced, so he continued. "I thought we were getting along well, with plans for the school and what-not. Since we seem to be stuck with each other for the time being, let us not waste any time in arguing."

"I wasn't arguing."

"You are arguing right this minute, Arianna. Alicia?"

She looked quite ready to pinch him again. "Shall I carry you to prevent further injury, or can you manage on your own?" he teased.

She snorted and marched up the stairs.

"You might, you know, tug up your dress and display some ankle so you don't trip on your skirts again. I promise I won't look."

"Hah."

She knew as well as he did his promise was hollow. He would have to master himself soon or he would go mad. He watched the voluminous fabric sway as she stumbled up the steps, bracing himself for another accidental encounter. But alas, she made it to the top of the stairs without incident. He heard Marc down the hall, singing to himself in his crib. It was an Italian song Miss Peartree had sung to him, her voice surprisingly lush coming from so slight an instrument.

Andrew could not remember a time his mother had ever sung to him. Perhaps she had, and other, less pleasant memories had layered and crusted over his early years making them impenetrable. Molly Rossiter had fallen so deep in poverty that her looks and spirits had deserted her, and then she had deserted him. Andrew owed his male beauty to her, but his survival skills were all his own.

He watched as Miss Peartree lifted a sleep-flushed Marc from his bed, his yellow ringlets damp and tufting. Andrew had decided to keep his own hair shorn; no point in looking like an angel when one had fallen so very far. There were no more lovers to exclaim upon his curls or run their fingers through his sex-rumpled hair—unless he could somehow persuade the nameless Miss Peartree to abandon her virtue and good sense.

A winter in this wild, desolate place just might do it. When Andrew set his mind—and his body—to it, all manner of things were possible. But it was best to keep Miss Peartree safe from his predatory nature. It was the least he could do to thank her for the miracle she was working with his son. As his dreams reminded him, it was far too late to work any miracles with him.

CHAPTER 8

Gemma snuggled with Marc close against her breast, wishing it was the father instead of the son she held so close. It had been a very near thing on the stairs, falling down and into Andrew Ross's embrace. She had let her temper get the best of her as usual and been rude to her employer once again, but really— he had taken advantage of her helplessness and her hideous dress and her own confusion.

Although she'd vowed to be wiser, it was futile not to want Andrew Ross. He was all attractive sin, wit, and mystery. He'd held her so carefully, his clear blue eyes looking down straight into her soul. He smelled of lime and oatmeal soap—and good enough to eat, really. If she ever wanted to devour a gentleman, Andrew Ross would be at the top of the menu.

She wondered about his unhappy marriage and his need to hide on this island. It wasn't as if this was his ancestral home or he spoke the language or he loved the wintry weather—if anything, it must make his poor damaged arm ache like the devil. She saw the white lines around his mouth, watched his eyes flash with discomfort every time he jarred it or attempted normal activities. It must be torture to hold his own child and hard on his pride when old Mr. MacLaren was far more capable than he was to make ordinary repairs.

Though she ached for him, she was careful not to show it. It had become a difficult chore to be as rude to him as she was. And now that her job looked secure—at least for two weeks, although she was sure he was only teasing—she would be shut up in this house with him all winter. He was temptation incarnate.

A gust of wind rattled the window frame. "No!" cried Marc. She carried him to the window. "That's right. It's snowing again. Pretty, yes? *Bella*? White. *Bianca*. I don't imagine he ever saw snow before coming here," she said to his father.

"No. He lived on the Mediterranean coast. Every day was filled with sunshine and gentle bay breezes."

"It sounds like heaven." Gemma imagined picnics, replete with wine and exotic foods. Andrew Ross might peel her a grape as she dozed on silken pillows under the sun.

Fat chance of that. She was a courtesan's daughter. No matter how pretty a word *courtesan* was, it simply meant whore. No decent man would ever want her.

Although there were many moments when she thought Andrew Ross was not decent at all.

"We should go out. Build a snowman. There seems to be enough of it on the ground."

Mr. Ross raised an eyebrow. "Do you think that's wise? What if Marc catches a cold?"

"Poo. I'll dress him warmly. Fresh air will do us all good. We cannot spend the entire winter indoors. We'll go mad. What do you say, sweetheart? Do you want to play outside? *Farla vuole giocare fuori?*"

Marc clapped his chubby hands and wriggled to get down.

"All right," Mr. Ross said reluctantly. "I'll meet you downstairs in half an hour. I'll tell Mrs. MacLaren to make us some flasks of tea, some warm milk for Marc."

"Goodness, we're not trekking through the Alps." Gemma laughed.

"Nevertheless, I don't want Marc to catch a chill. May I remind you there's no doctor here? He's only just recovering from his journey. I don't want to take any chances."

Gemma bit her tongue. It was clear Mr. Ross was a concerned parent, if overprotective. But a little boy needed exercise and activity. Since there were no leafy parks here in which to promenade with Marc, the wild outdoors would have to do.

She changed Marc's nappy and layered him into so many of his clothes he could barely stand up. Bringing him next door to her room, she did the same to herself, until she was weighted down with yards of ugly fabric. Once she was satisfied that no frozen tongue of wind would pierce her defenses, she carried Marc down the stairs carefully. She would not want to fall into his father's arms again. She might never find the strength to extricate herself.

Every time he saw her lately, he had to refrain from laughter. Miss Puffy Peartree minced down the stairs looking like a poor homeless waif who wore every bit of clothing she owned, layer upon layer of unmitigated ugliness. His son was little better in circumference, padded against the cold, although at least his clothes had been purchased from the finest French clothier. Andrew had put on several coats and scarves himself. He imagined he looked just as ridiculous as his two companions.

"We've sustenance," he said, gesturing with a basket. "Are you sure this is wise? Going out in the middle of a storm?"

"Absolutely! And I wouldn't even call this a storm. For once there's white, fluffy snow, not miserable needles of sleet. I haven't seen this much snow since Vienna."

Here was an intriguing tidbit to add to the paucity of his knowledge on the subject of his nameless governess. "I thought you said you lived in London."

Miss Peartree shrugged. "I've lived in lots of places. My mother traveled quite a bit in her later years and took me with her when she could."

"Did she perhaps give you an Austrian name? Heidi? Ana-liese?"

"Mr. Ross!" she said warningly, but her lip curved upward.

"All right, all right. I thought it was worth a guess. You are a stubborn chit. Let's go then." He made a show of taking a deep breath and girding his loins before he opened the front door.

They stepped out into a fairy world of snow frosting the usually bleak landscape. Great fat flakes fell, slow and silent, almost warm to the touch in comparison to the usual Batter Island precipitation. They walked a little ways from the house, the crushed shell path hidden by a thick blanket of drifting snow. Miss Peartree set Marc down with care. The snow was over his knees. He took a step and toppled down instantly.

Instead of crying, the little one laughed, his little hands flailing through the crust of snow. The sound was so rare and so precious, Andrew's heart squeezed. Miss Peartree joined in. Her laughter was rare and precious, too, transforming her face into something so pure Andrew had no words for it.

"Ah, look at you, my love." Miss Peartree brushed Marc off. "Are you all right? *La sono bene?* Come, and I'll help you up."

Marc giggled and crawled through the snow, perfectly happy as he was. He displaced a great deal of snow for a little boy, making a convenient track for the adults to follow.

"*Sono un cane!* Grr. Woof, woof!"

"He says he is a dog." Miss Peartree smiled. "Perhaps you should think about getting him one. He sometimes talks about the puppy you left behind, you know."

It wasn't as if Andrew could have gone back to the villa for it, what with Gianni's goons waiting to kill him. Poor Marc escaped with only the clothes on his back, and those exquisitely embroidered things had been left at the fisherman's cottage in exchange for serviceable traveling gear. Nothing remained of Marc's old world, and there was nothing Andrew could do about that but try his best to create a new one.

"That's a good idea. Perhaps someone here has a pup I can buy."

Miss Peartree scooped up a fistful of snow and tossed it into the air. "I've seen very few dogs here. Those I have seen are working animals, herding the sheep. Pet dogs are a luxury most of the islanders cannot afford. It's hard enough to feed themselves, you know."

Andrew bent and began to roll a ball of snow. "It's a brutal life here, isn't it? I wonder why they stay when they could live anywhere."

Miss Peartree looked down at him, her sharp little chin pointed, a snowflake melting on her cheek. "One might say the same for you, sir."

"Just as your name is your own, my motives are mine," he said curtly, dropping to his knees. He concentrated on packing a largish block as a base for a snowman, and not on Miss Peartree's bright brown eyes, which seemed capable of stripping his thin gentlemanly veneer clean away. "Come, Marc. Help me."

"*Piccolo cane, aiutare suo padre,*" Miss Peartree coaxed. With one last bark, Marc crawled over and sat down. He patted extra snow at the bottom, and Andrew praised him lavishly. Miss Peartree gave up her probing and started the second, smaller ball. They all worked together, Miss Peartree chattering to Marc in Italian with an occasional English word thrown in. Andrew tried not to feel left out, although it was something he was used to.

He could not remember a time when he felt he belonged. As a child, someone in Donal Stewart's household always reminded him of his humble origins. At school, he was set apart from the well-connected young lordlings as the ward of a tradesman, rich though Donal was. Nicky had taken advantage of Andrew's isolation and moved in for his easy conquest. When Andrew later prostituted himself—he could not call it anything else, really—he was simply the hired help, paid for his services yet not truly part of society for all the books he read and the clubs he belonged to. He was a man without a country, a misfit, certainly not a gentleman for all the airs he'd practiced for the past twenty-five years. He licked a snowflake from his lip in an attempt to remove the bitterness from his mouth.

He lifted his eyes from the misshapen clump of snow. Miss Peartree was obviously not reflecting on any sad past. She and Marc were rosy cheeked and laughing, their eyelashes silvered with melting snow. The snowman was coming into lumpy reality, its head listing precariously. Miss Peartree removed one of her scarves and tied it beneath the top snowball to better anchor it.

Marc clapped his hands. *"Pupazzo di neve!"*

"That's right. Snowman. He needs more than my scarf, Mr. Ross."

Andrew stuck a gloved hand into his breeches and pulled out a few coins. Why he still carried money with him was a bit of a mystery, as there was no place to spend it here. The village shop seemed never to be open any time he ventured down the track to the settlement.

But old habits died hard—he'd never be caught short, always have something to bargain with and stave off disaster. It was paramount that he never be poor again.

"Eyes," he said to Marc, pressing them into the snowball. "Nose." The child stood wide eyed in a lazy swirl of snow as Andrew tapped his own. "Now, what can we use for the mouth?"

Miss Peartree reached under her bonnet and pulled out a curved tortoise shell comb, releasing a charming amber curl in the process. Andrew stifled the impulse to tuck it back up. Or tear off his gloves and twist it about his finger. Or bury his nose in its fresh, lemony scent.

"Fearsome teeth," she said, showing her own. *"Denti.* He shall be the most ferocious snowman on the island. Here, Marc. Do you want to do it? *Farla vuole farlo?"*

Marc reached up but was not quite tall enough. Miss Peartree raised an eyebrow at Andrew. "Your papa will help."

Andrew lifted his son and steadied him as he stuck the comb into the snowman's face. "Well done." Holding the boy with his good arm, he took off his own hat and placed it on the head at a rakish angle. Marc giggled and snatched the hat off, putting it on top of his knitted cap. The hat fell over his face, making him giggle even more.

"Peek-a-boo," Andrew said, lifting the hat.

"*Il nascondiglio e cerca*. Well, that's really 'hide-and-seek.' I don't know how to translate peek-a-boo," Miss Peartree said, her eyes dancing. She put the hat back on the snowman. "A perfect work of art, don't you think? I think this calls for a celebration." She opened the picnic hamper and gave Marc his jug of warm sweetened milk. Marc took it, snuggling into his father's chest to drink. He immediately dribbled a goodly quantity down Andrew's front, but he didn't mind.

"Can you manage your tea one-handed, or do you want to put Marc down?"

Andrew didn't need tea at the moment. Having his son in his arms warmed him in ways he hadn't dared hope for. "I'm fine. You have yours. You're not too cold?"

"No! It's just glorious, isn't it? There's such a hush—the landscape is so perfect and silent. Even the ocean seems quiet today." She uncorked her flask and took a sip. "Do you want your hat back? You've gone quite white on top."

Andrew shook some of the snow from his hair. "As I said, I'm fine. In fact, it seems warmer today than it's been in ages. The wind must be on holiday for us." Apart from the odd gust, it had been almost pleasant to be outside, the snow falling like soft balls of cotton fluff.

The ocean beyond the verge of lawn was flat and gunmetal gray. Not even a seabird's cry broke the spell of the gently spiraling snow. Curious, Marc raised his pink face and opened his mouth, catching a snowflake on his tongue. Andrew was obliged to do the same to share the moment. The snow melted, and Andrew swallowed the crisp taste of winter—such a simple thing. Something he'd never experienced before in all of his many exploits. He winked down at his son, and Marc gave him a tentative smile.

Miss Peartree was stamping her feet, making a pretense of ignoring the father-son bonding. The brim of her ugly brown bonnet was coated with snow, adding considerably to its appeal. The snow was transformative, working its magic, washing the world clean, softening its edges. Would there were such a thing in nature to change a man.

A stream of Gaelic interrupted their blissful interlude. Mrs. MacLaren was at the front door, waving to them to come in.

"I suppose she thinks we're a bit mad," Andrew said with a grin.

"I wager she's never made so fine a snowman. But perhaps she's right. Marc may be getting overheated in all his clothes. Do you want me to take him?"

"No. Grab the basket. I don't seem quite so objectionable to him today. Isn't that right, little chap? Your papa is not a complete ogre now, am I?" Marc said nothing but relaxed in his arms. "Yes. It's time to get dry and warm."

A waft of cinnamon hit them as they entered the house, leading them straight back to the kitchen. A rack of cinnamon biscuits sat on the kitchen table, as well as a fresh pot of tea and more warm milk for Marc. Miss Peartree had located the family who owned the only cows on the other side of the island, and Gull House was now being supplied with fresh milk and butter. She made an exception for goat cheese, but plainly her insistence had made Marc much more robust than he had been when they'd first arrived.

It took them some time to divest themselves of all their layers, Mrs. MacLaren clucking all the while and hanging up things near the fire to dry. Eventually Miss Peartree's original hideous gray dress appeared, but her hair was half down, making her look like a schoolgirl. Its streaks gleamed in the firelight of the cozy kitchen, her cheeks and nose were a lovely shade of pink, and her wet lashes reminded Andrew of the day he caught her in the bath, all spiky and innocent like a fawn. He had to turn away.

Marc had climbed up to the table and was devouring his third cookie before Andrew had time to remove his ruined boots. His stockings were soaked through. Would it shock Miss Peartree— or worse, Mrs. MacLaren—if he removed them and sat in his own kitchen in bare feet? He didn't care. Balling the stockings up, he tossed them in a corner. Mrs. MacLaren mumbled something, probably along the line of "You'll have to pick those up yourself."

He imagined like most servants, Mrs. MacLaren said a great deal about them all he wouldn't wish to comprehend. Servants usually had a shrewd take on their masters, and Mrs. MacLaren seemed shrewder than most. What she thought of the scandalous Sassenach—for so he was to these people—was not likely to be without criticism. After all, he lived with a young woman, un-chaperoned. The fact that he was regrettably nowhere near Miss Peartree's bed all night long didn't make a difference. Andrew had as good as ruined his governess. But the islanders were not apt to go to London and spread their tales, and if they ever did, their Gaelic was an insurmountable barrier.

There was a certain advantage to not sharing the same language. Andrew thought of all the lascivious things he'd say to Miss Peartree if she couldn't understand him. How he'd lick the cinnamon crumb from her lower lip. How he'd strip her of that awful dress and lick the rest of her. He settled for a strong cup of tea, teasing the rim of the mug instead in secret substitution.

He admired the homely scene before him—his housekeeper bustling about the kitchen, his son's milk mustache, Miss Peartree holding her cookie between long, delicate fingers. He watched as her small white teeth took a bite and her lids dropped as she savored the buttery richness. He took his own bite, sharing the sensation across the table, which prompted Marc to grab another cookie in his chubby fist before his father ate them all. Andrew rose to the challenge. Before he knew it, he and his son had demolished the entire rack under Miss Peartree's fond observation.

Andrew remembered all the elegant dinner parties he'd attended as some peer's clandestine companion, but a plate of cinnamon biscuits and a stoneware mug of tea tasted better to him than lobster patties and champagne. His whitewashed kitchen was a happier place than the most silver-bedecked London dining room. His son was here, growing sturdy and less shy of him.

And so was Miss Peartree.

"You two have spoiled your supper. It's a wonder Mrs. MacLaren hasn't taken the broom to you."

"Then she shouldn't make biscuits as delicious as these." He caught his housekeeper's eye, rubbed his belly, and smiled. The woman frowned and waved him off, clattering a roasting pan filled with fish fillets into the oven, but he could tell she was pleased at the compliment.

Miss Peartree rose from the table. "I'm going to read to Marc now. I've made a picture book for him, you know. Sometimes he tells me what to draw, and then we say the words in Italian and English."

"Are you an artist, Miss Peartree?"

"Far from it, although I had the requisite water color lessons growing up. All young ladies do. My efforts met the minimum standards. But your son, thank heaven, is not a fussy art critic."

"I'd like to see this book of yours."

"All right. I warn you, I'm not much better than you are when you're drawing wrong-handed for the MacLarens." She got Marc down from his chair and brushed the crumbs from his shirt.

This time he didn't try to carry his son back upstairs. His arm radiated pain from his shoulder to his pinkie finger. But it had been good to get some exercise, better to carry his son like a normal father might.

What was he saying? Most fathers of his acquaintance barely saw their infants. Children were cloistered in nurseries, allowed out only for ceremonial good-night kisses. Even Marc had had limited contact with the *duca*, which had made Andrew's job somewhat easier. Giulietta, however, was a loving mother who channeled her loneliness into great affection for her son. They had been inseparable. How hard it must be for the little boy to be without her, but bless Miss Peartree for filling the void.

He followed behind them, focusing on his feet rather than folds of swaying dress that obscured Miss Peartree's pert backside. Entering Marc's room, he took note of the efforts Miss Peartree had made to make the place child-friendly. She had run up bright-colored quilts herself that served as window curtains and commissioned Mr. MacLaren to make a small red-painted table and chair. A tower of wooden blocks stood in one corner. Mrs. MacLaren had supplied a few ragdolls and what might be a bear, if bears were green. The room was still sparse, and Andrew felt a twinge of guilt that he'd been so anxious to hide out here he'd neglected to think of amusements for his son.

Miss Peartree went to a shelf and removed a stack of his writing paper, a pink hair ribbon looped through a hole in each sheet. She set it on Marc's table, and the child sat down to turn the pages. Here was the "book," each page covered with plain pencil drawings and words printed under each picture.

"I would have colored everything in, but my art supplies are in my lost trunk."

"Impressive. But surely he's too young to read."

"Of course, but it can't harm him to see the words with the objects. One day he'll be able to just see the letters and know what they say."

"What dis?" Marc asked his father, a finger pointing to a tree.

It must have taken Miss Peartree ages to draw in each tiny leaf. Despite her protestations, she was a fair artist. It was *she* who should have been drawing all of Andrew's little illustrations with the villagers.

"A tree." There were precious few of them on Batter Island— vegetation consisted mostly of heather and machair.

Marc nodded his head in approval. "*Si. Un albaro.*" He turned each page, querying his father and giving the Italian word printed underneath. Andrew wondered if Miss Peartree should be teaching him Italian as she taught his son English. It was always useful, just as she said, to know several languages, and it would be a shame if Marc forgot Italian entirely. He imagined them years from now sitting in his library reading Dante together.

This cozy fantasy came to earth as Andrew looked down at the next picture. There he was—Andrew Rossiter—standing on the cliff, the ocean behind him. Miss Peartree had gotten the angle as he favored his bad arm just right. Somehow even with gray pencil he could tell his eyes were meant to be ice blue and his shorn hair gold. The figure on the paper had a benign smile on its face, a look made to reassure a little boy that his father was not the devil who stole him from his happy home.

"Papa!" Marc said in triumph. He tapped at both words, identical in either language.

Andrew swallowed. Miss Peartree had achieved a miracle with her makeshift book.

"You underrate yourself as an artist, Miss Peartree. I'll have to start calling you Artemisia Gentileschi." He named a famous Italian painter, one of the very few females to make a name for herself in the Renaissance art world.

She smiled. "That's quite a mouthful, and I'm nowhere in her league. I hope you don't mind being a subject."

"I'd be delighted to pose for you anytime. Anywhere."

Damn. From the look on her face, all his restraint and useless scruples over the past hour were obliterated. But flirting was second nature to him, or had been. He was getting rusty if he came off as desperate as he sounded, even to himself.

"I'm sure you have better things to do," Miss Peartree responded in her crisp, governessy voice. "Please tell Mrs. MacLaren that Marc and I will take dinner together here in his room."

Relegated to another solitary meal. It was for the best. The less time he spent with the mysteriously compelling Miss Peartree, the safer she was.

CHAPTER 9

M r. MacLaren knocked on the open library door. Andrew was behind his desk, as usual, trying to concentrate on the list of figures before him. If only Miss Peartree had remained in her room, there might have been hope of reconciling them. But she had come for a book while Marc was napping, looking like an enormous ripe eggplant in a purple woolen dress. For the past ten minutes, she had taken down and rejected one book after the next until Andrew wanted to send her to the attics to his boxed-up pornography. Let her rummage through *that* and be as tortured as he. Her hair today was concealed by a plain linen cap much like the one Mrs. MacLaren wore. Andrew assumed it was her attempt at propriety, but it failed miserably.

Andrew knew what was under the cap—soft hair twisting into strands of melted brown sugar and gold, copper and amber. He'd never realized brown could come in so many riveting shades. Looking at her hair was like a walk in the autumn woods, each step bringing a fresh vista.

He wondered if he'd ever see a copse of trees again. Wondered how long he'd have to stay on Batter Island until his son would be safe. Gianni might forget about the boy, but the ton would whisper about his father for years yet. Andrew had cut quite a swath in society, certain pockets of it anyhow. Was he missed?

Longed for? It didn't matter. He couldn't—wouldn't ever—go back to his old life.

Mr. MacLaren bowed and handed Andrew a slip of paper. On it were three stick figures, a man, a woman, and a child. An arrow was drawn to a rectangle with a roof. There were tiny people inside the house and an odd shape outside on the grass.

"Artemisia, what do you think of this?" For lack of anything better, he had taken to calling her Artemisia to tease her. She still refused to tell him her name, which rankled more than it should.

But almost everything about his governess drove him to distraction lately. He'd been shut up indoors with her for days on end while the sleet blew horizontally across the front lawn. There had been no more snowmen or playful banter. Miss Peartree was all business, almost as frosty as the weather. The little cap was just one more barrier she sought to erect between them.

She frowned. "It looks like a pear, cut in half. It's devilish big, though, next to the house. Maybe it's a giant's foot?"

"There are no giants here, and where would these people get pears in the winter? I will say, Mr. MacLaren does not hold a candle to your drawing, Miss Gentileschi." Andrew shook his head at Mr. MacLaren and shrugged. The man lifted a gray eyebrow, stuck his left hand out straight, and with his right madly stroked the air, whistling a Scottish reel.

"Ah! I understand. The pear is a violin! They want us to come for a party. With music. A *ceilidh*," Andrew said.

Mr. MacLaren gave a semitoothless grin and nodded vigorously.

"Very clever, Mr. Ross. At this rate you'll surpass me in Gaelic vocabulary words."

"I *was* born here. Well, in Edinburgh anyway. But I never had much Gaelic, just the odd word here and there. My guardian frowned upon the old language. He wanted me to be more English than the English."

"Why?"

"I'm sure I couldn't say." Everything that Donal Stewart did was a mystery to Andrew. "Well, what say you, Artemisia? Shall we accept this invitation and kick up our heels?"

"It looks like we can bring Marc. It will do him good to see more people. Yes, of course."

"And how about you, Artemisia? You must be sick to death of my company."

She nodded too quickly in agreement. "You are a burden I must bear to care for your delightful child. You must have noticed how quickly he's learning. He's a very bright boy."

Andrew surged with parental pride. "Brighter than your previous pupils? You did say you were the governess to Barrowdown's heir."

Her eyes slid to the book in her hand, a mathematical treatise if he wasn't mistaken. Maybe *she* could work the figures that danced the tarantella all over the papers on his desk. "I do not wish to speak ill of the peerage, Mr. Ross. The Barrowdowns are a sorry lot. But at least one of Lord Barrowdown's children is as brilliant as I am."

Andrew laughed. "Modest little thing, aren't you? How long were you in the household?"

"Long enough, sir, to satisfy Lord Christie." A little "v" appeared between her brows. "Perhaps you should go to this party without me. I can't very well go in my potato sacks."

She *had* to come. He pictured her face, flushed from wine punch and dancing. For there would be dancing, he was sure of it. Of course, she wouldn't stand up with him—his arm still troubled him, even more now that the weather had been unrelentingly wet.

"Nonsense. Everyone will be dressed as you are. The island is not exactly the fashion capital of the world."

He examined her current dress, a virulent shade of purple,

rather like a fresh bruise. Probably every lass in the village had contributed in some way to her wardrobe, selecting the worst from their trunks. He'd seen the smirks as they caught sight of Miss Peartree plodding about in her ugly floppy clothes, sleeves tumbling over her hands, voluminous skirts trailing on the ground. Even after temporary alterations, since they had to be returned in their original condition, they were hopeless.

She'd be far better off in lads' clothing. He imagined Miss Peartree encased in a pair of snug breeches. That would stop the smirks but start something else altogether.

Unfortunately, the people here didn't have much to spare in the way of extra clothing. Perhaps he was being unfair. If malice toward an outsider—and an Englishwoman at that—had been intended, it was of a very minor kind. They didn't know tripping on her overlong skirts would result in her falling down the stairs into his arms. Well, his arm.

"Besides," he continued, "if you refuse the invitation, Marc will be reluctant to go, and then we shall offend the MacLarens. And if you do wish to impress people about this school idea of yours, you'd best put a smile on your face and convince them of your good character."

Miss Peartree looked uncertain. "I suppose you're right."

"I always am."

She lifted a brow but said nothing.

Was it possible he was warming her up? It seemed of late she was less apt to argue with him, although she was scrupulous at keeping him at arm's length. If he couldn't with clear conscience seduce her into his bed as a lover, it would be almost as satisfactory to have her as a friend. True friends had been in short supply all his life.

It was novel to realize that this tiny girl was becoming rather dear to him in the daytime. At night, she took on another form altogether, drifting through his dreams like a faerie sprite, wrapping her slender limbs around him, sliding her bare, cocoa-tinged skin against his. Kissing him with honeyed lips, sighing with pleasure. He'd invented the most complex couplings for his dream Artemisia, and she was always happily complicit no matter what task befell her. On her knees. On her back. Above him. There were days when Andrew longed for the sun to set so he could meet her behind his eyelids and beneath his covers.

"It's settled then. Yes, *cinnte*! Thank you for the invitation, Mr. MacLaren." He shook the man's hand vigorously with his left hand. Mr. MacLaren went off to tackle one more Gull House problem. "We'll have to bring something. Damned if I can think what. I can't very well ask Mrs. MacLaren to cook something here for her own party."

"I'm a disaster in the kitchen, so don't ask me. My mother never set much store by instructing me in domestic arts. I expect a few bottles of your whiskey wouldn't go amiss, though."

Andrew was rather fond of his solitary whiskey before bedtime, and sometimes even earlier. He wasn't precisely drinking away his sorrows, for in truth he was becoming content on his rock, apart from his raging erection every time he thought of a naked Artemisia. His job was *not* to think of her, *not* to want her, *not* to have her. It would do Marc no good to lose the anchor in his new life, for Andrew really couldn't see Miss Peartree acceding to be his mistress *and* his governess.

"No pasta? What a pity. But the whiskey's a good idea. I suppose you think I overindulge anyhow."

"It's not my place to tell you how to spend your time, Mr. Ross," she sniffed.

"That's never stopped you before."

She put the mathematics book back. "I've turned over a new leaf. I acknowledge I may have been altogether too bold for a servant."

Andrew slapped a hand against his heart in exaggerated shock.

"Pardon me. I think I'm having some sort of attack. I didn't quite hear you."

"Don't tease. We got off on shaky ground. But we understand each other better now. I know you have Marc's best interests in mind. You are doing the best you can."

"Faint praise," Andrew murmured.

"Not at all. All of us are limited in our own ways."

"I can't imagine what your shortcomings are. Aside from the fact that you are—short," he joked. But he liked his pocket Venus just as she was.

"My mother was just my size. She hoped I'd gain some inches from my father's side of the family, but obviously not. Were your parents tall? You're a veritable giant."

"I never knew my father."

"Oh! I'm so sorry. Did he die when you were a baby?"

"Something like that." It would do no good to disclose to Miss Peartree just how lowborn he was. He'd spent too much time and effort trying to elevate himself from the muck.

"I think Marc takes after you. I think he's grown a few inches in just the few weeks I've been here."

Andrew had noticed that, too. "I'm putting more children's clothing on the ever-lengthening list. Is there anything else you can think of to add to it? When the boat comes, I'll send my letters off."

"I'll have to think. Oh, I do hope my trunk comes this time. If it doesn't, I'm afraid you'll have to put some of my salary toward ordering proper clothing for me. I'm not a vain woman, but I don't know how much longer I can go on this way." She pulled at her bodice, exposing her smooth brown throat. "This itches like the devil. The wool must be mixed with wire."

Andrew wanted to say he'd unbutton her out of it immediately but held his tongue. "Just let me know what you need. Lord Christie can be depended upon. And Lady Christie is a renowned fashion plate. I'm sure she wouldn't mind purchasing you a few things."

In fact, Caro would probably want nothing whatever to do with anyone he was involved with—he'd caused her enough grief in the past. But according to Edward's letter, she was increasing now, and happy with her dull husband, so perhaps she had softened toward Andrew a little bit.

He couldn't go on begging favors from the Christies forever, though. He needed a contact on the mainland who could act as his factor. Hiring one would be the last thing he'd ask Edward to do for him.

Miss Peartree stared dreamily at the library bookshelves. "How exciting. A party. From the invitation it looks like everyone on the island is invited. I haven't been to a party since my mother and stepfather died."

"Now it's my turn to be sorry. Were there no other relatives to care for you? I presume that's why you have to earn your living."

"I have a stepbrother. He is the most loathsome man imaginable."

To Andrew's sensitive ears, her clipped words concealed deep hurt. He'd wager once she had not considered this stepbrother loathsome at all. He was now an inch closer to solving the mystery of Miss Peartree.

He wasn't sure why he cared, unless it was out of sheer boredom. His governess's past life was none of his business. He'd be a cur to meddle with her present, and she could not remain here in the future or he'd go irrevocably mad with lust for her.

For that's all it was. All it could be. Andrew couldn't afford to love anyone, save for his son.

"One's family can be a trial," he said neutrally, hoping for more, but Miss Peartree busied herself rearranging his books. It was foolish of him to want to stop her—he knew he was too particular with his personal things. It came of trying to exert some control over the chaos that had been his life, but he was master of his own island now, at least one-third of it. Until the Mac-Ewan turned up before Christmas to collect his rents.

Stephen MacEwan was probably laughing himself all the way to the bank for selling off Gull House and the surrounding acreage. Andrew could not imagine the bidding had been fierce, for who besides a desperate man fleeing from his past would want to live here? He wondered if the MacEwan would make an appearance at the *ceilidh*. The laird was spoken of with awe, but he hadn't done much to improve the lot of his tenants as far as Andrew could tell.

"I think I'll take these upstairs if you don't mind." Miss Peartree clutched three worn volumes in her hands.

"You'll find them desecrated, I'm afraid. I often scribble notes on the margins."

"So it *was* you. I wondered."

"Don't sound so surprised. I may not have gone to university, but I fancy that one should learn all one's life."

At first he'd read to make sense of the conversations he was exposed to around ton dinner tables, but he discovered he had a thirst for knowledge, not all of it carnal. This development would have stunned Reverend Raybourne and all the other pinched-faced masters at Reverend Raybourne's School for Boys, if the old buzzards were still alive.

"Very enlightened of you. Most gentlemen care nothing for the classics once they finish school."

"I'm not like most gentlemen, I'm afraid." He'd never spoken truer words.

Miss Peartree dropped those long spidery lashes to her brown cheeks. "Thank you for the loan of your books. We will join you at dinner tonight if you have no objection."

Yes, she was definitely warming up, and Andrew wasn't sure that was good. His self-control was a chancy thing. He nodded and went back to his column of figures.

Her lemony perfume was all that remained of her, and before

long that disappeared, too, beneath the scent of the peat fire in the library hearth. Scattershot sleet pinged against the window, and Andrew lit another lamp to dispel the gloom of the room. He was half-inclined to take a page out of his son's book and sleep the afternoon away, but his bed was lonely enough at nighttime.

CHAPTER 10

The morning was as black as any day this week, so it wasn't the sunshine that woke Andrew. But he'd heard the much-delayed boat was due this morning, and he was on a mission. He crept out of bed and dressed himself in the dark, forgoing break-fast, although he did light a roaring fire in the kitchen. He'd given Mr. and Mrs. MacLaren the day off so they could ready themselves for the party. It, too, had been delayed, waiting for the invited ferry passengers and the arrival of the MacEwan, clan chieftain and landlord of the island. The weather had been pre-dictably filthy for days, but for the moment only the wind was blowing. Andrew clapped a fisherman's cap on his head, having given up on his handsome beaver hat not going airborne, and marched down the path to the settlement. The sky turned to pearl gray as his feet left a trail in the frost.

He was not the only early riser. Someone was even playing a squeezebox at this ungodly hour as the community—seemingly every man, woman, and child—was swarming at the dock. The ferry had landed already as well as the MacEwan's private craft. Planks were being off-loaded from the latter, supervised by a red-headed giant in a garish green kilt. His long hair was tied back with a leather cord, his beard was fierce, and a large silver badge glinted on his plaid. All he was missing was his broadsword, the picture of a rough highlander come to life. The man stopped his shouting and turned to Andrew. Andrew was tall but had to look up to meet the Scot's eyes.

"Are you the Sassenach who's bought Gull House? I don't suppose you've come to help us then with your crippled arm and gentlemanly ways."

The man's English was excellent, the insult clear. Andrew's "crippled arm" longed to punch the MacEwan in his face.

"I was born in Edinburgh," Andrew said stiffly.

"You're a long way from the wicked city now, my lad. So, how do you like the place out here? Quiet enough for you? Or is the ghost rattling his chains?" MacEwan grinned, revealing startlingly white teeth. He might be a savage, but his dental hygiene was undeniably good.

"What ghost?" Andrew asked before he could stop himself.

"Och, the old gent who owned the house afore you. The birder. It's all nonsense, o'course, and has been a bloody trial to get anyone fool enough to buy the property. M'father tried for years. He must be smiling down at me from heaven for finally achieving what he could not. You're happy in the place?"

Andrew did not wish to engage in any way with the king of this little kingdom. After being called a cripple and a fool, he was not rising to the bait. He tried to catch the eye of one of the ferry crew but was unsuccessful. He was not about to stand here freezing to death any longer than he could help it, being quizzed and mocked by this shrewd-eyed stranger. "It suits my purposes. If you will excuse me—"

The Scotsman laid a hand on Andrew's arm to stay him. "That lawyer acting for you said as how you needed peace and privacy, but I don't guess you bargained for this dismal place now, did you, you poor fellow?" The MacEwan slapped Andrew on the back and nearly knocked him over into the ice-speckled water. "But I won't complain. Gull House has been empty since my father's day. I was glad to be rid of it and the ghost, too."

Andrew had no ready reply to this confession and fought the urge to brush off the sleeve of his coat where he had been touched. He watched the men carry the lengths of planed wood up the hill, and his curiosity got the better of him. "What's all this?"

"The lumber? My contribution to the party. I bring it out every year. I'd leave it, but my other islands use it, too, for their own celebrations. Wood's worth its weight in gold here, you know. No trees to speak of as far as the eye can see. My men and the islanders set up a kind of pavilion for the fete as you toffs might call it and then dismantle it the next day. Pretty soon the wood will be nothing but nail holes and fit only for the burn pile." He laughed, showing more of his teeth.

Andrew could hear hammering already. "Seems like a lot of trouble for a few hours of pleasure."

"Trouble? You've never been to a Batter Island *ceilidh*, that's for sure. You'll have the time of your life or my name isn't Stephen Angus MacEwan. You're Rossiter, correct?" He held out a large ungloved hand. Reluctantly, Andrew gave him his right one and was rewarded by an agonizing pain to his elbow.

"The name's Ross. There was a mix-up."

A bushy red eyebrow rose. "Don't be trying to weasel out of your sales contract. I won't take Gull House back even if the name is all wrong on the deed. It's yours and you'll die there."

"But preferably not today," Andrew said, nonplussed by this pronouncement.

"Of course not. Today is for living, aye? It must be a trial though to have a useless arm. Not convenient when mounting the ladies, I wager. But perhaps you let them ride you?" The MacEwan winked one brown eye.

Andrew had had enough. No wonder Donal Stewart wanted to knock the bloody Scot out of him if this rudeness was acceptable behavior. "As I said earlier, if you will excuse me, I came down to see if my governess's trunk arrived." He crossed to the other side of the dock and was sure he heard the MacEwan snicker behind him. The chieftain resumed shouting in Gaelic, and Andrew put him firmly out of his mind.

After some gesturing and a few shillings, he handed off a packet of letters and was in possession of an enormous battered black trunk, big enough to hide a grown man. Andrew looked at it with dismay. How he was to get it home when the island's wagon was being used to off-load supplies and every man was in servitude to the MacEwan was an unforeseen difficulty. He was not about to beg the laird for help.

Clearly, Miss Peartree had packed the trunk with boulders and lead weights. Andrew hoisted it up at an angle and dragged it behind him with his left arm, which soon felt just as afflicted as his right. The trunk bumped along over the uneven ground, rattling Andrew's own white teeth. Once he got out of sight of the village, he let the trunk fall with a thud and sat down on it to catch his breath. He nearly slid off the hump, adding nothing to his black mood.

He was in a temper. It wasn't often he let anyone get the best of him, but Stephen Angus MacEwan had managed to needle him. Andrew saw it for what it was—he was an interloper who needed to be taught his place by the Alpha male of the island. All this talk about ghosts—absurd. The MacEwan was used to his godlike status as reigning overlord of this portion of the Western Isles and didn't want Andrew to dream of intruding upon his territory.

Andrew had no intention of interfering. He was entirely disinterested in the village and would have holed himself up completely from society if it were not for Miss Peartree and her desire to see the children educated. But if the MacEwan forbid a school for some reason, Andrew had no doubt the villagers would obey his command.

So, Miss Peartree had better charm the laird tonight. And the thought of that did absolutely nothing to improve Andrew's state of mind.

"Miss Peartree!"

Good heavens, he was thundering this morning. What could she have done now to deserve his displeasure? They had not even seen each other over the breakfast table. Mr. Ross was gone by the time she and Marc had come downstairs to have their raisin-studded oatmeal in the snug kitchen. He must have started the fire himself—he had given the MacLarens the day off to get ready for the *ceilidh*, though Mary had walked up from the village and was now scouring the porridge dishes, gesticulating with soapy hands and chattering incomprehensibly about who knew what. The MacLarens and others had family coming on the boat today, so perhaps Mary was reporting on this morning's arrivals. The islanders had thrummed with energy and anticipation the last time she and Marc had ventured forth down the track. She was of the opinion that children needed fresh air, but lately the wind had been so fierce she worried the boy would be knocked off his feet and blown across the Atlantic, so they'd kept close to home.

She left Marc with Mary and his blocks and stuffed cloth bear and hurried down the hall from the kitchen.

Gemma could have wept with joy. Her worn black trunk stood in the empty hall, the initials G.A.B. inscribed in fading gilt. She'd taken a penknife to the "B" and removed the bottom bump to make it look as much like a "P" as possible when she had struck upon her scheme, but here at last was her missing life.

"Oh! I've never been so happy to see anything in all my life!"

"I thought you'd be pleased." Mr. Ross's disembodied voice came from the parlor, his velvet burr sending shivers down her spine. She looked into the room through the open doors to see him sprawled on the smelly sofa. He pulled the cap off his head, his damp blond hair sticking up every which way. "Forgive me if I don't rise in the presence of a lady. Whatever have you got in that damn thing? Rocks? A dead body?"

"Don't be silly. Just all my earthly possessions." She ran a hand lovingly on the curve of the lid. "Among them, *real clothes*, Mr. Ross. You will not be ashamed of me at the gathering tonight."

"I could never be ashamed of you, Miss Peartree," he said softly.

She felt her face go warm. Despite her every effort to rebuff him, the man was uncanny in his ability to make her lose her wits.

"But I, too, am very glad the trunk finally arrived. There are clues now." His light blue eyes twinkled with mischief.

She stepped into the parlor to see the twinkling up close. "What clues?"

"Why, your initials, of course. G.A.P. *Gap*. Very unfortunate, as I can see no vacuity or lack when I look at you. But at least now I have some letters to work with."

"Perhaps this was my mother's trunk," she retorted. "Or I bought it secondhand."

"No, it's yours. I'm quite convinced. Only a little thing like you would have so much *stuff*. Let me see. G. Something musical and Italian. Gabriella? Graziela? Or perhaps Germanic? There was that talk about Vienna. Gertrude? But you were born in London, so maybe it's very English? Gussie? No, then you'd be an Augusta, and I simply can't see that. Ah! I have it. Grace, because you're so very full of it."

It was he who was so very full of blarney this morning. "Gertrude! Gussie! As if I would have ever permitted my mother to call me such names. I have already told you—"

He raised his right hand, wincing a bit. It seemed he was recovering some strength to his injured arm, although his recovery was arcticly slow. How frustrating it must be for him.

"Yes, you wish to remain a woman of mystery, your deep dark past buried. But I aim to dig down to the bottom of it, Miss Peartree. Gloria?" he asked, hopeful.

Gemma bit her lip to stop from smiling. "You are reminding me of the Grimm fairy tale, where the little gnome's name must be guessed."

"You are not a little gnome. Little, yes." His eyes raked her, and she felt the familiar *frisson*. "You would make a fine climbing boy."

"I'll keep that in mind if I need to seek other employment. You have not threatened to sack me yet today, but it's still morning."

"I believe if you could see your way to helping me get the trunk upstairs, I'll keep you on at least another day."

Her trunk really did hold everything she owned, and it *was* big enough to store a fair-size body. Even between the two of them it would be difficult to get it up the stairs. "However did you bring it home from the landing?"

"Let's just say I hope there was nothing breakable in it. I dragged it behind me when I didn't kick it forward. My boots are ruined."

She was horrified. "Was there no one to help you?"

Andrew shifted on the sofa, looking discomfited. "The Mac-Ewan's boat followed in the wake of the island launch, and I'm afraid the villagers were much too preoccupied with his arrival to pay any attention to me, with all their bowing and scraping as if he were royalty. I was quite eclipsed. I needed the exercise anyway."

"But your arm! Surely it's too soon to strain it so."

He rubbed his shoulder. "I daresay I know that now. Between my arm and my broken toes, you'll have to find someone else to dance with you tonight. The MacEwan looks braw enough, and he's brought some of his clansmen with him. You can talk to him about your school."

"Dancing!" She stopped herself from waltzing around the sofa. Gemma hadn't danced in an age, not since the first weeks she'd returned to Vienna from Miss Meredith's. Her social life ceased soon after that when her mother died. "Do you really think so? The MacLarens' cottage isn't big enough to swing a cat."

"I think they'll find a way. They're building a sort of pavilion right now in front of the house with planks their laird brought over. The islanders are very keyed up, and even the ferry crew is helping, as they're staying over. I was subjected to an impromptu concertina recital on the dock and the banging of a hundred hammers. I'm surprised you can't hear them from here."

"A pavilion? How strange. It's not exactly summer."

"Maybe a dance floor is a better description. I gather the whole thing will be taken down tomorrow and the MacEwan will take his wood back home with him. This seems to be a yearly event, and the men know what they're doing. Half the floor was laid down before I knew it."

"But it's *December*. How can there be a party out-of-doors?"

"In just a few hours, we'll find out."

Gemma thought it the most peculiar thing she'd ever heard of. "So your letters will go off with the crew tomorrow then."

"If they're not too jug-bitten after tonight's festivities to shove off. There's the unpredictable weather, too. My arm says it's going to storm."

"When doesn't it? Really, I don't mean to criticize, but whatever possessed you to retire here? You could have stayed in sunny Italy where Marc would have been much more at home."

"There were reasons," he said tersely.

He may not have loved and lived with his wife, but the subject of Italy always caused tension between them and he clammed right up. She wondered what kind of woman would have the fortitude to reject Andrew Ross. To send him away without regret. Gemma knew instinctively he would be a masterful lover. He radiated masculine perfection, which distracted her even when she turned her mind to multiplication tables to block it out.

Talk about a "braw" man—Andrew Ross was every girl's dream. The village lasses made cows' eyes at him every time they saw him, and poor little Mary was so smitten she could barely put two words together in his presence. Fortunately, she chattered away to Marc with no problem and the child was becoming trilingual.

Mr. Ross's wife must have wanted him once, and he her. As yet, there was no trace of her in any of his belongings, and Gemma had snooped when she had the chance. Not a letter. Not a book. Not a lace handkerchief. No mementos of any kind for Marc to remember his mama by. Sometimes Gemma wondered if the woman had ever existed at all, but then she saw Marc's innocent face, so like his father's. To raise a boy who was the image of her estranged husband must have caused Signora Ross considerable pain.

Gemma wasn't going to get anything more out of him now, and was ashamed of herself for badgering him after he'd gone through all the trouble of bringing her trunk home. He was looking white around the mouth, too, a sure sign he was in pain again.

"Look, I think it will be much easier if I just unpack bit by bit and carry the items upstairs. That way, you won't have to stress your arm dragging the trunk all the way to my room. Your sling is in the kitchen, you know. Why don't you keep Marc company while I take care of it?"

He heaved himself somewhat unsteadily off the couch. Yes, he'd definitely overdone it this morning.

"You won't trip and fall down the stairs again?"

Gemma remembered crashing into the man's broad chest, his arms coming around to steady her, his warm breath in her hair. He'd held her a bit too long and too tightly as she recovered from her clumsiness, and she'd forgotten to protest in a timely fashion, although she made up for it by being as rude as she could manage once she'd retrieved her wits.

"I will be fine. If you leave me, I'll knot up this skirt. I shouldn't want you to see my ankles—it wouldn't be proper."

His voice was pure sinful silk. "If you recall, I've seen them. And a bit more besides."

"Well, you'll not be seeing them again, nor anything else." Not right now at any rate. But Gemma was very much afraid the time was coming.

As soon as he limped off to the kitchen, she fished the silver chain from underneath her rough wool jumper and drew it over her head. The key slid easily into the lock, making her fearful that someone else had been here before her, filing down edges and stealing her things. Once the trunk popped open, however, she was relieved to see a storm-tossed jumble of slippers and chemises and shawls. She rapped the side panel and it fell forward to reveal her little leather jewel pouch. Her *full* little jewel pouch. She blew a kiss to heaven with a trembling hand. She'd been afraid to think how she'd manage if she lost everything forever.

But her mother was in her heart, not trapped in cold stones.

She rucked up her skirts and scooped up an armful of sweet-smelling clothing. A vial of lemon verbena cologne had become unstoppered somewhere along the way, the perfume permeating the fabrics. Gemma buried her nose in velvets and silks with appreciation. Mixed in with the newly purchased proper governess attire were some of her mother's things. She and Francesca were the same height, although the mother had been much more liberally endowed than the daughter. From somewhere on the Barrowdown side, Gemma had been bequeathed her boyish figure, freckles, and sharp elbows. Francesca Bassano had been soft and supple in both body and spirit, the perfect attributes for a successful courtesan. But now that Gemma had her recovered treasure, she was determined to approximate her mother's charm as best she could, even if it meant more alterations.

She was going to dance, with Andrew and whoever else asked her—twirl and dip and glide—even if she was outside in the coming snowstorm. She'd be wearing a proper gown, probably improper for the island if truth be told, but certainly more becoming than the shapeless sacks she'd been forced to wear for weeks. The effect might be somewhat spoiled if she had to layer on shawls and scarves and cloaks against the weather, but there would be the joy of having her own things against her skin. It was almost Christmas, and it was time to celebrate the many things she was grateful for.

She had her possessions back, a job, a home, her own kind of family. One couldn't really ask for much more.

Yet for one moment she did, making a foolish, wistful wish.

"Mary!" she called. Gemma stuffed the jewel pouch in her apron pocket. Her clothes alone would be enough to overwhelm the girl without tempting her with the sight of diamonds.

The two of them trucked the contents of the trunk upstairs, back and forth so many times Gemma's knees ached. True to her expectations, Mary was goggle eyed at the finery. In an impulsive gesture, Gemma gave the girl a pretty pink spangled scarf.

"For the party. The *ceilidh*." She arranged it over the girl's sober brown smock, and Mary became quite useless, fingering the beading with wonder. Gemma folded and brushed and hung the clothes by herself, her rough hands catching on the smooth fabrics. Her mother would chide her for letting herself go, but her mother had never lived on bleak Batter Island caring for a busy little boy.

She wouldn't shame her mother's memory tonight. And maybe, just maybe, her wish would come true.

CHAPTER 11

The feeble sun held out longest over the Western Isles, turning the winter sky lavender before it dipped into the Atlantic. Dressed in all their finery, Gemma, Mr. Ross, and Marc had plenty of natural light to walk down the rutted track to the village. Even if they could not have seen their destination, the laughter and the music would have lured them ahead.

When they got to the rise over the little group of dwellings, they were rewarded with the scent of peat fires and roasting meat. Lanterns lit every doorstep, as if a hundred fireflies had descended from the dusk to join the festivities. An enormous tent-like structure stood in the crescent of grass in front of the houses. As they approached, Gemma knew this was the famous "pavilion," its walls sheathed in sailcloth tacked to posts. The door to the MacLaren cottage was thrown open, so crowded with food-laden tables a body could barely get in to get a bite, but that did not stop the villagers from trying. A spectacular fire was burning in the hearth, keeping the house and the food warm despite the open door. Marc toddled immediately to a plate of cake and was swept up by Mary and her little brothers.

Gemma stared at ironstone platter after platter of food. "Good heavens."

"Indeed. I don't know when I've seen such a spread. There's plenty of fish, but beef besides. I hope none of it was destined for Gull House and got waylaid."

"Oh, and what if it did? It's Christmas. You can share your riches with the islanders."

"I'd like to be asked first," Mr. Ross said grumpily. "I don't believe I got everything I ordered this time around."

He had unpacked the supplies himself when they arrived this afternoon, an afterthought once the ferry crew had helped with the party preparations. If he'd waited, they would have delivered Miss Peartree's trunk, and then he wouldn't be so cross and sore.

"Well, we'll just have to stock up—stuff our pockets with treats to bring home."

"You'll ruin your dress."

Not one adjective—not pretty, not lovely, not scandalous, and she knew the dress was all three. Gemma was disappointed. He'd not uttered one word when she'd come downstairs floating in bronze silk, topaz drops swaying in her earlobes and her mother's topaz necklace buried in her décolletage. For a second she thought she'd seen a flash of emotion, but he'd hidden it quickly. No trace of flirtation remained from their conversation this morning, no talk of exposed ankles or memories of a hug on the stairs. Mr. Ross was entirely proper tonight, her wounded employer and Marc's father, nothing more.

Without another word, he abandoned her, heading outside to where his whiskey sat on a table surrounded by loud men already under its spell, their breaths white puffs in the air. She smiled nervously at the other women bustling about, wondering if they'd let her help. She hadn't removed her cloak yet and was now a little afraid to. She'd spent the afternoon with a needle, taking in the figured bodice so that it fit her like a glove. Unlike a glove, it didn't precisely cover every inch of skin.

She watched Marc lick frosting from his fingers. He seemed

perfectly happy with the MacLaren children, and Mary waved her away with a smile. Gemma had nothing to do but go outside and listen to the lively music.

The makeshift ballroom was warmed by strategically placed braziers and the body heat of everyone who'd already eaten their fill, or was resting between courses. A small raised platform held several fiddlers, pipers, an accordionist, and a wizened old woman on a drum. At the moment they were all playing together, and the floor reverberated from the noise and stamping of feet. Dancing was already in progress, resembling no cotillion she'd ever attended. Gemma hovered near the entrance, marveling how the plain space was brightened by swinging lamps from the beams across the ceiling, illuminating the colorful clan tartans and flushed faces of the partiers. There were plenty of strangers, the ferrymen, neighbors, and relatives from the other islands she supposed. A bearlike red-bearded man in the middle of them spotted her and pushed his way across the floor. Instinctively, she curtsied to him, earning a dazzling smile of approval.

"I haven't seen you before, my beauty. You must be the English governess that's caused such talk."

Good lord. She had hoped Mrs. MacLaren wouldn't spread embarrassing rumors about her to all and sundry, but she must have been wrong. Gemma lifted her pointed little chin. "What have you heard, my lord?"

"That you live up in the big house all alone with a man, lass, and that you want to teach English to my people. Now, why would you want to do that?"

Gemma ignored the first part. "You speak the language so well, my lord. Why would you have objection to others following your fine example?"

"I've no use for the English as a people, but one must get on with them on occasion." His wink softened his words. "I tried to talk to your man this morning, but it must cost him a shilling for every word he says. Tight-fisted, he is."

"Mr. Ross is not 'my man,' sir," Gemma said, keeping rein on her annoyance. "He's my employer. I care for his infant son. I'm teaching Marc English, too. He was raised in Italy, you know."

"Was he? I've been to Italy."

Gemma's surprise must have shown, for before she could say anything, he frowned down at her, his caterpillary red brows united. Apart from his excess facial hair, she thought he was passably handsome. "What, do you think me a savage Scotsman? I was educated in France like so many of my kinsmen. *Parlez-vous francais, ma petite?*"

"*Bien sur*. And German, Greek, and Latin. Italian, of course. I'm trying to learn Gaelic as well, but your native tongue is very challenging."

"I'd be happy to give you private lessons on my native tongue." He licked his lips for emphasis.

His message was rather obvious. For all his French education, it had not taught him much finesse. Gemma decided she could spend part of her night teaching this man a lesson, and Mr. Ross one as well. He was brooding by the whiskey, ignoring her completely.

"I'm sure you won't have time. Aren't you leaving tomorrow?" Feeling somewhat cliché, she batted her lashes.

"I could stay on for a few days. If it was worth my while. Dance with me."

Gemma clutched her cloak. "We've not been introduced."

"And here you've been talking to me all this time without a thought of that. I am Lord Stephen Angus MacEwan, and you are Miss Peartree, or so the old biddies tell me. What's your Christian name?"

Gemma shook her head. For all she knew, Mr. Ross had put him up to this. "Miss Peartree will do, Lord MacEwan. I—I'm not sure I know how to do these dances."

"I'll teach you that, at least. Let me take your cloak, Miss Peartree. You wouldn't want to trip as I spin you around, and it's plenty warm. I've seen to it. Colum!" He called to one of his men and spoke rapid Gaelic. Before she knew it, he had divested her of her cloak and hat and scarves and Colum was walking away with them.

There was a collective gasp by everyone over the music as they saw Gemma's silk dress for the first time. The MacEwan only smiled, looking remarkably like the Big Bad Wolf.

How did the fairy tale go? *Why, Grandmother, what big teeth you have.* Maybe she'd picked the wrong wolf to teach.

It was worse than he thought. Andrew took another sip of whiskey, ruing the day he ever accepted this invitation. The liquor burned, punishing his throat as he deserved to be punished, but not dulling his vision in the slightest. Despite his best efforts, he was as sober as a judge, if not as dispassionate.

For the past two hours, he'd watched Miss Peartree flit like a copper flame through the pavilion on the arm of Stephen Mac-Ewan, scorching a trail to every man's heart. Evidently, her Italian mother never told her a young lady never partnered the same gentleman more than twice in an evening, for she'd stood up with the MacEwan for at least half a dozen dances, most of which involved showing much more than her ankles as he spun her about. She'd also been passed around to his kilted clansmen, with whom she was just as flirtatious as she was with MacEwan.

What a little democrat she was, treating the slavering men with equal delight, laughing and charming the kilts off them. Wallflower that he was, Andrew shifted in his hard chair to hide his own hardness. The damned chit was driving him to drink, although he couldn't very well stand up to go get more.

He'd sat through the thumping music, the off-key and on-key singing, since everyone had been welcome to display whatever measure of talent they possessed at this *ceilidh*. Some had sung and then departed, and the crowd had thinned considerably as Andrew's frustration rose. And now Miss Peartree, her face nearly as glowing as her dress and her hair tumbling in spiral curls from its clips, stood before the remaining guests, her hands folded piously as a nun. No nun would show her chest like that, however.

She began to sing an Italian song a cappella, a rather somber tune considering Andrew thought it had to do with kissing and roses. The baroque cadence sounded as though she should be joined by monks, or perhaps castrati. *Baci soavi e cari,* she began, her pure contralto placing a quiet spell on the crowd. She held the last note as well as a trained opera singer. In spite of his irritation, he joined the enthusiastic applause once she finished. She was surrounded at once by her admirers.

Andrew had had enough. All night he had watched her get maneuvered beneath the mistletoe kissing ball suspended from a beam. Her lips must be chapped by now. She might even be in pain. But that was not going to stop him from tasting her.

He shoved his way through the clot of men. Miss Peartree's female friends were currently in short supply, but she seemed oblivious of the hostile looks tossed her way.

He gripped her elbow. "I need to talk to you."

"Did you like the song? It was Monteverdi, meant to be a madrigal, perhaps not quite as cheerful—"

He stopped her with a kiss. They were still a good two feet from the mistletoe, but he was not standing on ceremony.

He realized at once he was too angry, but he could not stop himself. Her lips opened at once in surprise, and he swept his tongue in ruthlessly. He tasted wine and cake, or perhaps that was because he'd watched her drain her punch cup and lick royal frosting from her lips and just imagined it. She still was the sweetest thing he'd ever tasted, and he hungered for more.

Not satisfied with a quick kiss, he slid her under the kissing ball as the fiddlers struck up a tune. The dancers murmured and jostled them, but Andrew didn't care. His senses had overtaken his sense.

The kiss meant she would have to go, however, perhaps even on tomorrow's boat. His jealousy had ruined the night, but he could not release her even as she was feebly trying to pull away. Would she slap him? Shriek at him for embarrassing her in front of the village?

Even if she did, it had been worth it.

He uncovered her lips with great reluctance and looked down at her. Her eyes were wide, her lashes tangled, her lips red.

"Why did you do that?" she whispered.

"Your song was about kissing, was it not? I do know a little Italian."

He turned his embrace into a dance position, setting her at a decent distance, holding her as if they were waltzing even though the music was some complicated Scottish jig. He was an acclaimed dancer—ladies had swooned in ecstasy as he swept them around ballrooms, and gentlemen had turned green with jealousy that they could not partake of Andrew's skill publicly. Dancing was just part of his compendium of charms, designed to ensure his place in society and keep him plump in the pocket. But right now his feet felt leaden, his movements clumsy.

"Do you mean to dance with me *n-n-now*?" Miss Peartree stuttered. She lurched to the side with him, narrowly avoiding one of Lord MacEwan's men and his partner.

"Why not? You've been with every able-bodied man, and some not so able-bodied," Andrew shouted over the music. "It's a wonder that dress didn't give them a heart attack."

Miss Peartree looked down at the slight swell of *café au lait* breast that the tight embroidered bodice pushed up. "What's wrong with it?"

"Nothing. Everything. As you well know."

The little hellion grinned up at him. "Do you like it? You never said."

Andrew gritted his teeth. He was not going to indulge her vanity. She must know she was the brightest flame among all the candles and lanterns. She sang like an angel and looked like a courtesan. Every man on the island wanted to fuck her tonight, him included.

She had to go.

Tomorrow was probably too soon, for it was halfway here already and she'd need time to repack the trunk from Hades. Another two weeks would get them through Christmas. That would be better for Marc. Andrew might deputize little Mary to come daily if her mother could spare her until he could write away for another governess. Someone stout, about seventy, with a whiskery chin and negligible teeth. She might not even need to speak Italian as long as she didn't arouse him like the vexatious nameless Miss Peartree.

"I don't even know your damn name," he muttered. It began with a "G." He hoped to God it wasn't Giulietta.

"Pardon me? Ouch, you've stepped on my slipper!"

Couples were coming at them from all sides now, trying to elbow them and even kick them away. Andrew realized that he and Miss Peartree were still under the kissing ball, monopolizing it without following the rules. No wonder the other dancers were disgruntled.

"I'm going to kiss you again. Better this time," he said softly.

"What?" she shouted up at him.

He didn't explain further, but leaned down to brush her lips. It would be so much better if they were horizontal—kissing the tiny Miss Peartree was bound to give him a crick in his neck or a hump in his back. Age him before his time. For she was so fresh he felt ancient, as though all of his practiced arts seemed to be failing him.

Her lips were soft and warm. This time she didn't rear backward, but slipped a small hand around his collar to draw him down. There seemed to be a hot current from her tongue to his groin. He felt bathed in light, his skin receptive to the slightest touch. Her little freckled nose pressed against the side of his, setting his face aflame—he must be as red as the coals in the braziers. His neck cloth choked him, his jacket felt miles too small, his breeches strangled his manhood. He stood mummified as *she* kissed *him* with artless abandon, her eyelashes fluttering on her brown cheeks as he watched, cross-eyed and wild.

He could have kissed her forever except the blasted MacEwan slapped him on the back again. His teeth clicked against Miss Peartree's, and he steadied her before they both disgraced themselves any further and fell to the floor.

"Well now, Mr. Ross, you've stood here long enough with the lass. You're in the way of all these good people who want their share of romance. Shame on you. It's not as if you can't do this very thing at home when you're all alone. Save some of your kisses for the rest of us, Miss Peartree, won't you? It's only fair."

Not meeting anyone's eye, Miss Peartree put a shaky hand to her mouth as though she wanted to verify it was still there. The music continued to screech in the background, and Andrew's head buzzed with whiskey and noise and anger.

"Mind your own business, MacEwan."

"Laddie, everything that happens on this island is my business," the Scotsman warned. "If your little lady wants to set up a schoolhouse here, it's best the mothers don't think she's some kind of strumpet, rubbing up against you like a cat in heat."

"Oh!" Miss Peartree said, looking mortified.

"Now, now. It's a party, and all of us have spent some time under the kissing ball. Don't fret. I brought it myself on my boat for just that purpose. But it's time you danced with me again, aye?"

"You've danced with him enough," Andrew said to her.

"*He* asked."

She sounded hurt. Andrew knew her social success was his doing—he'd ignored her, left her to the wolves while he drank and felt sorry for himself. "I think we should go home. Several people have left already." Though how they could sleep with the racket at their doorstep would be a Christmas miracle.

"Perhaps that's best."

"Are you both mad? If you leave now, everyone will think you're off to finish what you started. No, no. Let Miss Peartree have a few more turns on the dance floor. The party's not quite over yet. Ross, you might ask some of your neighbors to dance. Don't be such a snob, sitting in your chair and looking down your nose at the simple folk. You *do* dance?"

"Of course."

"Get to it, then. I'll take care of Miss Peartree."

It was futile to argue. Andrew recognized with annoyance that MacEwan was right. If anyone could reinstate Miss Peartree to Batter Island society, it was the laird himself.

Another few minutes. He could manage. Despite MacEwan's exhortations, he had no interest in touching another woman. Andrew snaked his way around the merry stragglers and parted the canvas flap to exit the pavilion. A blast of cold air and a swirl of snow jolted him awake, reminding him the walk home would be wet and uncomfortable. He'd better find their coats and his son. He hadn't been at all hungry, but should compliment Mrs. MacLaren on the spread and have a last fortifying drop of whiskey if there was any left.

Most of the men were either in the pavilion dancing or snug in their own beds, but there were still a few outside clustered around the whiskey and ale, ignoring the falling flakes. Andrew nodded and filled his cup. He smiled to himself as they stopped talking—though he and Miss Peartree might be the subject of their gossip, he couldn't understand a word. Let them natter on. But he sensed their discomfort and his own. He was a stranger and always would be. Even if he learned their language, he'd never fit in.

He downed his whiskey in one gulp, then entered the cottage.

The tables had been well sacked and women were carting the leftovers away. Mrs. MacLaren came up to him instantly and threw her arms around him. She must have been at the whiskey, too, Andrew thought wryly. She held a finger to her lips and led him to the pile of coats on her bed. There was Marc, with two of Mary's little brothers, curled up fast asleep like a trio of puppies. A bleary-eyed Mary kept vigil over them.

Andrew found his and Miss Peartree's outerwear. He shrugged into his coat and then walked around the bed to untangle Marc from the clothing and other little boys. Mrs. MacLaren stayed his arm.

After some fierce whispering and a show of shivering, he gathered she was offering to keep Marc for the night in her cottage. The idea had appeal. It was snowing, not hard yet, but that could change any second. The walk in the dark would be difficult enough without carrying a cranky child ripped from a warm bed. Andrew wished he could crawl into the bed himself.

"Thank you. It was a lovely party," he said, kissing Mrs. Mac-Laren on her wrinkled cheek. She beamed up at him like a schoolgirl, understanding his meaning even if he spoke English.

Now it would be up to him to make Miss Peartree understand what the future held. They spoke the same language, but Andrew had a feeling she would not understand a word he'd say.

CHAPTER 12

Gemma had offered to help clear up, once the MacEwan had finished burnishing her reputation. Dogged, the laird had taken her around the dance floor until the last note of music, making small talk with the islanders. He translated the conversations, although Gemma was uncertain of his accuracy. The musicians had scattered, and most everyone save for MacEwan's men had left for the warmth of their own cottages.

Go now, Mrs. MacLaren gestured, practically pushing Gemma and Mr. Ross out the door. A hush had fallen on the island, along with a pristine carpet of snow on the ground. Tiny flakes were tumbling from the sky, confirming Mr. Ross's weather prediction. It looked to snow all night.

Marc wouldn't be coming back with them—he'd be cozy and safe while they would fight Mother Nature in the dark. But if they stayed, they'd sorely try the MacLarens' hospitality. There was room in their cottage for the sleeping toddler and his little cohorts, but with all the MacLaren family here for Christmas taking up every nook and cranny, it would be rude to commandeer a bed.

With a somewhat lecherous wink, Lord MacEwan had invited them to stay the night and sleep on the floor of the pavilion with all the other bedless revelers, but sleep would be impossible.

With the tacked canvas walls and freestanding camp stoves, it might be warm enough, but never proper for Gemma to spend the night with all those men. It was far too late to wander about the settlement knocking on doors to see who might have space for them, and Gemma was afraid she'd get the door shut in her face if she asked.

She had misbehaved. Badly. She supposed she could blame it on the punch. It had been a lovely pale pink color, concealing the strength of the wine within. She may as well have been drinking blood-red burgundy for the effect it had upon her. She had danced too much, laughed too much, sang too much, kissed too much. The bracing air was not enough to banish the lingering muzziness from her head.

But, oh! If she were honest, the punch had nothing to do with her euphoria. She'd felt like Cendrillon from the Perrault fairy tale, minus the pumpkin and the mice. Never had she been the center of attention as she was tonight. Her mother's dress had made a miraculous transformation of her dull little body, and the color was absolute perfection, catching the light and turning to molten fire.

The look on Mr. Ross's face when she'd come down the stairs earlier this evening was worth every bloody pinprick of the needle to her fingers as she'd altered the gown. But he'd quickly masked his response and turned into an icicle, so proper and stiff she wondered if he had a broomstick up his arse.

Until the kisses.

His first had taken her by surprise, though it was little more than a jealous kiss of possession. He'd glowered through the night watching her dance with and get kissed by beardless boys and withered fishermen. Their kisses were hesitant, wet or lusty, all profoundly unmoving. Andrew's second—well, there were no words in *any* of her languages to describe it.

It was thorough, mind-immobilizing, mind-*obliterating*. She'd half-forgotten her own name. It was as if she'd never been kissed before, which was ridiculous since nearly every man present had caught her under the kissing ball, and Franz had once made her lips—and most every other part of her—a priority.

They climbed up the path, Gemma holding tight to Andrew's arm before the wind sent her flying. The lantern swung at a crazy angle with each step, illuminating the snow that eddied around them like shimmering fairy dust. Encased in frivolous velvet, Gemma's feet were frozen before they'd gone very far, becoming so numb she slipped and slid, almost bringing Mr. Ross down with her.

With a grunt he stopped, put the lantern on the ground, and swooped her up into the crook of his left arm, squashing her hat in the process. She buried her nose in his woolen greatcoat, smelling cold air, whiskey, and lime.

"You'll have to hold the light," he shouted, tipping her down to pick it up.

"Don't drop me!" She giggled She wrapped one arm around his neck and held the lantern out in front of them with stiff fingers. Like her useless shoes, her satin gloves were inadequate for the weather. She should have dressed in a more practical fashion, but she had only concerned herself with looking pretty.

She had impressed everyone but her employer.

Gemma should have known better. She'd tried to catch Franz the very same way, gilding the lily so she was irresistible, and look where that had gotten her.

She would not think of Franz now, not when she was right where she had dreamed of being for weeks—in Mr. Ross's arms, even if he carried her like a sack of potatoes and refused to do more than mumble and curse. Each time they hit a bump on the path, he swore under his breath and held her a little tighter. She closed her eyes and curled into him, relishing the contact. Layers of fabric separated them—his gloves, her cloak and dress, petticoats, and stockings—but still she felt his tender imprint on her body.

His long strides got them home fast, and she was almost sorry when he dropped her abruptly to both frozen feet at the front door of Gull House. He lifted the latch and waited like a gentleman for her to enter.

For one moment, Gemma wished he'd pick her up again and carry her over the threshold like a winter bride.

Would he ever marry again? He was so solitary a wife could probably not ever penetrate his reserve.

The house was pitch-black and cold. Gemma placed the lantern on the hall credenza, reluctant to remove her layers. "It was a lovely evening, wasn't it?" she asked, brushing snow from her cloak before she hung it on its hook. Her bonnet was as ruined as her slippers, but she set it on the table to dry.

He occupied himself with his own coat, not meeting her eye, then dropped his gloves next to her hat. "It was all right."

"Come now! You must admit it was very merry—all the pipes and violins, and you seemed to enjoy the whiskey."

"Whiskey is a universal language," he said grudgingly. "And I've had too much of it. Good night, Artemisia." He left her standing in the shadowed hallway without another word.

She watched him climb the stairs, his back erect as though he hadn't carried her home all that way through the storm. He was so very, very handsome with glistening snowflakes in his golden hair.

Gemma wanted to brush them off as she had her cloak, twine her fingers into the damp curls that were forming. Trail a fingertip from between his frowning brows to the cleft of his chin. He would catch her finger as she passed his lips, suckle it as she wanted him to suckle her breasts. Her most private of places.

Now that would make it a very fine end to the evening indeed.

They had the house to themselves. And she had her trunk at last. She smiled, picked up the lantern, and danced up the stairs after him, nearly tripping. *Careful, Gemma.* He wasn't there to catch her now.

* * *

Andrew's room was so cold he could see his breath. He got his fire going, wondering if he should go to Miss Peartree's bedroom and get hers started as well.

There led disaster. Let her do it herself. She was probably getting undressed this minute, her taffy-brown hair falling down her back. The sight of her anywhere near a bed would be his undoing. No, it had been hard enough carrying her home. He hadn't trusted himself to speak, had done his damnedest to ignore her little sighs as she snuggled against him.

Flirting was second nature to him—possibly even first—but anything that could happen with Miss Peartree would doom them both. He was determined to stop playing any more teasing games. They were torturing him.

No more kisses under the mistletoe.

No more Miss Peartree.

She'd been irresistible tonight, like a metallic flame. Each time she moved, the witchy gown changed color, from amber to chestnut to russet. The candlelight had picked up the golden embroidery of her bodice, a bodice tight enough to push up what little bosom she had and accent it with sparkle. He'd been helpless to avoid looking at her and the topaz teardrop necklace that pointed the way to heaven.

Her dress and her jewels were not those of an impoverished governess. Andrew sensed a deeper mystery here, one he could not afford to investigate.

If her appearance had shocked him, the islanders were swept away with stupefaction. He was not at all sure after watching her dance and laugh and sing that they would view her school scheme with any favor, no matter how Stephen MacEwan rehabilitated her character. She was unlike any teacher he had ever imagined and far too dazzling for the straightlaced simple folk who lived on Batter Island. The women, young and old, had turned sour as the night wore on. Their men, on the other hand, emboldened by whiskey and blinded by accurate eyesight, had responded differently. They'd tripped over their feet to beg a dance with her.

Stephen MacEwan, that blasted barbarian, had singled her out, his ruddy face shining with lust every time he spun her around on the floor. There had been far too many kisses beneath the kissing ball. Andrew would not be surprised if tomorrow didn't bring a flock of suitors to his door, probably the bloody MacEwan himself, his hairy knees exposed for all the world to see. Andrew would turn them away without remorse.

Despite his pledge to her to keep her on, he would have to turn her away, too, and soon.

After Christmas. Marc was too young to know the holiday, and Andrew had not much reason to have room in his heart for God, but for once he wished to keep Christmas as others did. There were no holly or ivy or fir boughs to be found on this windswept crag, but Mrs. MacLaren and Miss Peartree had made fruitcake the other day, swapping cheerful insults as they wrapped the loaves in brandy-soaked cheesecloth. In addition to her artistic inclination, Miss Peartree was also crafty, making paper chains and an intricate set of folded stars for the parlor mantel. The house was beginning to feel festive.

He imagined himself as head of the family at the table carving a roast goose, Miss Peartree and his son opposite, candles bright. She might be wearing the bronze dress, a paper crown on her head. She would smile like a benevolent queen, and after the meal—

Ah, there was no point in carrying the thought any further. Likely, Miss Peartree would be pushing the goose around the gravy on her plate, claiming that she never ate meat. Marc would probably turn his own little nose up at the non-Italian fare. A gust of wind would blow down the dining room chimney, leaving them sputtering with smoke and coughing their heads off.

He struggled with his well-tailored clothing, both arms nearly useless after carrying Miss Peartree home, though she was hardly a heavyweight. Hiring a valet to help him was out of the question—he'd not subject another soul to Batter Island, and somehow he could not see pressing one of the fishermen to temporarily assist him in his bath or remove his wet boots or shave off his stubble. Andrew rubbed his jaw, wondering if his beard would be as formidable as MacEwan's if he let it grow. A beard might serve as camouflage if he had to return to England for any reason. He'd draw the line at wearing a kilt, though.

Sitting at the edge of his bed, he massaged the sore muscles, seeing Gianni's triumphant face in front of him in the darkness. He must be enjoying his dukedom despite the death of his henchman. If there was a God, Gianni believed Andrew and Marc had perished in the Mediterranean.

In a way, they had. No one would think to look for them here— it was the only benefit of the isolation. Perhaps one day he and his son could leave, once he was sure that all traces of his past were buried.

But even with a bushy beard, someone was bound to recognize him if he went to London. He'd lived an indiscreet life within his select circle. Everyone knew what Andrew Rossiter was capable of. Masterful at. Edinburgh held too many memories of dashed hopes and weakness. So even if he hid himself in some tiny rural hamlet, discovery was possible. The British Isles were not so very large, and gossip seemed a national pastime.

Best to stay here until the boredom was so acute he was forced to take action. Marc could be sent away to school, as all young gentlemen were. Andrew might travel on the Continent again. By then, his hair would be silver and the Batter Island wind would have weathered his face and no one would know him or want him.

Too exhausted to hang up his clothing, Andrew slipped under the comforter and waited for the tension to leave his body. But there was no rest for the wicked until he took his manhood in hand and pumped the dream of Miss Peartree into clearer focus, her bronze dress dropping from her shoulders. The firelight would limn her from her gold-brown hair to her bare feet, every inch of her available to his imaginary exploration.

He thought of all the places he was desperate to touch. The odd allure of her collarbone, where he could kiss the indentation. The beauty mark high on her left cheek, a permanent tear. The scattering of freckles across the bridge of her nose. Her slim hips. Her flat belly. The heavenly dark tangle between her thighs. He grew stiff picturing her beneath him, her legs parted. He would watch as he disappeared inside her, the honeyed heat of her passage enveloping him.

His strokes grew urgent, his need great. He wanted to see the bliss from his kisses in her eyes again. He wanted to make her come, call his name, spiral into toe-curling spasms.

His own orgasm ripped through him, starbursts of light and shadows behind his eyelids. He was fairly certain he'd been quiet, his gasping breaths muffled by the crackling fire and blowing wind. What would Artemisia say if she knew what he'd just done? Would she hold him in disgust, or offer herself up to sate his hunger?

Andrew vowed never to find out. Somehow, he'd get through the next few weeks, biting his tongue from telling her his fantasies, clenching his fists so he'd not be tempted to touch her. She was nothing to him, after all—just a little brown scrap of girl. If he weren't so damned lonely, she'd have little appeal.

Or so he told himself, rolling in the bedding until he finally fell asleep.

CHAPTER 13

Gemma didn't knock, but turned the doorknob as quietly as she could. If she lost her nerve, Andrew Ross would never know she was here. The light from her candle spilled into the room, bright enough already from the flickering coals in the hearth. She blew out the candle, then set the pewter holder atop the tall dresser and padded barefoot across the moth-eaten carpet.

He was dead asleep on his back, his breathing heavy, punctuated now and again by a rumbling snore.

Gemma smiled. He had a rather ordinary, manly vice. So he wasn't completely perfect, although in sleep he looked like a fallen angel, the chiseled planes of his face and the dent of his chin shadowed with the beginnings of a gilt beard. He'd tossed the covers off the bed and his physical beauty took her breath away. He was dusted with golden hair everywhere, his cock nestled in a thick thatch of it. Even in repose it was huge. Gemma could only imagine what it would be like erect when she made love to him.

For she would. She'd found nothing to prevent her from doing so. Whatever mystery he protected from his past, she had come to trust him.

Everyone had their little mysteries, even she. This time—this man—would be different. She was a woman now who knew her own mind and heart, not a silly besotted fifteen-year-old. She had tried to guard herself against Andrew Ross and had failed utterly. His kiss was her undoing. The wine punch may have emboldened her, but her head now was crystal-clear, her thoughts bright as the sparkling icicles that clung to the roof. Sharp. Dangerous.

And bound to fall and break. But he meant for her to leave—she could feel it. It didn't matter how good she was for Marc anymore. She was bad for him.

Did she remind him of his wife? Tempt him beyond restraint? Annoy him so much he wanted to throttle her? Gemma knew he felt *something*, no matter how hard he tried to hide it. His kisses had proved that.

There would be no youthful clumsy coupling tonight. Gemma was quite sure Andrew Ross was a master of seduction. Even when he distanced himself from her, she sensed his innate sensual power. She knew he fought against it and wondered if he wished to spare her reputation. As it was, she was as good as ruined here, sleeping night after night with only a toddler for chaperone. Marc slept like a cherub now, his bad dreams a thing of the past. She was proud of herself for supplying him with the security to dream in peace.

Now if she could do that for his father. She'd heard Mr. Ross—Andrew—pace of a night, had heard him call out in distress more than once. She wasn't fool enough to think warm milk with honey and whispers would assuage whatever wounds he had buried within. There was something dark beneath his glinting gold façade, something tainted behind his teasing.

His wife must have hurt him deeply.

What would it be like to be married to Andrew Ross? Gemma wanted to know—wanted to *be*. She had slid into love for him and his child far too easily. But if he was determined to send her away, as she was very much afraid he was planning, at least she would know a night of bliss. It was the only Christmas present she wanted.

She moved silently toward the bed, the pounding of her heart vying with his heavy breathing. With the utmost gentleness, she placed a hand on his warm shoulder.

And found herself thrown backward on her bum to the floor, Andrew Ross shouting a string of curses.

"Leave me be, you damned pervert!"

Gemma struggled to her feet. Unbelievably, he seemed to be still asleep, thrashing with the pillows.

"Fuck it! You're dead. I watched you die. Some might even say I killed you. Go back to hell and wait for me. I'll be there soon enough," he mumbled.

Gemma didn't dare to touch him again. "Andrew, wake up," she said, modulating her voice as if she were reassuring a child. "You're having a bad dream."

He shot up from the mattress, hands cupped over his member. At first, he looked at her as though he hadn't the faintest idea who she was. Then she shrank back a step when she saw the blaze in his eyes.

"What are you doing here? Is Marco all right?"

"*Marc* is in the village, Andrew, remember? Mr. Ross," she amended. Impossible to think of seducing him now, although she wished she could relieve his agitation as she did his son's. The man before her was far different from the collected gentleman she knew. She'd seen him imperious, she'd seen him playful, but tonight he was a stranger who scared her.

He talked of *murder*.

Some might even say I killed you.

"You. You touched me." His voice was as cold as the air outside.

Gemma swallowed. "I did."

"Why?"

"I told you. Y-you were having a bad dream."

He shook his head. "No. I know exactly what happens when I—" He broke off, giving her a twisted smile. "As I recall, my dream was very pleasant tonight, not my usual sort of nightmare at all. Believe me, I wake up on my own from those. But you touched me and I thought—Jesus. Get out of here right now, Miss Peartree." Glaring at her, he pulled the covers up swiftly, as though he had only just realized every inch of him was visible.

"Who did you think I was?" Surely he could not have thought she was his wife. The words he used had been filled with venom, hatred. His phantom attacker could not be the woman who bore Marc. And he could not have killed his own wife, could he?

He rubbed his injured arm as he so often did. The long scar over the shattered bone was livid against his skin. "It doesn't matter. Go away."

"You can talk to me. Tell me anything. I'll understand." If he admitted to being a murderer, she was nearly prepared to forgive him. He probably had valid reasons. Unhappy people were often pressed to do the unthinkable.

Lord, she was far gone, making excuses for the inexcusable.

"Look. You understand nothing, and you never will."

"Don't be so sure. I've lived in many places, speak all those languages. I understand a great deal about people, men in particular." She toyed with the fringe of her shawl. "I've observed all sorts of things. Unusual things. For all you know I'm the daughter of a courtesan."

There. She'd said it.

He snorted in disbelief. "Most unlikely. You're no woman of the world. An innocent girl like you cannot possibly imagine the life I've led."

"Then explain it to me."

"My God, Miss Peartree, do you know what time it is? You stand there half-dressed, expecting a midnight confession and who knows what else. So we danced. So we kissed beneath the mistletoe. It meant nothing."

She knew he was lying, whether to protect her or himself she hadn't a clue. "It meant something to me."

"Have you no shame? I'm sure one of the other men you kissed tonight might be more accommodating. Why don't you go back in the storm to find out and leave me alone! Lord Mac-Ewan won't turn you away."

She stood her ground. "I don't care about Stephen MacEwan. I care about you. Something happened. Whatever it was, it has left you—I don't even know how to describe it. I watch you wrestle with yourself. Over Marc. Over me." She lowered her voice, uncertain of her next words. "Part of you knows how good it would be between us. You flirt. You touch me with your eyes. And then you freeze up. The other part just pushes me away."

"Don't flatter yourself. You're not that tempting, believe me. I'm—I'm just bored."

Gemma lifted an eyebrow. "You are?" She unwrapped her shawl, heard Andrew's sharp intake of breath. Beneath the fringed shawl she wore her mother's favorite sheer nightgown, a peach confection embroidered at the neckline with tiny rosettes and seed pearls. She was as good as naked. Gemma knew he could see everything, as she had just seen him. She untied a ribbon, letting the fabric fall from her shoulder, felt her nipple pucker in the chill of the room. Andrew averted his eyes, but not before revealing his unexpressed desire by licking his beautiful lips.

She cupped the slight swell of her breast, remembering her mother's decidedly unusual advice. "*Let a man know what you want from him, cara. Do not just lie there like a dead thing waiting for him to make all the moves, do all the work. A man needs a bit of direction, especially at first. Be bold. Be shocking. We women get what we need so very rarely, and I blame foolish rules for it. If wives were not so cold, we courtesans would have no business. Not,*" she would interrupt herself, "*that I want you to follow in my footsteps, Gemma. I wish you to be a happy wife, and your husband even happier.*"

Like Franz, Andrew was not going to marry her. Like Franz, Andrew was going to send her away. Unless—

She closed her eyes and screwed up her courage. Gemma had been so much younger when she tried this approach on Franz. It had worked, but she was convinced he would have bedded her for spite no matter what she said all those years ago. In the end, she had just been a way for Franz to express his displeasure with his father's marriage and satisfy his male urges conveniently at home. She was surprised to feel no pain at the recollection of being used then, but perhaps that was because she was so nervous now.

She was not her mother, whose soft Italian-accented voice could make even reading a dull shopping list sound wicked and provocative. Nevertheless, she began, her voice getting stronger with each word.

"I want you to kiss me here, Andrew. I want to feel the warmth of your mouth on my nipple. You'll make me so wet with just one kiss to my body. I'm telling you this, but you'll want to make sure. Your fingers will slip between my legs and feel what you do to me. Only you."

This wasn't quite true, but he didn't need to know about Franz. Not yet. In any event, Franz had been a better lover in her dreams than he was when she was awake. She had forced her body to respond, convinced herself that any attention he paid her was sufficient, because she was in love.

What an idiot she had been.

Was she any better now? She would soon find out.

"And I'll want to touch you, feel the velvet and strength of you. You're hard for me already. Don't deny it."

She had gotten through her absurd little speech without a stutter. She opened her eyes to see the anger blazing on Andrew's face. He tore the blankets from his body. "Fine! You see how you tease me. I'm rock hard. Happy? Get out now, Miss Peartree, while the getting is good. A man like me doesn't care who he fucks. Men. Women. It's all the same to me."

She dropped her hand and stood very still. "What do you mean?"

"Do I need to spell it out to you? How do you think I made the money to buy this property, shithole that it is? On my back, on my knees, bent over a chair so I could be buggered more easily. I was corrupted by my so-called guardian. He picked me off the street when I was seven years old and gave me a taste for sin. When he died—in my bed, I might add, while I did not hurry myself to give him his medicine—I discovered that women weren't so bad, either. I almost fell in love, but thought the better of it. No. What am I saying? Let me be honest. She wouldn't have me, especially after I killed her brother when he botched the job himself. That's two deaths at my door. Shocked yet?"

He waited for her to say something, but her tongue was frozen to the roof of her mouth. Would she be his next victim? No one would hear her scream.

"But I digress. Here's what's really important. I fucked for my living, Miss Peartree. Did anything—anything you can imagine and more—for a watch fob I could pawn or a trip to the country or a stock tip. Sold myself—for a considerable fortune—so that the Duca di Maniero could have an heir. Sold my own child, and I had no right to him. I never would have seen Marc again except that Giulietta wanted my seed once more so she could have another baby. Only I and my magic cock would do. She and her husband were both quite in love with it," he said bitterly

He was in torment, no longer erect, his blue eyes clouded. Gemma was ashamed she had so thoughtlessly brought him to this confession, but how could she ever have guessed such dark secrets?

He spoke of perversion. And death. These were things that could not be made right by one night of naughty nightgowns, saucy words, and slow lovemaking. She slipped the nightdress back up, the ribbons wrinkling between her shaking fingers.

His son was indeed his, but Giulietta? Gemma had heard of the di Manieros. When she was alive, her mother always longed for gossip from home. Mamma had followed the Italian aristocracy through the newssheets, which often arrived weeks late. She would remark on people she once knew, or even once bedded. Francesca Bassano had moved in exalted circles once she gave up her virginity. Then the Earl of Barrowdown met her at a party in Venice and had installed her as his mistress in chilly London.

Gemma remembered the young duchess was reputed to be one of the most beautiful women in all of the Italian states. "You never had a wife, then?"

His face shuttered. "Who would have me? No, I'll never marry. And until you came, I was resigned to this new life of abstinence and duty." He had covered himself again, and she followed suit with her shawl, feeling like an unwanted virgin sacrifice.

But she wasn't a virgin and hadn't been for some time.

So, he hadn't loved his "wife." No wonder there was no trace of her in Andrew's belongings, and Gemma had searched diligently when she had a spare moment in her days. She'd put her hands in pockets and drawers and riffled through the pages of books. A horrible thought came to her, a reason why he had chosen to immure himself on the stormy, barren rock. "Did you steal your son away? K-kidnap him?"

He flashed her a hostile look. "I may be capable of much, Miss Peartree, but not that. His parents are both dead. Murdered. Because of me and what I'd helped them do. That brings my personal death toll up to four. I took Marc out of Italy so he wouldn't be his cousin's next victim, changed my name, got so far away I've fallen off the face of the earth."

She looked at the puckered red scar that blossomed beneath

his shoulder and ran to his elbow, the only blemish on his exquisite body. "Was that how you were injured?"

He flicked a dismissive wrist at her. "Yes, yes. Gianni's henchman's aim was bad. I was meant to die, too. I didn't. Oh, wait. That makes five. I killed him, too."

Five. But the last must have been in self-defense. The others—perhaps he twisted the truth to torture himself further. Fate had not been kind to him thus far. But she was here now.

He had been saved for her, but she didn't dare tell him that. He would think her quite mad, but she was a big believer in Fate. Her mother had often said things happen for a reason, even if the reason was not immediately apparent or seemed hopelessly wrong. It had been Fate that caused her to see the advertisement for a governess in *The London List* buried among the others, Fate that brought her to this isolated island splendor, Fate that had her standing trembling with nerves and cold by the side of Andrew's bed.

She had been so certain that one night with Andrew Ross would make her forget everything and everyone that came before him. That it would be enough to keep her warm when he sent her away, as she knew he would. Their mistletoe kiss had been tinged with recognition and regret. Gemma had been quite prepared to use him, much as one used an ivory back scratcher to satisfy an itch.

But what he had told her complicated everything. He'd already been used in unconscionable ways, had paid a terrible price no matter the amount of fortune he'd earned. More than his arm was damaged.

She could help drive his demons away, she was sure of it. But she had to convince him, and just at present he did not look ready to receive her with open arms. She sat down gingerly at the edge of the bed.

"Go away," he growled.

"No."

"Damn it! Is the truth not sordid enough for you? Must you examine me like a bug under a microscope? Getting your fill of what sin looks like?"

She swallowed back an inappropriate giggle. He was being so dramatically gothic, except it was impossible for him to look like a gargoyle. She would indeed like to examine him, touch his skin, brush away the worry lines on his forehead. Soothe him as she was able to calm Marc from a bad dream.

Gemma had never shied from a challenge, and Andrew Ross was the most challenging man she had ever encountered, far more frightening than her cold, aristocratic father or the devious Franz.

She leaned forward, so quickly he had no time to escape her, brushing her lips against his ear. "My name is Gemma. But I'm not Miss Peartree, not really. I just thought you should know in case you want to say something nice to me at some point or other."

CHAPTER 14

One answer, but so many questions left. She might have been speaking an African dialect. Right this minute he didn't care what her name was, or who she was, or why she was here. How was he to rid himself of her when she hadn't flinched at the truth? She darted above him like a golden butterfly, the filmy material of her robe gossamer against his skin, her hair cascading in molten waves in the firelight.

Gemma.

She was a jewel who shone so bright he had to close his eyes.

"Get *out*. I mean it. Gemma." Her name was as sweet as honey on his tongue. He could push her away—fling her really, like a rag doll. She didn't weigh anything, but his arms lay leaden at his side. Her fingertips skimmed across his chest, and he shivered.

"Did you not hear me? I'm responsible for five deaths, Miss Peartree."

"Gemma," she reminded him.

"Forgive me if I can't adjust to this fascinating new knowledge. I don't care what your name is anymore. I want you to go to your room and pack your bloody trunk. You'll leave on the ferry tomorrow."

"No. I really have nowhere to go. I am an orphan." The little witch lay down beside him, staring at the firelight dancing on the ceiling. Her chin was set at its usual stubborn angle, and her hands were crossed over her sheer negligee like an effigy.

"I don't give a damn. A man like me doesn't pay attention to petty details like that. Go back to England and sell oranges at Covent Garden for all I care."

Andrew tried to gather up his sheet to wrap it around him so he could get out of bed, but Miss Peartree—Gemma—was lying on it. He yanked, but she wouldn't budge. But hell, she'd already seen him in all his naked glory, her doe-eyes wide with interest. He bounced off the bed and put on his dressing gown.

"I will count to ten, Miss Peartree, and you will leave, or I'll open my window and pitch you straight down on the rocks."

"No, you won't," she said, quite calm.

"You will not seduce me, no matter how many hours you lie in my bed. I'll leave—I'll go sleep in another room."

"Your bed is very comfortable, isn't it? Mine is hard as a monk's. Maybe you can order me a new feather mattress the next time you make a list."

"There will be no next time, Miss Peartree. You are dismissed. Your position is terminated. You are relieved of duty. You will get the hell out of my house even if I have to dump your naked body on the boat tomorrow morning myself."

"Are you asking me to disrobe?"

"No, damn it! You are the most provoking little thing." He stopped pacing, realizing he must look ridiculous stalking about like a wild animal. He threw himself down on the ratty chair by the fire and snarled, "Onetwothree."

She didn't move. If anything, he thought she wiggled into his pillow to get more comfortable.

Did she not know how desperate he was becoming? Of course she did—she was a wicked faerie, an evil pixie, the Temptress of Batter Island. "*Please*, Gemma."

She leaned up on her elbows, baring her breasts beneath the diaphanous fabric. His mouth dried.

"If you're worried about someone finding out, they never will. When the MacLarens come tomorrow with Marc, things will be back to normal."

"Normal! Have you listened to a word I've said? I am not normal. And I'm not going to fuck you. Ever. Get out. I've asked nicely. I called you by your name. This has gone too far."

"We are both adults."

"I am your employer, that's all. Don't make me one of those blackguards who takes advantage of the servants."

By God, the little imp was grinning at him. "I believe it is *I* that is trying to take advantage of *you*. And you're making it most difficult."

He saw his entrée. "Are you trying to trap me into marriage? It won't work. I wouldn't marry you if you were the last woman on earth."

She sat up now, her hair cascading down her front, covering what he most longed to see. "I haven't said one word about marriage. I'm only proposing pleasure. It's clear to me you're wound tight as a spring. I could help relieve you."

He barked in laughter. "Really, Gemma. I have hands. I just jerked off in the bed you're lying in."

She actually raised her nose and sniffed like a dog. By God, he was going to throw *himself* out the window and fall to the rocks.

"Did you? No matter. I'm sure your manhood has had sufficient time to recover. Although I shall expect you to withdraw like a gentleman in any case. It would not do for me to fall pregnant just yet."

"Just yet? Just yet!" he sputtered.

She waved a small white hand. "You know what I mean. I suppose at some point I will have to consider matrimony. I'm not too keen, to be frank. People like my mother—like *you*—are temptations most people can't resist. Fidelity is a rare commodity. I could go on being a governess indefinitely, I suppose. I'm good with children, and I love Marc. But someday I might like a child of my own."

This conversation was growing more fantastic by the minute. "And who will be the lucky father?" Andrew sneered.

"I have no idea. I wouldn't like to saddle myself with someone too dull and worthy. We should not suit."

"Any man who marries you should be clapped in Bethlem Hospital with the rest of the unfortunates."

"You're hardly in a position to judge. Some might call you the lunatic. You have a willing woman in your bed and there you sit, your dressing gown tied up to your chin. We are quite alone. No one will descend upon us for hours and hours. What harm can we cause each other? If you are determined to send me away, why not say good-bye properly?"

She sounded so damned reasonable. She looked so damned beautiful. He tried to conjure up the first day he met her, when she was a filthy, smelly little ragamuffin, and failed.

He was so very tired of being good.

"I will not marry you. And you *will* have to leave after."

"So you said. Please don't repeat yourself. I might become bored."

Andrew was across the carpet in three strides. In seconds, both his robe and the transparent nightgown were tossed aside and Gemma's gamine body covered his. She was surprisingly smooth and warm for such a bony little thing, pouring over him as though she were vanilla custard. But there was nothing bland about the kiss she gave him. She cupped his face, licking the seam of his lips like a starving child.

It was he who was hungry. He held her to him so there was not a sliver of space between them, stroking her back and her bottom. Her skin was velvet, her kiss victorious. He had no will to fight as she nipped and parried and swirled.

He was perfectly content to lie back and let her kiss him. She was so good at it, with just the right amount of pressure on his lips, delightful wiggles against his body and endearing, enthusiastic groans. Her hair fell like a silk curtain around them, filling his senses with lemon. She tasted of tooth powder and innocence, although someone must have taught her to kiss. No one was born with such skill. Andrew was the beneficiary, and he had no complaints until her soft lips left his. He stayed his objection as she traced her tongue down the column of his throat. His pulse point jumped, and he felt her smile over it as she kissed him back to life.

He was rock-hard again, his manhood jutting into her flat belly. He might come just from the sweet friction of her skin against his like a schoolboy, though Gemma was no schoolgirl despite her diminutive size.

It had been so long since he'd allowed himself to feel anything. Most coupling was simply perfunctory—he had a job to do, and he did it for any fleeting sensation and the permanent benefits at the end. His bank account was proof that he, too, was good at what he did, good especially at convincing himself that all pleasure was equal. But Gemma was a distinct departure from his usual conquests.

He had not even tried to seduce her. Not in his waking hours anyhow. Yes, he'd teased her. It had been impossible not to. Impossible not to kiss her tonight, when every other man had and grinned like fools after.

Impossible not to kiss her now, as he pulled her back up before he spilled his seed as she kissed her way down his chest. A few more inches and her mouth would be on his cock and the night would be over before it started. Enticing as the act was, he wanted to be inside her. Needed to be inside her.

She slithered on top of him like a sinuous golden serpent, squeezing his heart, a heart he'd ignored far too long. He'd give himself this one night. An early Christmas present. He had the self-discipline, and more important, he still had a shred of sense.

Andrew could not embark on a full-blown affair with his son's governess. Such a plot might end happily in gothic novels, but in real life he could not marry Gemma or any woman. He'd been bent so long he couldn't remember ever standing tall.

But tonight was not for reminiscing or recriminations. Tonight was for desire.

He skimmed his hands down her sides to her narrow hips.

"Gemma," he whispered against her mouth.

Her lashes fluttered against his cheeks. "Mm."

"Get on your knees. Straddle me. Do you know what I want?" He watched the blush sweep across her delicate features as she nodded.

He would watch her rise and sink above him. His cock twitched in anticipation.

She scrambled up on her haunches, self-consciously twisting her hair to one side to fall at her waist. He flicked back a curl. "Don't cover yourself."

"There's nothing to see."

Her nipples were large and a shade darker than her tawny skin, her breasts the merest hint of curve. "You are exquisite."

"And you are a liar."

"I don't think so. You're a pretty little package."

"I look like a boy. Oh! I didn't mean—" She put a hand over her mouth.

"Like no boy I've ever been with. It's all right. I can't change my past."

This was the strangest encounter he'd ever had, awkward yet oddly liberating. His cards, dingy as they were, lay on the table. There was no pretense between them, no promises. He'd fantasized long enough about this very scenario. In minutes—seconds—he would either be thrilled or disappointed.

When she took his cock in her hand, he had his answer.

Heaven. But she stroked him far too gently.

"I won't break," he ground out. Covering her hand with his,

he set the pace, aware of her warm weight resting on his thighs. Was it his imagination, or did her wet center weep on his skin? A probing finger assured him she was as ready as he.

Her kisses and touches had shown artful intent, and her original proposal before his confession was shocking indeed. All that talk about kissing her breasts, which he had yet to do, unfortunately. He guessed she was not still a virgin, for which he was grateful. Much the better. He had no wish to hurt her as he lifted her over his cockstand. As she guided him into her tight, slick sheath, every inch of him was alert to that artful intent. She contracted around him, a shy yet satisfied smile on her rose-tinted lips.

Gemma was the antithesis of her ragamuffin self. Somehow she'd turned into a pocket Venus, wise beyond her years and skilled beyond his dreams. She eased up and down, gliding effortlessly, almost mechanically, squeezing his cock with delicious precision. When her hand slipped down between her brown curls, Andrew realized just how selfish he was.

Bracing himself with his good arm, he pushed up to sit with Gemma firmly impaled in his lap. Her eyes blinked with questions, but he gave her the answer as he bent to take a peaked brown nipple in his mouth and work his fingers on her clitoris. He was rewarded with almost immediate unpracticed shudders of pleasure as her hands smoothed over him, her passage clenched tight around him.

He didn't even have to move. She drew him in deeper, milking his cock until he couldn't think to do anything but kiss her. Every place he could reach, and that would never be enough. He was drowning in Gemma—her scent, her wet softness. He was gloved tight within, her perfection a stark reminder that he didn't deserve her. Deserve this.

But if he stopped, he'd simply die. So he suckled and stroked using all his skill and more until her crisis came and she shivered against him, crying his name.

Crying real tears, too. Sweet rivulets of silver that mixed with the sweat of their bodies. He kissed them away, then fell backward on the bed to reap his own reward. His balls seized, and he attempted to lift her away. Despite what she had said, she hung on, riding him through her bliss to his own, writhing over him with abandon until he had no choice but to spill deep within her. He should be, but was not, sorry.

"My name is Rossiter," he said, surging up into her. "Andrew Rossiter." It seemed only fair that he introduce himself, too.

CHAPTER 15

Andrew lay on his back, spent. Gemma was still perched on top of him, her tiny body quaking. Her nipples had darkened, swollen from being tugged between his teeth and tongue. Her skin was the color of sherried cream in the firelight, flecked with bits of chocolate beauty marks. He had never felt so perfectly seated in any human being—it was as though this little brown sprite had been constructed bone by delicate bone just for him to wipe away the years of excess. Flushed with orgasm, she was so exquisite she took his breath away.

It took him a while to find his voice, and longer to find the right words. In his previous life, he would have assured his partner that he had never before experienced such ecstasy. Tonight, those words seemed truer than they ever had, but he dared not say them. He settled for neutral; she could interpret any meaning she chose.

"*That* was a surprise."

She misunderstood him, looking embarrassed.

"You are wondering why I wasn't a virgin, aren't you?"

Blast. If anyone was to feel guilt, it should be he. "No, not at all. I—"

She put a finger to his lips. "You told me all your secrets. Now let me tell you mine."

Yes, he'd told her too much already and still hadn't repelled her. But she didn't know everything and never would—he could scarce remember all the dismal details himself. "It's none of my business, Gemma. I can hardly make accusations in my position."

She smiled down impishly. "I rather like you in this position, Mr. *Rossiter*." She had been paying attention. "You are exactly right where I want you to be."

To punctuate her words, she contracted her muscles one last time. Andrew thought his head might explode.

"I will tell you about my wicked past, only it's not so awfully wicked. My stepbrother was the first. And only. His name was Franz."

One lover. If Gemma asked for a list from him, he would be unable to recall half of the men and women he'd serviced, having deliberately blocked them from memory. She had no reason to be embarrassed—it was he who had the wicked past. But he'd revealed enough tonight and would volunteer no more.

Gemma relaxed on his lap, causing him one more slide of glory. His cock never wanted to leave her warmth, so he would lie and listen to her tale before he made her leave. Which he would. Had to.

"When my mother married Herr Birnbaum, I fell in love with him at once. I was stupid. Fifteen." She sighed. "Girls at fifteen should be locked up."

At fifteen, Andrew had fallen in love, too, or at least in lust. He and Nicky had carried on their clandestine relationship while they were at school and after, when Andrew went to live with him and Caro. That had been disaster for all three of them, ending in Nicky's death.

Would his usual tripartite nightmare come tonight after Gemma left his bed? He almost felt he deserved the torture.

She was waiting for him to say something, so he did.

"Did he force you?"

She rose up suddenly and wrapped her shawl around herself to shield her body from his gaze. His cock missed the hot honey of her, but his mind was glad she was talking. Moving away. They could not do this again. Ever. He pulled the sheet up, matching her in modesty.

She picked at a thread from her shawl, pulling until the fabric bunched. "Oh, no. I was quite willing. Insistent if you must know. You have just seen what happens when I make up my mind." Her lips quirked. "I set my cap for him and hoped to become his bride. That's where I got the name Peartree, you see. It's my own little joke. Birnbaum means Peartree in German, not that I want to be married to Franz now. Heaven's no, not at all. But the name seemed nice and conventional and suitable for my new life as a governess."

She lay back down beside him, still worrying the fraying thread of her shawl. "Anyway, after our parents found out—which they did with almost instant alacrity because we were horribly, foolishly indiscreet—Herr Birnbaum sent me to school back in England. I begged to come home, but he wouldn't let me, not even for Christmas. My stepfather had high hopes for his son, you see. It was one thing for him to marry my mother. No one knew what she was in Vienna, and he was so very proper and powerful he would have frozen anyone out had they ever criticized her for one second.

"But I was not good enough to marry his precious Franz. The bastard daughter of an Italian courtesan? Unthinkable. So they kept me away."

Gemma, a courtesan's daughter? By God, she was telling the truth earlier. He'd paid it no mind. The two of them, children of sin.

The irony was not lost upon him. But he didn't dare laugh after what she had just done to him. He'd never in his life been so mastered.

He frowned. An expensive Italian courtesan was quite different from an Edinburgh streetwalker. He was still fathoms beneath her.

Andrew ripped his self-pitying thoughts away. He pictured a skinny, lonely girl in Bath, spending holidays with the headmistress and spinster teachers. "How old was Franz when he took your maidenhead?"

"Twenty-four."

"But you were so much younger!" He was outraged for her. A decade at that age meant the difference between being a child and an adult. She'd made a choice, though. Andrew had not had the opportunity.

Gemma leveled her gold-flecked eyes at him. "I was the daughter of a whore, Andrew. I knew what I was about. I'd watched my mother seduce even the hardest of hearts. Sometimes she had to, to keep a roof over our heads. Quite frankly, I believe Mamma was a little proud of me for the first time, although she would never admit it and jeopardize her new marriage. I was always a bit of a disappointment to her. She was so very beautiful."

He stilled her nervous hands. "As are you."

She shook his words away. "I am nothing like her, nothing at all." Her hands trembled and he held them tighter. "My stepfather wanted me to stay at school, to teach. He offered Miss Meredith quite a bit of money to have her keep me, but I was not suited. I left a year ago when I turned twenty-one. Miss Meredith said she had no lessons left to teach me and didn't dare turn me loose on the other pupils for fear I would corrupt them. I went back to Vienna, vowing to be good. But then our parents were killed in a carriage accident. Franz took me to bed again the night of their funeral. I thought we would marry."

"What happened?"

She shrugged. "The usual sort of thing. I worshipped him like a panting puppy, but he just used me. He told me—he told me a few months ago he'd never really cared for me, but I was handy at fifteen and handy now. I wasted years of my life pining for him." She tugged her hands away and knotted the shawl. "He's engaged to someone now, a perfect little blonde fraulein from a good family with a big dowry. I couldn't hang around waiting for the wedding, so I sold some of my mother's jewelry and went to London. To see my real father."

"Who is he?"

She bit a lip. "The Earl of Barrowdown."

The same name of her previous employer? Before he could question her, she hurried on. "My mother was his mistress for many years, but when she became pregnant, he suddenly found his moral compass and threw her out. He has a wife and real children and has never claimed me. Needless to say, he was not at all sympathetic to my situation when I told him what Franz had done. Like mother, like daughter, he said. Told me it was a pity I didn't share her looks because it would be hard going for me as a whore."

Her bottom lashes were tipped with tears, but her stubborn jaw was set. "So I forged his reference. Said I was governess to his grandchildren—he's quite old now, you know. Miss Meredith helped me, bless her. Lord Christie was very impressed."

If Andrew was ever in Vienna, he'd make a special visit to Franz Birnbaum to knock out a few teeth. The Earl of Barrowdown would be next.

"You little liar." Andrew swept his thumb across her cheekbone. She leaned into his palm and shut her eyes.

"It takes one to know one."

"I've never claimed to be honest. But you— I don't even know your name, except it's not Miss Peartree."

"Gemma Anna Bassano."

"And yet you are so very English. How did you manage it?"

"I grew up in London, remember? My mother found other

men to keep her after I was born and made sure she was never caught with child again. We even lived on Jane Street for a time. You've heard of it?"

Andrew nodded but said nothing. He knew it well. Jane Street was the most notorious street in London, where only the most exclusive mistresses were kept. Gemma's mother must have been very accomplished, but he doubted she was anywhere near as perfect as her daughter.

"We traveled, too, when Napoleon was not at our heels. My mother met Herr Birnbaum at a spa in the Tyrol. Good hunting ground, she said, and she was right. Even after he discovered her past, he was smitten. My mother was—oh, I can't even describe her. Full of life and joy. Short like I am, but her figure was superb, even at forty. Every man fell in love with her. Herr Birnbaum didn't stand a chance."

"Franz must have been jealous."

"Yes, he was. Franz was his father's golden boy. Literally. He was tall and blond and the center of his father's universe until my mother came into the picture. He resented her, and he didn't even know about her background, though I think he suspected. Even if I had not been determined to sleep with him, he would have found a way on his own. To get some sort of revenge despoiling the virgin daughter of his unwanted stepmother. I wanted so very much to be despoiled, though," she said, wistful.

"It was just sex. It meant nothing," Andrew said. He'd told himself that tale for decades.

She looked up at him. "I know that now. I know what it means to lo—to care about someone."

Love? She didn't mean it. Couldn't. But she was nestled in his arms, her hair a satin fall of burnt umber and gold, her slender body pressed against his, her lips bruised from kisses and truth.

She felt too perfect in his bed. He had to get rid of her.

"Did you hear me, Andrew? I almost just said I love you.

Please say something back, even if it's to tell me you're putting me on the next boat."

He pulled away. "I'm putting you on the next boat. I cannot love anybody, Gemma. I'm not made that way."

"Nonsense. You love Marc. You saved his life."

"That's different! And some might say I'm depriving him of his heritage. He could be a duke." He ran a hand through his hair, desperate now to get her off the bed and out of the room. Out of his life.

She smoothed his hair down. "Your curls are growing in. What a curse you have—such male beauty. You probably think I lo—care about you only because of your appearance."

She was "almost" saying it again. For most of his life, Andrew had been an attractive, charming chameleon, adapting to whatever role was required. Surely he could become someone unattractive, uncharming. A lizard of the first order. He slipped on the mask. "You don't love me, Gemma. We've just been stuck here. Trapped, with no one to talk to and nowhere to go. You're bored, just like I am. It's only natural that this nonsense has happened between us."

"Define 'this nonsense.' "

"The fucking," Andrew said brutally. "It's been a long time without for a man like me. I could have fucked Mrs. MacLaren as she bent over to sweep the hearth just as well. As your stepbrother said, you were handy."

"Don't do this, Andrew," she whispered.

"Gemma, Gemma. I told you before I fucked you who I was. You went into this with your eyes wide open. And your mouth. And your cunt." What else could he say to drive her away so he wouldn't have to see the shock and pity on her face? "I *do* want you on the next boat, Gemma. I'll write you a reference, though. Maybe your next employer will think you're a good fuck. I've had better."

She looked at him. Scornful, not hurt. She wasn't running from the room or cursing at him for his cruelty. "Now who is the liar? You won't get rid of me so easily, Andrew. You don't fool me for a minute."

"What the hell are you talking about?"

She stood up, regal in her shawl. "You need me. Your son needs me."

"I'll get somebody else for Marc. I've always planned to."

"I won't go. I told you that weeks ago, and now I'm even more sure."

"Why? Because I made you come? That's what I do, Gemma. I make *everybody* come. It was just sex. It meant absolutely nothing."

"We'll see. Pleasant dreams, Andrew. I'll see you in the morning."

Before he could argue, she shut the door behind her. *Bloody hell.* What was wrong with the girl? He'd been a perfect prick. Insolent. Contemptuous. He'd taken her and then thrown her away. She didn't seem to know it.

He'd have to be resolute. Now that he'd scratched this itch, he needed no more of Gemma Anna Bassano. He knew what it felt like to be embedded in her heated slit, knew how sweet her mouth tasted, touched her velvet skin, inhaled her lemon verbena fragrance. Watched her as she came apart over him again and again, her face lit with fierce joy. He may have been able to make her come—as he said, that's what he did. But he had nothing else to give her.

Chapter 16

For a rejected mistress, Gemma spent a peaceful night, dropping off to sleep almost the instant her head touched the pillow. She was not going to take Andrew's words to heart, for she knew he didn't mean them. And she would need all her wits about her in the morning when the battle began again.

Without Marc to wake for, Gemma slept much later than usual. It wasn't until the front door slammed that she came to abrupt consciousness in the cold room. The day was not bright, but the snow had stopped falling. She stretched, still naked beneath her blankets, and evaluated her circumstances. There was no headache to remind her she'd had too much punch. Her body was pleasantly sore from lovemaking and dancing. Her unbraided hair was a dreadful tangle, but she'd soon remedy that if she got the courage to get out of bed. How pleasant it would be if there were a maid to light the fire and bring her a cup of chocolate and the gossip pages, but she would have to fend for herself.

Wrapping up in a worn woolen robe, Gemma stirred up the coals and coaxed the fire along. The house was dead silent—Andrew must have been the door-slammer. Perhaps he'd gone to the village to fetch Marc or, worse, arrange for her to sail on the ferry. She couldn't possibly leave today. She'd only just unpacked.

Her hair required a good ten minutes of attention. Then Gemma dressed in one of her proper gray governess gowns with a starched white collar and cuffs, forgoing the prim little cap that went with it. As tempting as it would be to wear something more fetching for Andrew, she had decided to set the tone. By day, she would be Marc's teacher and companion. But the nights would belong to Andrew.

Whether he wanted her or not.

Oh, he wanted her. There was no escaping the hunger in his pale blue eyes. But he didn't think he deserved her, foolish man.

Overcoming his past would be a formidable challenge, one that Gemma was not sure she was equal to. She needed her mother's sensible advice even more than her scandalous nightgown.

The kitchen was empty, the hearth dark. Gemma lit the stove and boiled water for her tea. She was too nervous to swallow more than a mouthful of toast, wondering what Andrew would say to her when he came back. Wondering what she would say to him. She had visions of him carrying her down to the dock, perhaps even locking her in her trunk with express instructions to let her out only when the ship was miles out to sea.

But surely the ferry had left by now. The crew might not be in the finest fettle after the late night, but they had a schedule to keep. They would return in two weeks, just after the new year. Gemma had fourteen days to convince Andrew that she should stay.

Last night she was ready to settle for one night. Now she knew one night was not enough.

Andrew Rossiter was a man who had done everything with everybody. Gemma was not vain enough to think she could truly turn his head by the usual female tricks. She had neither pulchritude nor fortune, great beauty nor great intellect. What she had was determination, a stubborn pride, and a past of her own. She had thrown her virginity away. Andrew's was taken when he was a small child. How dreadful to grow up with such a "benefactor." How hopeless his life must have seemed. It was no wonder he'd floated in polluted waters like so much jetsam until he'd washed ashore on Batter Island.

Into her arms.

Into her heart.

Was she silly to believe herself in love? She'd known the man barely more than a month. It had not been a *coup de foudre*—if anything, she'd held him in dislike at first. But now—

Now she liked him very much indeed.

A sharp knock at the front door interrupted her reflections. It was not like the MacLarens to come in that way, and in any event they had a spare key. Gemma brushed down her gray skirts and hastened down the hallway.

It was the MacEwan himself filling all the space in the doorway, kitted out in a fresh plaid and jaunty cap, which he held down with one hand against the wind. "Good morning, lass. I saw your man down in the village and thought to sneak up here and have a word with you."

"He's not 'my man,'" Gemma said again. Unfortunately, despite last night, that was still true. "Come in."

"With the greatest of pleasure. I forget just how bad the weather is out here." He removed his cap and gloves, stamping his boots on the hall rug. "At least it's not snowing anymore." Gemma wondered if his legs were cold in spite of the thick cable-knit stockings that came to his knees. He followed her into the icy parlor, saw the lack of a fire, and immediately set to building one.

"You don't live on the islands?" Gemma asked, watching him work efficiently. He seemed the sort of man who could kill and cook dinner without blinking an eye, but she was reluctant to welcome him into the warm kitchen. He was the laird, after all.

"Nay. My people did, o'course, years ago, but we had the sense to move to the mainland in my grandfather's day." Mac-

Ewan stood back to admire the flames, rubbing his hands. "He built this cottage for a Sassenach friend. Keen on birds, he was. When he passed, my father had trouble keeping tenants. The house is too fancy for the islanders and not fancy enough for a gentleman. Except for your man."

"He's *not* my man."

"So you keep saying, but I've eyes in my head now, don't I? However, I think I stopped the tongues from wagging too badly. The villagers think you both had a wee too much to drink and lost your heads for a minute under the mistletoe. Just too much Christmas spirits as it were. Mrs. MacLaren seems to think the world of Ross. I don't see it myself, but no matter."

"What does she say about me?"

"Oh, she tolerates you for what you're doing with the boy. Says you both started off on the wrong foot but that perhaps she was mistaken in what she thought she saw. And what was that anyhow? She wouldn't say." He lifted a red brow.

Gemma's skin burned with embarrassment. Thank goodness the woman had not revealed the shameful truth to anyone. "As she said, we had a misunderstanding when I first arrived on the island. We get on well enough now. Did she say when they were bringing Marc home?"

"Aye, that's one of the reasons I'm here. Her grandchildren from away have taken a great fancy to him. They'd like to keep him another night."

Another night alone with Andrew. It seemed too good to be true. "Mr. Ross will have to give his permission."

"I left her with him drawing those pictures, so I knew he wasn't lurking about."

"He lives here!" Gemma protested.

" 'Tis a mystery why the fellow chose to settle here when he has no Gaelic. Says he's a Scotsman, but he talks like the bloody king," MacEwan said with disgust.

"I believe he's spent most of his adult life in England. And traveled, of course." To Italy, where he was paid to father a child. She firmly pushed the thought out of her mind.

MacEwan settled his bulk on a fading chair near the fire and looked around the room. "Hasn't done much with the place, has he? Doesn't he have the blunt?"

"Mr. Ross has written to his friend. With a list of things to purchase for the cottage. And my school," she said brightly, trying to steer the conversation to safer territory. "Did you explain the idea to your people?"

"Aye. You'll have better luck getting the girls to come, I think. But I'll drop a few more words before I leave."

"Thank you. You must want to spend Christmas with your family."

"I would if I had one. My men are a poor substitute. I don't suppose," he said with a devilish grin, "you'd like the job of Lady MacEwan?"

Gemma swallowed hard. "You are not serious, my lord."

"Who says I am not? You're a taking little thing, although I liked last night's dress much better."

"But—but I—"

"Dinna fash yourself, Miss Peartree. I see where your interests lie. I'll not be playing second fiddle to your employer, though he should make an honest woman out of you if you live alone in this house together."

It was inconceivable that Lord MacEwan knew what had transpired last night, yet somehow Gemma was certain he had guessed. Did she look different this morning? More womanly? Well-pleasured? She crossed her arms over her chest, locking her hands around her elbows and put on Miss Meredith's sternest expression.

"I assure you, sir, that there is absolutely nothing untoward going on in this house. My first and only priority is Marc. I am a v-virtuous woman."

The MacEwan threw back his head and laughed. It was on this note that Andrew entered the house, slamming the door once again. He paused at the threshold, taking in the MacEwan sitting comfortably on the tatty chair and Gemma looking daggers at him.

"What's all this?"

"N-nothing, Mr. Ross. Lord MacEwan came by to discuss the school plans."

Andrew frowned. "The school."

"Aye. The school. I told your little governess that I've spoken to the islanders. She tells me you made a list of supplies for it. Did you get it to the ferrymen this morning before the boat went off?"

Andrew's gaze dropped to the floor. "I gave it to someone yesterday. The boat was gone by the time I got to the landing today," he muttered.

Clearly, he was unhappy about that, but Gemma experienced a jump of joy. He couldn't get rid of her quite yet. Unless—

"MacEwan, would you consider taking a passenger back with you when you leave?"

"As long as you know I've one more stop to make before we head home. What's your business on the mainland, Mr. Ross?"

"It is not I we're talking about. Miss Peartree has decided her position does not suit."

"I have not!" countered Gemma. She was not going to let him force the issue in front of MacEwan and meekly submit to his edict.

"There seems to be some difference of opinion," MacEwan said, stretching his long legs out before him. "Perhaps I can act as judge. As laird, I'm often called to settle disputes between tenants on my land."

"You forget you sold me this property, MacEwan. I'm not your tenant."

"Och. The legalities. Perhaps I can act as a friend, then." He winked at Gemma. "What becomes of the school then if Miss Peartree leaves?"

"I don't give a damn about the school. Miss Peartree, I'd like to speak to you. Alone," Andrew said pointedly.

Gemma looked from one man to the other. MacEwan was enjoying this contretemps far too much. Andrew looked ready to throttle someone.

"Go on then," MacEwan said expansively, relaxing in his chair. "I'll just wait for the verdict. But you should know we leave this evening. Time and tide tarry on for no man. Or woman."

Gemma followed Andrew down the hall to the kitchen. Her fire was crackling merrily, but she was cold nonetheless. "You cannot send me away!" she burst out.

"I told you I would." His voice was level. Calm. Dispassionate, and Gemma wanted to take her fists to him. Or kiss him. She wasn't sure which.

"I'll go, but not today. I—I can't. I feel most unwell."

Andrew's concern showed for a moment, but then his mask slipped back on. "No doubt it's the fault of all the punch you drank. You'll be fine."

"I can't leave Marc. Not like this."

"This is exactly the best time to go. He's with the MacLarens and won't be disturbed by your packing. I'll give you plenty of money, Gemma. You needn't worry about starving. More than enough to tide you over until you find another situation."

He sounded resolute. Gemma was desperate.

"You can't send me away with Stephen MacEwan. He asked me to marry him. I said no, but I don't trust him an inch. He'll— he'll take advantage of me. I know it. He's a brute."

"Did he touch you?" Andrew snarled.

"Yes." *But not today.*

"I knew it! School be damned. The bastard!"

Blood would not improve the parlor's décor. Gemma did not

want to be the cause of any, fearing it would be Andrew's that would be spilled, brawling with a man who was taller, heavier, and had the full use of both his arms. She touched his elbow. "Don't confront him. I promise you I will leave on the next ferry in two weeks' time. That will give me time to pack and plan, and for you to arrange for a woman from the village to care for Marc. Surely you can put up with me for two weeks. It's almost Christmas. You can't turn me out at Christmas. I have nowhere to go." She fluttered her lashes, making it look as though she was blinking back tears. If he sent her away, she would cry for real.

Andrew hesitated. She was playing on his sympathy, being such an object of pity. Soon she would do everything in her power to make herself irresistible. But today, she sniffed loudly and wiped away a nonexistent tear. Francesca Bassano would have been proud.

Gemma was spared from finding out whether her dramatics were successful when the kitchen door blew open. "Mamma!" Marc cried, bundled up in Mrs. MacLaren's arms. His face was scarlet, and Mrs. MacLaren made a vain attempt to wipe away the snot under his little nose. "*L'ho mancata!*" He burst into tears. Gemma dashed across the room and grabbed him, wet and lumpy, kissing his cheeks and murmuring in Italian.

Mrs. MacLaren erupted in a torrent of Gaelic. The commotion was loud enough to rouse the MacEwan from the parlor. He towered over the housekeeper as she gestured, pointing first to Marc and then to Andrew. MacEwan nodded sagely.

"What's the matter with him? Is he ill?" Andrew asked, a touch of panic in his voice.

"Not at all. Mrs. MacLaren said he was fine, playing with her grandchildren until you showed up. Then he decided he missed Miss Peartree. And you, I suppose. He's been shrieking his head off ever since you left the village. She thought it best to bring him home."

Gemma snuggled with the boy. He'd called her mamma, said he missed her. Andrew couldn't possibly turn her out today. He'd have to have a heart of stone.

"*Grazi, bambino,*" Gemma whispered in his ear. "Thank you." Marc gave her a snotty kiss and hiccupped.

"See here. I know you think it's none of my business, Ross, but that child will have a fit if you send Miss Peartree away. Just look at them, like a Madonna and child, if the baby Jesus was wearing a sweater. I'd think twice about dismissing her."

"As you said," Andrew ground out, "it's none of your business. I'll see to my own servants."

"And that's another thing." MacEwan threw an arm around the housekeeper protectively. "Mrs. MacLaren will return tomorrow. Her nerves are quite overset what with Marc carrying on so and all the revelry last night. She's going home to take a nap. That's if her grandchildren can quiet down. Marc evidently spurred them on to a bit of a riot."

A muscle twitched in Andrew's cheek. "Bloody wonderful. I suppose we'll manage."

MacEwan grinned hugely, reveling in Andrew's obvious discomfort. "Well, I'll just get my hat and gloves and escort Mrs. MacLaren back home then, aye? I'll be out again in the spring to collect the rents. Keep warm over the winter. Miss Peartree, it was pure pleasure meeting you. If you need anything, anything at all, I'm at your service."

"Th-thank you," Gemma said faintly. With a few whispered words to the old woman, he left with her by the front door. Marc burrowed down into Gemma's shoulder, ignoring the tension in the kitchen.

"I'll just bring Marc upstairs," she said, breaking the silence.

"Don't think this is the end of it," Andrew growled. "You'll leave in two weeks. No stratagem will change my mind."

We'll see about that. With a brisk nod, Gemma left him alone to stew.

CHAPTER 17

He'd waited in his empty library. Waited and drank until his empty stomach rebelled and his mind emptied of everything save the pain in his gut.

He listened. The house was never quiet—there was always the rattling of window frames, groaning floorboards, the blasting wind and splashing water outside. But right now it was as still as it was apt to ever be. Hours ago he'd heard Gemma sing to Marc—Italian lullabies mixed with snatches of songs that seemed familiar to him. Her voice was as sweet as the rest of her.

She would be asleep by now. It was safe to go upstairs and spend the night staring at the bedroom ceiling rather than the library ceiling. There was a damp patch that he could focus on by candlelight. Perhaps the whole bloody thing would fall on his head and put him out of his misery.

He took off his boots and climbed the thinly carpeted stairs. It wouldn't do to wake his son. He had refused a nap all day, clinging to Gemma like a monkey, afraid to let her out of his sight. Preventing Andrew from having a civil conversation and laying down the law about the rest of the time that remained. He wondered if Gemma had used his son as some sort of shield.

No. Her feelings for Marc were genuine. She'd worked won-

ders with him in the month they'd been stuck out here. He was
now sleeping through the night. There had been no night terrors
or accidents. He babbled in English. All Gemma's doing, not his
father's.

He pushed open his bedroom door and paused on the threshold, his heart stopping along with his feet. The firelight in the
grate flickered, revealing an odalisque rivaling any artist's rendi-
tion.

Gemma slept in his bed, her hair braided to the side and tied
with a scrap of green ribbon. Her narrow back and bottom
curved in invitation. If she woke and looked over her shoulder at
him, he would be undone.

The covers were folded back neatly. The exposure—this revelation—of her body was not accidental. She must know the
image she presented anyone who walked through the door. But
there was no one but Andrew to discover her, no one but Andrew to tempt beyond bearing.

The bloody girl wouldn't take no for an answer. It was as if
she'd lost all her facility with the English language even as she
taught it to Marc. Andrew had been blunt. Dismissive. Cruel.
About the only thing he hadn't done was take his fists to her, and
only because if his hands drew near, they would forget to be in-
struments of pain and turn to her pleasure. His pleasure, too.
She'd lit a spark within him he had thought long extinguished.

Gemma might be an orphaned courtesan's daughter with a
rackety upbringing, but she deserved more than Andrew could
give her. If she wasn't so bloody pigheaded, so bloody perverse,
so bloody *perfect*—

She turned in her sleep, one small hand still tucked beneath
her ear. She was on her back now, her chest rising and falling, her
nipples stiff from the cold room despite the fire. Andrew stared
as the shadows danced across her creamy skin, flitting fingers
pointing to each gentle curve, each tiny chocolate birthmark,

each gilt strand in her loosely bound hair. He'd been so wrong about her before. She wasn't simply brown all over, but bronze and gold, almond and apricot, chestnut and copper.

"Get out." He'd intended to bark, but his mouth was so dry his voice was barely above a whisper. She slept on, her face as innocent as a child's, her straight brows relaxed. She seemed to think the better of her position in her dreams, and presented him her lovely arse again as she rolled to her side.

If she wouldn't get out, he would. He stumbled down the stairs like a blind man in perpetual darkness. He should have gone to one of the spare rooms, but it was too late to mount the stairs again when it would only lead him closer to Gemma.

The parlor fire had died hours ago. Andrew worked it to feeble flames and sat down on the sagging couch. Gemma had slept here when she first came. He could, too. With more whiskey anything was possible. There was a bottle now here as well as his library. One in his bedroom. Several in the kitchen, always at hand for a man who was trying to drive his demons away. He poured himself yet another glass, then set it abruptly back on the table.

Overindulgence in spirits had never been one of his sins. In the past, he'd needed his wits about him to make sure events unfolded in precisely the ways he wished them to. Drink was for the weak or the merry, and he was neither. Marc was too young to notice he had an incipient sot for a father, but Gemma would know. She'd seen him in his cups since that misbegotten *ceilidh*, bit her beautiful lip but said nothing. She had to know she was the reason for the current fall from his graceless state.

No. He couldn't blame her. She had some misguided notion that her love would heal him, as if a quarter of a decade of sin could be erased by a faerie's solemn kiss.

Andrew had not let her utter another word about her dismissal, and now she'd taken matters into her own hands and into his own bed. It was Christmas Eve, and she lay like a present, already unwrapped.

He knew now what it felt like to be buried inside her. To touch her bare, dusky skin. To smell the lemon fragrance as her body heated. To hear her call his name. To watch her come apart. He was denying himself what he most wanted, but he could not give in to his desire again. In a little more than a week he would never see her again. Best to have their one night to savor as he spent the rest of his life doing penance.

Marc would be fine. Andrew would find another relative of Mrs. MacLaren's to help young Mary with his son. The child would forget Gemma soon enough.

But would Andrew? He'd carried a torch for Caro for years. He was steadfast, in his fashion, still able to satisfy others sexually while he fantasized about his first love. But Caro hadn't once intruded in his mind the other night. It had been Gemma, and only Gemma.

He buzzed her name between his lips, able finally to put a name to the piquant little face and body that had so enthralled him. It suited her. She was like polished topaz, golden amber. Citrine. Cat's-eye. Cut perfectly into spare angles and planes.

Groaning, he picked up his glass again, swirling the liquid. The color reminded him of Gemma's eyes.

He was simply going mad.

What state would he be in a year from now, alone with Marc and makeshift nursemaids? He pictured himself wizened and wild eyed, his arm still useless. He'd not be fit to be anyone's father.

Maybe Caro and Christie could take the boy, hire Gemma back, and raise him as their own. Caro loved children, and Christie would see it as his Christian duty to save Marc from his sinful father. Marc would lead a normal life with a normal family, not be set adrift on Batter Island to be forever in isolation.

It was the ideal solution—Andrew wondered why he'd not thought of it before. He'd write the letter tonight. He drained his glass and set it on the rug.

Could he give up his son? He had before. But then, Marc had been an abstract infant, faceless in Giulietta's occasional letters. Now he saw himself in his son, the Rossiter cleft in his chin, his fair curls, his ice-blue eyes. Someone vigilant was needed to protect him from the predators that were sure to be drawn to Marc's angelic good looks.

Virtuous Edward Christie would do better than amoral Andrew Rossiter. He may have changed his name to Ross, but he was still the same man underneath.

Andrew felt more than a moment of regret, but he went into his library and penned his plea by candlelight. Any favor Christie owed him had long been returned, and asking this was surely too much.

The words did not come easily, and he went through several sheets of foolscap until he got the right tone. The clock struck one. Some happy Christmas, when he was giving his only treasure away. But it would take weeks to hear back, and then the answer might be no.

Without the responsibility to protect Marc, he could go anywhere. Be anybody. The thought should have lifted his spirits, but it did not. Instead, he was strangled in a kind of sorrow he'd never before experienced.

The kind of sorrow that made one's life seem pointless.

The kind of sorrow that made one desperate. Reckless.

The kind of sorrow that pushed one into the arms of the willing woman waiting for him upstairs.

He would deny himself everything. Later. His child. His woman. He'd go back to his old life, collect his money, breeze by without a care in the world. But tonight—

It was Christmas. A night of stars and miracles.

He left the ink to dry on his letter and navigated through the dark house. His door stood open as he'd left it, a spill of firelight into the hall. To his great disappointment, Gemma had pulled his coverlet up. The sound of her even breathing told him she slept, unaware of his presence or his desire. But she was not here by accident, by a wrong turn, or by mistaken invitation. She knew what his intentions toward her had been and had defied him, unrolling nude like Cleopatra from her rug. But she'd wrapped back up. He would have to remedy that.

He dropped his wrinkled clothes to the chair, wishing he'd availed himself of a bath earlier. Gemma would have to take him as he was, punchy from too little sleep and too much whiskey. He wiped a hand over his face, feeling the golden bristles that had been undisturbed by a razor since the night of the *ceilidh*.

If he thought to turn himself into a beast to repel her, he'd failed, for here she was, lit by flickers of light, her lips set in a dreamy smile. No matter how he'd growled at her the past few days, or ignored her as if she wasn't even there, she had paid him no mind. Took no offense. Went about her business as though they lived in a normal household and he was a normal master. As though the threat of banishment didn't loom. As though they had not spent a few blissful hours in each other's arms before Andrew ripped himself away.

Which he was determined to do again. Gemma Peartree was leaving after the new year. He would grant himself one more chance to feel her body against his, to slip inside her, to lose his loneliness. But he didn't dare taste her mouth again, for his thirst would not be quenched so casually.

Peeling the covers back, he fitted himself behind her, drawing her bottom to his rampant erection. She made a happy sigh and wiggled against him. He feasted on her shoulder and neck as his right arm curved around her to reach for her curls. He might not have full use of it, but he could still bring her to orgasm with a few well-placed flicks and circles of his thumb. He pictured her pink bud in his mind's eye, wished it was between his lips. She would be sweet and tart on his tongue. But again, like her kiss, one taste would not be enough. He settled for the smooth flavor of her back, her earlobe, her throat, nibbling as he stroked her. She was slick, wet, ready. When her muscles contracted and her bud trembled on his fingers, he coated himself with her juices and thrust deep within.

His hand returned to her center, holding her captive, spurring her to ride through wave after wave. She clenched around him, pulling him along to her tide. *Time and tide tarry on for no man.* Andrew could do nothing but follow her to the bottom of the sea, drowning in breathless sensation, struggling to keep his head clear enough to withdraw against her soft bottom. Instinctively she pressed hard against him, simulating as best she could the stricture of her silken inner walls. He savored the rush of his seed, his hand cupping her slight breast, his troubled mind untangling too briefly.

Andrew had never felt such comfort. All the more reason for this to never happen again, for it would become impossible to keep walking away. He could not let her innocent ardor wear him down.

"Merry Christmas," Gemma whispered. A flare-up of coals hissed and popped in the fireplace. She settled against him, relaxed, while every nerve in his body went on alert. She would expect capitulation after this, deserved it. But he could not allow himself to trust the happiness. It would curdle, constrict them both once daylight shone upon his many sins.

But it was still dark, a scattering of diamond-bright stars visible through the windows. He held her to him, his chin resting upon the top of her head. She smelled of lemons and soap and sex. He closed his eyes, breathing deep, and in minutes was fast asleep.

Gemma felt the rise and fall of Andrew's chest against her back, the weight of his arm around her waist. She had taken a risk but had been rewarded. Since the night of the *ceilidh*, Andrew had vacillated between chilly reserve and imperious bluster. All her efforts to talk to him had met with failure. Either he said too little or too much, and never looked her in the eye. He refused to consider any other alternative than her leaving on the next sail.

But tonight he'd taken her bait and joined her in bed. Joined *with* her. Even in the odd position of being on her side, so far from his lips, unable to watch his face, she had gloried in his every stroke. Andrew filled her so completely, his touch so sure, she could not imagine her life without him in it.

Without him inside her.

Gemma frowned in the dark. Once she'd felt the same about Franz. But that was before she had been so thoroughly mastered by Andrew. Even being the daughter of a courtesan, Gemma had been naïve when it came to evaluating sexual prowess. She realized now that sex with Franz had been more of a triumph for her mind than her body. Too eager, she had orchestrated her own seduction, assuming it would end in marriage. Marriage was the ultimate goal of any young girl, especially one like her who'd been raised in such unconventional circumstances. Gemma had yearned for respectability—and yes, boredom. But thank goodness she was not tied down to her Austrian stepbrother.

Comparing the two men did not set Franz in a flattering light. From his unfortunate history, Andrew seemed to know how to do everything that Franz did not. Gemma wished she could discuss his expansive sexual skills with her mother so she could arm her own arsenal of sensual persuasion.

She would have to rely on snatches of memory. Her mother had been frank to the point of sometimes frightening the impressionable, inexperienced Gemma. Francesca had described all manner of physical acts possible between a man and a woman, between two women, between two men. Or, Gemma shuddered, more than two in any combination thereof. According to Andrew, he'd been a willing participant in such schemes.

Nothing she could ever do with Andrew would be wrong, but she didn't want to share him with anyone, no matter their gender.

She was jealous.

She—she *loved* him.

And she also knew with all her heart that Andrew felt something for her, something he fought against. How to turn his flight from feelings to freedom to love for both of them?

Gemma couldn't trick herself into believing she was the answer to every man's prayer. She was sharp tongued and plain as a hen peacock when she didn't borrow the cock's feathers. She had, as Andrew pointed out, the body of a climbing boy, utterly devoid of roundness in any of the accustomed places. Despite once having had a lover, her practical knowledge didn't really amount to much. She was no femme fatale.

But perhaps that was just what Andrew needed. Gemma was like a slice of crisp, tart apple, meant to cleanse his palate after a heavy and indigestible meal.

She giggled silently at the absurd metaphor, not wanting to wake him. He'd fallen asleep instantly, oblivious to the sticky semen on their bodies. Snuggling into him, she let the cadence of his breaths lull her to her own dreams, secure for the moment. It was Christmas morning, and all was well.

CHAPTER 18

Andrew fought his way up through the layers of semi-consciousness, as though he was swimming against rough waves to the shore. There was something warm and soft—and snoring?—draped over his body, weighing him down.

Gemma.

Still asleep. He was wide awake now, his hand entangled in her hair, his erection pressed into her belly. They had passed the night together, or what remained of it after he had lurched upstairs. The room was smoke gray, the sky beyond the windows equally so. Too late for regrets, too early to rise and break the peace.

Marc would be rising soon enough, wondering if La Befana had filled his stocking with sweets. When they were still speaking civilly as employer and governess, Andrew had asked Gemma about Italian Christmas traditions. She'd told him the story of the lost old woman who looked for the Christ Child and left her gifts with every child she came across. In time Marc would benefit from both Father Christmas and La Befana. This year presents were in somewhat short supply, but when he went to live with the Christies—

Andrew swallowed. He'd had a touch too much to drink and had been beset with a kind of madness, yet the idea still had undeniable merit in the light of day. His past had poisoned any chance of him being a proper father. He'd tried, but deep in his heart Andrew knew it was hopeless. He simply wasn't worthy to be trusted to raise an innocent child. His son would adjust to his new life with the Christies—look how quickly he'd taken to Gemma. But what had seemed like the most beneficial solution to his problems last night gave him no relief today.

He was a master at compartmentalizing his thoughts, and he swiftly pushed the fate of his son out of his mind. Better to concentrate on the girl in his bed.

Last night was meant to be a singular occasion, a temporary truce between his conscience and his needy soul. If he had to, he could claim the whiskey blurred his boundaries—he still tasted its bite on his tongue. But he was entirely sober now, blood singing beneath the surface of his skin, hot and wanting what he shouldn't.

Once more.

And then, that would be the end of it.

He'd resisted for days.

He'd resist again.

He skimmed his fingers down her spine, touching each bump. Stirring, Gemma gave a muffled groan and tried to roll off. He could not permit that. He cupped her bottom and brought her closer, whispering nonsense in her ear. Women liked nonsense.

He was unprepared for the elbow to his gut.

"Let me up!" Her voice was husky, sin itself. Letting her up was the last thing he wanted to do.

He relaxed his hold and she scrambled off the bed, a blush on her sleep-wrinkled cheek. In pointless modesty, or perhaps because she was cold, she covered herself with her hands. Andrew stared anyway.

"I have to—you know," she said. Her discomfort was acute and rather endearing.

"The chamber pot is behind the screen."

"I can't go here!" Gemma said, scandalized. As though every inch of her was not now on display, although it was too dark to see much. As though he hadn't explored her rather thoroughly twice now.

Soon to be three times, he hoped.

She needed privacy. Very well. He could concede that.

"Do whatever is necessary," he shrugged. "And then I want you back."

"For how long?" Her voice was sharp, all traces of sleep-lust gone.

"Pardon?"

"For how long, Andrew? For a quick fuck? For the day? For the next week until you put me on the boat?"

Yes to all of them. But she was asking for a promise he couldn't give.

"Just come back. We'll argue as long as you want then." She could slice him with her tongue, but he wouldn't change his mind.

She blundered about the room, searching for her dressing gown. He watched her belt it as if she'd never take it off again. What happened to the houri in his bed? An attack of conscience? Smart girl. She was wise to have regrets.

She fled the room, and he took advantage of her absence to take care of himself and stir up a fire. It was brutally cold without the warmth of Gemma's body near his. His manhood was suffering along with the rest of his goose-pimpled skin. By rights, he should go downstairs and light the stove and hearth in the kitchen, too. Mrs. MacLaren was not due until later to fix the Christmas luncheon. She still had her houseful of company to take care of and was probably just as anxious as he for the ferry to come to rid herself of responsibility.

Batter Island was lucky in that it had a deep harbor and a long pier. Most of the other islands could not be serviced by the ferry without passengers rowing out to it and goods rowed back in. It would be much easier to walk Gemma down the dock than watch her bob off in the distance in treacherous water toward the waiting vessel, her little brown hat flapping in the wind. He might even feel the urge to dive in after her, and that would never do. If the temperature of the water didn't kill him, the current might sweep him out to be dashed on the jagged rocks that ringed the island like rotten witch's teeth.

She would leave—he had willed it to be so. But right now he waited for her return from her room. He'd worry about the kitchen fire—and her departure—later.

Andrew climbed back into bed, bringing the covers up to his whiskery chin. It would do no harm to have her once again. He'd make her understand.

If he could understand himself.

She was taking an inordinately long amount of time to freshen herself up. He listened for any sound of Marc, who usually babbled a bit in his cot before he was lifted out for breakfast. The house was quiet, the sky lighting fractionally. What was keeping her? Impatient, Andrew threw the covers off and put his robe and slippers on. He padded down the hallway. Gemma's bedroom door was open, but she was not within. He paused at Marc's door, but heard nothing.

A pop and crackle below told him she had decided to warm the house herself, for which he was grateful.

But not as grateful as he would have been if she'd simply come back to bed.

"Gemma?" he called at the bottom of the stairs. No answer. The parlor fire was flickering, casting shadows on the small pile of presents heaped on a wingchair.

She was probably in the kitchen, stirring oats or making tea. He wandered down the hall, stifling his annoyance. Passing the library, he noticed she had lit the fire in there, too. And she was still there, frowning over his desk in the corner.

"What are you doing? I got tired of waiting for you."

She looked up at him but didn't return his smile. "What's this?"

She held out his letter to Edward Christie. The room was just bright enough so he could read his own scrawl quite clearly. Damn him for not sanding and sealing it last night.

But he'd been anxious to get back upstairs. Get back to her.

"Are you in the habit of snooping in my personal things, Gemma?"

"Yes, of course," she said without shame. "I've been snooping ever since I met you, every chance I got. I kept trying to find something that would help me understand you. But this"—she dropped the letter to the desk—"I don't understand this at all."

"It's perfectly self-explanatory. I even made provisions for *you*."

"You truly would give your son away?" Her voice was barely above a whisper, yet her revulsion and horror were plain.

"Why not? I did it before. For the money he brought me from the Duca di Maniero. It's for the best, Gemma. I don't know what I was thinking trying to raise him myself. I'm unsuitable in every way to be a father. Christie has children. Three and one on the way. Marc would have a normal family life. Be with other children. Proper children for the son of a duke."

"But what about my school? He'll have plenty of chances to make friends if you let me stay."

"Fishermen's and crofters' children," he said dismissively. "You said yourself I'm the only gentleman on the island. And now you know I'm not even a gentleman, but a male whore. Marc would have advantages I cannot give him. And you are not staying," he added.

Gemma looked as gray as the light that enveloped her. "You cannot do this, Andrew. You cannot give up your child and send me away as though we mean nothing to each other."

"Oh, spare me the drama! I have told you and told you what kind of man I am. Don't be such a naïve little idiot."

Gemma flew at him, her fists pummeling his chest. It was like wrestling with a squirmy tortoiseshell kitten, but at last he set her back with some difficulty. "Really? Do you think assaulting me is going to make me change my mind? What will you do? Bite me next?"

She punched his bad arm with a vicious jab. "I've not yet begun to assault you, you great fool! You are not the man you think you are, Andrew."

He cocked a brow, ignoring the throb of pain radiating from his shoulder to his elbow. "What manner of man am I, Gemma?"

"You love your son. As you were never loved, so perhaps you don't think you know how. Loving is not about money or possessions or position in society. Lord Christie could give Marc the moon, but it wouldn't be better than living here with you. Marc has come so far—and so have you. And then, there's me."

Her smug wisdom dared him to contradict her, so he did.

"You have nothing to do with this."

"I suppose you didn't want me back in your bed this morning?" she asked, scornful.

"What if I did? It means nothing. You are someone who can scratch my itch, Gemma, nothing more. The fact that I fucked you after you threw yourself at me again only proves what a bastard I am."

Gemma shook her head. "You are deluding yourself, but I know the truth. We can raise Marc together, Andrew. We need not marry if you don't wish it. I don't care what people think. But you cannot give up your son and return to your old life. You're better than that."

"Better? I'm disabled. With this arm I'll have to be propped up on a mounting block to service my clients." He was deliberately crude, hoping to shock her. Instead, she shocked him.

"We managed. Quite well."

Oh, lord, but she was difficult. Stubborn. Stupid. He opened his mouth to tell her so.

There was a thud from above, a shriek, then the patter of footsteps.

"Oh, goodness! He's figured out how to climb out from his cot!"

Gemma disappeared up the stairs, her robe flying behind her. Andrew followed, sure that since there was no continuous screaming, his son had survived his descent. Marc was already in the hallway, clutching his bear and his blanket. Andrew could smell the reek of his nappy from yards away.

"Emma! Papa! *Stapag!*"

"Oatmeal," muttered Gemma, sweeping his damp son up in her arms without flinching or apparent need of a clothespin for her nose. "Did you know the Gaelic word comes from the Norse *stappa*? You have a book in your library."

He did? One he'd never felt the need to read, obviously, although now that he lived out here, he should familiarize himself with the island's Norse roots.

No. He was leaving. Gemma was leaving. Marc was leaving.

"*Buon Natale*, Marc," Gemma said. "Happy Christmas! We'll go downstairs and see what La Befana left you as soon as we clean you up."

Andrew felt misgivings when he heard the "we."

"Go fetch some water. There's some warming on the stove."

Miss Peartree was back, ever practical, snapping out orders. Andrew wondered how she could transform so thoroughly from the role of jilted lover to nursemaid. He went downstairs to do her bidding, returning with a pitcher and some towels he found drying in a corner.

At the sight of him, Marc screamed, "No bath!"

"No indeed. Just a little wash-up," Gemma said soothingly. "What a big boy you are, to get out of your crib! Bravo! But every morning you should call for me first, so I may watch you do it. I will clap my hands like this!" She repeated the sentences in Italian, putting Marc's chubby fists together to clap.

"Bavo! Bavo!" the child said, grinning. He was so busy clapping his hands he held still for the nappy change.

She was clever, getting Marc to look before he leaped. Playing up to his inborn male pride, yet getting him to do exactly what was best for him. But that tactic would not work on Andrew.

Since Marc was awake, there was no question of repeating the intimacy with Gemma. Perhaps that was just as well. He would find his self-discipline and exercise it as he used the hard leather ball he got in Paris.

"Do you suppose Marc remembers last Christmas?" Gemma asked, buttoning his last button.

"I doubt it. I can hardly recall what I was doing myself." He'd been quite alone for the day, his so-called friends in the bosom of their families. Andrew's presence would have shined a light on their unusual tastes.

"I was in Vienna, skating on the Danube. It was glorious. Here, can you manage to carry him downstairs? There's something I want to get from my room." She didn't wait for an answer.

"Well, little chap, so you want some oatmeal. We'll leave that to Miss Peartree, but I believe I can toast you some bread." Marc curled into Andrew's chest, clutching the collar of his robe. No doubt they'd be considered quite indecent if they had morning visitors—the only one of them dressed properly was Marc.

The kitchen was warm thanks to Gemma's efforts. Andrew set Marc down in his high chair and fussed with bread and tea leaves. He'd made do without a manservant for years, due to the nature of his profession. Most servants were too high in the instep to work for a male prostitute, no matter how well paid they'd be. Quite frankly, there was too much Scots blood in Andrew to countenance throwing money away on a judgmental valet when Andrew could fend nearly adequately for himself.

He was joined by Gemma within five minutes, and they worked in tandem and in awkward silence, placing bowls of oatmeal and plates of toast on the table. Andrew had half an idea to take his breakfast into the library, but one look at his son's jam-smeared face changed his mind. There would not be too many more mornings to witness such greedy, innocent pleasure.

Andrew checked the clock on the dresser. Soon he'd be banished from the kitchen when Mrs. MacLaren came to prepare their luncheon. Gemma would help her, having the final say as she always did, even though Mrs. MacLaren couldn't understand her. When Gemma went with Marc to the Christies, at least she'd be surrounded by people who spoke her language. Offered some civilization. She and Caroline might even become friends.

Marc tapped his spoon on the side of his empty dish. "Regale!"

"He wants his presents," Gemma explained to Andrew. "What do you say, Marc?" she asked, stern.

"Per favore! Pease!"

"Now that you've asked nicely, we'll go into the parlor. Are you ready, Andrew?"

He stared down at his toast and cup of tea. He had no hunger for anything but Gemma's body, and that was denied to him. But at least he could watch her face when she unwrapped Caroline's latest novel. He lifted his son from the high chair, and Marc scampered off down the hall.

Gemma folded her napkin into neat squares. "I'll clean up after. Mrs. MacLaren will give me the devil for going about her kitchen and leaving a mess."

"We *did* have to eat breakfast."

"You didn't actually have much. Do you feel all right?" Gemma asked.

What a question. No, he was sick at heart but really didn't see the need to explain.

"I'm fine. A bit tired."

"After last night, I should think so," she said saucily.

He was happier when they were not speaking. "Gemma, it won't happen again."

"Andrew, you remind me of the wind, blowing north and south. You were perfectly ready to bed me earlier."

"It was a mistake. All of it has been a mistake."

"If I believed you, my feelings would be hurt. Come along, before Marc rips open everything. He can't read the tags yet, you know."

Andrew felt like he was flinging verbal darts that missed their target. Whether Gemma was well armored or simply side-stepping, it was obvious she didn't accept a word he said.

He wasn't used to being managed. It was he who set the stage, he who drew the boundary lines. It was his gift that others assumed they were in control, that Andrew acquiesced to their demands. He'd walled off his core for so long he'd truly thought his heart was petrified, like a lump of coal in a bad child's stocking.

Speaking of stockings, Marc had already upended his.

"Caramele!"

"Si. Candy. Eat just one now."

Gemma was crouched on the carpet admiring the stocking Mrs. MacLaren had knitted for Marc. Knitting, whether it was socks or fishing nets, passed the time in winter for the island women and brought them coin in the spring. His housekeeper was particularly proficient. Marc's stocking had an intricate design and had been filled with sweets and small wooden soldiers carved by Mr. MacLaren. They all had tumbled out and lay scattered on the battlefield of the rug.

"I gots sojers from La Befana!"

Andrew picked one up. From the tiny buttons on the uniform to the curling mustache on the resolute face, the attention to detail was extraordinary. "I see. This is very fine work. Mr. MacLaren could charge a fortune."

Gemma's face lit up. "What a good idea! I wonder if he could be persuaded to sell some. They're really little works of art, aren't they? They would bring him extra income. Improve his circumstances."

"Gemma, stop meddling. I'm sure he has enough to do. These people are happy as they are."

She paid him no mind, turning the knitted stocking over in her hand. "And just look at the quality of this! The pattern is lovely. We could sell these, too. Think of all the country squires who have need to keep their toes warm in winter. You must have connections, Andrew. People who could help us to lift these people's lives from poverty. We could sponsor a cottage industry out here."

"Good lord. You sound like a reformer. My old friends would not trouble themselves over socks and toy soldiers, I assure you. And I repeat, everyone here seems happy with their fishing and farming. Look at the party the other night. It lacked for nothing."

"Didn't you know? The MacEwan paid for most of it and provided much of the food. He transported more than just the pavilion."

The notion that Stephen MacEwan's largesse had filled his stomach did not sit well. "I suppose he bragged about it to you."

"Not at all. He had so many people come up to speak to him while we danced I was curious. So I asked. It's his way of making sure his tenants have enough to get them through Christmas. I imagine he gives out more in charity at this time of year than he collects in rent."

"Well, there's the man for you, then. Talk to him about—hell, what am I saying? You are *leaving*."

CHAPTER 19

M y, but he was being tiresome. Andrew stood over her, arms crossed, looking like a tyrant. This was hardly the way to begin Christmas morning. She much preferred him warm and relaxed in his bed.

But she had muffed her chance there, getting up and then getting the fires started. She had not meant to take so long, but that letter—

Unthinkable that he intended to give his son away, and pack her up with him as if she were one of Marc's toys.

Gemma had nothing against Baron Christie's household. His mansion in Town was impressive. The man himself seemed unobjectionable if a bit stiff-necked, but he was a peer, after all. There was no doubt in her mind that Marc would be well-cared for in such a situation, and employment in the Christie residence would not necessitate her leaving a warm bed and a more-than-willing partner to start fires before they all froze to death. There would be upstairs maids and downstairs maids, nursery maids, a proper housekeeper. Places to shop. Congenial conversations with people who spoke English.

But there would be no Andrew Rossiter.

"Do stop scowling so. You'll frighten Marc."

Andrew looked over at his son, who was bashing two soldiers' heads together, blissfully unaware of any tension in the room. "I believe he's otherwise occupied." He picked up a small parcel tied with twine from the chair. It was not festive—not like the other gifts. Gemma and Marc had decorated their plain paper with colored lines and squiggles in the absence of wrapping paper.

"What's that?"

"Something that came over on the last boat. It's for you, but I'm not certain you deserve it now."

Gemma was surprised. Though she had a gift for Andrew, she had not expected to get anything from him. "We can call it a going-away present, if that helps you decide whether to give it to me or not."

"I won't change my mind about you leaving, no matter how hard you try to charm me," Andrew said.

Gemma took due note of the stubborn set of his dimpled chin. She did not want to spend the day arguing with him, but she had no intention of seeking other employment. "Very well. But make this Christmas concession for me please, if you will. Until Marc's guardianship is settled, let me stay here and take care of him. If he is to be ripped from the life he's used to again, there's no telling how it will affect him. He's already lost his mother. The man he thought was his father. If he loses me and then you, he will not understand why the people who love him always leave. Betray him. If Baron Christie accepts the role you've asked him to play, then Marc and I will go together and you won't have to set eyes on me ever again."

Something washed over Andrew's face—relief? Longing? Gemma thought it was the ideal solution. For Marc, certainly, and for her, too. It would give her more time to change Andrew's mind about his son and his relationship with her, which after last night she was more than ever determined to do.

"You must admit my idea has merit. Think of Marc," she said, her tone reasonable.

The parcel bobbled in Andrew's hands. "I *was* thinking of Marc."

"I know you were. Perhaps he would be happier with the Christies, but right now, he seems very happy here."

Marc was lining up his soldiers, paying no attention to the adults settling his fate above him. Gemma held her breath, and then Andrew nodded slowly.

Encouraged, Gemma stepped off the cliff. "And there's no reason whatsoever to deny the attraction between us. I'm prepared to be your mistress until we go to London."

She could see the temptation in Andrew's eyes. Was it unfair of her to offer herself to a man who had been starved all his life of love? She didn't care about playing fair. She wanted him—more, she wanted him to know what he was truly capable of. Gemma knew he would be—was—an excellent father, and being his lover would never be boring.

"Nothing you could do to me or say to me will make me love you any less, Andrew," she continued. "Nothing you have done in your past disgusts me in any way."

His brow rose in disbelief. "You can't mean that. You have absolutely no idea."

She pushed a ribbon of hair behind an ear. Clad in a warm gray robe, she was hardly dressed for seduction, but she knew this moment might never come again. "You were honest with me the other night. I understood you perfectly well—I'm not some green girl. We are both of us adults, with adult needs. You may not love me, but you desire me. Perhaps it is out of boredom, as you said. But I'm willing to be used, for I'll use you right back."

She watched his Adam's apple convulse as he swallowed. She had robbed him of speech. Good. Gemma wondered if her mother would approve of her boldness. She was laying her cards on the table, waiting to see if she won this round or whether Andrew would toss them and her aside. There was not much she could do in front of Marc, although he was so preoccupied with his new toys he probably would not notice if she flung herself into his father's arms.

"Well, what's it to be? A practical arrangement for the duration of my stay? Or will you insist on noble self-sacrifice?"

"Jesus, but you're incorrigible."

"Is that a compliment? I've had better."

"Gemma, this is not a game. I'll not rise to your dare."

Deliberately, she cast her eyes downward beneath the belt of his robe. "I believe you have already risen, Andrew."

He surprised her by laughing. "I'll take your proposal under consideration. You know, I once thought you like a little brown terrier. I was not far wrong."

"And now you're calling me a bitch?"

"Only in the best possible way. Here. Open this." He thrust the package toward her.

From the feel of it, it was a book. She tore the paper off.

"Oh! Lady X's latest! Your friend, correct?"

"Latest, and probably last. She has given up writing for the time being."

"Thank you very much. It's a very thoughtful present."

"You did tell me she was a favorite."

"And you remembered." That fact pleased Gemma enormously. Gave her hope that if she kept up the pressure, she would get what she wanted.

Andrew.

He bent over the chair. "Let's see what else is here. Look, Marc!"

The child fumbled unwrapping the rest of his presents—some picture books from his father, and a bear that Gemma had quickly stitched up from a length of brown velvet she found in her trunk. She'd made it as close in size as the green one that Marc dragged everywhere.

"Now your bear will have a friend, too!" She put the bears' faces together and made a kissing sound. Marc giggled and went back to his soldiers. Even an almost-three-year-old male preferred the martial to the marital.

Andrew read the tag on the last flat parcel. "From Marc." Inside was an inky handprint on a thin scrap of wood, with Marc's crude lettering beneath it. "He must have enjoyed making this."

"He did. I had a devil of a time getting his hand clean after." Gemma had thought it a stroke of genius to come up with a present at all for Marc to give his father. It was not as if she could run around to the shops.

"It's hard to believe my hands were ever once so small."

"Think of how tiny they must have been when he was a baby."

"I never saw him," Andrew said, pensive.

"Well, now you'll have something to remember this moment in time," Gemma said briskly. "You can't change the past. Just make the most of the present." Which would, she hoped, very much involve her.

"Happy Christmas, then," Andrew said, standing awkwardly by the chair.

"There's one more present for you." Gemma reached behind the sofa cushion for the roll of paper tied with one of her hair ribbons. She watched as Andrew unfurled it. He was silent for so long, her anxiety provoked her to speech. "Don't you like it?"

It was a careful pencil sketch of Andrew and Marc, sitting in a chair with a book. She had drawn it from memory, capturing the look on Marc's face as he looked up at his father. She remembered the day well. Andrew had been pointing to the illustrations, saying the words in English. Instead of paying attention to the pictures, Marc had gazed at his father, finally poking a finger in the crease of his chin, then touching his own. Gemma believed that was the day Marc truly made the connection that this stranger was his father. It was all the more bittersweet now that she knew their true history.

"It's extraordinary." Andrew's voice was raspy.

"We can get Mr. MacLaren to make a frame for it. There wasn't time."

Andrew said nothing. He studied the drawing intently, shifting the parchment to catch the early-morning light.

"I could do a more formal portrait if you wish it," Gemma offered. "If we could get Marc to sit still long enough."

"This will do. You really are quite talented."

"Oh, I've just the usual schoolgirl accomplishments. Miss Meredith was an enviable artist herself and saw to it that all her pupils learned to draw."

"Don't be modest," he said gruffly. "I think I prefer you when you presume to know it all."

"You must think me a shrew."

"I think you are just Gemma." He lifted his eyes from the paper. They were such a pale blue, almost colorless, like melted snow. "Thank you for this. For the gift of the handprint as well. When Marc leaves, I will at least have something."

Gemma held her tongue. Even if she *was* a shrew, she didn't want to browbeat him about his ridiculous plan. She would have to finesse the future, arranging it as precisely as she had the portrait with each stroke of her pencil. Shading, contouring, balancing. Burnishing until the paper of his life was completely filled in, its surface smooth and shiny.

"Will you watch Marc while I go get dressed? Mrs. MacLaren will be shocked if she finds me in such a state."

"You look perfectly fine. That robe would suit a nun."

Gemma grinned. "I purchased it for just that reason. It's part of my governess trousseau. That was when I wished to ward off the unwelcome advances from my employer. Before I discovered his advances weren't unwelcome at all."

Andrew ran a hand through his unruly curls. "Gemma, I cannot be what you wish me to be. I'm sorry."

" 'Never make a defense or an apology until you are accused.' Those are King Charles the First's words, by the way. I have said nothing about my expectations."

"I know what you're thinking."

"Do you? I doubt it."

"You think you can heal me. Stitch me up somehow like you did Marc's bear. Well, you can't. I've had a full quarter century of sin." He picked up the fireplace tong and adjusted a brick of peat, then poked at it viciously. A shower of sparks flew up the chimney. His back was still to her when he said, "I'll not deny you arouse me. You have practically from the first. But anything more than physical gratification between us is impossible."

She wished she could see his face as he spoke, look for the trace of truth in his words. She didn't—couldn't—believe him.

"I'm not asking for a lifetime commitment, Andrew. Just a little comfort while we endure part of the winter out here. For all you know, your letter won't reach Lord Christie for weeks once it's sent, maybe a month or more. It's winter in Scotland. Roads are impassable. You may be stuck with me until spring." Lord, she hoped so.

He straightened up, towering over her. "You're giving yourself away cheap."

"That's my prerogative, isn't it? I have a mind and body of my own. What I do with them is my business."

"You are a modern thinker, aren't you?"

She took a step toward him, inhaling the sweet smoky aroma that clung to him. "Look, Andrew, you know the fate of a fallen woman as well as I. I am the illegitimate daughter of a courtesan. I was willingly ruined at fifteen. No decent man would have me. So I suppose I'll have to settle for you. You're not decent, you're handy, and you're handsome. You may even teach me a thing or two my mother overlooked."

Andrew shook his head slowly. "Franz never stood a chance against you, did he? I begin to feel sorry for the bastard."

"Don't waste a thought on him. His little fraulein is stuck with him. Wait until she finds out how poorly endowed he is. You are very, very much larger." She pressed her palm flat on his chest but did not move her hand where it wished to be.

He covered her hand and swung it aside. "Flattery will get you nowhere."

"I don't wish to get anywhere at the moment. Mrs. MacLaren is due any second, and Marc is wide awake. But later, after lunch, when Marc is napping, we'll discuss this further. In bed."

She whirled away, feeling quite proud of her blatant insouciance. Andrew would not know how her heart hammered in her chest as she channeled her mother at her naughtiest. Gemma had never been so bold in her life, or so desperate to have what she wanted. What he needed.

Her hands shook too much to dress quickly, which was fine. Let him think on her words. Weigh her suggestion. Imagine what might be. What would be, as soon as the last dish was washed and Marc tucked into his cot.

She imagined her mother behind her, brushing out the kinks in her hair as she had done for the first fifteen years of Gemma's life. "He's not an ordinary man, Mamma. I don't know if your advice will work on him." She twisted her hair into two loops and pinned them up, turning from wanton to respectable. "Have I gone too far? You always said men were easily bored and liked the unexpected. That a shy miss might lose her chance. But I was so brazen. Maybe too brazen," Gemma whispered, noting the hot flush of her cheeks in the mirror. No rouge would be necessary today. She arranged a crisp white fichu over the scooped neckline of her bottle-green gown and took a step backward. "I look like a governess now. Mrs. MacLaren will approve at least."

Gemma picked up her sketchbook and removed the portrait she had made of the MacLarens. She'd placed them in front of the kitchen hearth, both with knives in hand. Mr. MacLaren was whittling with his, and Mrs. MacLaren was peeling potatoes. It was a homely scene, depicting their quiet companionship.

Gemma wondered what womanly arts Mrs. MacLaren had used to lure her husband to marriage all those decades ago. Perhaps it had been something as simple as being the girl in the neighboring cottage—the population was so small they must have been limited for choice. All but one of their sons had left Batter for greener pastures and wives they weren't related to.

Would Gemma have pledged herself to Andrew if he had competition? Yes, she believed she would. He was beautiful, true, but beyond his beauty was a kind of wounded dignity that fascinated her. He'd been through so much, yet he'd not turned dark. He may have thought his soul was black, but she knew better.

She rolled the paper up and fished out another ribbon from her dressing table drawer. She'd better get downstairs and tidy up the kitchen, give Andrew a chance to get dressed. It was Christmas Day, and the present she most wanted was within reach.

CHAPTER 20

The remains of their Christmas feast lay before him. The day was not going precisely as Andrew had envisioned it weeks ago. Then, he was the happy father at the head of the table, enjoying the unaccustomed customs of the holiday. It would mark his first foray into a truly normal life. Instead, the day had taken some unexpected twists and turns, the most notable being his decision to send Marc away and Gemma's foolish declaration.

He knew what she was trying to do. There were moments when he felt he was in one of Caroline's novels with a feisty heroine who "risked all for love." Gemma had flirted outrageously over the leg of lamb—no goose could be found to be sacrificed—casting burning glances that made it difficult for him to hold in his laughter. She was outrageous, as far from a subtle seductress as he'd ever encountered. It was clear, despite what she said, that she wanted to marry him. Did she not know he had played every game there was to be played? His only urge was to turn her over his knee and spank the silliness out of her.

Now *there* was an image to relish, her pert bottom pink beneath his hand. He shook his head to clear it.

Gemma meant to tame him somehow, but she underestimated his wildness. A few weeks of her company in his bed would not solve his problems. He would never be domesticated—the move here and this morning had proven that. He was going half-mad, lusting after a boyish hoyden. Now that Andrew had bedded her, he knew he needed to pull back for both their sakes. If he accepted her proposition, he would doom them both.

He was not cut out to be anybody's husband. Oh, he'd been faithful in his time—purely for financial reasons. But he always got bored and was grateful when circumstances changed. He was used to a revolving cast of characters, and surely one slip of a girl would not satisfy him for a lifetime.

But he found her irresistible right now under the necessary candlelight in the dining room. The sky outside was black as night even though it was the middle of the afternoon. The weather had turned foul, driving Mrs. MacLaren back to the village before they sat down to lunch. The salty scent of the roiling ocean had wafted through the cracks in the window frames along with the icy nip of wind. The candles sputtered as Marc drooped over his plate, still clutching one of his soldiers in a sticky fist.

"You should take him up to bed. I'll clear the table."

Andrew rose and hoisted his son from his chair. "When he's settled, I'll help you wash up."

"Oh! You needn't come down. Wait for me upstairs."

The siren had returned, batting her long lashes.

He didn't argue. Over dinner he'd come to the simplest of plans—he would frighten her away. It should not be too difficult. The grim day leant itself to a gothic scenario—the isolated house, the roaring sea, the driving wind. A madman and an almost-innocent. Andrew suppressed a chuckle. Caro could have written the plot with ease.

He trundled Marc upstairs, leaving Gemma to stack the plates and carry them to the kitchen. How long would he have to prepare her surprise? He supposed it depended upon whether Mrs. MacLaren had washed the pots before she left.

Marc fell into bed without protest, no song or story required.

If he was true to form, he'd sleep at least two hours, giving Andrew time to convince Gemma she'd made a mistake. He went to his room and quickly gathered up what he needed. It was all too available and well used, stored away in his trunk. The water in the jug was cold, but he didn't want to arouse her suspicions by heating any in the kitchen. Unwinding his tie, he debated about getting undressed, decided it best to keep his shirt and breeches on. She would be shivering. Naked. He'd be in control. Dominant. Show Gemma just exactly what she thought she wanted and make her change her mind.

He picked up a book and settled himself in a chair by the fire. After two minutes of watching the words run together, he tossed it aside. The sooner Gemma came up here, the sooner she'd leave. He rolled up his sleeves and went down to the kitchen.

Gemma had discarded her limp fichu first thing. The heat of the kitchen was oppressive despite the violent storm outside. Needles of sleet battered the kitchen windows, the crackling sound a steady buzz in her ears. She could not see the water off the point for the frozen fog but could hear it thrashing like thunder against the rocks. She hoped Mrs. MacLaren was home safe and snug in her cottage, surrounded by jolly grandchildren and bowls of Christmas pudding.

The housekeeper had left a neat tower of roasting pans and pots soaking in the deep slate sink. Gemma filled a kettle of water from the pump and set it to heat on the stove. Covering her dress with a fresh apron that fell to the floor, she scraped the dishes and packed away the leftovers. There was a great deal to do, and every minute was precious. Marc would not sleep forever.

For the first time, she wondered how her mother had balanced raising her with her obligations to the various men who kept a roof over their heads. But then, she had Caterina to take over minding Gemma when duty called. Francesca Bassano's own loyal nursemaid had shared the life of shame once Francesca fell from society's good graces. But Gemma could never remember Caterina complaining, just spending a great deal of time on her knees praying for patience. Gemma had been a mischievous child, and now—

Caterina would be praying fervently again if she were still alive, making signs of the cross and kissing her crucifix in the vain hope that Gemma would behave.

"Not done yet?"

Gemma spun around, catching her foot on the apron hem. Andrew lounged against the door frame. He'd lost his cravat, waistcoat, and tailored jacket, the golden column of his throat visible against his unbuttoned lawn shirt.

"I've hardly begun," Gemma said ruefully. She brushed a damp curl from her forehead.

"Leave it, then. Like you did the breakfast dishes."

Gemma looked at the sink and its ominous content. "No. Marc will want his tea later. I won't be able to wade through the battlefield to make it."

Andrew gave an exaggerated sigh. "I'll just have to help you. Step aside."

"You're joking!"

"Do you think I've never washed a dish? You'd be surprised what I know how to do."

The way he said it made Gemma think he was not talking of household tasks. "All right." The sooner she got out of the hot kitchen and out of her constricting clothes, the happier she'd be. And Andrew would be unconstricted with her.

She worked with unseemly haste, desperate to get upstairs and get her hands on him instead of china and drying cloths. Within fifteen minutes, the kitchen was more or less clean and Gemma was flushed with anticipation.

Andrew hadn't said much, just cast her sinful looks as she tried not to drop the slippery plates. She was mesmerized by corded arms, the span of his hands as he scrubbed a serving dish. Soon his arms and hands would work their magic on her.

But all her bravado had deserted her, and she was beginning to feel some misgivings. She had laid it on awfully thick today, and the truth was Andrew's sexual history was formidable. But, she counseled herself, he had always made love without love. She would change all that.

She wasn't prepared when he swept her up, apron and all, and carried her through the hallway and up the stairs.

"My," she said breathless, "you are as anxious as I am, aren't you?"

"More." He shouldered his way into his bedroom. The fire burned bright, and the bed had been turned down. He deposited her on it and pointed. "Not one word."

He must have been thinking of his son, napping a few doors down the corridor. He turned the key in the lock, and the click seemed very final.

"Undress," he growled.

Gemma sat up on the bed. "You're being awfully bossy," she whispered.

"I told you to be quiet. Do as you're told."

This was a side of Andrew she hadn't seen, and she wasn't quite sure she liked it. She rolled the apron off and began unhooking the side of her dress.

"Hurry up."

"Maybe you can help me." She tried to lighten the moment by winking.

Andrew kneeled on the bed, tore the remaining hooks from their thread eyes, and wrestled her out of the dress. With one vicious tug, her short front-lacing corset was untied and she was left shivering in her chemise, stockings, and slippers.

Andrew held the corset up with contempt. "Why do you wear this? It's not as though you have need of it."

"My lack of pulchritude didn't seem to bother you before," she retorted, stung.

"Any port in the storm. Getting you out of all this is a bother. From now on, as my mistress, you'll make yourself accessible. No corsets. Certainly no drawers." There was an evil glint in his eye.

"I don't wear drawers."

"Good. I like the idea of you open at all times for me."

Gemma scrambled off the bed. "Now, wait a minute. I never agreed to be a convenient plaything, ready to be swived whenever you catch me in a dark corner."

"Swived? I'm surprised. I never expected such a word from you. Then what, pray tell, was your plan?"

"I—I—we're going to have an affair. A perfectly pleasant affair, like two civilized people. Satisfy our mutual needs. Act as friends."

Andrew shook his head in mock dismay. "Gemma, Gemma. Number one, I am not civilized. Number two, I'm a selfish bastard. I care nothing for your needs. Number three, you are not my friend, but my mistress. You've offered me carte blanche to fuck you. If you don't like my way of going about it, feel free to leave at any time."

Ah. His brutish behavior was instantly clearer. All this caveman business was a method to scare her off. Drive her away again. He must think her fainthearted indeed to go through this charade. This *farce.* Well, two could play-act. She stepped onto the stage to interrupt his solo performance.

Her eyes dropped to the ground. She hoped she was the perfect picture of penitence. "I'm sorry. I'll do whatever you say."

"Excellent," he said, although there was a trace of doubt in his voice. "Take off the rest of that muck and lie down on the bed."

Gemma complied, hiding a smile behind a curtain of hair. In short order she found herself tied, her hands bound above her head and her legs spread hideously wide and lashed to the bed-posts. This was an entirely novel experience, and she was deter-mined to enjoy it as much as he did not want her to.

Andrew stood over her, his beautiful face inscrutable. Then he turned away to his dresser and came back with a tray holding a bowl, scissors, and a wicked-looking razor. She had a moment of doubt herself when he held his razor up.

"Is that to cut through the ropes when we're done?" She tried to smile.

"No."

"Wh-what are you going to do?"

"You said nothing I could do would make you love me any less," Andrew reminded her.

She had. Now her words sounded idiotic. He'd warned and warned her, and she paid him no mind, sure that she could some-how bring him back from the brink.

Gemma hesitated. The razor looked particularly sharp, gleam-ing silver in the candlelight. "Surely it's too dark in here for you to see to shave. And I don't mind a bit of stubble when you kiss me."

"It's not for me. And I see very well in the dark. My reputa-tion has always depended on it."

Was he actually making a joke about his past? She tried to relax on the mattress but jumped a mile when his hand covered her mons. His fingers looped through the golden-brown curls, his thumb finding the center of her womanhood. But with one quick brush, it was gone.

She raised her head from the pillow. Andrew picked up the scissors, and she watched in stupefaction as he began to cut tufts of her nether curls and drop them into a handkerchief. She bit a lip. How proud she'd been when she'd spotted the first wiry dark hair on her body. Her mother said she'd soon be a woman. Gemma had waited, but nothing much happened except the tan-gle at the juncture of her thighs and the pain of her menses. She grew no beautiful full womanly breasts like her mother, despite exercises and creams and the mysterious Italian prayers of Caterina. At twenty-two, she was almost as flat as she'd been as a child.

When he seemed satisfied that he cut away as many of her curls as he could, he took some soap from the bowl and lathered her pubis. His fingers stroked her inner folds for good—or bad—measure and she felt herself growing ever more fascinated by the look of concentration on his face and his gentle, expert touch.

"I'm going to see what no other man has ever seen," he murmured. "Unless your nursemaid was a nurse*man*."

"Don't be silly." She felt the firm scrape of the razor and flinched. "You won't cut me?"

"I'd rather slit my own throat. Lie still, Gemma. I'll be finished soon." His voice was gravel-rough.

She closed her eyes, aware of each line of the blade as it slid over her skin. He lifted her and she endured further invasion. When he was done, she felt the warm scrub of a cloth.

"Bella. So, so beautiful." Barely a whispered breath. Gemma was not even sure she heard him or imagined it. It was odd to think of Andrew speaking Italian, but he must have said something endearing to his son's mother. To the duke, too. She squelched the flare of jealousy. Neither of them could go backward, only forward.

"And now, I will show you why this was necessary." His golden head disappeared between her legs.

She knew men did this to women. She knew everything, after all—she was a courtesan's daughter. But Franz had thought only of his pleasure, and she'd been much too shy to ask.

She wasn't shy now.

"Oh. My. Yes."

His tongue was ruthless. She felt like a juicy split fruit as he parted her, swept in, and suckled. He inserted two fingers into her passage to join his assault, and her hips flew off the bed, urging him to go deeper, harder, softer, more—the words didn't matter because everything he did was indescribable. His wicked mouth covered her bud, teasing and tasting. His breath was so hot, his fingers so skilled, her need so great.

If this was his way to warn her off, it was a hopeless failure. She wanted more, wanted it all. Always. She wasn't frightened of the passion he engendered, but welcomed it. She only wished she could touch him as he licked his way to her core, but she was tethered and helpless.

His power over her gave her the ultimate freedom to receive without giving anything back but her ragged cries. She crested again, choking back a scream so she wouldn't wake Marc. This was sublime torture, wave after wave. She was awash in sensation, every inch of her alive.

And then, his weight shifted on the bed and he stood up, wiping his mouth on the sleeve of his shirt. He picked up the razor and wordlessly sliced through her bonds. She untangled the fraying strands of rope from her wrists, rubbing the pink lines that she had caused herself straining against them. Andrew went to stand in front of the fireplace, his back to her.

"Aren't you going to undress?"

"Why should I? You got what you wanted."

She sat up and sighed. Her nipples were hard points, but she looked now as she had as a young girl, bare and smooth and curiously sensual. "Oh, Andrew. Please don't do this. I know what you're trying to do, and it won't work. You will never be as great an ogre as you are pretending to be."

"*Stop*, Gemma. Just stop making excuses for me. It does you no credit."

"You cannot tell me you don't want me."

"I can, and I do not."

"Oh, for heaven's sake," she said in impatience. "I admit, I tried to trick you into letting me stay. I thought I might worm my way into your heart just a little bit, and then we could all live happily ever after together as we deserve. I was heavy-handed, flirting too much. You needn't teach me this lesson of domination and indifference to get rid of me. It does *you* no credit."

He turned. "Do you think this is a game?"

"Of course it is! I've watched you too long to believe you would do me harm."

His mouth curled. "What if I told you I had devices of torture in the chest at the end of my bed?"

"I would ask you to show them to me."

He stalked across the room and threw the trunk open. Brandishing a black quilted-velvet paddle, he tossed it on the bed. "See this? A certain marquess was very fond of using this on me, but even happier when I used it on him. He would get hard when I spanked him, and then I had to suck him off."

Gemma nodded, careful not to show distaste. "My mother told me of men like that. I don't think I would care for it very much, but if you're determined to spank me to prove something, have at it." She rolled on her stomach, shut her eyes, and prayed.

"Damn it, Gemma!" She heard a shower of objects fall to the floor but didn't move an inch.

Then there was nothing but the wail of the wind and the hiss of the fire. After a few minutes, Gemma flipped over. Andrew sat on the floor amidst a display of sexual weaponry she really didn't care to investigate. "Why did you keep it all?" she asked softly.

"I wanted to remember. Everything." His face was bleak.

"You did what you thought you had to do. What that man trained you to do. But that's not who you are, Andrew."

"You don't know me."

"I know you love your son, more than most men do. No father I ever knew changed his son's nappies or sang him bawdy songs to sleep. I've heard you."

Andrew flushed. "They're the only songs I know, I'm afraid."

"And it's a good thing Marc is still not totally fluent in English, or I would not permit it. Don't you see? Fate has brought you here. Fate has brought me here. There truly isn't anything you could tell me to shock me—my mother took care of all that. I am the perfect woman for you."

For a second, she thought he was laughing, but the firelight lit a silvery tear beneath one eye.

She slid off the bed to join him on the floor, paying no mind to the fact that she was naked and he still dressed. She touched his cheek. "It's time for you to be happy, Andrew. I think we can be happy together. I didn't plan to fall in love with you, but I have. Won't you love me back?"

CHAPTER 21

She made it sound so simple. So natural. Just as she was, heed-less of her state of undress, like some woodland nymph who danced by the light of the moon. She was exquisite, her taste still filling his mouth and preventing him from thinking clearly.

"You can't love me. You don't know me."

"Then tell me your secrets, Andrew."

"They're all around us."

She picked up a marble dildo. "These are just things, Andrew. They don't have a life of their own. You can pitch them into the sea." She dropped the "he's at home" to the carpet and it rolled beneath the bed.

"What if I need them again?" he asked bitterly.

Gemma placed a small hand on his bad arm. Was it his imag-ination, or did the ache decrease? "Then use them on me to ex-orcise your demons."

"God, no!" He stumbled to his feet. "You—and my son—are the only pure things in my life. That's why you both need to leave."

"Are you afraid you'll corrupt us?"

"Look what I've done to you already!"

"And I enjoyed it very much. Andrew, I've been seducing *you*, not the other way around. I've been a veritable hoyden. It would take a better man than you to resist a Bassano when she wants something. Although," she said with regret, "I was much too obvious today. I must work on calibrating my skills."

Andrew returned to the chair by the fire. "Look, I understand what you're trying to do. And I appreciate it. But I've been fooling myself these past weeks. You can't make a silk purse out of a sow's ear."

Gemma raised a brow. "Who's the pig? You or me?"

"Oink. I've been bent so long I'll never be straight again, Gemma. I've tried—God knows I've tried—but this affair with you just proves I cannot control myself."

"Now wait a minute. I know you said I was just a handy diversion, but I don't believe you. You *do* care for me." She suddenly seemed to realize she was naked, and crossed her arms over her breasts.

"Of course I do! I've dreamed of nothing but you ever since you climbed out of that bathtub!"

"That's lust, Andrew, not affection. Flattering as it is to know my body doesn't repulse you. I'd like to think you *like* me."

He closed his eyes. "What I feel for you is a bit more complicated than 'like.' You argue over the least little thing. You always must have the last word. But you're a wonder with Marc. And an excellent dancer." He paused. "You taste like heaven."

"Oh."

He knew how absurd his words were. Had he ever loved? Perhaps Nicky and Caro, but he'd been so very young and tormented it was hard to know what his feelings for them were. He'd spent the rest of his life bobbing in the ocean, going in whichever direction the current took him. He'd washed ashore now and simply didn't know what to do with himself.

"I haven't given affection much thought, truthfully," Andrew said. "It wasn't useful in my line of work, investing emotion in the relationships I had. They were engineered to end when the parties got what they paid for. I've always been able to separate the physical from the mental. I learned to do that as a child."

"You were lucky then."

"Lucky!" he snorted. "That's not the word I'd choose."

She scooted over the rug on her bottom to his chair, stopping at his feet. She looked up at him, her little face so earnest. "What if you had allowed yourself to feel? You would have been even more miserable than you were, brokenhearted all the time."

"That's one way of looking at it, I suppose." He took a breath. "I don't think I'm capable of that happy ending you talked of. It's just not in the cards."

"How do you know if you don't try?" she asked, her voice soft.

Her eyes shimmered in the firelight. Tears for her, too? He hadn't cried in years, had stopped himself before he disgraced himself further. He hardened his heart. Again. This time he felt the pain of it snapping shut on the brief flicker of hope he'd allowed himself to flirt with.

"I don't want to try, Gemma. I stand by my earlier decision. Marc will be better off with the Christies, and I'll be better off without you dogging me, trying to reform me. I'm a lost cause."

"All right." She leaped up, surprising him, and gathered up her clothes. "Marc will be waking soon. I can manage a simple tea if you want to join us later."

No argument? She was up to something. Again.

"I'm still full from Christmas lunch. I think I'll just stay up here and read."

"As you wish. Merry Christmas, Mr. Ross."

The starchy governess was back, even if she merely had clothes in front of her slim body and not on it. She walked stoically to the door and turned the key. Andrew committed the line of her back and bottom to memory. He would not be seeing that view again unless she tied him down with his own ropes.

I am a coward, plain and simple. All his life he'd taken risks, but this was one he did not feel equal to. Gemma might not hold him in aversion now, but the day would come when he'd see disgust in her eyes. He might feel an urge she could not comply with. Hell, he felt one now as she disappeared through his door.

He strode across the room. One by one, he picked up the implements of his past and dropped them into the chest. "Gifts" the men—and some women—he serviced had bestowed upon him. At least a decade's worth of images blurred together, some amusing, some rather frightening.

How long would he last out here alone once Gemma and Marc left? It would be easy to go back to London and slip into his old life. He'd have to be discreet, so Gianni would not discover he was still alive, but discretion was practically his middle name. And once in London, he might have word of his son. Catch a glimpse of him across a park or through a window.

He would sell Gull House to the MacEwan. *Give* it back to him if he had to—he had plenty of money left. Andrew thought of the furniture and books he'd ordered, then dismissed the waste with no regret. Better to learn now he was unsuited to this hermitage.

The islands had long been home to hermits. They were considered holy places, their isolation and stark beauty conduits to spiritual communion. For centuries religious men had found solace out here, but alas, Andrew was not one of them. He was in a hell of his own making, and there he would stay.

He is a coward, plain and simple. Gemma was furious with him, furious with herself—she tried to give her heart and body to a man who did not deserve her. It was all she could do to not brain him with a candlestick as he sat in the chair feeling sorry for himself.

True, terrible things had happened to him at a tender age. She imagined Marc in a few years and shuddered that such innocence could be ruptured. The thought probably frightened Andrew out of his wits, too, wondering if he could protect his child.

But no one was ever completely safe. An ague could turn into lung fever, a cut could become septic, a mother could die in childbed. Love faded, fortunes were lost. Life's only guarantee was that it would end—for some sooner than later. Damn Andrew for his false martyrdom.

He may not have been born to privilege and position, but he had looks, money, and charm in abundance. He had a beautiful child. And he was willing to give it all away.

If he left Batter Island and resumed his old life, he would truly leave his soul behind. He was fortunate indeed that his escapades had not resulted in disease, but how long could that last if he continued to test society's boundaries? Gemma wasn't all that fond of rules and regulations herself, but there were reasons to be prudent. Her mother had been very particular choosing her protectors and had long cautioned Gemma to be careful.

Well, she'd ignored her mother's good advice again and had nothing to show for it but a patch of bare skin and a bruised heart. She would not think of Andrew's tongue and fingers, of the few minutes of bliss they brought her.

Gemma folded her green dress and set it deep in her trunk. Christmas was over, and it was time to return as the little brown governess. To make tea for Marc's supper and sing him back to sleep. She took a drab woolen gown from a hook and dressed quickly, braiding her loose hair into uncompromising order.

She would try to persuade Andrew to let her stay for Marc's sake, but there would be no more frolicking beneath his sheets. She would not throw her self-respect away again, not try to cajole him to embrace a new life, a new beginning with her.

Not today at any rate.

She slumped down on her bed and did up her sleeve buttons. It wasn't like her to give up, and once the red haze cleared she might change her mind. Right now, she wanted to slap herself for thinking she had the power to change the past.

She thought of lichen on a gravestone, spreading and altering until the words were obscured. Andrew's past had taken over his present, the lichen covering the man beneath. It was a pity, but she had no effective tools with which to scrape off the parasite. If raising his son was not sufficient motivation, she could not expect her less-than-perfect body to do the trick.

"Gemma! Gemma! *Guardarmi!* Watch me. I get out now."

Marc had remembered her counsel. She couldn't bear it if anything happened to the boy in her charge—the poor mite had had enough tragedy and was probably due for more. She hurried to his room to see him standing at the railing of his cot, one leg hooked over the bar. Maybe it was time he slept in a regular bed, although he might roll off in the night and hurt himself.

There was no guarantee of safety, she reminded herself.

She smiled at him, ruffling his wayward curls. "Thank you for calling me, Marc. Be careful." She took a step back and folded her hands to stop from trying to help him. He climbed out with the agility of an acrobat and held up his arms to be picked up and hugged.

Gemma could not resist him, although he was getting heavier by the day. She sniffed. Marc was still dry, thank heavens. She set him down at the chamber pot where he proudly peed, his aim more or less accurate.

"Let's get your hands clean." Gemma gave him a damp cloth from the washstand, and he scrubbed.

"Where is Papa?"

"He is tired, Marc. He reads and sleeps. *Dorme e legge.*"

Marc went right for his new soldiers and spent a happy hour making them shoot, with a full complement of sound effects as he dropped them from imaginary cliffs. Gemma didn't need to do much but utter an occasional encouraging word.

When it was time for his tea, Gemma and Marc went downstairs to the kitchen. The room was still very warm, and the full kettle whistled low on the stove. Gemma scattered tea leaves in the pot, poured water, and let it steep. She buttered a slice of bread and cut a thin piece of mild cheese for each of them, although she wasn't hungry at all. After putting applesauce in a bowl for Marc and pouring him a cup of tea weakened with milk and sugar, she set him in his high chair.

"*Bene,*" Marc said, surveying his feast. "Thank you."

"You're most welcome." English came more easily to him now, and it amazed her how much Gaelic he'd picked up from Mary, Mrs. MacLaren, and her grandchildren. Gemma thought Marc was rather brilliant. At least the Christies would not be stuck with a stupid boy.

Gemma wondered about Marc's babyhood, the sunny villa he was raised in, and the many servants who must have cosseted him as the ducal heir. He'd made a remarkable transition to these reduced circumstances and would have to adjust again into a normal tonnish English household. She didn't doubt that he could do it—he was a resilient, even-tempered child. Something of a little miracle, really. If he could stay that way, his future would be a happy one.

She stirred sugar into her tea, watching the pewter spoon circle and disturb the tiny flakes that had settled to the bottom of the cup. When Gemma was a little girl, her nursemaid Caterina had made a game of predicting the future by reading tea leaves. Gemma could not recall ever being told that she'd be marooned in the stormy ocean, a nursemaid herself. She had wanted to be a princess. Thus far, she'd met no princes and was unlikely to. Gemma had seen the king once when he was still Prince George, but she would not have wanted to trade places with his wife Caroline for all the tea in China or the tea leaves in her cup.

She took a bite of bread, then pushed her plate aside. Marc

was busy enjoying his simple supper. He swallowed a spoonful of applesauce and pointed to the table.

"What wrong?"

She had not meant her gloom to transmit across the table. "Nothing, sweetheart. I'm not very hungry."

"Maybe I'll finish it for you."

Gemma startled, splashing a bit of tea on her skirt. Andrew came up behind her and snatched the bread and cheese from her plate.

"Hallo, Papa!" Marc said cheerfully.

"Hallo, yourself. You don't mind if I join you?"

"I thought you weren't hungry," Gemma said stiffly.

"Changed my mind." He pulled up a chair close to Marc. "Umm. Applesauce." He opened his mouth expectantly, winking at his son and patting his belly. Marc carefully scooped up some to feed his father. Andrew made appreciative noises, then settled in to eat Gemma's food.

"I can get you some applesauce of your own," Gemma said, rising.

"No, no. I'm fine." He waved the bread. "This will be enough."

"Some tea then?"

"Please."

She went to the Welsh dresser and took a mug down from its hook. Pouring the tea gave her something to do, something to look at besides Andrew's long body lounging in the chair. It was a pity he took no milk and sugar to keep her mind and hands occupied longer. She passed the mug across the scrubbed table, not meeting his eyes.

"Thank you, Miss Peartree."

"You're welcome, Mr. Ross."

So, it had come full circle, the two of them in the kitchen. Strangers. At least she was cleaner tonight than the first day she met him.

CHAPTER 22

There was a chill between them, like the blanket of icy fog that rose over the shoreline. Gemma and Andrew passed each other in the hallway, sat opposite in the warm kitchen for meals, but their conversation was limited to Marc's activities and "please pass the butter." The days were much the same, short and sunless, with Mr. and Mrs. MacLaren arriving early to escape the mayhem in their small cottage. The boat had been delayed again due to the blustery weather, and their relatives were stranded on Batter. Mrs. MacLaren even seemed to welcome Gemma's help in the house as a pleasant diversion from her daughters-in-law. Mary and the two women spent time baking and cleaning, with Marc playing happily with his soldiers, blocks, and bears.

Andrew and Mr. MacLaren were consigned to the attic, where they were attacking the roof from the inside. Thin and sometimes thick fingers of daylight were visible, and until the weather improved enough for Mr. MacLaren to climb atop the roof with new slates, he and Andrew were closing the gaps. It was the first time in his life that Andrew could remember being rained on indoors.

And not just ordinary rain. Dagger-sharp and frozen, enough to make a man long for the Tropics.

And then it hit him, as he steadied the ladder for the older man. He could begin again in the New World. Find another is-land—warm this time, lush with exotic flowers and rolling green hills. A place where Marc could run outdoors in bare feet, not wrapped like a mummy against the cold.

Where no one would spot Andrew walking on the street and remember seeing him in quite another position on his knees.

Sailing across the ocean would accomplish just what he had envisioned for the Western Isles, except he'd be under the hot sun with other English-speaking people. Breathing in flower-fragrant air and gentle sea breezes. Sipping rum in the afternoon shade. Dining on fresh fruit and vegetables rather than dried and preserved muck stored against the ferry's schedule. The simplic-ity and seductiveness of the idea was so sharp he wondered why it had not occurred to him before.

A part of him had wanted to return "home" to Scotland, where he would be safe from the ton's opprobrium, but after these past few months he knew he'd made yet another lapse in judgment. It was an ingrained habit, making these mistakes. But perhaps it was not too late to turn over a new leaf. Something tropical. Banana? Palm? He broke into a smile.

Mr. MacLaren glared down at him and mumbled, and An-drew remembered to pass up the tar pot. He should be doing this job himself. Surely a warmer climate would ease the ache in his arm and bring about his recovery all the quicker?

There was only one person left to make his plan perfect. And last he'd seen her, she'd been stitching a new shirt for Marc out of an old sheet.

He might be too late. Andrew had rejected Gemma pretty firmly, had gone extra steps to withdraw and make himself, if not disagreeable, generally aloof. They only took meals together in the presence of Mrs. MacLaren. At night, Andrew locked him-self in his library with a sandwich or whatever had been left for his supper. Gemma's talents lay in reheating food only—she was not about to cook him anything, but Mrs. MacLaren saw to it they didn't starve once she walked home at dusk.

Which came in the middle of the afternoon. Winter days on Batter were short. What would it be like to watch a huge golden sun dip into a deep purple bay late in the evening? See a thousand stars above? The image was seductive, particularly as a drop of rain landed on his upturned face.

Andrew held the ladder impatiently. Somewhere among his books was a travelogue on the West Indies. Why, he could trade his Western Isles address by changing just a few letters.

He bided his time until the holes were plugged and Mr. Mac-Laren seemed satisfied with his handiwork. Clambering down the attic stairs with the ladder between them, Andrew was treated to an incomprehensible lecture on what he should do about the roof come spring.

By spring, he might not even be here.

Winter crossings were tricky, that much he knew. He might be on board a ship for six or seven long, dangerous weeks. Marc had fared very poorly the last time they traveled by water, and the open Atlantic was bound to be much more inhospitable than the English Channel.

Perhaps it would be better to wait until spring. That would give him time to fix his leaky roof, find a buyer, and make inquiries about properties in the islands. Andrew had no idea how to go about any of it, but he had no doubt Edward Christie would.

And that truly would be the last favor he asked of the baron. He'd be thousands of miles away and on his own. Independent of anyone's direction. Master of his own fate.

Gemma had talked about fate when she was so eager to persuade him they were meant to be together. Could he persuade her now?

Before he went off half-cocked, he went into the library and shut the door. His letter to Edward was folded in his top desk drawer. Andrew had pulled that drawer open every day for a week, fingering the sharp edges of the folded paper. Today, he picked it up and tore it into tiny pieces, dropping them onto the coals in the fireplace. They flared with brilliance and then disappeared.

He could not abandon his son, no matter that the child deserved a better father. Ironically, Gianni had given him a chance to know his son as he never would have before. To think, Andrew had been prepared and paid to father another child, to walk away again as if he was not responsible for the life he'd helped create.

Giulietta might even have been carrying that child when she was gunned down. If she was not, it would not have been for the lack of trying. Andrew had been assiduous in his attentions to her, with poor portly Alessandro hovering beside them on the bed.

Andrew shut his eyes against the image. That life was over. Whether Gemma forgave or believed him, he would never go back to his old ways. He knew it now with a fierce certainty that washed over him from his scalp to his booted toes.

He riffled through his shelves until he came to the book he remembered, *The American Universal Geography, or A View of the Present State of All the Kingdoms, States and Colonies,* this edition only recently published in Boston. The title was long, the goal ambitious for a mere two volumes. Andrew had bought entire lots of books for years, taking advantage of bankrupt peers or sons who did not appreciate their fathers' libraries. His collection was eclectic to say the least.

Thumbing to "The Caribbean Islands," he skimmed the overview of the original natives and their fearsome customs and went directly to the paragraphs describing each island. He read of sugar, indigo, and rum, of forts and sheltered harbors. The Leeward Islands—the very name meant peaceful and protected. Quite a change from the thunderous ocean at his doorstep and the driving, daily sleet. He took a few notes of things that caught his attention among the dry lists of exports and local government.

When he had selected a few islands to explore further, he closed the book and leaned back in his chair. An unaccustomed tingle of hope surged within. He'd been so desperate before to hide Marc that he'd not considered the ramifications of being marooned on this bit of volcanic rock. If he was going to be marooned anywhere, why not in a more forgiving climate?

Oh, he knew there were hurricanes in the Caribbean. He'd just read of the destruction of Bridgetown in Barbados. And worse than the weather was slavery, which flourished unabated. He had been piqued by the approval by the landowners of Antigua to allow the Moravian missionaries to educate the island's slaves. That was something in their favor, he supposed. But if he were to purchase property, anyone who worked for him would be freed. Andrew knew only too well what it was like to feel enslaved.

Not that Donal Stewart had owned him. Andrew could have left the comfort of his Edinburgh home at any time. But the shame of what he'd done—of what he'd been forced to do—from the age of seven on made him disbelieve there were any alternatives.

God, he'd been a fool then. And a fool now, as recently as last week. But he'd come to his senses this afternoon standing in the attic looking at the gray sky through a slit in the roof.

There were stirrings in the back hall, an indication that the MacLarens were getting ready to leave for the day. Andrew was glad they had each other for company while they went back to the village on the icy track. He didn't envy them a stroll in the dependably daily storm. He poked his head out of the library door and wished them a good evening and a Happy New Year, then went to hunt down Gemma.

He had no idea what he was going to say to her. For an orderly man who planned everything down to the last detail, that should have terrified him, but he was almost looking forward to her giving him the cutting edge of her tongue.

Gemma's eyes were tired. She was no needlewoman, just as she was no cook. It really was a pity her mother had spent so much money on her schooling when she had learned so little of the domestic arts. Miss Meredith hadn't cared—she was more concerned with a girl's mind than her manners and had excused Gemma many lapses. True, Gemma could sew a crooked seam when she had to take a garment in, or embroider a lumpy leaf on a napkin, but making Marc's shirt from scratch had been a bit of a nightmare. The thought of slicing through the fabric to make buttonholes gave her palpitations, for she was quite sure no matter where she placed the button, it would never match up with its hole.

She abandoned the shirt to the workbasket and checked on the soup that was warming on the stove. It smelled delicious, as did everything Mrs. MacLaren made. Gemma really should take advantage of her present situation and learn how things were done in the kitchen. Mrs. MacLaren accepted her help only grudgingly, relying on Mary much more than she did Gemma. It was lowering to think a thirteen-year-old girl had more expertise than she did.

The spoon slipped from her fingers when Andrew surprised her by entering the room. He'd kept to himself for days, which was only fitting. She couldn't bear to look at him. And she was now suffering from unbearable itching as her nether hair grew back. It was too vexing for words, when she had nothing to look forward to for her discomfort.

He cleared his throat. "I take it Marc is still sleeping." His voice was raspy, as though he hadn't spoken to anyone in ages. He certainly had not said much to her.

"Yes." She retrieved the spoon from the stovetop and continued to circle the carrots and potatoes around.

"That smells good." Andrew peered over her shoulder, close enough for her to detect his lime cologne. The scent of the soup was nothing compared to the tangy scent of Andrew Rossiter.

"Um."

"I'd like to talk to you if you have a minute."

"I don't really. Marc could get up any time. If I'm not there to watch him, I'm afraid he'll hurt himself."

"He calls for you, does he not? You've trained him well."

"Little boys are unpredictable. Much like men," she said tartly. "He could decide to jump out without me there."

"Come into the parlor with me then. You can hear him if he calls down for you."

Gemma couldn't argue. She should have stationed herself near the bottom of the stairs to listen for Marc anyway instead of being in the back of the house. She'd moved a chair there for just such a purpose, where she could read by flickering candlelight on the hall table while the chill draughts from the front door numbed her feet.

"All right." She followed him down the dim hallway to the double parlor doors. A listless fire had been ignored too long, and Andrew set about poking up the coals and adding a brick of peat, a wasteful indulgence as she didn't plan to be there long enough to get comfortable. She sat down on the stiffest-backed chair in the room and folded her hands primly. "What is it that you want, Mr. Ross?" If he was about to tell her she was going without Marc, she would be very irritated indeed.

He remained by the fireplace, warming his hands. They were stained with ink, probably from writing letters in ever more clever ways to get rid of her and his son.

"It's New Year's Day tomorrow."

"Yes. What of it? You don't expect us to burn a bush in a field, do you? There aren't any."

"No, nor do I expect you to drop egg white in water to see who your love will be."

Gemma could feel her face heat. She would not hope for an "A" to form, truly she wouldn't. She waited. He seemed tense, rubbing his bad arm now as if it pained him. It pained her to watch him.

"I don't quite know how to say what I want to say," he said at last.

"Perhaps you should write it down and then read it."

"I doubt the words would come any easier. Gemma, I've made a terrible mistake. Well"—he chuckled ruefully—"not *a* mistake. Many of them."

"I don't appreciate being called a mistake, Mr. Ross. But if you are worried that there were consequences from our times together, you needn't be. My—my courses have come. You have no further obligation to me."

He looked so stricken she thought for a moment he was sorry there would be no baby.

"You misunderstand me. I've—I've been completely muddled. I've ignored your advice when I should have listened. You're very smart for a mere girl."

"I'm two and twenty. On the shelf."

"Yes. Vastly ancient. I've over ten years on you, but you put me to shame." He ran a hand through disheveled golden curls. "There's no good way to say this. Gemma, will you marry me?"

Gemma shook her head like a dog with water in its ear. Whatever she had expected, it was not this.

"Absolutely not" were the first words out of her mouth.

"Maybe I should explain." Andrew went on as though she had not refused him. "Hear me out. I've come up with an idea. We can leave this house, go to the Caribbean. You've said yourself I was a bit mad to settle out here. I wanted somewhere remote and safe for Marc, but Batter's *too* remote. You're the only person who can understand what I say, and the damned weather is colder than a witch's t—toe. Perhaps it's heaven in the summer, but I really don't think I can last that long. Ever since I had the chance, I've always seen to my creature comforts. I may be shallow, but I'd rather roast under the sun than freeze to death."

"The Caribbean?" she asked stupidly. *Turquoise waters. The rattle of palm leaves in the breeze. Hairy spiders. Scorpions.* Herr Birnbaum had been something of a naturalist, and he had collected shadow boxes full of oddities from his trips abroad. Gemma's mother was not the first item he'd acquired as he traveled the globe.

"Think how good it would be for Marc to be raised in such an environment. Why, he could run barefoot on the beach every day."

"Sand flies," Gemma murmured. Herr Birnbaum had been quite emphatic about the mosquitoes, too.

"We can make a fresh start." Andrew's pale eyes were bright as diamonds. "Tuck ourselves away on a plantation and sip rum on the veranda."

"Slaves."

He seemed to finally hear her. "I won't countenance that. You should know me better, Gemma."

"I don't know you at all!" she cried. "Three hours ago you looked down your nose at me, and now you want to marry me. Forgive me if I'm a bit confused." She stood up so quickly the chair toppled to the carpet. "You are as variable as the weather, Andrew. Mr. Ross. A week ago you planned to give your son away and release me from my employment. You bedded me, then spurned me. I'm not some—not some doll you can play with and then toss aside." She balled her fists tight but really wanted to punch Andrew Ross's—Andrew *Rossiter's*—dimpled chin and add another hole.

"I know. I've been an idiot. Don't you see? I've had a revelation. I can still keep Marc safe, keep our anonymity, but in a much nicer place. No one will know what I was before—there would be no shame for you if you married me."

Gemma opened her mouth, but nothing came out. *That* was why he rejected her? That she would somehow be tarred with his past?

She watched him pace along the edge of the worn carpet. It was true that there must be much *nicer* places on earth than Batter Island and Gull House. But she had become accustomed to the howl of the wind and the bite of the sleet. The scent of damp and ocean permeating the furniture and even her clothes, now that she had some. She thought ahead to spring and summer, when the island would be carpeted by yellow stars of tormentil and bog asphodel. The frozen streams and pools she'd seen on her walks would be flowing. Seals would bask on rocks and geese would return to honk overhead. Each season in Scotland had a distinct chapter—Andrew was just now in the most difficult part of the book.

"No matter how far away you go, the past goes with you," Gemma said. That applied to her as well as the harebrained man before her.

"I know all that. But can you honestly say you could live here for the rest of your life?"

Gemma bent to right the chair and sat back down. "If I were with the people I loved, I could live anywhere."

"Well, then." Andrew's smile was triumphant. "Come with me to the Caribbean, Gemma. There are thousands of islands to choose from. I'll let you decide."

"You'll *let* me." She didn't have time to ask him what else he was prepared to *let* her do, because Marc chose that moment to call for her.

"We can talk about this later tonight," Andrew suggested, not realizing he'd been saved from a scathing set-down. No man was going to *let* her do anything. She didn't need Andrew's permission to make decisions. She would do what she wanted, and right now the temptation to shove him into the fireplace was strong. If he wanted to be warmer, that just might do the trick. The man had proposed, talking of his child and the weather, without a word of his feeling for her. Oh, he didn't want his name to bring her shame, but that wouldn't keep *her* warm at night. That was no basis for a marriage, even if it was the only offer she might ever get.

She flounced up the stairs, so agitated she had to hold on to the railing. This was one time she didn't want to fall into his arms.

CHAPTER 23

Gemma hesitated at her bedroom door. She was well-wrapped up in two flannel nightgowns and a robe, with nubby wool socks on her feet and a scarf tied over her ears to keep out the cold. Even with the fire rippling in her hearth, the new year was beginning on an arctic note. Because her hearing was obstructed, she could only imagine Andrew's footfalls as he climbed the stairs. The closer she thought he came, the more indecisive she was. Just when she figured he must have walked the length of the hall and reached for her doorknob, she turned the key in the lock.

She waited for a knock. An imploring word. There was nothing. Tearing off the plaid scarf, she listened for any sign of him, but only the pervasive wind rattled the windowpanes.

Good. She'd kept him at bay all through dinner, speaking in monosyllables and declining a warming tot of brandy to celebrate the end of 1820. She'd tucked Marc in bed and retreated to her room, where she armed herself with layers of off-putting clothing. Her final step was to lock herself in. She was not ready to discuss Andrew's abrupt transformation.

He had proposed. Words that she'd wanted to hear for a month, but now that they had been spoken, Gemma's heart was oddly disengaged. He was still *wrong* somehow, as wrong as he'd been when he denied she meant anything to him, as wrong as he'd been when he wanted to send Marc away, as wrong as he was to think he didn't deserve happiness.

Perhaps she was being overly fussy. A proposal was a proposal, and Andrew's was the first she'd ever received. Franz, to his credit, had never promised marriage—it had been Gemma who'd fantasized he was thinking the words he never said.

Gemma draped her robe onto a chair, crawled into bed, and drew the covers up around her ears. The quivering flames made a dozy random pattern in the ceiling, but it was not enough to lull her to sleep. In five minutes, she decided she was hot and removed one of the nightgowns. In another five, she kicked off the socks. After rolling around in the bed like a die tossed in a game of hazard, she pulled the last nightgown over her head, got up, and unlocked the door.

She was almost asleep when a shaft of light from the hall cut across the bedclothes. Andrew was at the door, holding a small glass oil lamp. Gemma blinked at the brightness.

"May I come in?"

"What choice do I have?"

He didn't move. "You can say yes. Or you can say yes."

"Just as I thought. I suppose you have a key for my door, too."

"Yes. I would have been up earlier, but I had a devil of a time finding it. I'm glad I didn't have to use it."

Gemma sat up on the bed, clutching the quilts over her chest. "I'm not dressed."

"I'm glad."

He smiled then, and Gemma's heart stuttered.

"Do you have the proper answer to my question, Gemma?"

"What question was that? I forget. You've said so much nonsense lately I barely listen to you."

"I've been an ass. Don't argue with me."

"I wasn't going to," Gemma said dryly.

He came to her, placed the lamp on her bedside table, and sat down heavily. Gemma tried to stop herself from pitching into him and failed. His warm arm came around her, his lime scent engulfed her, and she whispered, "Yes."

"I beg your pardon?"

"N—nothing."

"Between the crackle of the coals and the howl of the wind, I distinctly heard you say something."

"You are mistaken."

"Well, I've felt for weeks now this place was driving me mad. Now you've confirmed it."

"What's wrong with Gull House, precisely?"

Andrew scooted back on the bed and plumped pillows against the headboard, still managing to keep a hold on Gemma.

"There are numerous disadvantages to the property. It's falling down faster than Mr. MacLaren can fix it."

"He's made considerable progress, considering the weather."

"Ah, the weather. You asked what was wrong? Look out the window."

Gemma didn't bother to turn her head. "It's too dark to see anything."

"Exactly. Even if there was a moon, those damned clouds would obscure it. It's always storming. A man likes to watch the stars when he can. I haven't seen a star in ages."

Gemma imagined Andrew as a boy, gazing up at a sooty Edinburgh sky. "I'm sure it doesn't storm year-round. From what I've read in those bird journals, the weather becomes quite lovely. And the flora and fauna improve, too, with blossoming plants and the migration of geese."

"Could have used one for our Christmas dinner."

"We could celebrate Christmas in July again." Gemma rested her hand on Andrew's chest.

"The people here would think we're cracked. But then, no one speaks English. Another point in its disfavor, and I'm too old to learn Gaelic."

"Nonsense. One is never too old to learn anything. Education should be a lifelong occupation. And once my school gets going, the children at least will have some facility with the language."

"That's months and months away. Who do I talk to in the meantime?"

"Marc. And me."

"You'll grow sick of me." He waited hopefully for her to deny it, but she wouldn't. Not yet.

She felt his chin rest on her head and curled her body into him. He was very still, as if he didn't trust that she was not fighting him off tooth and nail. Gemma watched the fire lick and tremble for some long minutes before she spoke again.

"I will consider this Caribbean business, but I think we need to make more of an effort to settle in here. The people have been very kind to you, and Marc is happy. It seems a shame to keep uprooting him."

"This is the same argument you used about Marc going to the Christies. And how can you say the islanders have been kind? Think what they gave you to wear."

"I have thought. And cursed over it, too. But they gave me what they had, even if it was stupendously ugly. I didn't have to run about naked."

"You're naked now." Andrew's hand drifted under the quilt from her shoulder. She didn't push him away when he found her nipple with casual exploration. She peaked between his thumb and forefinger, shivering.

"Are you cold?"

"A little," she admitted. Her body was in an utter state of confusion, first cold, then hot, now balanced between the two.

"I can fix that."

She heard the desire in his sinful rumble. There lay the way to madness.

Abruptly, she extricated herself from his embrace. "Andrew, I know we are compatible physically. You know precisely what to do to cause pleasure, and any woman who marries you will be lucky indeed. But I want to be courted. I've never been. If anything, I courted Franz with silly letters and gifts. No one has ever taken the trouble for me."

"Pardon?"

"You don't have to love me—I don't expect that. I know you've asked me to marry you because it's the practical thing. I'm here; you're here. I'm good with Marc. And for some reason I don't repulse you. You're looking for a steady life, and that's to your credit. Really, I quite admire your change of heart." Her words jumped around the room like drunken grasshoppers. Andrew stared at her in shock, watching her lips move as she rambled on as if he couldn't quite hear her. "But if I marry you, I want to remember the days before everything turns to tedium. I want my heart to flutter. I want stolen glances. I want poetry."

What she really wanted was an entire new brain. Her speech sounded absurd even to her own ears. But she wanted to give Andrew time to adjust to his newfound quest for respectability. This sudden turnaround made her nervous. If it didn't stick, marriage to him would be heartbreaking, because while he did not love her, she was hopelessly, helplessly in love with him.

"You want poetry." He spoke as if he were rising to the surface from a deep well.

Gemma nodded. "I don't expect Shakespeare, but any few couplets will do, even if you copy them out of one of your books."

"This is ridiculous." He rolled off the bed. "We suit, Gemma. We can make a go of a marriage, even through the 'tedium,' as you call it. Why dress our relationship up with poetry and flowers? Flowers," he snorted. "Just where do you recommend I get some?"

"There will be plenty of wildflowers in the spring."

"Spring! I don't want to be stuck here indefinitely waiting for you to consent to marry me."

"Andrew, stop your pacing. We barely know each other. Yes, yes, I know," she said hastily, "we have carnal knowledge of each other. And it is—extraordinary. But we've been at odds more often than evens. You want to make a fresh start—well, I suggest you start with me. Show me that you want me."

"Damned ridiculous," Andrew muttered, raking a hand through his hair. "I suppose you won't let me fuck you, either."

"Would you say such a thing to a woman you'd just met?" she asked, giving him a glacial stare.

"We haven't just met, you little fool! You want me to play games with you, when all my life I've had to, one way or another. Pretend to be someone I'm not. Do things I didn't want to. I'm a bloody master at playing games, Gemma. I doubt you could hold up under them. I'd have you eating out of my hand and on your knees in a day. But that's not how I want it to be. It's—it's more of the same, and I won't stand for it!" He slammed the door behind him.

That didn't go well. What a speech! Gemma picked her nightgown from the floor and shoved her head into it. She was right. She knew it. Andrew needed to analyze why he thought this marriage was a good idea. So far, she was not convinced that *he* was convinced.

Perhaps by spring, she wouldn't even love Andrew anymore if he didn't do better than this. It would pain her to deny him her body, but it was for the best. She didn't mind a marriage of convenience—but damned if she were to be used without some sop to her woman's heart.

*   *   *

Andrew threw back a brandy and waited for it to burn some sense into him. He had proposed marriage once before, and it had been even more disastrous than this. When Nicky lay dying from his self-inflicted wound, Andrew had asked Caroline to marry him. The look of horror on Caro's face had driven him to drink then, too. Andrew had loved Caro, but Nicky had loved him, and there was no way to rescue any kind of respectability out of that triangle. And when he'd helped Nicky at the end— Caroline could not forgive him or herself.

What he'd done at twenty was his greatest sorrow, worse than what had been done to him before and after. He'd been so sure it would guarantee him a trip to hell, what did it matter how he lived his life from then on?

But now—now he had a child to raise. A child he couldn't give up no matter that virtually any other man would be a more proper father and role model than he.

He thought Gemma understood his flaws. He'd been honest enough. Brutally honest. Even after hearing it all in its bare, warty truth, she'd said she loved him, stupid little thing. She was usually so levelheaded. No-nonsense, apart from her weakness where he was concerned. So why was she insisting on a false courtship, with honeyed words and trinkets of affection? Of course he wanted her—thoughts of her had tormented him for weeks. Months, now.

But love? Andrew couldn't do love. And Gemma needed to understand that.

He swallowed the dregs from his glass. A man who kept whiskey in his bedroom was not a man you could depend on. He owed more to Marc. And to Gemma if he expected her to marry him. Shoving the stopper back into the decanter, he stared into his fire until thin gray light pierced the ever-present clouds.

He went to the window. The sea was flat and calm, shimmering silver. There had been many New Year's Days in his life where he'd been up to see the dawn, muzzy-headed and thoroughly debauched. Today was slightly different, although the weight of his past still fractured his thoughts. He needed an hour or three of sleep before he tackled 1821.

This year would bring the coronation of the king, a man who'd overstepped his own bounds for decades. If George could elevate himself, perhaps Andrew could, too. The subjects in his tiny island kingdom were few but challenging. If he was equal to the task of changing a filthy nappy, surely he had it in himself to crib a line of poetry and wait for Gemma to fall.

It wouldn't take long. Andrew's fabled charm was rusty from disuse, but he'd buff it enough to accede to Gemma's foolish wishes. Then they'd leave this inhospitable spit of land and seek their fortune under a tropical sun. He longed to see Gemma's dusky skin deepen, her adorable freckles spread like stars in a clear sky. He'd kiss every one and make her glad she'd agreed to be his wife. Marc would thrive under her motherhood. When he was old enough, he could go to school in the Americas where there was little chance to discover his less-than-savory background. Andrew would find new ventures in which to invest in the New World to keep a roof over their head and food on the table.

He ignored the rumble of his stomach. He wasn't ready to see Gemma in the kitchen yet, to watch her burn the toast or lump the oatmeal while she "helped" Mrs. MacLaren. Andrew hadn't yet decided what his first tribute would be—best to sleep on it for a few hours. This was the first day of the rest of his life, and for once, he wanted to get it right.

CHAPTER 24

Gemma groaned. She could have stayed in her warm bed forever, could understand why people turned to laudanum to blur the edges of their days away. But Marc was calling with his usual note of pride.

She scrambled into her robe and thick socks without a thought to her vanity and watched him climb out of his crib like a little blond monkey. She made her usual fuss, applauding and praising, then spruced him up for breakfast. She held his hand as he walked downstairs. He was proud of that accomplishment, too, and she was relieved he was becoming so independent. He was getting too heavy anyhow to carry down the flight of stairs, and Gemma had been terrified of tripping over her overlong skirts and plunging them both to death or dismemberment.

The house was unusually quiet, the fireplaces gone cold. Odd. Generally Mrs. MacLaren and her husband had arrived by now. Gemma didn't think Andrew had given them the day off, although perhaps he had. They may have indulged with their family welcoming in the new year, too. Fiddles and whiskey could have put a damper on their steps up the rise to Gull Cottage.

The boat was due to arrive today, finally taking away the MacLarens' guests. Perhaps they were saying their good-byes, although usually the crew unloaded the boat of its cargo and spent the night in their cramped little cottage down by the quay to sail on the morning tide. Mary wouldn't be coming at all today— she'd caught a cold from her little brothers and Gemma had told her to stay home, taking pity on her as well as trying to protect Marc from illness. Whether Mary could rest in a household full of sick little boys was anyone's guess.

Gemma wouldn't wait for the MacLarens to come to start the fires. She could see her breath indoors, although the sky was pale blue and the wind had ceased wailing. She told Marc to sit back a safe distance from each fireplace as she coaxed the coals to spark, then laid kindling and peat in the grates.

Next on the agenda was breakfast. Gemma really was a dreadful cook, but there was half a loaf of yesterday's bread and water to boil. Marc would be satisfied with some honey and but-ter on untoasted bread and milky tea. As for herself, she was not hungry at all.

She'd been up hours wondering what Andrew would say to her when he came downstairs. He'd been so angry. If he had slept as little as she had last night, he was likely to be a bear, even less willing to sweet-talk her as a courting swain.

Was she selfish to insist on something more than pure lust as a basis for marriage? Most women would consider themselves for-tunate and settle for the kind of unbridled sex Andrew was more than capable of. Had spent an eternity perfecting. A lifetime spent in his bed would weaken the morals of anyone. But Gemma had let lust rule her life once before. Some might have called it calf-love, but she'd been very determined to lose her in-nocence to Franz. As the daughter of a courtesan, she was com-pletely cognizant of the repercussions of desire. This time, she needed something less physical and more—mental? Was that the right word? She wanted to be more than just a body beneath the covers that temporarily subdued Andrew's demons.

Her disjointed thoughts were interrupted by a knock at the

kitchen door. It was far too early for company, not that anyone from the village ever plucked up the nerve to come up here. Gemma tied her robe a bit tighter and pulled the door open.

She recognized one of Mr. MacLaren's sons, the one who spoke a few words of English. He was a shepherd on one of the other islands, a solitary life that enabled him to teach himself some handy phrases. She had danced with him at the *ceilidh*, and he'd tried out every one with her. But this morning, he was not trying to shyly charm her. Once he finished blurting out the reason for his visit, he refused a cup of tea and hurried back to his mother's house.

Andrew came down a few minutes later, fully and exquisitely dressed. His hair had been dampened and the curls brushed down, his shirtpoints jutted to his cheekbones, and his cravat was tied in something so complicated Gemma had never seen its like. She was acutely aware that her old robe was sticky from Marc's honeyed fingers as he sat in her lap, finishing his breakfast.

"Who was that on the path?"

"One of the MacLaren sons. David, I think. He said his mother has broken her leg or hip—I'm not sure which, and they're taking her off to the mainland today to stay with another of her sons, the one in Oban. She needs a doctor. Apparently, she slipped on the path when they were walking home last night, and poor Mr. MacLaren carried her all the way to their house. At her age, such a thing can be dangerous."

"I'll go. See what I can do." Gemma nodded. She would have done the same as soon as Marc finished his breakfast. He grabbed his heavy coat from a hook near the back door and disappeared down the hallway. She heard him rummage about in his study, the sound of drawers opening and shutting. From her snooping experience, she knew he kept money between the pages of the old birder's journals. That fact had given her some comfort—if she were ever forced to leave without a reference or salary, he might not notice a pound note or two missing. Now that she was officially a thief and a fraud, stealing from Andrew had not seemed so very awful. If she had to resort to such a thing, he would undoubtedly deserve it.

Gemma wiped Marc's sticky face and fingers and then went to take stock of the pantry. If Mrs. MacLaren wasn't here to feed them, Gemma was very much afraid she would be enlisted. She didn't much care for what she ate, but Andrew and Marc would not be satisfied with cold bread forever. She lifted the lids off crocks and sniffed at the contents. If she was judicious, she could probably get them through the next week on what Mrs. Mac-Laren had put by.

Gemma didn't think Andrew's library boasted a cookery book, and even if Mrs. MacLaren had left her written recipes—if in fact she was even literate—Gemma could not have read them. Once Mary recovered from her sniffles, she could make some basic dishes to keep their bodies and souls together. Mary was a capable child—she'd shown great aptitude in everything. But Gemma couldn't turn the running of Gull House over to a thirteen-year-old girl.

She pictured the inhabitants of each of the cottages down below. There were far more children than adults, and few women with whom she'd feel comfortable enough even if they could spare the time to work here. She'd called the community "kind" to Andrew, but their feelings were much kinder toward him and his son than they were to Gemma.

Maybe Andrew was right. If they went across the ocean, they might have an easier time of it. But there was no point feeling sorry for herself right now. She'd just have to make the best of it in the kitchen. She knew her way around a fire, and that was half the battle, wasn't it? Fresh eggs and milk were delivered every couple of days, and eggs were easy.

She blushed, remembering Andrew's taunt about the New Year's egg, watching the egg white form the letter of the man you were destined to marry. If Andrew had his way, no eggs would be necessary.

She chattered to Marc as she searched through the supplies, turning her quest into a lesson, supplying the English and Italian words for everything she found. Marc dutifully repeated them but would not be satisfied with a menu list forever. She needed to dress and get on with the business of playing with Marc.

And wait to see what Andrew would say and do next.

Hours later, he let himself in the back door. The kitchen was warm but empty. Andrew had spent the morning pressing money upon the MacLarens and writing a letter to the only physician he knew in Scotland, a bisexual fellow named Larrabee who owed him a favor. The money he enclosed would ensure that Larrabee remembered. Andrew had been Peter Larrabee's secret for several years every time the man came down to London without his wife. They'd shared an odd sort of friendship, and Andrew was certain if Mrs. MacLaren needed anything out of the ordinary, Larrabee would see to it himself or arrange for someone else to. Peter spoke Gaelic, an added bonus for the MacLarens, who'd made very few trips in their lifetime off Batter.

It had seemed insensitive at the moment to inquire in the village about a replacement for his cook-housekeeper, and no one had volunteered their services. Andrew had done for himself for years, although he'd had plenty of dinner invitations to keep him from total starvation. His social life had been incredibly full— Venetian breakfasts, afternoon teas, routs, cotillions, and midnight suppers. There was always a need for an attractive extra man in his devilish circle, and Andrew had made sure there was a need for him specifically.

He poked at the stove, stomach growling. He'd left before breakfast and refused all offers of sustenance at the MacLarens' cottage, which was confusingly crowded. Travel trunks were heaped about everywhere, and Mrs. MacLaren's daughters-in-law were withering under her direction between some rather blood-curdling groans to pack up what she needed for her departure to Oban. The woman's leg might be broken, but there was nothing wrong with her tongue. She had enough pep left to give Andrew a smile and thank him for his help, then ordered a son to see him out. He'd spent the rest of the morning walking in what had been the best day in ages, cold but clear, the sky above a dull, bleached blue. It was more vigorous exercise than he'd had since the walk home in the blizzard.

Or in his bed with Gemma.

There was last night's soup left over and a heel of bread. He heated the pot, cut himself a slice of cheese, and poured ale into the single pewter tankard he owned, one that had come with the odd assortment of kitchen equipment belonging to the house. Gull House's original owner must have been even more solitary than Andrew was.

He was just sitting at the table when Marc burst into the room, a harried Gemma trailing after him.

"How is she?"

"She's in considerable pain, but very tough. She was frightening the wits out of her grown children when I left." He dipped a spoon into the broth and swallowed. "There's hot soup in the pot, enough for both of you, I think." He busied himself with his meal while Gemma set Marc in his high chair and gave him a small bowl and a handful of crackers.

"Nothing for you?"

"I—" she rubbed her hands nervously. "No."

He couldn't very well sit here eating while she hovered. He was supposed to be wooing her, taking care of her. What would a gentleman do for his lady? "Come sit down and join me, Gemma." Andrew rose from the table and ladled soup in a bowl. "You must eat. I insist. This may be the last decent victuals we have for a while."

Gemma's dimple appeared for a flash and then was gone.

"I've taken inventory. I think we shall be all right for a while, if you don't mind very plain fare."

"How plain?"

"Well," she said, finally obeying him and unrolling her napkin on her lap, "I've never made bread, but I'm willing to try. There are quite a lot of root vegetables, and jars and crocks of all sorts of things. Some hams. Cheeses."

"Then we shall eat like kings. I can cook, you know."

She looked doubtful.

"It's true. Many years ago I lived with two friends. Orphans. We didn't have a pot to p—puree in," he amended, with a quick glance at his son. "I had a bit of skill in the kitchen, and before we were able to hire a cook, I shared kitchen duties with my friend's sister."

The color leached from her brown cheeks. Yes, she remembered his confession from that first night of sex. God, he'd been a fool, telling her his darkest secrets. He hadn't gone into detail then, but he didn't want her to dwell on the fact that the man who had asked her to marry him might be considered a murderer in some circles. So he launched into a breezy recitation of all the dishes he knew how to fix. She kept her eyes on her bowl, occasionally fishing something out and putting it to her lips.

"So, if you want to be courted, I can do it with food, Gemma. I'm told I make an excellent pie crust. Light and flaky." He winked at her.

"I thought the way to a *man's* heart was through his stomach."

"I can teach you so you can turn the tables on me." He got up and carried his bowl to the sink. Marc raised his arms as he passed.

"*Finito*, Marc? All finished? Uh-oh, I see a carrot. Quick!" Andrew plucked the vegetable up and pretended to eat it.

"Mine!" Marc opened wide, and Andrew dropped the bit in his son's mouth. "Good boy. You'll grow big and strong. *Grande e forte*." He freed the child from his chair. Marc headed immediately for the tower of blocks that had a place of honor in the corner.

Gemma put her spoon down. "You've been fibbing about your Italian language skills."

"Not really. I know a few words. *Bacio* means kiss, for example. I can think of a few places I'd like to kiss." He leaned over the table and touched the beauty mark on her left cheek. Gemma blinked, her long lashes brushing his finger. "Here," he whispered. His finger drifted to the corner of her lips. "Here, too." His thumb stroked the soft flesh beneath her pointed chin, and he lifted her face to him. "Really, I'd like to kiss you all over as I think on it. You would taste much, much sweeter than pie." For a second he thought she was yielding—she had a drugged look in her wide brown eyes. No, they weren't altogether brown. There were gold bits, floating around enormous black irises. She blinked, her feathery brown lashes tipped with gold, too.

"That was well done. But there will be no kissing," Gemma said, her voice not entirely firm. *Progress.*

"As your suitor, I would expect *some* token of affection. Perhaps you'll let me kiss your hand."

Gemma stared down as he took her hand in his and turned it palm up. He traced the lines with an edge of fingernail. "Hm, what do I see here? A very long life. A handsome gentleman. A trip over water."

Gemma snatched her hand back. "You can't read palms!"

"How do you know what I can do? As you said, we barely know each other. Give it back."

When she made no move to do so, he took her fist gently from the table and pressed a kiss on each knuckle. Her hand trembled at each point of contact.

"Now then." He uncurled her fingers and touched her palm with his forefinger. "This is your lifeline. It's very long, deep and unbroken. No illnesses to speak of. No tragedies. You will live to bedevil me until you are an ancient crone."

"That sounds like a fate worse than death for you."

"Not at all. It's a vast improvement on what I expected early in life."

"Did you ever have your palm read?"

Andrew laughed. "I did. And then I learned how myself. I told you, I lived with a brother and sister in their family home in the wilds of Cumbria. A ramshackle place, but we fixed it up as best we could. Then we ran a sort of hotel, providing amusement for members of the ton with too much money and too few morals. We hired a fortune-teller once for the entertainment of our guests, and I persuaded her to teach me her tricks."

"I can only imagine your method of 'persuasion,'" Gemma said, sniffing.

"There you would be wrong. She was an ancient crone herself. It's rather obligatory in her line of business, you know. But she took one look at my palm and took pity on me. Apparently a palm reader can read the past as well as the future. She told me I'd need all the skills I could acquire to get ahead, and then proceeded to instruct me on fate lines and the Mount of Venus. You'd be amazed how many earls and countesses want a simple answer to their problems, and a few readings of their palms brought me closer to amassing my own fortune."

"You told them what they wanted to hear."

"Of course, just as I am acting the love-struck beau as you requested. I always do what is expected of me to further my ambition."

Judging from her gasp, he'd gone too far. He didn't mind exerting his charm, but having to force it was unexpectedly irritating.

"I don't want you to lie to me!"

"What is courtship then, if not a shiny false face presented to lull the object of desire into submission? I want you, Gemma. That should be enough without me jumping through hoops. I'm tired of life on the stage. I'd like to be myself. Whoever that is, with whatever faults I have. And there are many, as you know."

Gemma worried a lip with two small white teeth. "I see I was wrong in what I asked of you. I'm sorry, Andrew."

"Then you'll marry me?"

To his disappointment, she shook her head. "I don't want a shiny false face. I simply want us to get to know each other better. You can dispense with poetry. But a palm kiss would be quite lovely."

"I won't want to stop there."

Gemma eyed Marc, who was occupying himself by building blocks up and then knocking them down. "I probably won't want you to." She sighed. "But we owe it to ourselves not to make any more mistakes. I want to know that you don't see me as just some port in the storm, Andrew. I'm afraid you convinced me altogether too thoroughly that what's been between us is just a convenient dalliance. I'm finding your turnabout a little perplexing."

Andrew found it perplexing himself. But he didn't want to deal with rational thought now while Gemma sat in her chair looking up at him with hope in her eyes. Instead he brought her palm to his mouth, expelling a breath of air on its surface. Then his tongue drew a slow circle on the center of her hand, his lips pressing down, his fingers kneading hers. She tasted of honey and soap. He replaced his mouth with his finger and swirled over the spot where he'd kissed her, following the lines etched into her little brown hand. "I see palm trees," he said gruffly.

"You do not."

"I'd like to. When Marc takes his nap, come into the library. I can show you some maps."

"Oh, all right. I might learn something. You know how I value education."

He did. And there was so much he wanted to teach her.

CHAPTER 25

The wintry days were busy. Poor Gemma was up to her gilt-tipped eyelashes in one domestic chore after another, cementing her grudging respect for Mrs. MacLaren. Her hands were rough, her back was bent, her nose was red from sneezing through the dust. She still looked adorable to him.

The kitchen was the one place she was spared from tending to—true to his word, Andrew was wooing her with food. When Mary was finally well enough to return, he commandeered her away from the nursery a few hours a day and made her his assistant, slicing and dicing. Gemma seemed to enjoy glimpses of him as she bustled about. She was not put off by his rolled-up sleeves or the sheen of perspiration on his throat as he patiently explained things to Mary as if she could understand him. And actually, the girl was beginning to.

Mary was Gemma's first island success. As she expanded Marc's vocabulary, she always involved Mary. The little maid was even picking up Italian. Gemma said she thought it all boded well for any school she might start.

If they stayed.

He had not won her over to his tropical island retreat as yet But any school she dreamed of would have to wait. Just the day-to-day living was proving to be a challenge. Gemma was far too immersed keeping Gull House clean and caring for Marc to have time to worry about anybody else. Including, unfortunately, him. He was still kept at broomstick's length from her, and he was growing impatient.

They had fallen into a routine at the end of the day, once Marc was in bed. It was their courting time, but utterly devoid of romance no matter how high Andrew turned up his charm. Instead they sat together before the fire in his cozy library talking of mundane things, often with geography books in their laps. Gemma was sometimes so exhausted she fell asleep sitting up in the worn wing chair in the middle of one of his sentences, like tonight. The girl knew how to deflate one's sense of consequence.

It was toward the end of January, a night of inky darkness inside as well out. The supply of candles and lamp oil was running a little low, and Andrew had not wanted to be wasteful. A single candle flickered at his elbow, casting the room into smoky shadow. Fierce storms had prevented the boat from returning since it ferried Mr. and Mrs. MacLaren to the mainland, a usual winter occurrence according to Mary. It might be another month or more before the regular trips resumed.

He had been spoiled from the age of seven on by having some measure of comfort—there had been no worry about candles or coal in Donal Stewart's opulent house. For years Andrew had convinced himself the trade-off of being warm and fed was worth what happened beneath the covers every night. Even as a child, he'd been supremely practical. The son of a whore had to be.

So he understood Gemma's reluctance to settle for second-best, to be the practical choice, the port in the storm as she called it. And in truth, there was nothing much practical about her. She couldn't cook, was opinionated, bossy and, although every inch of her drove him to distraction, she was not a great beauty. She'd disappear in a drawing room full of feathered plumes and silks, jewels, and décolletage. Nevertheless, he was determined to marry her and take her away from this frozen wasteland as soon as the weather improved or she woke up, whichever came first. If he could, he'd snap his fingers and transport them instantly across the ocean.

He thought of nudging her, to watch her wide brown eyes blink in confusion like a sleepy fawn as she emerged from her exhaustion. Instead, he gently took the book from her lap and set it face down on his desk. He had carried her before—she weighed so little it was barely a strain to his bad arm. He slipped a hand around her waist and gathered her up against his chest. She gave a little huff and buried her face in his shirt, making no protest as he blew out the candle and headed down the hall.

She was warm and soft and smelled of lemons. When he got her to civilization, he'd make sure she always had as many bottles of scent as she needed. No expense would be spared to get a dressmaker to design clothes to set off her petite figure to advantage, to buy as many gothic novels as she wanted, to make her feel secure and treasured. Thorny though she might be, Gemma was his rose, and he took another breath of her hair as he carried her up the stairs.

Why deposit her on her own bed when she would awaken to a chilly room? Far better for her to remain tucked into him to share his bed tonight. His fire was dependably roaring, his mattress big enough. He would simply loosen her laces and take off her slippers, spread her scented hair across his pillow, and listen to his heart pulse with desire as she lay beside him. Andrew was almost sure he could control the urge to skim her skin with a fingertip, trace the line of her pointed little chin down the column of her neck to her sharp collarbone. He would certainly not push past the fabric of her bodice and palm a perfect swell of breast, her cocoa nipple jeweled against his hand. He would not bend to part her lips and taste her—

"Mmph!" Her fist flailed on his shoulder. "What are you doing?"

"I am kissing you, Gemma. It's long overdue. You can pretend to be asleep and let me."

"You would make love to a corpse?"

"If the corpse was you. I've been good too long, Gemma. Night after night we sit together talking when all I want to do is fuck you."

She narrowed her eyes. "How flattering."

"I mean it in the best possible way. Until I came here, I'd pretty much lost interest in sex." He saw her look of disbelief and hurried on. "It's true. Oh, I could certainly perform, but I wasn't especially engaged. I've been told some women make shopping lists as their husbands pump over them. It was like that with me, as though I was a mindless machine, detached from the task at hand, thinking of something else entirely."

To his dismay, Gemma rebuttoned her bodice. "What did you think about?"

He flopped back on the bed and tried unsuccessfully to kick off his boots. "It rather depended. When I was with a man, I'd often think of a woman I knew. With some women, I thought of men." He felt his face flame making such a confession. "But when I'm with you, I think of you. Only you."

"That's a relief," she said dryly.

"It is. I think about you all the time, Gemma, even when you've got soot on your nose or a wet diaper in your hand. It's as if you've bewitched me."

A corner of her lip quirked. "Ooh. Pretty sentiments if not pretty words. This is a very satisfactory conversation, even if you don't think much of the whole courting ritual."

"I'm not courting you now!"

"I admit the bit with the wet diaper lacked delicacy. But you're speaking from the heart, and I like that."

Andrew snorted. "I have no heart."

She didn't argue but raised herself up on an elbow to look at him in the firelight. "If I let you make love to me tonight—"

"Have sex," Andrew corrected.

"Again, a failure of delicacy. If we have *carnal relations*, I don't want you to think I'll succumb to every pretty word you say and fall into your arms with regularity. We are still getting to know each other, and I need to preserve some semblance of propriety."

"Not an inch of you is proper, Gemma. You are the most vexing, the most maddening, improper female I've ever met."

"Good." She sighed happily. "You may ravish me."

"I'm not sure I want to now."

Gemma punched him. "Take off your clothes this instant! I might change my mind, too. Any minute."

Andrew pulled his watch from his pocket. "One . . . two . . . three . . ."

"Oh! You are insufferable! Never mind then. Who knows when I'll lose my head and let you take advantage of me again." She tried to roll off the bed, but Andrew's arm shot out to hold her down. "Release me, you great brute. I'll scream."

"You'd wake Marc, and you wouldn't want to do that." Andrew knew he had her there. She was much too conscientious when it came to his son.

"I won't enjoy myself," she said stubbornly.

"Oh, I think you will. I know *I* will. This is all I've dreamed about for weeks."

"What do you mean by 'this'?" she asked, her voice faint.

"*This*," he said, nipping an earlobe. "And *this*." He took advantage of her blink and kissed an eyelid, feeling her lashes tickle his chin. "Touch me, Gemma. I've never been harder for anyone."

Her hand came between them to caress his rigid shaft

"How is it that you can be so aroused when we've been arguing?"

"I'm hard all day for you, Gemma. I've just said. Devilish uncomfortable every waking hour. When I'm asleep, too."

She looked at him, her expression sober as a nun's. "It can't last. The lust, I mean. You'll tire of me."

He brushed a strand of hair from her cheek. "No doubt. And you'll tire of me. Let's see how long it takes for us to tire of each other, shall we?"

She bit a lip. "This is not the time for honesty."

"I won't lie to you, Gemma. I've lied too much all my life. There very well may come a day when I look at you over the breakfast table and wonder why such a scrawny little brown thing ever drove me to such madness as marriage. By then, though, you may be fat. And gray. Possibly toothless." He kissed his way along her jaw and watched her pulse jump.

"You will be bald and have a paunch yourself," she said, gasping as he lifted her skirts.

There simply wasn't time to undress—he'd spill into his breeches unless he got inside her right this instant. Her little hand worked to unfasten his falls, and he sprang to freedom.

"I can't wait. Sorry." He stroked her folds. Short, sharp spears of hair had grown back in since the time he had shaved her. He would tend to them again later so he could feast upon her without obstruction. His mouth watered at the thought, but right now his other end was desperate. He plunged in two fingers. She was as slick and wet as he was hard. "Arguing seems to be an aphrodisiac for us." He balanced over her, looking down. Her eyes were open, assessing. "I'll make it up to you later. With more delicacy."

"Do you hear me complaining?"

"Not yet." He thrust into her, sliding back quickly, teasing. She clutched his rump and pushed him in again.

Tight.

Hot.

Heaven.

Their eyes locked as Andrew drove into her, twisting and pressing himself against her sheath, the distance between them disappearing into jagged bliss. He even relished the splintering pain in his arm as he held himself above her. He could watch her face this way, her sweet face, kissed by tiny dark beauty marks and golden freckles. Her lips were slightly parted, a damp curl spiraling on her cheek near the corner of her mouth. He kissed it away and then plundered, his tongue matching the stroke of his cock, deep, deliberate, slow. Her eyes flickered and shut, and a low moan trembled in her throat.

He held to this tortuous, fevered rhythm until her hips lifted and her heels dug frantically into the small of his back. Her capitulation was glorious. The scent of her sex filled his head, made him increase his pace and edge her over. She writhed helplessly beneath him, gasping into his mouth, her own hand thumbing her bud. She was shameless and perfect and tasted like sin.

No, not sin. To kiss her like this could not possibly be wrong. In fact, he felt closer to right than he ever had.

Too good. Too perfect. It was almost too much.

Breaking the kiss, he raised himself up again. Sweat poured from his body, causing him to regret his hastiness to get inside her. His linen shirt was stuck to his back, and Gemma was crushed by yards of tossed-up skirt. They should be naked, skin to skin. But he could still see the flush spread from her cheeks to her throat to the tops of her breasts beneath her buttoned dress. The rest of her was pink, too, including the exquisite muscles that clenched around him, forcing his pleasure. She still keened and shuddered under him, greedy and heedless, squeezing his cock until he had little choice in the matter but to spend endlessly inside her.

Her eyes opened, her focus pure. Though they glittered with tears, her smile cleaved his heart.

But he had no heart. He'd just said so.

This was simply passion. Gemma was good for him, and good for his son. He could manage to cobble together the qualities of a husband for the sake of his child. Gemma was inventive and attractive and intelligent. A fine companion—when she wasn't dressing him down or falling asleep on him.

He lay atop her, steadying his breathing, although if she kept twitching like that he would not be responsible for what came next.

"You did not even remove your boots," she complained into his cravat.

"I told you I was in a bit of a hurry. Shall I get off you? We can do the whole thing in reverse until we're both undressed, and then we can begin again."

Gemma's eyes clouded. "I don't think that would be a good idea."

"I assure you, madam, my recovery time is the envy of every other man of my acquaintance."

"Brag all you want, but I think we've made a mistake."

He rolled off. "A mistake! Now I'm offended. Just because I was a little precipitate doesn't make the act wrong. You told me to ravish you, and I obliged."

"Andrew, the point of our courtship is to get to know each other. We already know that we're compatible in the bedchamber. As you've often pointed out, you're compatible with anyone."

"A direct hit." He said it jokingly, but he truly was stung. He did not need her to remind him of his shortcomings. He resolutely stared at the shadows on the ceiling instead of her earnest little face.

"I see what you're trying to do—you think you can seduce me and tie me up in knots so I'll have no objection and do your bidding, whatever it is. Marry you. Follow you to—Antigua? Is that what you've decided on? Or is it Barbados? It changes every night. But you can still get my company as Marc's governess

without marrying me. Marriage lasts a lifetime. I shouldn't want
to be forced to smother you in your sleep if you disappoint me."

"Now I'll have to sleep with one eye open. How have I disappointed you, Gemma? I'm being as honest with you as I can."

She sighed and wiped the tears away. "I know. I just wish
you'd realize—" Her vexing little mouth snapped shut. "Never
mind. I'm being a shrew. Thank you, Mr. Ross. The encounter
was lovely."

" 'The encounter was lovely,' " he mimicked. "You make it
sound like we took a stroll together. And do stop calling me
Mr. Ross when no one else is around. You know what my true
name is."

"I do it so I won't make a mistake, Andrew. What if those
men are still looking for you?"

"Jesus." He pushed his hair from his forehead. Now she'd
given him something else to worry about. That afternoon on the
boat had joined his triple-nightmare to become a quartet of uneasy dreams. It was just as well Gemma refused to sleep beside
him—she'd bear the brunt of his thrashing and shouting.

Odd that he never felt an instant's guilt about the death of Gianni's henchman. But Nicky, and even the old bastard Donal
Stewart, still haunted him.

Oh, he was becoming maudlin. This encounter, as she called
it, was supposed to relieve his tension and soothe his black soul.
Now she'd stirred up memories he'd crossed the Sea of Hebrides
to avoid. He sat up.

"If anything happens to me, Gemma, I want you to take Marc
to the Christies. They'll take care of both of you, not out of any
love for me but because it's the right thing to do. Edward
Christie is the epitome of duty, and Caro has a foolishly warm
heart when she's not throwing things."

Gemma's eyes were wide. "I'm sure nothing will happen to
you. The Italians have probably forgotten about you by now."

Andrew shrugged. "Gianni must know I'm still alive. Word surely got around about our stay in the fisherman's cottage. He pawned my jewelry for me so I'd have enough to travel on."

"Didn't you tell me he'd say that he found your body washed up on shore?" By now, Gemma knew virtually every one of his secrets from their nightly talks. He'd not even spared her stories that shone a very dim light on his character. If she was to marry him, she'd said reasonably, she wanted to touch all his invisible warts. The confessions had been oddly liberating, and it was amusing to watch Gemma try to come up with some girlish scrape to vie with his years of wickedness. Her relationship with Franz was the closest she had come to falling off the straight and narrow path, and he dismissed it as childish infatuation. Everyone was entitled to make some mistakes, even if the number of his rather strained his allotment.

Andrew gave a twisted smile. "That was the plan. I had to make drawings for him, too. It seems the only person lately who understands me is you."

"I do understand you, you know, and I like you just the same."

Andrew was relieved she didn't say she loved him. There'd been no more talk of love since New Year's. He had the feeling she was thinking it, though, when she came apart a few minutes ago. Women cried when they thought they were in love, and Gemma's eyes had been filled with liquid crystal.

How many times had Andrew been the recipient of tears and entreaties from past lovers? He'd never softened, just counted his money and moved on. He had plenty of money now. Beyond his investments, he'd been remembered kindly in an old duke's will, much to the mortification of the man's children. Andrew didn't bother to explain that he'd played chess with His Grace more often than let him suck his cock. The duke was lonely despite his enormous wealth and privilege, and Andrew had time to be a friend. He'd be lying if he said he never expected recompense, but the amount had been a most welcome surprise.

"So marry me, Gemma, if you like me so much."

She rolled her eyes at him. "I'm considering it. You really ought to stop pressing me. There's no one to do the deed here anyway. The priest is not due until the spring."

"Can't we stand inside a ring of stones and chant something?" he teased. "You know I'm a heathen."

"These islands have been considered to be holy places for centuries. There's something quite mystical about them. That probably would work."

"Yes. I've read up. I know I'm not the first hermit to live out here."

"Some hermit you are with a woman in your bed."

"Right where you should be." He skimmed a finger across her lip. "We could go to the mainland to marry."

"How? Walk on water?"

"Don't *you* be a heathen. The Lord will smite you if you mock." He grinned at her look of outrage. "At some point, my dear, the ferry will return. All of us could take a trip. Make a holiday of it. We'd have to spend three weeks somewhere for the banns to be read."

"But we're not members of any parish."

"Details, details. I can afford a special license, though. Perhaps that might be best. And then we could go on a honeymoon—somewhere warm. Tropical. Turquoise waters as far as the eye could see. Why, we just might like it so much we'd stay forever."

"I should have known this is just a ruse to get me to agree to go to the Caribbean."

"I don't see why you're so reluctant. Batter Island is hardly paradise. We haven't been outside for days."

"I haven't time to go outside! Oh, I do wish Mrs. MacLaren

would get well and come home." She looked at her red, rough hands with resignation.

"I've had no luck getting more help, Gemma. I've drawn so many damn pictures my hand is sore."

"I know." She sighed. "I don't understand why people are opposed to coming here."

He may have been telling her everything night after night, but this one little nugget he had held in reserve. "Best as I can tell, it's because of the ghost."

Gemma sat straight up to join him against the headboard. "What?"

He patted her shoulder. "Calm yourself. We've seen nothing untoward, but apparently—" he lowered his voice to an ominous rumble—"the ghost of the old birder haunts Gull House." He grinned. "Or at least the islanders think it does. That's why everything was left just as is here for decades."

"Ridiculous! I don't believe in ghosts."

"I quite agree. But you must admit the house is rather noisy. The people here are a superstitious lot. You said it yourself—the island is one of those 'thin places,' where the spiritual and the temporal worlds collide."

"Wind. Uncaulked windows. Faulty construction."

"Yes, yes. Your practicality does you credit. A pity the natives are not blessed with your attitude. So you'd better get used to the domestic drudgery if you insist we stay here. At least you have Mary to help you. She isn't frightened—a ghost is probably less fearsome than all her little brothers."

"I can't believe people here would turn down your money on the basis of some silly ghost story."

"I'm surprised myself." He unbuttoned his shirt and pulled it over his head. "But where would they spend it? They haven't much, and are used to it that way. They're happy enough to eat shag and puffins, and Lord knows they're plentiful. I've never seen so many birds in my life, even in the dead of winter. I thought birds were smart enough to head south. Just as we should." He winked at her.

"You are incorrigible." She made no effort to undress or leave the bed, and Andrew was encouraged to finally take off his boots, stockings, and breeches. He didn't miss the keen interest she showed in his naked body as he warmed himself before the fire.

"Stay with me tonight, Gemma," he said softly.

"Tell me more about this ghost, and I might."

"You want a ghost story to frighten you enough to give in to me?"

"I can take care of myself against any old shade. No, I'm just curious."

Andrew sat back on the bed. "Shove over. I want to get under the covers." Once he'd arranged himself so that his manhood was properly covered from Gemma's speculation, he began.

"I don't know much, really. From what I've been able to piece together, the old man who lived here fell to his death from the cliffs. I gather he was looking for nests. Probably slipped on bird droppings, poor fellow."

Gemma's brow wrinkled. "That's *it*?"

"Remember the language barrier, love. As far as I know he didn't place a curse on the house when he fell, but no one's lived here since. I do know the MacEwan was over the moon to find an ignorant sod like myself to buy it."

Gemma sniffed. "That's not a very good ghost story at all. Caterina would have done much better."

Andrew knew Caterina was Gemma's childhood nurse. He settled against the pillows and drew her to him. "So tell me one of hers, then." Idly, he fingered Gemma's buttons, and she didn't slap his hand away.

"Let's see. Two boys were once walking in a beautiful garden.

There were bougainvillea and oleander. Cypress and cedar trees, marble statues. Wisteria tumbling from arbors. Roses of every color—"

"I don't mean to interrupt, but I don't think boys would care about all the flowers. Now the statues—if they were of naked goddesses—that might be a different story."

"Be quiet. The boys were walking in the most fabulous garden in all the world, with flowers of every description, which they noted because they were training to be scientists, when they saw a woman in the distance. She was *not* naked, but veiled and mysterious. Because they were training to be scientists their curiosity was piqued, and they followed her even though their parents had told them to never speak to strangers."

"I sense a moral coming."

"Of course. Everything Caterina told me had a point, even to making me look up names of flowers," Gemma said. "Now, are you going to let me finish?"

"I can't wait," Andrew murmured. Her bodice was now down and her nipples swollen and luscious from his attentions.

"The woman turned and gestured to them. They were now in front of the most beautiful mansion in all the world, equal to the garden they had walked through. And there was music—the most beautiful music they'd ever heard."

"Is nothing just average in this story?" Andrew asked before fastening his lips on Gemma's left nipple.

She inhaled sharply but continued. "Nothing. Everything is the most beautiful, the most wonderful—oh! I don't know if I can finish the story if you keep doing that."

"Try," Andrew whispered into her skin.

Gemma cleared her throat. "The boys followed the woman up the stairs to where the musicians played. They were all masked and played like angels. The woman turned to one boy, then the other. She danced with each of them, spinning them around and around in the room until they were dizzy and happier than they'd ever been in their lives. The only thing that would make them happier, they decided, would be to see the face of the woman who had given them such pleasure. Ahh."

"Go on."

"Um."

"Pleasure was your last word." He suckled hard and felt her go slack in his arms.

"They begged her and b-begged her to remove her veil, and she just laughed, the most beautiful laugh in all the world. She gave them wine to drink—"

"The most delicious wine—"

"Y-yes. And the most delicious food. The boys were drunk and their stomachs were full, but she made them dance with her one more time. This time she held both their hands, and they danced from one end of the ballroom to the other.

"The clock struck midnight, and the boys realized they had been gone all day without a word to their parents. And they still did not know what the woman looked like. They got down on their knees and pleaded for a kiss good-bye. The wine had made them bold, you see, and the woman had bewitched them. She laughed again and tore off her veil. To the boys' horror, she was a skeleton. She had no eyes, no nose, just a hideous mouth that laughed and laughed at them. And then she bent to kiss them, and they died."

Andrew reluctantly stopped what he was doing. "Good heavens. That's grisly."

"Oh, yes. But instructive. See if you can figure out why Caterina told it to me."

"For the flowers, so you would know your horticulture." Gemma nodded. "To warn you that not everything is as it seems. To never follow strangers. And—let me think. Not to drink to excess. Not to kiss skeletons." He returned to his earlier task.

"Very good. Oh, that's *very* good."

He feasted for a while, then came up for air. "And to be careful what you wish for. Although I've wished for this, Gemma, for more nights than I can count. I'm not at all sorry." She lay pliant as he removed each piece of wrinkled clothing. "Promise me you won't tell that story to Marc."

"I p-promise. What will you promise in return?"

"This. And this. Every night. And I keep my promises, Gemma. Always. I don't make many of them, but when I do"—his tongue swept ruthlessly down her belly, pausing every few inches for a gentle nip—"I honor my obligations."

And making love to Gemma was one obligation that was pure, unadulterated pleasure.

CHAPTER 26

Their evenings had taken on a different atmosphere now that Gemma had agreed to return to Andrew's bed. There was less geography and more ghost stories. Instead of sitting in the library for hours after supper, they climbed the stairs, with or without books, and lay in each other's arms, whispering in the dark. It had become a point of pride for Andrew to try to top Caterina's lurid Italian folktales, and then top Gemma with his sinfully beautiful body. She had nearly forgotten why she'd held him off for so long, but the end result was they knew each other better.

Andrew was now her friend as well as her lover. He'd been completely honest in revealing each raw detail of his previous life, and though she'd flinched inwardly, Gemma showed nothing but acceptance. She was waiting for the perfect moment to tell him she'd marry him but was in no hurry. In between the frank conversations, he continued to surprise her with sweet if not spontaneous romantic gestures. Once she agreed to marry him, he might stop trying to woo her, and treat her like every other wife she'd ever observed—respected but not cherished. Gemma was filing away each sentimental memory for the future.

She might even overcome her fear of great hairy spiders and slithery snakes and move with him to a hotter climate. Goodness knows she'd unearthed plenty of braw Scottish spiders right here as she swept corners and dusted.

It was odd that she felt such an attachment to Gull House despite its imperfections. When she'd first been directed here, exhausted from travel and missing her trunk, she thought the dwelling was a grim, forbidding place. It hadn't helped that Mrs. MacLaren had looked at her as if she had two heads, and the two weeks Gemma had fended for herself had done nothing to improve her affection for her new surroundings. But now it really did feel like home, drafty hallways and all. When there wasn't rain or snow or fog to obscure the view, the expanse of ocean was breathtaking. Inside the house, each room now held a happy memory of Marc playing or Andrew exercising his considerable sensual prowess. If she could learn all those other languages, surely she could learn Gaelic and act as translator if they stayed here.

If she could find someone to instruct her. Mary was willing, but she was more interested in picking up English than teaching Gemma. If anyone wanted to leave Batter Island, it was this thirteen-year-old girl, who saw a brighter future for herself than becoming like her mother, providing son after son to help with the fishing.

Gemma turned down the bedcovers. Andrew would be up in a few minutes, sooner if the weather worked into him. It was bone-chillingly cold, but he'd gone outside to look at the stars. For once the night sky was clear, a black velvet blanket sparkling with diamonds, a fat moon leaving a pearlescent path on the rippling ocean and lighting the glowing snow. He'd invited Gemma— a proper amorous offer if there ever was one—but the cold February air had deterred her from accepting. Instead of wrapping herself up in layers of clothing, she wanted to get *un*dressed and fall into Andrew's bed.

She went to the window and saw him at the point, his hatless head thrown back as he looked above. Her fingers itched for a pencil; instead, she watched while he stared as the universe wheeled overhead. She wondered if he felt humbled or perceived himself as the master of his own little universe. It was possible to feel both, she supposed.

She pressed a hand to the icy pane of glass and shivered. Yes, it was much too cold. After stirring up the fire, she poured each of them a small glass of brandy and brought the tray to the bedside. His drinking didn't worry her anymore—the blackness that had overcome him when he felt inadequate to parenting and loving had gone.

Not that Andrew had admitted he loved her. And she had wisely held her own tongue as well. Gemma didn't speak of Fate and love. *Destino.* There was no point in adding pressure when she was watching him grow before her eyes. He even looked much less careworn, more carefree. Andrew laughed more, and if he was still too stubborn to realize he loved her, time would cure him of that. She would work herself into his heart if it was the last thing she ever did.

The draft from the window drove her to get undressed quickly, put on her warmest nightgown, and dive under the pile of blankets. Her body was so ready for Andrew that even the brush of the flannel gown puckered her nipples. She was bone-weary, but never too tired to deny herself what she needed—Andrew's cock and tongue and fingers working in concert to make her see her own set of stars behind her eyelids. Her anticipation was keen—she was, shamelessly, her mother's daughter.

Andrew's footfalls on the stairs only increased her desire. She raised herself up on an elbow as he entered the room. He was still in his greatcoat, his hair scrambled from the wind, his cheeks ruddy.

"Do not dream of touching me until you've warmed yourself," she warned.

Standing over her, Andrew chuckled. "You should have come. The cold wasn't so bad." He stripped himself of a fur-lined glove and reached for her cheek.

She darted back. "I mean it! I've only just gotten comfortable myself."

"Drink your brandy. That should help." Andrew passed her the glass and picked up his own, drinking it in one swallow. He then proceeded to give Gemma an agonizingly slow show of divesting himself of his clothing. Every button was caressed with deliberation, every garment folded with precision. Gemma knew he was teasing her and denied him satisfaction by sipping her drink, focusing on the fireplace instead of the golden man before it. He was almost too perfect to look at anyway—like staring at the sun, Andrew Rossiter could burn one's eyes with his beauty.

He swung his long legs into the bed and drew her to him. "It was a perfect night, Gemma. I don't know when I've seen so many stars."

"I'm sure there are pictures in one of the books downstairs."

"Secondhand knowledge. Nothing beats seeing them overhead. Makes one feel like a very small part of history. Imagine primitive men trying to make sense out of their everyday existence. Charting the cycle of the moon and watching the tides. It quite boggles the mind."

"I suppose we're lucky to live in the modern age."

Andrew snorted. "There's not much modern about Batter. The people here are doing just what their great-great-great grandparents did. More greats than that. There's plenty of Viking blood here, and before that Pictish warriors defending their territory. Fighting and fishing and farming for centuries."

"Don't forget the sheep."

"No, indeed. Although they blend in rather nicely with the snow at the moment."

"Marc will love it here in the spring. All the lambs sprinting about."

Andrew gave an exaggerated sigh. "You persist in tying us to this rock forever, don't you? I should think you'd like to be someplace warm. Why, your body is colder than mine, and you've been inside the whole night long." To prove his point, he pressed her to the length of him, his hand sweeping down her side and settling on her bottom. His skin was warm and scented with crisp air and lime.

"I'm ready for my story," she said, snuggling into his heat. "Nothing too scary, mind."

"Spoilsport. All right, since we're on the topic of sheep, I've an appropriate story. This happened a hundred years ago, somewhere in the Western Isles. An old shepherd rowed his sheep ashore one silent summer night. I defy you to say that three times, by the way."

"An old shepherd rowed his sheep ashore one silent summer night. An old shepherd rowed his sheep ashore one shilent shummer—oh, very well." She giggled. "Go on."

Andrew kissed her temple. "The shepherd was running away from the island he'd lived on for half a century. Just him and his sheep for decades. He was a bit of a hermit. In his youth, he'd fallen in love with a beautiful girl who had no use for him. He had a squint, you see, and a very casual acquaintance with soap and water. The girl married someone else, and the shepherd moved to an island far out in the Sea of Hebrides, as far as he could sail with a boatload of sheep without falling off the edge of the earth."

"The earth is round."

"He didn't know that. Remember, he was just a simple, unwashed shepherd. All was normal, year after year. He tended to his sheep on the island and shipped them off to the mainland when the time came, having very little to do with any humans. Then everything changed the night of the summer solstice—the longest night of the year. It was then that the shepherd awoke in his hut to the sound of women's laughter."

Gemma yawned. "Witches, I suppose."

"So the shepherd thought. He crept out of his hut and followed the laughter. Soon it was all around him, but he couldn't see a soul. But he could feel them—their warm breath on his neck, their hands slipping under his shepherd's smock. He tried to beat them off with his crook, but the laughter only grew louder."

"I should think he'd welcome the attention. Fifty years is a long time with only sheep for company."

"Come now. Don't be so sarcastic. Our shepherd's heart was pure, but the night was dark and the magic overtook him. Before he knew it, he was stretched out on a stone, naked as the day he was born."

"And the witches had their wicked way with him."

"Who's telling this story? Now, where was I? He was frightened half out of his wits but whistled to his faithful dog to come to his aid." Andrew took a breath and blew softly into Gemma's ear.

"You never mentioned a dog."

"All shepherds have dogs. It's a requirement."

"So there was a dog as well as the sheep in the boat the old shepherd rowed ashore on the silent summer night."

"Precisely. The dog came running, barking his head off."

"I would have thought the dog might have barked earlier. When the witches began to laugh."

"He was a sound sleeper, exhausted from chasing sheep all day. His hackles rose, and he growled like the most ferocious lion, frightening the witches away. But not before they marked the shepherd with a cold witch's kiss. Right about . . . here."

Gemma permitted Andrew's amorous assault on her throat. She'd hide the mark from Mary tomorrow with a scarf, although the whole island must know by now that Gemma and Andrew were sharing a bed. And it wasn't just because the nights were cold and they could bundle together. Andrew had become a sort of addiction—Gemma could see why he'd been so successful in his previous career.

Satisfied that he'd demonstrated the alleged power of the witches, he continued. "The only sign that they had ever been there beside the bite to the shepherd's neck—because, after all, he couldn't bite himself now, could he?—was the trammeled grass all around the stone. When the shepherd climbed down, his feet froze to the ground. He knew if he stayed they would find him again, so he packed up all his belongings at daybreak and rowed and rowed until the sun set, passing one neighboring island after another. He rowed until his arms ached and his heart was about to burst. When he could row no farther, he stopped at a settlement and begged the islanders to let him graze his sheep. He told them about the witches and showed his mark, which was a huge mistake."

"What did they do to him?"

"Oh, they let him stay but made him keep away from the village, remain far up on the crags with the seabirds. They thought he was cursed, you see. So there was the poor shepherd, near people for the first time in fifty years but lonelier than ever. He died alone, with only his faithful dog for company."

Gemma wrinkled her nose. "Andrew, this is a terrible story, and I'm having difficulty finding the moral to it."

"There is no moral. It's just a tale told about the islands. No one is quite sure which island the witches inhabit, but it keeps young fishermen from exploring too far afield."

"Like the stories about the Blue Men."

"Aye. You don't want your boat to stray into the Stream of the Blue Men. They'll drag you and your boat down."

Gemma settled into the crook of Andrew's arm. "We're afraid of strange places, aren't we? We make up goblins as an excuse to stay put. Stay safe."

"I see you've found the moral after all."

"Andrew Rossiter! I am not afraid of new places! I'm here, aren't I?"

"So you are. But my bed is not so strange anymore. Batter is as familiar now as an old boot. It's time for greener pastures, Gemma. Sunshine." He kissed the tip of her nose. "What say you? Let's row from one island to another."

Why not? There was no earthly reason to stay here, working her fingers to the bone. She tried to remember what sunshine felt like on the top of her head. Imagined water that was warm enough to bathe in. Gemma felt a pang at the thought of her school, but maybe Mary could be persuaded to come with them—she could improve at least one life.

"We wouldn't make the same mistake the shepherd did. No one would have to know about our pasts. And we'll need to get a dog when we get there. For Marc."

The look on Andrew's face was comical. When he shut his mouth and could get his lips to work again, he said, "You *are* telling me that you'll marry me, aren't you? I was expecting more of a fight."

"No more fighting," Gemma whispered. *Only loving.*

She brushed the dimple on his chin, his golden stubble tickling her fingertips. He captured her hand and kissed her palm with a fierceness that told her everything she needed to know. And then his lips covered hers, seeking, searching, finding his own answer in the sweetness of her tongue. Gemma's every pore was open to receiving him, to joining him on whatever journey they would take together. To islands, wherever they were. To beds, hard and soft. To the solemn ground when God was done with them. There would be days of delight, and days of despair, but they could get through any difficulty as long as they had each other.

Gemma's blood sang and Andrew swept her nightgown up over her thighs, his hand heading unerringly to where she needed him most. She felt the burst of moisture as he stroked, his tongue and fingers tangling her thoughts until there was nothing left but feeling. Another nip to her throat, a finger thrust in her passage, a thumb at the pulsing center of her universe. She touched him back, reveling in his smooth hot skin. His cock jutted against her hip, so close yet too far. Gemma grasped him, barely able to wrap her small hand around his magnificent thickness. In minutes it would somehow miraculously meld into her, but for now, she pressed her thumb on the bead of fluid at its tip. Andrew groaned his satisfaction, turning so she could gain greater access.

She lifted her eyes to his. He returned her gaze, his blue eyes as clouded as a frosted windowpane. She knew what he wanted—what he needed—without any words. Slipping from his hold, she pulled her nightgown over her head and bent to take him in her mouth.

She'd not had much practice—Andrew had been assiduous in seeing to her needs as their courtship progressed, and she'd let him take the lead. But her mamma had advised her that every man would fall eternal victim to a woman's mouth—it was the ultimate mark of acceptance, of completion. A man need do nothing but receive, and that itself was a gift of great price—to take the reins from him, to take control yet subjugate herself thoroughly.

Andrew seemed to have no objection to her uncertainty or her clumsiness, his hand threading through her hair not so much in guidance as in blessing. She tasted salt and soap, and something darker, earthier. His body was no longer cold from his time under the stars—the heat of him as she stroked him and cupped his stones spread over her own skin, dancing like teasing darts of flame, flushing her cheeks and her breasts. She trembled at his power as he lay so still on his back, her power over him. A strangled sound escaped—from whom she wasn't sure.

She concentrated on every swirl of her tongue, every movement of his manhood, as he responded to her touches. A tender grazing of teeth, the resulting hiss of pleasure. A gentle squeeze, the tightening of her cheeks around him. His taste, his scent, was addictive, his breathing ragged, the sight of him sprawled beneath her exquisite in the firelight. His bright eyes were open as if he didn't quite believe what she was doing. She smiled up at him through her curtain of hair, and his face reflected his pure desire.

There was no barrier between them, nothing to slow the inescapable pleasure for both of them. Some might find this an odd way to seal their engagement, but Gemma knew she was blotting out other nights, other partners who'd sought Andrew's soul. He had ceded that soul to her, if he only knew it. And when the torrent of his seed erupted on her tongue, she drank greedily, heedless of any sin. She was a courtesan's daughter.

And a woman in love.

CHAPTER 27

February brought a break in the weather and activity in the harbor, as the island fishermen returned to the sea to catch cod and ling. The ferry resumed its hop between the islands and Mrs. MacLaren returned home, but not to work. It was Gemma who went down to the village with Marc to bring a pan of Andrew's chowder and fluff the pillows. The woman even seemed happy to see her, so homesick she had been.

The island was waking from winter, though still mortally cold at night. But Andrew kept Gemma on fire with his touch and entertained with his plans for their future.

Unfortunately, in order for the future to become the present, he felt obligated to go to the mainland for a stretch. Passage needed to be booked, real estate purchased, funds transferred, the fate of Gull House settled. All these tasks would keep Andrew busy in Glasgow for some time. There was a possibility he might even go to London if the weather cooperated and the roads were clear.

It was decided that Gemma would stay home with Marc, who would not fare well with all the inconveniences of travel. So with the greatest reluctance one drizzly morning in February, Andrew passed his apron on to Gemma, packed a small trunk, and set off for civilization. Gemma waved to him from the dock, watching the ferry sails turn to specks before she trundled back home with a wet and cranky Marc.

Each time they returned, the crew had delivered plenty of supplies sent by Andrew for Gull House—food and books and newspapers, clothes for Marc and drawing material for Gemma. She had plenty to occupy herself in the days to come, if she could but push her loneliness aside.

It wasn't like her to be mopey. Her mother wouldn't have tolerated it. To Francesca Bassano, every moment was to be savored, to be greeted with joy. Gemma reminded herself of that as she scrubbed the blackened treacle from a baking dish. She had been foolish enough to try to make a pudding for Marc. He was napping now, digesting the indigestible, poor lamb. Gemma blew a wisp of hair off her forehead and attacked the pan with Francesca-like vigor. Her mother had always encouraged her to go all out—it was just Gemma's luck that she seemed to be perfecting the very worst possible ways to cook.

Andrew had been gone a mere four weeks, but it seemed like a lifetime. There had been a letter from him in the mail that the crew had delivered yesterday, which she had read so many times she could quote it from memory.

It had been a very satisfactory letter, filled with practical facts but also embellished with lovely turns of romantic flights of fancy. At the time it was written, Andrew was negotiating for a piece of property on Antigua and was fairly sure his offer would be accepted. And he missed her—so much that he described in minute detail things about her person even she was not aware of. Andrew Rossiter had not omitted a freckle or a fold, nor what he planned to do to them once he returned. He made mention of chartering a boat, not waiting for the ferry in his impatience to get his hands and other parts of him on her again. Gemma supposed he could walk in at any second and wished he would, although a bath for her was definitely in order. She smelled and looked like a charwoman.

A stack of out-of-date newspapers had come along with his letter. They were folded on the bench near the hearth, ignored as Gemma had mooned over Andrew's missive. She dried her hands on her apron, collapsed in the rocking chair, and picked up a paper. The fire was fitful at best, but she was too tired to lift one more stick of wood at the moment. Mary would be by tomorrow to give her some respite, and she could wait to be warmer then.

If Andrew were home, he might be standing behind her rubbing her shoulders. But knowing him, he wouldn't stop his rubbing so far north. She smiled at the thought of his large, capable hands moving down her bodice to cup her breasts. She felt her nipples pucker with desire.

Good lord. She was now completely unsuited for celibacy, not that she had ever claimed to be pure. Franz had seen to the details of that, but Andrew had worked his way into her heart so that her entire being thrummed with passion. For this, at least, her mother would be proud. Gemma was going all out—was hopelessly in her lover's thrall and very glad of it.

The Scottish newspaper was more than a month old. There was a boring article on the presentation of a paper before the Highland Society of Scotland, touting the marvel of a wheel odometer, whatever that was. Gemma supposed if Andrew planned on becoming a plantation owner she should bone up on farming and surveying techniques, but today was not the day. She skipped through an equally obscure article filled with legal terminology over the disposition of 316 boxes of sugar. That vast amount would sweeten quite a few cups of tea, which prompted her to put the paper aside and get the kettle on.

She rummaged through the other papers for news in London and was rewarded by the mention of her father speaking before the House of Lords concerning the King of the Two Sicilies. Surely one Sicily was enough? There was still grave unrest in Europe—perhaps it *was* best that they seek their fortunes on the other side of the world.

And the thought of actually being hot for a change had some appeal—perspiring from the sun rather than the labor she had immersed herself in since Mrs. MacLaren's accident. Of course Andrew was welcome to labor all he wanted. He might be forced to bare his chest as he worked in his fields, and that was a delightful image to hold on this gray March afternoon.

Gemma drank her tea and read every word of the newspapers in the dim afternoon light, even the boring bits, grateful that Franz had not placed an advertisement anywhere accusing her of theft. Even he must realize that her mother's valuables rightfully belonged to her. No Bow Street Runners had turned up on the ferry landing, and if she was lucky, he'd never find her on Antigua as Mrs. Andrew Rossiter.

Gemma closed her eyes, imagining herself standing at an altar with Andrew, a bouquet of spring blossoms trembling in her hands. She supposed it was silly that a church wedding meant so much to her, but she was determined to start anew. In deference to the father who never wanted their daughter, Gemma's mother had raised her in the Anglican church. Andrew's horrible guardian had been a hypocritical, strict Scots Presbyterian, but Andrew had no preference. He had pretty much reconciled himself to ending up in hell, but Gemma had other plans for his afterlife.

Sin could be, would be, forgiven. Gemma had spent some time on her knees in contemplation and came to the conclusion that Andrew was reformed. She harbored no worry that he might be tempted and reverting to his past ways in Glasgow as he arranged for their future. He loved his child too much and seemed content enough with Gemma, if his letter was any indication.

Setting the newspapers down, she went to the sideboard, where a fresh sketch pad and charcoal pencils intermingled with twine-wrapped romance books. Andrew had been thoughtful in his shopping for clothes for a rapidly growing Marc but had not gotten around to sending her any ready-made dresses. Gemma drew her chair nearer the fire, lit a lamp, and added a few more sticks of wood. She was going to design her wedding dress, one modest ruffle at a time.

A few lonely nights later, Gemma stirred uneasily in her half-sleep. She missed Andrew's warmth, his steady breathing, most of all his lovemaking. She couldn't seem to settle herself without him.

He would be back soon, probably earlier than the next scheduled ferry. That certainty gave her a smile, and she slipped her hand under the pillow to touch a corner of his letter. The folded sheet was tearing at the seams, so often had she read and re-read each line. For a man who had derided romance as all lies, he'd been unsparing in his declaration of affection.

Or at least desire. That would have to be enough for Gemma at present. Love could come later, under a sultry lemon moon.

They might have children together, playmates for Marc. Babies Andrew would know from birth to make up for what he missed before. Gemma grinned thinking of a small mob of tow-headed, azure-eyed children chasing each other in a lush tropical garden. Andrew would be in the thick of it, childish mischief his most pressing problem. His painful past would fade with the blessings of fatherhood and marriage.

Was she being naïve to dream that Andrew could have an ordinary life? She hoped not.

Some minutes later, when she had nearly convinced herself to stop thinking, she heard a thud below stairs and blinked in the darkness. The windows rattled as usual with the brisk spring wind. Something must have fallen from a shelf. It couldn't possibly be Andrew, come home in the middle of the night. Even if he'd arranged for private transportation, not many men cared to navigate the Sea of Hebrides after dark. Currents could be treacherous, winds unpredictable, rock outcroppings like giant teeth waiting to bite into the bottom of a boat.

And she knew without a doubt it was not any Gull House ghost come to prove his existence.

Gemma sprang out of bed, not bothering with her dressing gown. She thrust a paper spill into the waning fire and lit a candle to check on Marc.

Silly. He was spending the night with Mary and her brothers, no doubt sleeping peacefully in their bed, his precious stuffed bears tucked under his chin, lots of little arms and legs entangled. The silence and emptiness of the evening had driven her to bed much earlier than was usual—no wonder she'd had such trouble lulling herself to sleep.

Hurrying barefoot down the stairs, her heart beat a tattoo of excitement. It would be just like Andrew to take a risk to surprise her, to chart his course back home under a starry sky. But it was well past midnight and a most foolish thing to do. She was afraid she was about to deliver a very wifely lecture once she'd kissed him senseless.

"Andrew?" she called, reaching the bottom step. "Is that you?"

There was no reply. The front door was bolted just as she had left it, locking up being an old habit. It was rather silly when the inhabitants of Batter Island were the least materialistic people she knew. They were not apt to creep in and steal. But sleeping alone in the house had made her a bit nervous. Not for the first time did she wish for a canine companion. A dog would be good for Marc, too. She and Andrew had discussed it but never settled on a breed, or whether to get a puppy or a full-grown animal. Gemma was not overly fond of the process of housetraining a dog—it was hard enough getting Marc weaned away from his nappies. Now the acquisition of an animal would have to wait for the move across the ocean. She'd not have a sturdy Scottish dog but something from the New World.

Standing in a pool of light from her candle, Gemma listened to the house groan and creak around her, just the usual Gull House symphony. She'd been spooked for no reason. Tomorrow in the daylight she'd probably find a picture that had fallen from a wall or a book that had slipped from the arm of a chair. She was halfway back up the stairs when she heard a hissed whisper.

"*Maledizione!*"

"*È calma.*"

At least two men. *Italian* men.

Her entire body felt leaden. For too many seconds she stood in the hall, her feet frozen to the flagstones. And then she flew up to Marc's room, as far down the hall as she could get from the top of the stairs. His cot was mercifully empty. She prayed he was safe where he was, oblivious to the danger downstairs. Frantic, Gemma ran to the dresser and fished the key out of the top drawer where she had hidden it from Marc's busy fingers. She locked the door, put the candle down, and, using strength she didn't know she had, shoved the dresser against the door. The slide made a grinding noise as wood hit wood, announcing her presence to the men below as clearly as if she had screamed. Marc's toy trunk and other bits of furniture joined the pile. Gemma's arms shook and back ached with strain as she waited for the footsteps up the stairs.

But she heard nothing but the rapid beating of her own heart and the buzzing in her ears.

Gemma tried to remember every word Andrew had said about the di Manieros, which wasn't much. He had been loath to revisit the incident that wounded him and made him out to be a hero in Gemma's eyes.

There had been a murderous cousin who was now the duke, one who had wanted Marc's death as well as his parents' to ensure his succession. A man who had tried to kill a child and would stop at nothing to do so. Was he one of the men downstairs, or had he sent assassins to act for him?

Gemma had nothing to bargain with. Her mother's jewels were in her nightstand drawer, easily accessible to everyone in the house but her now that a mountain of furniture stood in front of the door. There was no escape, unless she intended to climb from the window onto the roof of the kitchen ell.

It was pitch-black out. The slate roof was slippery. She was barefoot and practically naked. It was not a plan that held much promise at the moment.

Think, Gemma, think. She struggled to sit still in the padded chair near Marc's fireplace. The hearth was cold, but nothing would be hot enough to erase the icy fear that clutched at her, preventing sensible thought. The house that had been so noisy was now quiet as a graveyard, the only sound the steady buffeting of wind.

How had the Italians found them? Did Andrew's trip to the mainland somehow trigger their discovery? It didn't really matter—the men were here.

She would not tell them where Marc was—could not let them harm him. She had a bloody vision of them going cottage to cottage, searching for the child among the islanders. There were many fair-haired children in the village, proof that Viking lust had left its trace. How many children would be hurt before someone gave Marc up to them?

No, Gemma had to keep the men here at Gull House somehow. Surely she could reason with them, explain in Italian that Andrew had no intention of setting Marc back into the dukedom's path. If they wanted money, Andrew had plenty of it. They could wait until he returned—

There was a scuffling sound in the hallway. Gemma reached for the fireplace poker, watching her hand tremble uncontrollably as she did so.

"Artemisia."

The voice was raspy. Rusty. But undeniably Andrew's. He had

not called her that name for months, not since the first night she allowed him into her body.

Gemma rushed to the jumble at the door. She heard a sickening *thwack*. A suppressed groan. A few Italian curse words and then a vicious chuckle.

"Tell her to open the door."

"You heard them. But don't do it." Andrew's defiance earned him more attention. Gemma closed her eyes but couldn't cover her ears, both hands gripping the poker.

"*Idiota*! We'll burn the bloody house down no matter what, you fool. Get your slut and your bastard out here. Now."

Andrew said nothing. The men conferred in rapid Italian, each word causing Gemma's hope to sink like a stone into a well of despair. They were going to kill them all—from the conversation, Andrew was half-dead already.

"Marc isn't here," she said in clear, slow English. "I'm afraid I have some bad news, Mr. Ross." She lay the poker down and began the task of pushing the furniture aside, finding it far more difficult to move now that she was truly frightened. Time seemed to pass in liquid amber, her every movement sluggish and slow. She ignored the shouts on the other side of the door, mostly because the pounding of blood in her ears muffled their meaning. She would break Andrew's heart and save his life if she could in a few minutes and needed all her fractured wits about her. There was no point in succumbing to threats or thoughts of imminent death. Fate would decide her future.

She would not confront those monsters in a transparent nightgown. Grabbing Marc's blue knitted blanket, she tossed it over her shoulders like a shawl, then fell to the floor. The scent of little boy gave her confidence, and it proved an ideal place under which she could conceal the poker. She put the key in the lock and turned the knob.

Her heart stilled at the sight of Andrew's face. He must have fought for his life—the life of his son—and lost. She didn't care if he ever regained his male beauty—he was hers. She loved him. Now more than ever.

But she had to hurt him, too.

She clutched the blanket firmly in place with one hand and looked up at the men who towered over her. "What is the meaning of this?"

"We've come for the little brat." The shorter of the men knocked her away from the door frame. "Where is he? What have you done with him, eh?"

Gemma looked at Andrew. Only Andrew. Her voice softened. "He is dead, Mr. Ross. You remember he was unwell when you left. He died of a fever. I am so sorry."

Andrew's blue eyes had been beaten nearly shut, but he blinked and then stumbled backward, nearly taking down the brute who kept hold of him.

"No."

"I did not know how to reach you, or when to expect you. He's buried in the churchyard. I can take you there when morning comes."

"*Che dice?*" *What did she say?* This from the man who had a knife at Andrew's ribs.

"*Il ragazzo è morto. Bene. Un meno di uccidere.*" *The boy is dead. Good. One less to kill.* Gemma shivered but pretended not to understand. She twisted her hands in the fringe of the blanket, not having to pretend distress.

"Who are these men, Mr. Ross? What do they want?"

Gemma hoped Andrew would understand what she was doing. But he was so brutalized it was impossible to tell.

"Did he not tell you what he really is, *mia cara*? A man who sticks his *pene* into anything. He sold his own son to my cousin to pass him off as a *duca*, to rob me of my inheritance. My birthright. I am the true *duca* now." Gianni spat on the floor, far too near Gemma's bare feet. "I heard your 'Mr. Ross' and the child had escaped after I sought my vengeance. That is not even his name, you know. He has deceived you as he has deceived everyone."

Gemma feigned shock. "How horrible. But poor little Marc is dead. You have nothing to worry about now. You can leave the island today and take me with you. If he is what you say he is, there is no reason for me to stay." She gave Andrew a contemptuous look. "I suppose you never planned to marry me, either."

Gianni laughed and lifted a strand of hair from her shoulder. Gemma willed herself to stand still and look the young man in the face. His black eyes were soulless. "Oh, he did. He had a special license in his pocket when we took him. It was his mistake. His undoing, the trip to get it. *Errore stupido.* I had my spies on the lookout for him everywhere. You are Miss Bassano, yes? *Lei parla l'italiano?*"

Gemma did not fall for the trap. "I am Miss Peartree. Artemisia Peartree. Who is this Miss Bassano, Mr. Ross?" He'd gone to get a special license. He would have had to give her true name to the archbishop's representative, but by calling her Artemisia in front of the *duca* and his minion upstairs, he had tried to protect her. Distance himself from her. The lies they were both weaving for each other made her head ache.

"The woman I love," Andrew mumbled.

"Well!" Gemma stamped a foot. "I should have known better than to believe such a pretty face! But you're not very pretty at the moment, Mr. Ross. Even if you are a liar, you need some bandaging. You," she said to the man guarding Andrew, "bring Mr. Ross downstairs and tie him to a kitchen chair so you can sit down and relax. I think we can all do with some tea. Perhaps even a dram of whiskey. Our Scottish whiskey is considered very fine, Your Grace, but I imagine you're used to wine. We haven't any, I'm afraid. But I can make you all a sandwich and we can wait for the sunrise. You can see for yourself the boy's grave, and then we can leave this place. And good riddance, I say. Did you come by a private boat, Your Grace? Is your crew waiting for you? We should get a message to them." She paused for breath.

Gianni stared at her as if she were a bedlamite. And if things went bad she would be. Or dead.

"*È una donna matt. È troppo stupida di sapere che siamo qui per,*" Gianni mumbled to his cohort. Yes, she was a crazy woman, but knew perfectly well why they were here. "*Andare di sotto, Paolo. Vuole cucinare per noi.*"

She had not promised to cook, merely make sandwiches, but an idea began forming that was rather compelling. She brushed by the men in the hallway and bounded down the stairs, hoping no knives would be thrown at her back. She practically raced to the kitchen, where she shoved the poker behind the pantry door. The men were on her heels—at least Gianni was. It took a bit longer for the other fellow Paolo to get poor Andrew down the stairs.

"*Signorina,*" Gianni said, a bit breathless, "we have not come here for a tea party."

Gemma dropped the blanket and smiled as coquettishly as she knew how. "Why of course you haven't. You came to teach Andrew Ross a lesson, and I believe you have. You've beaten him to a pulp." Andrew had been dragged to the kitchen bench, where he was slumped over the table. His minder stood over him, the knife shining in the lamps that Gemma was lighting as she flitted about the kitchen like a drunken butterfly, giving the men a show of her too-slender body. "But the man has just lost his only son. I think that's punishment enough, don't you? He won't bother you about dukedoms in Italy or anywhere else. Look around you, sir. He has nothing. He lives in the middle of nowhere. How did you get here, anyway?"

Gemma chattered, undoing a few buttons of her nightgown. She pumped water into a kettle and filled the stovebox with coals and anything else she could bring to hand, including one of Marc's ragdolls that had somehow wound up in the kindling. As she shut the damper, she prayed the duke had lived such a life of privilege that he'd never been near a kitchen range before and would have no idea what it was she was doing.

"*Fermare per parlare!* Be quiet, you foolish thing. I have come to kill my enemy, and I will kill you, too!"

"How positively banal. We are not in some melodrama, Duke. Andrew Ross is not your enemy, and you are most certainly not going to kill me. I have nothing to do with any of this. Tell me, do you want ham or chicken?" She batted her eyelashes, feeling rather desperate. Her mother would be doing this far better than she. "Help yourself to the whiskey on the sideboard. I'll just go into the pantry to get the soup—"

"Stop!" Gianni roared. "Sit down and shut up."

Gemma turned to him, eyes blazing. "How dare you, sir! Forgive me for taking umbrage, but I am not one of your Italian subjects to order about! You are in my country now and have no authority over me whatsoever. I've offered you sustenance, and perhaps something more—" She slid her hand down the worn linen of her shift in a provocative manner. "And what do I get but uncouth behavior? No wonder your cousin sought to exclude you from his line. You come into my home in the middle of the night with threats and knives. Why, you've probably got a gun, too!"

As she feared, Gianni pulled a pistol from his breast pocket. It was small, but lethal enough.

"How smart you are for a governess." There was a loud popping sound behind her, and Gianni startled. "What have you done with the stove? There is smoke."

"It is an old stove. Temperamental. There is always a little smoke in the beginning." Billowing black clouds belied her words, and she grinned inwardly. They would not be sitting in the kitchen for long, or indeed anywhere in the house. "There is a tool in the pantry I use when it acts up like this." She looked pointedly at the gun. "If you will permit me to get it?"

"I will go with you."

Even better. Then she wouldn't have to run across the kitchen floor, wielding the poker like a bayonet.

The pantry was as dark as the underside of hell. "Now, where did I put it? Perhaps you should fetch me a candle, Duke. I cannot see a thing." Gemma could feel him hesitate behind her. "I swear I won't hit you on the head with a crock of pickles. I'm not ready to get myself shot quite yet."

"*La sparerò comunque. Dopo che la violento.*" *I'll shoot you anyway. After I rape you.* Lovely. Well at least her flirtation had been successful, or he was attracted to crazy, angry women.

She positioned herself behind the door, the cool metal of the poker shooting through her blood as she raised it as high as she could. She would have just one chance to get this right. Gemma waited for the telltale flicker of candlelight. Her job became easier as Gianni coughed and sputtered entering the storage room.

"Where are you, you bitch?"

Well, that kind of language was unnecessary. Gemma drove the spike end down as hard as she could against the back of Gianni's dark head. Both the candle and gun slipped from his hands as he fell to the floor. An alarming quantity of blood gushed from the wound, but he rolled on his back, his face murderous.

It had been too much to hope that she had killed him, but he screamed in pain as the fire from the fallen candle licked at the sleeve of his coat. She did not bother to stamp it out. Gemma snatched the gun up and bolted him into the pantry. The latch would not last forever—it was not meant to keep criminals incarcerated, but small boys from helping themselves to too many sweets.

Andrew had lifted his head from the table, his expression dull. Gianni's man held the knife to his throat.

"*Fare cadere il coltello o la sparero.*" The man's eyes widened at Gemma's command of Italian. But he didn't drop the knife.

"You will not shoot me," the man replied in his language. Gianni howled behind the door. "Let the boss out or I will kill your lover."

"*Parla l'inglese?*" He shook his head.

Gemma had to make sure. "Your mother is a whore."

There was no response.

"You can fuck me on the kitchen table if you let him go."

"Jesus, Artemisia." Andrew seemed to be repressing laughter.

"Andrew, Marc is safe. Alive. Do something."

He didn't have to be asked twice. He twisted on the bench, the knife skimming his throat. Droplets of blood appeared instantly, but he reared and butted Paolo backward. The goon landed flat on his back, his head making a grim chunking sound. The knife skittered across the stone floor. Andrew stumbled from the bench to grab it and ground Paolo's hand into the floor with his boot. The man did not even flinch—he was out cold.

"Now what, Artemisia? You seem to have all this well in hand."

She went to him, touching his ruined mouth. "I love you, Andrew Rossiter."

"I love you more." Andrew blinked. "My God, I do."

"It took you long enough to say it."

"I thought I would get us both killed. You were magnificent."

Gemma waved the gun. "Enough of that romantic drivel. What are we going to do with them?" The kitchen was filled was foul-smelling smoke, and Gianni's screams were quite distracting.

"They planned to burn the house down after they killed us."

"You want to burn them *alive*?" Gemma asked.

"Well, yes, but I can tell from your tone you don't think it's a good idea. Tell you what. Give me the gun and run down to the village. Tell people what happened, however you can. Wake up Mary and she can translate. We'll get Mr. MacLaren and some of the fishermen to deposit them on one of the uninhabited islands at daybreak."

Gemma grinned. "The one with the witches."

"We can only hope," Andrew said grimly. "And then we'll be leaving. Immediately. I had booked passage for us on a ship heading for the West Indies a month from now, but we'll go to the mainland early. Get married. Have a honeymoon." He was pulling curtain cords from the windows and tying Paolo to a leg of the iron stove as he proposed, but Gemma didn't mind. She opened the damper and all the windows. Let Paolo freeze to death instead.

"You still have the special license?"

"It's in my valise. In the rented boat I had to row out here, Gianni and Paolo holding a gun to my head for days. I tried to take a detour, but the bastards had sea charts. The boat's beached in the cove below. We had to take the long way away from the settlement. I'm pretty tired, Gemma. Sorry if I was not more active in our rescue."

"I'm so sorry about telling you Marc was dead. It was the only thing I could think of to slow things down."

"It was brilliant. I admit I felt a terrible despair, agony, made even worse by the thought of losing you, too. I was formulating an escape plan, but you beat me to it."

Gemma cloaked herself and picked up a lamp. "You'll be all right?"

"I'll shoot him if he gets out. Did you hear that, Gianni? I won't think twice."

Gemma didn't bother to translate the Italian curses. She hurried out the kitchen door, down the path to the village. Scattered stars winked above, and her cloak billowed behind her. Spring was in the air, sharp, fresh, green. It would be light in a few hours. Whatever the day held, she was ready for it.

EPILOGUE

Antigua, 1822

The French doors to the veranda were open to the evening, a gentle sea breeze rattling the palm leaves in the garden. Andrew's stars were out in force in the purple velvet sky, perfectly visible from the bed where he lay with his wife and children. A lantern flickered fitfully on the porch, casting just enough light for his ghost story—a very mild one, safe enough to send Marc to sleep in boredom while Gemma nursed Francesca against the pile of lace-trimmed pillows. She looked down happily as Francie suckled, her rosebud mouth pumping milk like a tiny pink machine.

"I have breasts now, Andrew! Isn't it exciting?" she whispered in the shadows.

Andrew cradled Francie's head as she fed. It was his opinion that while Gemma was very slightly fuller, she was still his woodland nymph, tiny yet tough in every way. She had saved his life in too many ways to count.

"You've always had breasts, love." And he'd always loved them, just as they were, from the moment she'd risen like a Fury from the bathtub on Batter Island.

"But not like this! I thought all normal men liked a bit more up top."

Normal. His heart stuttered, corrected, and resumed its steady tick. "I'm not a normal man, Gemma."

"No," she said, "you're not. You're so much better."

Andrew shut his eyes. He knew nearly perfect happiness at this moment, in bed with his wife, his newest child, Marc dozing next to him. He'd never trade one misstep of his past if it meant being robbed of this present. Present in terms of time, present in terms of the gifts that had been bestowed upon him. He'd been bent and hammered, torn and mended. With Gemma beside him, he'd been given another life. In this new incarnation, anything at all was possible.

"It's time to put the children in their own beds, wife."

Gemma's gilt eyelashes flicked. "What do you have in mind, husband?"

He stroked his daughter's cheek. She had fallen asleep at Gemma's breast, a bubble of milk in the corner of her lips. All the work to feed herself had been exhausting. It was Andrew's turn now, to feast not upon his wife's breast but on every other delicious inch of her. He raised a brow. "I think you have some idea. You did tell me you were a courtesan's daughter."

"And an earl's. How odd it was that Barrowdown remembered me in his will."

Gemma would never need any pin-money from Andrew again. The unexpected bequest had only sweetened their plans for their children.

And there would be more of them, perhaps one even begotten tonight, once Andrew carted off his son to the nursery and Gemma laid Francie in her bassinet in the dressing room. Andrew's reformation was thorough indeed.

But one thing would never change—his lust—his love—for his wife's slender brown body beside him. And he had hours—a lifetime—to prove it to her.

Have you tried the other books in Maggie's Courtesan Court series?

Mistress by Mistake

Scandal is only the beginning . . .

Charlotte Fallon let her guarded virtue fall once—and she's paid dearly for it ever since. She swore she'd never succumb to men's desires again. But even a village spinster's life miles from temptation can't save her from a sister with no shame whatsoever. Or a heart that longs for more, whatever the cost . . .

Sir Michael Bayard found more than he expected in his bed when he finally joined his new mistress. He'd fantasized about her dewy skin and luscious curves, assured her understanding that what passed between them was mere dalliance. But he didn't expect the innocence and heat of her response in his arms. Nor her surprisingly sharp tongue once she was out of them . . .

A few days of abandon cannot undo the hard-learned lessons of a lifetime. Nor can an honest passion burn away the restraints of society's judgments. Unless, of course, one believes in nonsense like true love . . .

Mistress by Midnight

First comes seduction . . .

As children, Desmond Ryland, Marquess of Conover, and Laurette Vincent were inseparable. As young adults, their friendship blossomed into love. But then fate intervened, sending them down different paths. Years later, Con still can't forget his beautiful Laurette. Now he's determined to make her his forever. There's just one problem. Laurette keeps refusing his marriage proposals. Throwing honor to the wind, Con decides that the only way Laurette will wed him is if he thoroughly seduces her . . .

Then comes marriage . . .

Laurette's pulse still quickens every time she thinks of Con and the scorching passion they once shared. She aches to taste the pleasure Con offers her. But she knows she can't. For so much has happened since they were last lovers. But how long can she resist the consuming desire that demands to be obeyed . . . ?

Mistress by Marriage

Too late for cold feet . . .

Baron Edward Christie prided himself on his reputation for even temperament and reserve. That was before he met Caroline Parker. Wedding a scandalous beauty by special license days after they met did not inspire respect for his sangfroid. Moving her to a notorious lovebirds' nest as punishment for her flighty nature was perhaps also a blow. And of course talk has gotten out of his irresistible clandestine visits. Christie must put his wife aside—if only he can get her out of his blood first.

Too hot to refuse . . .

Caroline Parker was prepared to hear the worst: that her husband had determined to divorce her, spare them both the torture of passion they can neither tame nor escape. But his plan is wickeder than any she's ever heard. Life as his wife is suffocating. But she cannot resist becoming her own husband's mistress . . .

And don't miss the first of a new series by Maggie Robinson,

LORD GRAY'S LIST,

coming next November . . .

December 5, 1820

"This is the outside of enough." Baron Benton Gray tossed *The London List* on the floor beneath his breakfast table, where the new footman quickly scurried to pick it up.

"Burn it! No, wait. What is the business address of the infernal thing?" He should have paid attention to that two years ago, when the first of the scurrilous stories about him appeared in print. Ben had assumed the attention would eventually fade away.

He'd assumed wrong.

Callum the footman blanched and smoothed the newssheet between his spotless white gloves. "I dinna know, my lord. I canna read, my lord."

"Enough of the my lording, if you please. Tell Severson you want some reading lessons after your duties. All men should be allowed to read. Except I devoutly hope they turn the pages of something far more edifying than this rag. Give it over."

"Aye, my l—" Callum blushed and thrust the wrinkled paper into Lord Gray's large hand. His gloves were now streaked with gray from the cheap ink that was spilling into Ben's life every Tuesday and ruining it.

"I need nothing else, leave me be. Colin, is it?"

"Callum, my l—Lord Gray."

"Come down recently from Castle Gray, have you?"

"Yes, sir."

"How is the old place?"

This gave the young footman pause. "Old, Lord Gray."

Ben didn't doubt it. His ancestral home in the wilds of Scotland had begun as a humble fortified tower on a rocky promontory overlooking the sea. Centuries of wind and neglect had driven his mother back into the bosom of London society as soon as his bellicose father had the courtesy to meet an early end. Consequently Ben had not been raised to tramp the hills in a kilt and kick sheep out of the way. No, Baron Benton Gray was a modern, cultured man, prosperous with his investment in Sir Simon Keith's railroad scheme and suitably celebratory. How dare *The London List* make him sound like he was the veriest devil? Veronique had had no objection to—well, Ben reflected, she never objected to anything. She was paid well not to.

Perhaps it was time to give her her conge. Let the talk die down. She'd been his mistress for seven months and that thing she did with her hips was beginning to feel old hat.

Ben scowled. How did his morning decline from smug satisfaction over his bacon to this depressing state? He was not going to give up Veronique!

Unless someone better came along.

Not a wife. Ben had avoided the slavering mamas—except for his own—for over a decade. He'd been successful, for the most part. One did not reach the advanced age of thirty entirely unscathed, however. There had been that misunderstanding with the Crittendon chit a few years back, and he didn't allow himself to ever think of Evie.

She must be over thirty now herself. Probably running and ruining some poor man's life so that he longed for an early death. Ben hadn't heard a thing about her for ages. He'd stopped looking for her dark head in a London crowd once he'd found out she'd gone back to Scotland. Evangeline Ramsey was one reason he so much enjoyed living in London as a confirmed bachelor and with as many mistresses as he could handle.

Enough of the sentimental journey down memory lane. Ben poured himself another cup of coffee and opened up the distasteful newspaper. He skimmed the advertisements, chuckling only briefly when he came upon "*A young woman from a respectable family, honest, hard-working, country bred, would like to correspond with a city gentleman for amusement and possibly more. Physical attributes are unimportant, though it would be helpful if said gentleman is under forty and in possession of most of his teeth and a modest fortune.*"

Ben swiped his tongue over his even, fully intact teeth, dislodging a morsel of toast. He supposed he was a prime candidate, not that he was going to mix himself up with some uncivilized wench who probably had a hairy mole on the end of her chin. He pitied the poor people who were desperate enough to use *The London List* to try to solve their problems.

Blast! Where were their offices located? He began squinting again at the front page of the slender publication, avoiding the prominent article mentioning his recent activities in such lurid detail. He might have all his teeth, but he wondered if he was becoming eligible for reading glasses.

There was nothing the matter with his nose however. His mother was on her way into the dining room, her lily-of-the-valley perfume announcing her arrival quite a bit before she stepped through the door. He hastily shoved the paper underneath his bottom and plastered a smile on his face.

"Benton, darling, good morning!"

Ben angled a smooth-shaven cheek for his mother to kiss. Lady Emily Gray was a well-preserved forty-seven, her nut-brown hair only beginning to silver. She had practically been a child when she married and was brutalized by his father. The fact that

Ben was the image of the man—large, tawny-haired, green-eyed—did not seem to stop her from holding her only child in deep affection. Sometimes too deep. She was most anxious to become a grandmother, and never ceased to remind Ben of his duty to his title, such as it was.

Lady Gray's slate blue eyes swept the table. "Where is it?"

"Where is what, Mama?"

"*The London List.* It's Tuesday. For that matter, where is Callum? Though I suppose I'm still capable of fetching my own breakfast."

"Let me get it for you, Mama."

Ben recognized his error immediately. If he rose to get her a plate from the sideboard, she would see the newspaper he had taken such pains to hide. For the life of him, he could not see its appeal. But everyone from the loftiest viscount to his valet seemed addicted to the thing. Tuesdays could not come soon enough. There was much speculation in the clubs as to the identities of the blind items, and servants were always seeking greener pastures in the employment columns. Ghastly young poets could pay to have their ghastly poems published, too. Something for everyone, whatever their station in life.

There were plenty of people to write for and write about. Ben was extremely tired of finding himself on the front page week after week. It was almost as if the *List*'s publisher had a particular grudge against him.

He was saved from discovery as his mother waved him away and attacked the sideboard herself. She was pleasantly plump, convinced that she kept wrinkles at bay with a few extra pounds. Ben watched her pile her plate high with eggs, mushrooms, bacon and toast, then returned to his own food, which was sadly cold after his paper-pitching fit. But if he got up for a fresh helping, he'd be right back in his pickle. Sorry now that he'd dismissed Callum, he took a sip of lukewarm coffee.

"Did *The London List* not come with your post this morning? I knew we should have ordered more subscriptions."

Ben clinked his cup into its saucer. "More? Just how many do we get?"

"Well, Cook insists on her own copy. Severson as well. The maids share theirs, except for my dresser Barnes, who is far too top-lofty to share with anyone. I doubt she'd share with *me*. I believe a copy goes out to the stables. One for the footmen—"

"Callum does not read," Ben interrupted.

"Oh? I'll make sure Severson is apprised of that, although I'm sure he knows. He knows *everything*. He mentioned as I came downstairs that you managed to make the front page again."

Damn. So much for keeping his household, especially his mother, in the dark. If he'd counted correctly, he was paying for seven bloody subscriptions to announce his every peccadillo to the world.

"It's all a pack of lies!"

His mother raised a sculpted brow and took a forkful of egg. Once she swallowed, she said, "You are a grown man. How you choose to spend your time is, I suppose, your business. But you will never get a decent woman to marry you unless you curtail your notoriety. As it is, you're verging into desperate widow territory."

"Mama, I don't want a decent woman or a desperate widow. I have no interest in marriage, as well you know."

"Just because your father was a brute does not mean you will follow in his footsteps," his mother said, her tone remarkably mild.

Ben's father had died when he was a child, but not soon enough. He could remember every blow he and his mother suffered under Laird Gray, and the pervasive feeling of hopelessness and helplessness had never quite gone away. His father's temper had been legendary, which was one reason Ben worked so hard to control his. To cultivate an attitude of laissez-faire. To permit the unpermittable without much fuss or bother. He was the epitome of utter affability. Nothing would ruffle his feathers.

Except for the damned *London List*.

"Perhaps I've not yet met the right woman," Ben parried, his tone equally light. "Maybe I'm not holding out for a desperate widow but a buck-toothed virgin with spots."

"There are plenty of those this year." His mother laid her fork down. "Let us be serious for a moment. I made a mistake in my marriage—or rather my parents made it for me. There were whispers about your father, but they ignored them. The Gray fortune was temptation incarnate."

"It still is."

"I'm not questioning your stewardship, Benton. Everything you touch turns to gold. Which is why if you put your mind to it, I know you could be an adequate husband. And father."

The portion of his breakfast he had eaten turned to a hard lump in his stomach. "I will count that as a compliment, Mama. High praise indeed."

"It is meant to be. I have faith in you."

His poor mama. He supposed all mothers were easily gulled. Even his paternal grandmother had probably loved his father.

Ben changed the subject. "What are your plans for today?"

"Well, I'll have to cadge a copy of *The London List* from one of the servants. One can't start one's Tuesday morning without it."

With a sigh, Ben shifted in his chair and drew out the crumpled copy.

"Benton Alexander Dunbarton Gray! You devil!"

"I wanted to protect your delicate sensibilities, Mama. The article about me is pure rubbish." *Mostly.*

"My delicate sensibilities have gone the way of your good judgment. Hand it over."

His mother slipped her reading glasses out of a pocket sewn

specially for them. For the next five minutes Ben was subjected to his mother's pursed lips and head-shaking. It seemed she needed to read the story about him four times, if following the pattern of her finger was any indication. But she was mercifully silent. Ben was relieved when she turned the page to the paid advertisements.

"If you don't plan to give me a scold, may I be excused from the table?"

His mother looked up, her eyes wavery under the thick lenses. "I'll scold you later. I wonder who is in need of "*a strapping young valet whose hands and teeth can make quick work of neckcloths and falls?*"

"Mother!"

"Oh, do be quiet, Benton. It's not as if I can shock *you*."

A pity she had such a low opinion of him, but she was right. *Mostly.*

Ben left his mother to her gossip and speculation. Braving the kitchen and Cook's opprobrium, he snagged an extra scone and her copy of the newssheet. Over his crumbs he found the offices of the paper buried between advertisements for the improvement of manly vigor and custom reupholstery.

R. Ramsey, Publisher. An odd coincidence that the bane of his existence shared the surname of his lost and unlamented love.

He had nothing better to do today but defend his honor and demand satisfaction or retraction. He was *not* going to sit in his club and endure the jibes of his so-called friends as they reminded him that he was the number one topic of conversation in the ton. Bad enough Severson gave him a gimlet eye as he assisted Ben with his coat against the raw December wind.

It would do him good to walk the distance to the newspaper's office. Work up his umbrage and indignation. His calves would get exercise too. Ben wouldn't let a few nights of dissipation wreck his carefully-crafted body. It was damned hard to stay fit in Town, but Ben did by fencing regularly at a private *salle d'armes.* Using his fists was far too reminiscent of his father's proclivities, so he left Gentleman Jackson's to others.

In a matter of half an hour, he had traversed quite a bit of fashionable London and stood before the impeccably scrubbed front window of *The London List.* He could see clear to the back of the rear brick office wall and the hulking black printing press which would be idle for the rest of the week. A young gentleman, his black hair cropped brutally short, shirtsleeves rolled up and jacket discarded, appeared to be tinkering with the source of Ben's choler. If the infernal machine was broken, that would save him the trouble of smashing it himself.

No. Ben had other methods of persuasion. He would make the fellow, or his employer if he had one, an offer no sensible person could refuse.

Ben startled at the tinkle of bells over the door as he entered. The printer turned abruptly to him, his welcoming smile quickly draining away, looking ready to faint onto the wide pine floor-boards.

By God and the saints and all that was holy. The young gentleman was no gentleman. Ben felt light-headed himself as he stared into Evangeline Ramsey's parchment-pale face.